FOR KIM -

THE HEART DIDN'T FALL, IT FLEW!

Pam Godwin

Editor: Jacy Mackin
Interior Designer: Pam Godwin

Visit my website at pamgodwin.com

For my husband,
my freedom,
my warm spark to hold forever.

Chapter 1

Tonight was the night. Nervousness might have been a natural response in her position, but bending to it wouldn't change a damned thing. Liv sucked in hard. A lungful of smoke pushed past her unsteady smile and tumbled into a halfhearted cloud against the glare of stadium lights. Force of will pinned her bowed lips in place.

Another drag. Exhale. She stretched her neck and rotated her shoulders.

Whistles and cheers roared from the stands. Green and gold banners rippled to the stomp of thousands of feet on metal bleachers. Wedged between a trash barrel and a concrete wall, she smashed the cigarette on the *No Smoking* sign bolted to the railing at her hip.

To blend in as a Baylor University Bears fan, she wore a green t-shirt and dark jeans. Her alcove was field level, out of the path of foot traffic, and the best vantage to observe her mark.

The boy.

A goddamned saint.

He likely hadn't known a night similar to the one he was about to have. Her stomach quivered in a war of dread and anticipation.

The scoreboard counted down the final five minutes of the game. *Le Male* aftershave wafted from the nearby huddle of guys. The scent of store-bought pheromones mingled with their sweaty excitement and the nachos clutched in their hands. Smelled like fucking team spirit. Right now she hated *Nirvana* and everything musical expression had once meant to her.

She shouldn't begrudge the college boys their thrills. To be fair, a number of them, with their athletic frames and juvenile energy, could have been her next delivery. But she'd already chosen. A fucking holier-than-thou virgin boy.

The tone of cheers exploded in volume and urgency, drawing her attention to the field. Green jerseys descended upon the turf, cleats kicking up mud, the rush of testosterone led by number fifty-four, the Bears' star linebacker.

He jogged to midfield in long-legged strides, the seams of his sleeves straining to contain his biceps. She leaned over the railing, eyes glued to his gait. Self-assured and powered by trained muscles, he covered the field like he owned it. Given the whoops of his fans, he did.

His helmet, rib protectors, and shoulder pads concealed his pale green eyes and black hair while enhancing all six-foot-two inches and two hundred and twenty pounds of masculinity and sexual innocence that met the *client's* conditions. But she knew everything about the twenty-one year old. She had been watching Joshua Carter for weeks.

Daily surveillance had put her in the woods surrounding his parents' farm at five every morning, stalking the campus halls during his classes and football practices until four, and back in the cotton fields until dusk.

In his four-year college career as a linebacker, he had caught a record twenty-three interceptions. As a trained sex slave, he would catch seven digits in an offshore account.

While his predictable schedule made him an easy capture, his notoriety on the team magnified the risk. But it was the raw beauty in his seductive eyes and honed physique that passed a whisper between her ears, the kind that couldn't be unheard once acknowledged. He was the one.

A stolen password gave her access to his university records. As the only child of poor farmers, he would've needed every bit of financial aid offered had he not received a football scholarship. His scholarship essay supported his pursuit in earning a degree in Religion, stating it would *equip him with the tenet and fortitude to effectively fill a professional ministry role.*

His righteousness chafed her heathen ass, but it avowed his virginity. Not an easy find these days, especially not in one so potently masculine and easy on the eyes. Which was why she'd sought this particular job on Baylor's Christian-centric campus rather than her usual hunting grounds in the slums of Brownsville and Killeen. Besides, he would forget all about his godly endeavors by day two in chains. Just like all the others.

The visiting crowd moaned. Their quarterback lay on his back, the football wobbling beside his grass-stained helmet. Beside him, number fifty-four stretched out a hand to help the guy to his feet.

"A terrific defensive play by number fifty-four, the Bears." The announcer's enthusiasm reverberated above the hoots of Bears fans. "Results in a sack."

Anticipation twitched her shoulders. She came to watch him steal the spotlight. He didn't know it would be the last game in his career, but she would remember the high points for him. She would remind him of his glory right before she peeled it away and rebuilt him into the sum of the buyer's requirements.

Sixteen- and seventeen-year-olds were her forte. Not too young to make her stomach roll with pedophiliac queasiness and not too old to resist her methods. Though, with enough time, she could find the chink no matter the age. The buyer for this job demanded a boy in his twenties, virtuous in his relations with women, and a body disciplined to accept and please a man.

Number fifty-four sprinted to the defensive line, quadriceps flexing against his compression pants. As he bent at the waist, the spandex stretched over jock strap lines and the glorious divide of his ass.

Payday was in sight. She lit another cigarette and curved her lips through the exhale.

"If beautiful smiles could kill," said an unfamiliar voice behind her, "you'd be a spear through the heart."

The lame pick up line sent her molars slamming together. If she looked, she'd find a smirk that needed practice. If she gazed deeper, she'd find an entitled college kid, one who didn't appreciate his family-funded education. No mind-reading required. Seven years and seven captured slaves had taught her how to detect weakness in a voice and smell the waste in its words.

She brushed a length of hair forward, using the thick curls to cover the left half of her face and the four-inch scar there. It was her permanent reminder, not that she needed one. Her insides were gutted.

With deliberate slowness, she turned her head and confronted the annoyance.

Stiffly crooked lips and nervously blinking eyes belied the confidence he was attempting to exude. Hands fidgeting in the pockets of his jeans, feet a shoulder-width apart, the kid was no older than eighteen, at least six years her junior, and in need of a lesson on stranger danger.

She tiptoed her gaze down his puffing chest and paused on the bulge below his longhorn buckle. With a muffled sigh, she reminded herself she was there for a job. That didn't include informing some douche drip that her smile was especially dangerous when wrapped around a cock. She flicked her eyes to his and shed the smile.

"Oh, come on. I'm writing a paper on the life of Moses." He licked his lips. "Let me demonstrate how to part the sea with my staff." His gaze slid to her metaphoric sea.

The fact he wasn't choking on his own douchery was a prick to the nerves. He didn't know she tied people up and fucked them with rubber dicks for a living. With a grab and twist of his nuts, she could humiliate him. But she couldn't draw that kind of attention. She curled her fingers around the railing and shaped her expression into a mask of cruel arrogance.

Whatever he saw in her gaze pinched his face. He shuffled backward with deflated shoulders. Pathetic. If she had thirty minutes and an empty classroom, she'd show him things more painful than a bruised ego.

She turned back to the game and scanned the field.

Number fifty-four sprinted past the five-yard line, leapt to intercept a long pass, and caught the ball mid-turn.

"Interception," the announcer yelled as the crowd jumped up, their cheers as wild as the beat of her heart. One second remained on the clock.

She wanted to clap with the fans, but knowing it was his last victory crushed her celebratory spirit. Truth was, she didn't have a viable reason for being there. She couldn't exactly snatch him out of the crowd. But after weeks of watching him on the field, his games had become something to anticipate.

The ambience of the cheering crowd, the camaraderie of friends enjoying a favorite pastime, and the view of athletic boys showing off in tight pants nourished her longing for the youth that had been stolen from her. Seven years ago, she was the innocent girl who stood before the crowd singing the National Anthem at her high school's football games.

The memory fluttered in her belly and dulled her awareness. She snapped her spine straight. Fuck, she was losing track of time.

Lighting another cigarette, she blew her sentimentality into the night sky and slipped out of her recess. Striding up the stairs toward the parking lot, she twisted to catch a glimpse of number fifty-four running off the field.

Cheerleaders enveloped him on the sideline, hopping and mewling for his attention. He tugged off the helmet and rubbed a hand over his face, his complexion gilded so exquisitely by the Texas sun. He glanced at the scoreboard above her head. If she were watching through her binoculars, she would've been staring into the unusual glow of his innocent sea green eyes. The ones she was about to change forever.

"Excuse me, ma'am?"

What the unholy fuck now? She pivoted and met the narrowed glare of a middle-aged man. Dressed head-to-toe in Baylor swag, he was probably some overzealous alumni reliving the *glory days.*

He waved a flabby arm. "This is a smoke-free property."

She raised the cigarette, inhaled, and released a plume of *fuck you* into his scrunching face.

A dramatic cough accompanied another flap of his arm. "The university has strict guidelines—"

"Are you the smoke police?"

A fury of red bloomed from his buttoned collar to his blotted cheeks. "You can't do that here."

Bet his virgin ass clenched as he said that. She shifted to move past him, irritation skittering across her skin.

He stretched an arm out to block her. "What's your name, young lady?"

Before she did something that would get her hauled off in handcuffs, she blew him a smoke-ringed kiss, pushed around his arm, and wove into the exodus of spectators.

Past the cooling charcoal grills and trash-littered tailgates, her ten minute stroll took her to the edge of the parking lot. In the farthest corner, beneath a broken street lamp, she circled a nondescript sedan. No one loitered. No witnesses to connect her to the car. She tapped on the passenger window.

The locks released and the door swung open.

"How many times did you get hit on?" Van Quiso's timbre bordered on growly.

On a good night, calm reason eclipsed his jealousy.

She struggled to remember a good night.

"Wouldn't you love to know?" She winked at him, dropped into the seat, and shut the door.

Despite the consequences, she got off on tormenting him. A desperate and pathetic attempt at revenge.

A toothpick protruded from the opening of his charcoal hoodie where his mouth was, probing the air in restless circles. "You smell like sex."

"I banged three linebackers during halftime." She buckled her seat belt.

"Your sarcasm is juvenile."

"So is your suspicious resentment."

The stench of his possessiveness saturated her skin and bled into her veins. The more he took her, consensual or not, the farther she followed him, down, down, down into his twisted reality.

She rubbed her arms and focused on the empty lot. "The boy is here."

He leaned back and stretched a leg along the floorboard. "The kid's never missed a class or a practice, let alone a game."

"It's flu season, Van. People get sick." At least, that was the argument she'd given him to get one last chance to see the boy play.

The toothpick bobbed and stilled. He fingered the keys where they dangled from the ignition and lowered his hand. "Look at me."

Tension crept through her limbs. She itched to reach over and start the car. The confined space, in the dark, with him, had her crawling out of her skin with reminders of what he'd done to her, what he continued to do to her. His cock stretching her ass, his whip burning across her back, his fist in her face, the tenderness of his lips kissing her wounds.

She pushed her shoulders back, pulled out her phone, and checked the time. "The coach should be finished with his post-game speech. The boy will be showered and headed out soon. We need to go."

"Look. At. Me."

The heat in his command cracked her shell of bravado, tightening the muscles in her face. Only two people in her isolated world had a stronger strike than hers, and Van knew he was one. His breath sawed in and out with enough vehemence to sharpen his teeth as he watched her, poaching her air, waiting.

Avoiding his stare was a means of gaining distance, but ignoring him only delayed the inescapable. She made her face relax and looked at him straight in the eyes.

He stared right back, the toothpick jogging low in her periphery. It could've been the press of shadows in the car, but meeting his gaze was like straining to see into the reaches of the moonless night. Maybe something terrible lurked in there, something malicious enough to end her life in unspeakable ways. Maybe it was her imagination.

The rotating toothpick froze, caught between his molars as he spread his lips into a grin. His hooded sweatshirt hid his high-and-tight cut of brown hair and sharp features and struggled to contain his mountain of muscles. The severe angles of his face added to his dangerous beauty. An unsuspecting glance in his direction promised a double-glance, usually followed by a prayer to God that he didn't catch the admiring look and use it to his advantage.

He seemed to embrace the mold of a convicted criminal, but he had never been convicted. And despite the prayers to ward him off, his sexy smile could coerce a virgin girl's thighs into a spread-eagle sigh.

But that girl no longer existed.

A timeworn ache awoke in her chest. She masked it under a steady breath and let her eyelids half-droop in a display of boredom.

He slid back his hood to his hairline just behind the comma-shaped laceration that connected the outer edge of his eye to the crook of his mouth. Even in the dark, the deep red gash stood out, a threatening brand against the perfect symmetry of his features.

His hand lifted to her cheek, smoothing her hair away. She held herself immobile as he traced the scar that mirrored his. When he stared at it, did he ever regret the events that led to their matching punishments?

"You're sleeping in my bed tonight." The touch of his fingers and the command in his tone jabbed like a knife.

She leaned back, throat dry, and forced her eyes to remain on his. "I have a job to do. If I fail, you'll be digging my body out of the backyard to fuck it."

The skin around his scar strained. "He doesn't bury bodies back there."

"Yet."

He plucked the toothpick from his mouth and pointed it at her. His lips parted to speak and a gust of frustration grooved his face. He knew if she didn't meet their deadlines her threat was a dead-on promise.

Whatever he was going to say was abandoned as he dropped his brow to hers and pressed the seam of his lips to her bottom one. She fought a shiver. This bond wasn't romantic. It was unwanted, sad, and it thrived on her fear of him.

The slide of his tongue along her inner lip hitched her breath. He wouldn't fuck her here and sabotage the mission, but he always made time to fuck *with* her. To speed it along, she remained pliable in her stillness.

With a disappointed sigh, he returned the toothpick to his mouth and started the car. "Let's go get your boy."

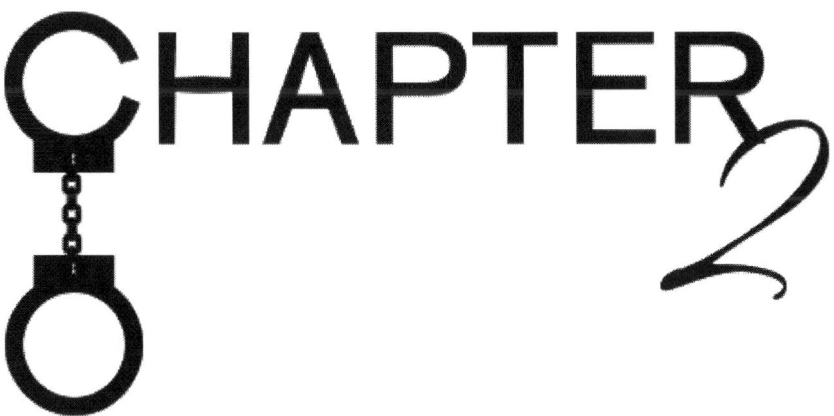

CHAPTER 2

Liv wanted to be anywhere but in that car, on her way to uproot another life, facing the next ten weeks behind a whip and a mask. She trained them. She delivered them. And after?

They were dead to her. They had to be. Sometimes, it was the lies she told herself that kept her going. Believing anything else made her a danger to the captives she sold.

She pressed her fingertips against the window. If only she could find the strength to end her own life.

The suburban conveniences of Waco, Texas, swept by in the form of drive-throughs, water towers, and churches of every denomination. As Van drove toward the outskirts of town, the scenery transformed. The wide-open freedom of the crop fields, cut by a swath of tarmac and hangars beneath the moonlight, haunted her vision.

Memories took shape, a tapestry of the private airport in Austin where Mom instructed skydiving courses, the adjacent corn field and its maze of childhood adventures, and the acres of paved airstrip where local teens roller-bladed until dusk.

Until one of the kids was taken.

The old sore in her chest opened. Her exhale

erupted in a choke, and she feigned a cough.

Van's hand swung into view and collided with her throat, squeezing. Oh God, her mind wasn't on the job, and he had the unnerving ability to mark every fucking move of her body.

She tried to draw air, an empty effort against the vise of his fingers on her windpipe. His *I-control-your-thoughts* conditioning was a technique that once worked on her, and experience taught her the best reaction was no reaction.

Lips pinned in silence, she sought out her defense, a song, any song, and grabbed hold of "Gods and Monsters" by *Lana Del Rey.* Saturating her thoughts with the lamenting chorus, she sang in her head. The rippling effects numbed her heart—and her throat beneath his fingers. Singing was her tonic, the only trace of self she had left.

"Is your head on straight?" He tightened his grip, gave it a shake. "Feels like it is."

Lungs burning, fingers digging into her thighs, she steadied her pulse to the slow beat of lyrics spilling through her mind.

The clamp vanished, and his hand returned to the wheel. She let her lungs fill with quiet stoicism and loosened her muscles limb by limb.

"Your mind is wandering." His impatience pulsated between them. "Pull your balls out of your cunt."

She wanted to hate him, but he was all she had. She wanted to love him, but memories tore deep and scarred. "My head is straight. Balls are out. What other body parts are you concerned about?"

Passing headlights illuminated the stone set of his

jaw, his eyes piercing the road. "Tell me what you were thinking about."

That command had more power than it should. She summoned a reply with control in her voice. "Your first capture."

"My first…" His hands tightened on the wheel, slackened, and a sick kind of attachment slithered into his tone. "My favorite capture." He squeezed her knee.

Mom used to say no one had truly evaluated their life until they looked at it from 10,000 feet. Liv's arrangement allowed her a certain amount of freedom, so she still skydived between jobs. When she did, her falls always retraced the same path of *should-haves*.

Should have jumped with Mom that day instead of staying behind to roller-blade. Should have skated away from his car when he stopped to ask directions. Should have screamed instead of getting in when he aimed the gun.

A wave of revulsion surged through her. "Your first capture was just a stupid girl."

"A stupid girl who incorporated the client's requirements. Tight seventeen-year-old ass, perky tits, all that innocence bouncing up and down on skates." He hummed. "I have no regrets."

Regret would have gone a long way in their relationship.

He shifted closer and reached for her thigh. She jerked out of the path of his hand and pressed against the door.

Black fields smeared by. If the cold glass against her cheek was the only barrier between her and those fields, she would be sprinting through them as fast as possible away from this car.

He reached again, a full-body lean, veering the car onto the edge of the shoulder. The car righted as his hand made contact, shoved between her legs, and cupped her.

That hand had been her undoing so many times. She was stolen innocence, following the rules of monsters. Somewhere along the way, she'd become one.

The faster he rubbed, the harder he pressed against the denim seam protecting her bundle of nerves, the looser her hips became. It was his words, however, that had the power to own her and destroy her, from the inside out.

"I want to spend the rest of my life looking at you, touching you. Christ, I have to touch you to make sure I'm not imagining you."

She ground against his fingers, hating herself. Her hips shifted up and down, pelvis rolling out, thighs opening, responding in defiance of her own volition.

His voice lowered to a murmur. "Why is fucking you the only way I can reach you, Liv? I want more. More than this."

She released a moan, a sound practiced to seduce. But she couldn't stop her heartfelt yearning from bleeding into the edges of her voice. She covered it by dragging it out into a longer, more robotic groan.

He yanked his hand away. "Save your fucking fakeasms for the new bitch boy."

A shaky breath tingled past her lips. She hadn't been faking, not completely, and that was more revolting than the act itself. "Maybe I won't fake with this boy."

The sudden stiffness of his posture betrayed the calmness in his tone. "The client was very specific about who will be fucking his property."

Of the twelve requirements in the contract, the

buyer's first demand took an audacious detour around the usual kinkativity.

Requirement One. Slave has never experienced sexual intimacy with a woman. Slave is heterosexual but hates women. He desires only his Master.

There wasn't a buyer who didn't make her shudder, but this one was so openly sexist, he notched a new level of loathing, and she hadn't even met him yet. "His first requirement is so fucked up. I don't like it."

"He's probably some scorned man and wants a slave to sympathize with his misery. He's not any different than the other kinky, fat-wallet pig fuckers you've contracted for."

"Maybe. But this one's a whole new breed of creepiness."

Their previous contracts were straightforward, listing desired physical attributes and demanding the usual kneel-grovel-suck-my-cock training. The cost for that training was ludicrous, and she never saw a penny of it. But everyone had a price. Hers was more valuable than money.

"The job's the same." His voice snapped through the car. "The slave you deliver will be *exactly* as he ordered."

Or she would lose the only two reasons she buckled on a parachute when she jumped.

He wiggled his toothpick. "Though it definitely would've been easier if the contract had allowed us to nab a homo."

Jesus, the world was already a predatory asshole, and here they were discriminating who it should feed on next. The client wanted a twenty-something, straight, virgin male with all the usual attractive, athletic qualities.

The fishing pool for such a demand was spectacularly small. Boys who grew up without families didn't retain their virginity.

"I don't like taking this boy from his parents." It fucked up her delicately woven strategy, the only secret she managed to keep from Van.

"So," he said, smirking, "because your previous captures didn't have families who missed them, that makes them less human?"

Absence of loved ones was her own personal requirement when she went through the selection process, but that did *not* make them less *at all*.

His laugh greased the air. "The irony of your ethics is perverse."

The irony of her life was perverse.

He relaxed into a sigh, his head dropping back against the seat. "We make an invincible team, Liv. Just do your thing until the mere presence of your pussy makes him vomit."

With the previous captives, Van held the reins, driving the level and direction of the training. But the first requirement in this contract was sticky. To condition the slave to hate women, they'd agreed that she would be the brute force.

Her stomach wobbled. "Think you can stay out of the way while I handle this one?"

"Yep. Just call me in when your devout jock-bag is ready to suck my cock."

Requirement Two. Slave will service Master sexually with exceptional skill, and his body will be prepared to make it easy for Master.

She and Van would play a depraved game designed to turn a straight, virgin boy into the embodiment of the client's twelve requirements. Virgin boys were beyond her expertise. Joshua Carter—with his pious upbringing and family support—was a tangle in their operation, one that could endanger her arrangement. The unmistakable shiver of panic lurched through her.

He eased off the gas. "I think we're here."

Up ahead, a smudge of trees breached the flat horizon of rural Texas.

She checked the signal on her phone. "We're in the dead zone. This is it."

He parked on the shoulder where the trees crept closest to the road and turned on the hazard lights. She stepped onto the gravel, the stir of dust settling around her sneakers. When she raised the hood of their car, he removed a fuse from the engine compartment and tucked it in his pocket. Then they waited.

Wheat fields reached around the woodland and stretched beyond the mantle of night. The lonely cry of a mockingbird pierced the dark hush.

The nearest resident lived two miles down. She knew them through the lens of her binoculars. Daniel and Emily Carter couldn't leave their nightly chores to attend their son's football game. She knew they expected him home soon.

A distant rumble drew her attention down the desolate road. Given the ease at which sound traveled over the vacant fields, she should see his headlights in about two or three minutes.

Van's big body blocked her view, pressing in, violating her comfort zone. She raised her chin and searched the depths of his hood. Shadowed and vacant, his expression mirrored her presence of mind.

The back of his hand made a slow trace of her scar, brushing her hair from its path. When he reached her lips, he coiled several strands around his finger.

She grabbed his wrist, and the tendons in her grip turned to steel, immovable. She closed her eyes and braced.

He yanked, sparking a burn where the follicles gave way.

At the sound of his retreating footsteps, she opened her eyes and watched his broad back move toward the trees. "Someday, we're going to talk about those fetishes of yours."

Without acknowledgment, he continued in a slow, dispassionate stride until the shadows between the trees swallowed his silhouette.

The purr of the approaching vehicle grew louder, followed by the spit of gravel and bobbing headlights. She leaned against the fender and hummed to the tune of her bludgeoning heart.

CHAPTER 3

The truck slowed and stopped. Liv held up a hand, greeting the darkened interior and the boy who lingered within.

Her mark.

When the door remained closed, she worried her lip. Were her assumptions about him wrong?

With each unanswered second, her nerves mounted. What if he had a passenger? She'd been so sure about this part of the plan.

Relief came with the creak of his door. It had been just her anxiety making it feel longer.

He hopped out, and the interior light illuminated the empty cab. "Hey there. You need help?"

His voice reverberated through her chest for the first time. It exceeded all her imaginings, a deep underlying elixir, the perfect embodiment of his powerful, masculine frame.

"Hi." She wiped imaginary grease on her jeans and gestured at the engine. "Started clanking on I-35. I pulled off, got turned around." She spread out her arms to indicate the expanse of nothingness around them and quickened her rambling with a display of panic. "I'm lost. Dang car crapped out, and I can't get a signal on my phone."

A chuckle vibrated in his chest, and there was something unnervingly soothing about it. "You definitely got turned around. You're miles from the interstate. Want me to take a look?" He pointed at the engine and cocked his head, his luminescent eyes dancing in the headlights.

Several feet separated them, the closest they'd ever been in proximity. At almost a foot taller and a hundred pounds heavier, he commanded the space he stood in, as well as hers. He could overpower her with sheer strength, which was why she had to lead him to chains by his own accord.

She regarded the ground and tapped the toe of her sneaker on the tire. "It's the alternator. Last time this happened, the mechanic told me I needed a new one. It's expensive, you know?" She peered at him through her lashes. "I'll have to tow it."

"There's cell service about a mile up the road. I can give you a lift."

Soon, he'd give her more than just a lift. Time to zip on the helpless-girl suit.

She inched forward until the beam of light caught the hideous damage on her left cheek.

His Adam's apple jumped, and he seemed to wrestle with dragging his gaze from the scar to her eyes. Sympathy, or perhaps pity, softened his expression. She deserved the latter, especially after she used it against him.

"My dad…he…" She placed a palm over her cheek, cradling it, and trickled out an award-winning whimper.

"Hey." Loose rock scraped beneath his tentative approach. "What's wrong?"

"It's just…Dad was so much harder on my little

sister." She stroked the scar and hunched her shoulders. "She's all alone, and she needs me."

There was no Dad, no sister, but a family boy like him needed something he could sympathize with.

"I left Dallas as soon as she called, and now I can't get to her." With a shuddering breath, she gave him her back and wrapped her arms around her midsection. "This can't be happening." A whisper.

"Where's your sister?"

"Temple." She released a sniffle into the darkness.

His silence struggled around her. If she had chosen the right play, he would be working out all the dire possibilities that would justify her driving two hours back to Dallas with a bad alternator. And if she'd chosen the right boy, he would offer a solution that delivered him into her hands.

"Is she in danger?" he asked.

If yes, he would call the cops.

She shook her bowed head and curled further into herself. "She's unstable. I don't think she'd hurt herself, but her mind's in a bad place." A deep breath for effect. "I'm the only person she has."

The scuff of his feet moved in the direction of the truck. "Temple is only thirty minutes from here. I can take you, if you want?"

Touchdown. The victory pulled at her lips.

She relaxed her mouth and pivoted slowly, facing him, her features arranged in a portrait of disbelief. "Really?"

He opened the passenger door and held it in invitation. "If you're okay leaving your car for the tow service. No one will bother it."

No one would bother it because Van would replace

the fuse and follow far enough behind to not be seen. She snagged her wallet and phone from the car and shuffled toward him with deliberate caution in her steps.

What would a normal girl in her position say?

"You're not going to kidnap me and rape me, are you?" The twisted callousness in that suggestion tightened her throat. She wanted to retract the words, despising what the end of the night would bring for him.

"No, ma'am." He shifted out of the way as she climbed in. "But there's Mace in the glove box. Help yourself." The corners of his full lips inched up. "Pretty as you are, you can't be too trusting."

A frigid clamp closed over her heart. *Stupid, stupid boy.*

Seated behind the wheel, he turned the truck around and drove toward town and I-35. When the bars appeared on her phone, he held up his. "I need to text my folks and let them know I'll be late. Would you mind?"

As expected, his law-abiding refusal to text and drive put his phone in her hands.

She accepted it and tapped on the call log. Last call was to his mom prior to the game. "Of course. Is it under—"

"Mom. Should be right—" He cut his eyes at her finger on the screen. "Yeah, that's it. Just tell her I'm giving a friend a lift to Temple and I'll be home by eleven-thirty."

It was remarkable how unabashed he was about living with his parents. He didn't know she knew the reasons. That they depended on him to work the struggling farm morning and night. That staying in his childhood bedroom saved them on-campus housing expenses despite some of the offset his scholarship awarded them.

He let her imagine whatever she wanted about a twenty-one-year-old checking in with Mom on a Friday night. His confidence wasn't boy-like at all. It was admirably mature. And problematic. It would require breaking, likely through physical humiliation.

The pang from that thought hit her stomach, and she calmed it with the reminder that to succeed in an important aim, it was acceptable to do something bad. Or lots of somethings bad.

A discreet glance confirmed his eyes were on the road. As she typed out the text, she worked the cover off the back of the phone, let the battery drop between her legs—thank God it wasn't an iPhone—and closed it up. The screen went black, the text unsent.

She placed it face down in the cup holder. "Sent."

"Thanks. Do you need a number for a tow service?"

"I'll call in the morning."

His thumbs drummed on the steering wheel and stopped. "Name's Josh. What's yours?"

She always used her real name. No reason not to. "Liv."

"Liv." He pursed his lips. "L-I-V."

"L-I-V."

Shove it between *DE* and *ERER*, and she had a job title. Mr. E had a jolly cruel laugh about it when he promoted her to a deliverer by way of blackmail.

Josh's face creased in a smile. "Do you believe in meaningful coincidence?"

Absolutely not. "Why?"

"I play football and my jersey number is fifty-four. Your name is L-I-V."

What was his deal with the spelling? She cocked her head at him. "And?"

He shrugged. "The Roman Numeral LIV is number fifty-four."

His jersey number. Would she know these things if she'd had the freedom to earn her diploma or attend college?

"I take it you believe coincidence is meaningful?" she asked, curious.

"I think it's plausible. There's comfort in believing there are things in the universe that defy the odds, that something beyond common sense can pivot into place and fill an inner need." He angled his head to glance at her, studying her face. He wouldn't find anything meaningful there. He returned his attention to the road. "What do you think?"

The focus of conversation was expected for a boy pursuing a career in ministry. Still, she scrambled for an answer and settled on the truth. "Coincidence is nothing more than cause and effect. You jump. You fall."

He'd unwittingly jumped from his path and fallen onto someone else's. What she had planned for him would challenge his notions of coincidence and every other damned thing in his life.

CHAPTER 4

Josh sensed Liv's huge brown eyes making furtive sweeps in his direction. Addictive eyes, the kind that tunneled through his outer shell and scrambled his mind until he forgot where he was going.

There were moments in his life when he wanted to bypass the road chosen for him. He was staring at one now. The most attractive woman he'd ever seen. In his truck. Watching him.

The scar dividing her cheek flickered beneath a passing streetlight. It didn't distract from her beauty. It was a delicate emblem of her life, of whatever had happened to her. He burned with curiosity to know her story.

"Take 35 south. I'll tell you where to go when we reach Temple." She shifted her gaze to the speedometer. "Watch your speed."

No *please* or *thank you*. Just a quiet authority that stroked his ears and urged him to test her limits. "How 'bout you just sit there, look pretty, and let me drive?"

"The cops are all over, shooting radar. I can't afford more delays tonight."

This girl seemed a lot less vulnerable than the one trembling on the road. Her voice was soft, musical even, but clipped at the edges as if repressing something beneath her scarred exterior, something beyond the hurt. Outside of her fleeting glances, there was a peculiar apathy in her stillness. Like a dormant animal, resting, waiting.

His discomfort swelled, feeding on all the unsaid things about her family. He merged onto the interstate. "Do you want to talk about your sister?"

"No."

He scratched his stubble and grappled with her reserve. "It's a good thing I came along when I did. I'm the only one who passes through there at this hour."

The wind rustled against the windows as the truck gathered speed.

This was when a normal person would pick up the thread of friendly chitchat. Her silence challenged what he knew about girls and their self-involved monologues. He wasn't usually a nervous talker, but seriously, her lack of conversation was growing more awkward and irritating by the second. "I live just down the road a piece from where I found you."

She stared out the windshield, her fingers seemingly dead on her slender thighs. "Mm."

Pity she didn't want to talk. He had thirty minutes with this gorgeous girl. Thirty minutes to speak openly, to be himself in the company of a stranger. "I'm majoring in religion at Baylor."

A sigh whispered past her lips. "Why?"

"Why what?"

"Why the Jesus career?" Her lips rolled as if constraining judgment.

"I promise you, the reason is completely and wholeheartedly…absurd."

She glanced at him. Not just a flick of her scrutinizing eyes. He won a full-on head turn.

A tousle of chestnut curls clung to her face and spilled around her… Sweet Lord, he shouldn't have been gawking, but her chest was very, very mature. He was certainly not immune to feminine attributes, but watching her mouth part, tipping up at the corners and stretching her scar, was hell on his focus. Confusion looked seductively X-rated on her.

A low-burning fire stirred in his groin, a sensation he'd never tried to sate with a girl. He could've blamed his abstinence on Christian principles and a demanding workload. Truth was, he derived pleasure from the exertion that hard work put on his mind and body. The girls hanging around his practices didn't arouse him like the bruise of a tackle, the pains of farm labor, or the mental strain that accompanied religious stringency. He'd accepted his unconventional urges long ago and locked the darkest ones deep inside. If his parents knew the kind of thoughts he entertained, it would destroy them. His chest tightened.

He moved out of the passing lane and merged into an opening between two slower cars. He'd admitted to her the reason for his career choice was absurd. Might as well tell her why.

"My folks tried to get pregnant for years. When they reached their mid-forties and found God, they prayed, made promises, and nine-months later…" He gave her a raised eyebrow.

"You arrived."

"Yep. Here to fulfill their promise. They'd made a deal with God. If He gave them a child, they vowed to raise their miracle to be a servant of His church in Baptist ministry."

She laughed, a sweet sound for such a glaring expression. "Absurd."

"Told you." And telling her seemed to dislodge it just a little from his chest. It wasn't that he didn't believe in God. He just wasn't fanatical like some of his classmates. Like his parents.

"So young to allow all your choices be dictated by a promise to God."

"*My* promise is to Mom and Dad."

"Whatever. It's a promise that controls you. Doesn't that make you angry?"

"It challenges me, makes me a better person. I'm good with that."

A lull settled over her, and her gaze lost focus as she stared at him. She raised her hand, tentative at first, and reached for his face, fingertips resting on his cheekbone. When she traced his jawline, it was a caress so alluring he had to put all his concentration in keeping his eyes open and his hands on the wheel.

"Your life has always been predetermined, huh?" Her words were as perplexing as her touch.

"Mom and Dad gave me life, an honest one. In return, I accept the path they want for me." He leaned ever so slightly against her fingers and murmured, "It's just a job. You never know, it might lead to something extraordinary."

She yanked her hand back, and her attention snapped to the road.

The absence of her touch left a cold shock. He rubbed his jaw on his shoulder. "Did I say something—"

"Take the next exit."

Unease burrowed in him. What the hell happened?

He exited, replaying the conversation in his head. Perhaps leaning into her touch had been too forward.

"Five miles up, turn right into the *Two Trails Crossing* subdivision."

He passed Temple's main drag, the emptiness of the streets seeping into the truck. His body knew she was sitting right beside him. Hell, it pulsed to close those few inches. But she seemed so very far away, lost in her thoughts.

Then she began to hum. It started with a tremor, out of the blue and shocking to his ears. Was she singing to avoid conversation or to slice through the quiet?

The fluttering harmonic built into a haunting rhythm. The tune was unfamiliar, yet the notes shifted through him as if breathed from the most secret part of her soul.

"What is that?" he whispered. "What are you humming?"

The enchanting crescendo cut off, and he immediately regretted opening his mouth.

She cleared her throat. Then he heard it. The a cappella melody of a voice so piercing and peaceful it jolted a chill through him, sparking every cell in his body. The shiver faded too quickly but not for long. Her voice pitched, and an electric surge fired down his spine. He held his breath, spellbound.

In unerring key, she sang of wishes and stars and souls that couldn't be saved. Her octave carried a tinkling quality, profound and lonely at the same time. It transported him to the farm, to the isolated pond on a rainy day. Her voice was the pattering of drizzle on the misty surface, infused with nourishment and despair and acceptance.

She closed with a hum and a delicate exhale.

"That was…" His tongue knotted, heavy in his mouth.

"'Lullaby' by *Sia*."

"I was going to say exquisite, bewitching." *Carnal.* "Do you sing for a living?" He slowed at a stoplight and twisted to look at her.

"No." Complex and unflinching, her eyes held his and the key to his secrets.

The light ticked green, and she broke the connection, pointing at the brick archway on the right.

Lopsided letters clung to a wooden sign in tired welcome. *Two Trails Crossing.* He turned in.

Massive elms darkened the rows of lower middle-class homes. Dated wrought-iron gussied up the doors and windows. A couple left and right turns led them to a cul-de-sac, where she nodded at the small single-story at the end. "That's it. I'll go in through the rear."

He followed the skinny driveway alongside the house, around the back, and parked in front of the rear garage. The engine rattled, and he willed it to choke and die. He didn't want to let her go in just yet, and why was that? As the most sought-after bachelor on the football team, he had more female attention than he knew what to do with.

It wasn't that he didn't want a girl. In fact, he was so aware of the way the female body moved with its ample curves and forbidden places that it was often unbearable to hang out with the opposite sex. He was a guy in his prime, for heaven's sake. His restraint had its limits. So he fended off the handsy girls, accepted dates with the proper girls, and late at night, alone in his bed, he gripped his erection and gave into his primitive needs.

Something he would be doing when he got home, because Liv was the summation of all those girls, and more. What was it about her? She sang like a choir of angels and didn't proposition him like the girls at his games, yet her eyes promised experience and indulgences that reached beyond the boundaries of his folks' expectations for him.

She licked her lips, and they glistened in the dim glow of the porch light. "Come in."

Go in with her? Hell, he couldn't think past the pull to kiss her. He realized he was leaning toward her when she spoke again.

"My father isn't here, and I don't expect anything unmanageable with my sister, but just in case?"

The thought of spending more time with her sped his pulse. The uncertainty etching her heart-shaped face decided it. One thing first.

He closed the final inches and tasted her lips. Her exhale caressed his mouth, and her fingers swept through his hair, pulling him closer. He fought the urgency to work his tongue past her lips and kept it chaste. Since kissing was the breadth of his experience, he'd stolen countless lip-locked moments, each one growing bolder but never out of bounds. Though the sensation of her lips whispering over his went beyond that point of contact, spreading south.

He cupped her cheek, holding her to him. Shuddering waves of need heated his insides and gripped his groin. If the kiss continued one more second, his vow to his parents would be put to the test. He broke the kiss.

The seam of her lips separated, the delicate lines of her face magnifying her allure. He grabbed his phone from the cup holder and jumped out. He wasn't a slave to his desires, and she'd asked him to come inside because she needed a friend. That he could do.

She joined him at the garage keypad and punched in the code. By the time they reached the interior door, he'd managed to wrestle down his libido.

A dark hush greeted them in the kitchen. There was a trace of mustiness in the air, the staleness of vacancy, but the red sauce smearing the dishes in the sink appeared fresh.

He trailed her confident pace over the worn brown carpet to the sitting room. A single lamp illuminated dark wood panels, a paisley couch, matching armchair, and a clunky tube-style television.

"This place is familiar." He rubbed his jaw.

Creases formed in her forehead. She scanned the room but didn't really seem to be inspecting it, her gaze more inwardly focused.

"*That '70s Show* was filmed right here in this living room, wasn't it?" He grinned, amusing himself.

Not a hint of a smile on her distracted face. "Poor people have poor ways."

A reminder he didn't know what she did for a living, and he'd probably offended her, dammit. He didn't know anything about her. Except the smooth silkiness of her lips.

"Sis?" She ambled down the hall and poked her head in each of the two bedrooms. "She must be in the attic."

The room chilled, and he shivered. "The attic?"

"She feels safe there." She paused at the enclosed staircase that led up from the mouth of the hallway and held out her hand.

He rubbed the back of his neck. "Sure you don't need a few minutes to talk? I can wait down here if you want privacy."

Her hand remained outstretched, her rich brown eyes watching him with a pleading kind of intensity that told him his presence was important.

He joined her and twined their fingers, her palm cool and damp. What could he do to ease her nervousness? He tightened his grip and followed her up, the unlit stairwell closing in around him. "Where's the light-switch?"

She stopped them on the top stair, the darkness as heavy as her silence. Her clothes rustled. Beeps followed. A small red light blinked on the wall.

Apprehension crawled over him, tickling the hairs on his arms. "Was that a keypad?"

A door opened, and he squinted into the fluorescent glare escaping from inside. Her grip on his hand tugged him over the threshold, and he followed, compelled, curious. *Shocked.*

His attention landed on the center of the room, and he struggled to process what he saw.

A teenage girl knelt before them, completely nude. Her white-blond hair and fair skin looked nothing like Liv. But what sent dread through his veins was how she lowered her brow to the floor, hands behind her back, thighs spread.

The door clicked shut behind him, snapping him out of his stunned paralysis. He averted his eyes to the cot in the corner and the steel rings bolted in the wall above it. Dear God, what was this place?

His pulse roared in his ears, his voice strangled. "That's your sister?"

Liv cocked her head, a smirk pinned on her face.

Holy crap. Did she lie to him? Why?

Realization sank his stomach. She lied to lure him there.

He spun, yanked the door handle. No give. He slammed a fist on the door, a muffled thump. Solid wood. Reinforced with a steel jamb. "Let me out."

"No."

No? She was refusing to release him? His blood drained to his legs, leaving a trail of ice in its wake. He pawed at the keypad on the brick wall. His heart rate redoubled. Surely the naked girl was there voluntarily. Maybe they just wanted to have some fun with him, and he'd given the wrong signals.

He turned, pressed his back to the door, and tugged out his phone. "I'm not into this…whatever this is."

The buttons wouldn't respond. Black screen. He jammed his thumb against the power switch. Nothing.

A hard swallow caught in his throat. He raised his eyes, found her watching him with that terrible stillness about her. When she spoke, the voice didn't belong to the girl with the silky lips and enthralling lullaby.

"You will learn, practice, and become the twelve requirements demanded by your Master." She crouched to stroke the girl's head, who hadn't moved or glanced up.

It had to be a sick joke. Just some swinging neighborhood debauchery. He needed to hear her admit it, because imagining the alternative was kicking his heart rate to dangerous levels.

"So you lured me here for some kinky game where I play gimp boy to your…your…she-Master?" He released a laugh, and it was strained and desperate. "Sorry, babe. You've got the wrong guy."

She rose and stalked toward him, her stride commanding, her expression blank. "I am a deliverer. I deliver the strikes that enforce your obedience."

Her voice, sweet Jesus, it was so cold, so wrong.

He slid to the side of the door, choking on panic, and smacked the keypad. "Open the door."

"I deliver the sexual training that justifies your purchase price."

If he screamed for help, would anyone hear? "What's really going on here, Liv? If you're in trouble, I can help you. I know people you can talk to."

She stepped into his space, the wall pressing against his back. "In ten weeks, I will deliver you to be sold."

His breath caught. "You're insane."

What he saw in her eyes wasn't insanity. Deeply-embedded resolve held her pupils immovable.

"Requirement number three," she said. "Slave will keep his eyes down unless Master requests otherwise."

The impulse to fight strengthened his spine. He was a linebacker, trained to run and tackle, so he lunged. Grabbed her shoulders. Slammed her chest into the wall beside the keypad. She didn't fight, didn't squeak under his rough handling.

"Enter the pass-code." He pressed against her back and gripped her neck.

Her body slouched, free of tension beneath the brace of his arms. She wasn't fighting him, and he realized why when the door swung open.

He swiveled, muscles heated to bolt, and met the short barrel of a revolver.

A hulking man strode through, his face shrouded by the hood of his sweatshirt. He kept the pistol aimed between Josh's eyes and closed the door. "Release her."

Josh let go of her neck, his jaw clenching painfully. She'd let him pin her, knowing she held the upper hand.

He took two steps back, hands up, and searched her face in a Hail-Mary hope her rigid mouth would crack into laughter and say, *Ha, ha. You've been punk'd.*

Her hips rocked in tight circles, slowly, seductively, as if an erotic dancer had taken over her body. She sashayed to stand beside the man with the gun and raised her chin.

The chill in her voice stopped his heart. "Eyes. Down."

CHAPTER 5

"Joshua Carter no longer exists." Liv gave him a second to absorb that, though the firestorm thrashing in his eyes told her he might need more than a pregnant pause.

Her heart rate threatened to rob the strength from her knees, and that kind of weakness pissed her the fuck off.

She gathered control over her features, arranging them into the stoniest expression she had. "For the next ten weeks, your name is whatever I want it to be."

"Let me go." Despite the pallor blanching his golden complexion, he glared down at her with the composure of a fearless man.

His maturity was emphasized by the whiskers darkening his square jaw and the carved contour of his rigid muscles.

She needed to think of him as a boy. Boys were malleable, unsteady, and less attractive. "For now, your name is *boy*."

Standing by the locked door as if its proximity could save him, he set his jaw, green eyes sparking with defiance. Van kept his position beside her, the gun level with the boy's head.

"Eyes down, boy." Not that she expected him to

obey. That progression had to be paved with his blood and tears. The thought stabbed a terrible pain in her chest.

His unwavering stare continued to press against her skin, and there was so much force in it, she didn't think she could endure it much longer. She would, though. She would do anything for the hope that awaited her at the end of the night. The hope that would feed her famished heart.

In the center of the room, the girl remained folded on her knees. Since her training neared completion, she could demonstrate some expectations for the boy.

Liv approached her, injecting her command with unfeeling iron. "On the cot, slave. Cuffed."

The girl crawled to the cot and lay on her back, hands reaching above her head to grasp the handcuffs on the wall. She locked in her wrists. The cuffs connected to steel eyehooks and were sturdy enough to restrain the strongest of struggling slaves.

The boy's glare ticked between the girl and the gun, tension rippling over the hard lines of his body.

He closed his eyes, opened them, and met Liv's gaze, nostrils flaring. "I kissed you."

Her insides tightened, and Van's finger twitched on the trigger. Just a twitch. Van's role that night was to keep quiet and ensure her success in confining the boy in the box. The rational part of her was glad Van was there. If she were alone with the boy, she might've anchored her thoughts in the intimacy they'd shared. She might've weakened under the resentment of her betrayal.

Van's presence kept her frigid, focused mask in place. But he was undoubtedly raging with jealousy. *Too damned bad.* He knew the job and what it involved.

She reached up and slid back his hood, caressing his scar. The affection catered to his possessiveness, calming his inward battle, evidenced in the subtle slackening of his finger on the trigger. But unveiling his expression also served as a warning for the boy. Van outmatched him in muscle and cruelty, and under the fluorescents, she knew Van's eyes were blades of silver and cut just as deep.

The boy swallowed. "You said something about—" He gritted his teeth. "You intend to sell me? Like a…a slave? This isn't a game?"

No way did the boy fully grasp what was going on. He was probably still clinging to the hope of release when they were done with him.

"Let him go, Liv." Van scratched his neck. "You got the wrong kid."

While Van was attempting to win the boy's trust, it didn't quite soften his razor eyes. He sucked at being the passive captor, though to his credit, he'd never had to watch from the sidelines before. His sadistic control-freakery was probably tearing him up inside.

"Just stand there and hold the gun like you're supposed to, Van." She met the boy's steadfast expression with her own. "You will be trained. Then you will be sold for sex."

"I can pay." He raised his stubborn chin. "I can come up with the money and cover whatever they're paying you."

Hell, he didn't have a dollar, and certainly not two million of them. His illogical offer meant he was still in the panic stage. She remembered the confusion and how the uncontrollable trembling and desire to escape had made her crazed, hyper-aware, and desperate.

Witnessing him experience the first horrific phases of capture was why she'd avoided conversation in the truck. She hadn't wanted to connect with him as his equal, as a friend. Connections like that birthed concern and sympathy and other touchy-feely detriments to her arrangement.

But she'd returned his kiss. At the time, she'd reasoned it was a luring tactic. Until their lips separated, and she was left with a lingering taste of something she'd never have.

"Follow me." She didn't wait for the boy's obedience. Van's gun would ensure it. She strode to the soundproof wall that divided the attic into two chambers.

At the door, she punched her code into the keypad. She and Van had separate codes to move through the rooms within the house, but only she had a code for this one.

She walked through the long, narrow room. Once her prison, it was now her sanctuary, her bedroom, and the only place she could escape Van. When Mr. E promoted her from slave to deliverer, he allowed her request to hold the only combination to the room. And why not? He could reach through any door with the threat he held over her. But Van could not.

Tossing her phone on the threadbare mattress in the corner, she moved past the open shower, toilet, and sink along the front wall. Reaching the coffin-sized pine box opposite the unenclosed bathroom, she turned and waited for the boy to join her.

There was an illusion that he could walk freely into the room, but it was psychological bullshit. Van wouldn't shoot if the boy slipped-up, but any number of the non-lethal weapons hidden on his person insured compliance.

The brick at her back made the attic feel inescapable, as was intended, but the true barrier was the sound-deadening concrete forms veneering the exterior walls. Its effectiveness was tested by her own lungs during her first year in this room. No one had come to save her.

The boy crossed the threshold with Van's gun at his back. His arms lolled at his sides, his expression growing more wary and alert with each step. What would he do? What was he thinking? Planning?

He scanned her room—the room she would be sharing with him—and his gaze seized on the phone on the mattress, flicked to the horizontal box, and returned to the phone.

"The phone is locked." She kept her posture still and straight, her voice detached.

A storm of frantic ideas churned in his icy eyes. He could try to dial 911, but the modifications Mr. E put on her phone disabled things like the camera and the ability to make emergency calls while it was locked. This allowed her to keep her phone with her, one of his requirements. He used it to track her every call, her every move. At the end of the day, she was just as trapped as the boy.

Van nudged him with the gun, moving him forward.

The boy stopped a foot away from her position beside the box. His breath evened in what seemed to be an attempt at deference. Too many emotions clouded his face to predict what he was planning. But his choices were no longer his.

"Requirement number four. Slave will not wear clothes unless Master requests otherwise." She exhaled slowly through her nose. This would not go over well. "Strip."

His expression emptied. Was it shock? Was he masking his terror? If so, he was doing a damned good job. Maybe he already worked out it would come to this. When she was forced to strip the first time, she'd already played out the worst scenarios in her head. Surrendering her clothes had paled next to her imagination. Hadn't stopped her from pleading for her modesty.

"Why did you skip requirements one and two?" His voice was calm. Too calm.

Had he already reached the compliance stage? That usually took days to weeks of unrelenting pressure. Perhaps he was just being vigilant and probing his hopeless situation from all angles.

She inhaled deeply through her nose. As a cold-hearted deliverer, she couldn't answer his questions. She kicked his knee, hard enough to make him stumble. "Clothes. Now."

He glanced at Van, the gun, back to her. "If I refuse, do I get a matching scar, too?"

The little shit actually grinned. It was shaky as hell, but he had brass balls. Her stomach sank at the thought of breaking them.

Van laughed, playing the part. "Only if you're really lucky. You'd have to fall in love and break the virginity clause to earn one of these." He stroked his scar.

She closed her eyes. The love thing was one-sided, and he'd left out the most important part, the piece that held her there. For that, she was grateful.

When she opened her eyes, the boy was watching her with a demeanor she couldn't interpret.

"Just take off your clothes, man," Van said. "Do

what she says, and no one will scar your pretty face."

The boy held her gaze as he yanked his shirt over his head, toed off his work boots, and dropped his jeans and boxers in one shove. He didn't cover himself. Just stepped out of his pants and let her peruse his body.

His thick neck expanded into cut after cut of muscle down his torso. Sinews and tendons stretched the skin in his arms and legs. It was a physique developed through rigorous labor and exercise, wrapped in golden flesh. And his cock… Her breath caught. In its flaccid state, it lay over a loose, full sac and reached a few inches beyond.

"Look at that." Van circled to stand beside her. "And you thought it was the jockstrap straining his pants."

The boy's eyes widened, likely in realization that this wasn't a spontaneous kidnapping. Yeah, she knew all about his jockstraps, but she'd never mentioned his package to Van. Didn't mean she hadn't thought about it. Warmth swirled, uninvited, through her body.

When she was sure she'd mustered strength back into her voice, she tapped the edge of the box. "Get in."

A twitch in his socked foot was the only response.

Van rotated the aim of the gun down, up, left to right, as if deciding what body part to shoot. He settled the sights on the boy's balls. "Liv, you sure Mr. E doesn't bury the bodies in the backyard?"

Fear was the cruelest weapon. It victimized the mind and bred inaction.

She despised the idea of scaring the boy. Fuck, she was scared every damned day of her life, but she maintained the bitchy role she was required to play. "I don't want to know what he does with the bodies."

Truth was, Mr. E no longer needed to dirty his gloved hands since he'd acquired her. His visits were rare, his identity masked.

"You won't shoot me." The boy rolled back his shoulders, flexing his pecs. "How much money will you make off me?"

She leaned up on tip-toes, using the nearness to examine the depth of his bright eyes, the sun-bronzed skin dipping in the hollows of his cheeks, and the velvet pillow of his lips. He was raw, unblemished beauty. Mesmerizing. Distracting.

Relaxing her feet, she dropped back. "Emily Carter has a doctor's appointment tomorrow morning. Your mom goes every Saturday for her weekly allergy shot."

A hitch shuddered around his mouth.

She reached behind Van, slipped her hand under his sweatshirt, and removed the Taurus PT-22 from its wedge between his spine and waistband.

"The clinic's not in a very good part of town." She held up the .22, aimed at the ceiling. The intent wasn't to shoot him. It conveyed a much grimmer purpose. "Would be a shame if she got carjacked."

He stared at the gun, at the pink wood-grain grip. Horror tightened his face as he recognized his mother's pistol. "No." A heartbreaking whisper. "Please, no."

Though he gave her the response she needed, her heart felt like it was shrinking. She relaxed her mouth in a painful smile. "I stole it from her glovebox a few days ago. She's unmolested. For now."

His breath wheezed hard and fast. A moment later, his lungs slowed. He looked at the box, and a long, deep inhale widened his nostrils. He blinked slowly, eyes lowering.

Then he jerked forward, fist reared back and aimed at her. Expecting it, she dropped in a crouch, dodged his punch, and slammed her shoulders into his knees.

The .22 clattered to the floor, a deliberate maneuver to distract him. He wobbled, skirting around her, and scrambled for the gun. She let him. After all, it wasn't loaded.

As he bent to retrieve it, Van pressed a boot on his back and shoved the loaded revolver against his nape.

From a small trunk by the box, she gathered locking metal cuffs and a coil of chain, the clanking drawing his attention. "Van's gun is loaded. Your mother's gun is not. Go ahead. Check."

He did, wrinkles forming on his forehead. After a second check of the magazine, he set it on the floor and slumped under the weight of Van's foot.

"In the box." She kicked the .22 out of reach as he climbed in, his movements wooden.

The cuffs went on first, cinching tight. Next, she wrapped the chain around his wrists until the full length was used. The excess binding was more psychological than practical.

He allowed her to move his limbs where she wanted them, his eyes squeezed shut. What was he feeling? Frustration, denial, hope of rescue, utter terror? Her time in that box had covered the gamut.

With the ends of the chains hooked together, she raised his bound arms above his head and locked the cuffs to one of the many eyehooks lining the wood slats.

The box was a device in repression, used to send a degrading message. She controlled his actions, down to every sensory detail. In twenty-four hours, he would emerge sleep-deprived, hungry, and, with no access to a bathroom, humiliated. Weakened and at the mercy of her commands.

She removed his socks and repeated the shackling with his ankles. He stiffened each time her finger brushed his skin, likely repulsed by the feel of her. She swallowed around the knot in her throat. She didn't blame him.

A yank at his arms and legs confirmed the detainment. She stepped back, followed Van to the door, and entered the code.

As he pushed it open, he swayed toward her, slanting his cheek against hers.

She tensed. With his mouth so close, would he kiss her or bite her?

His nose slid through her hair, inhaling her scent. "I'll let Mr. E know we'll be ready for the videos in five."

The gentleness in his tone and the meaning of his words loosened some of her stiffness. On nights like these, when they watched the footage together and he shared in the assurance it delivered, she could feel the tender caress of affection poking past her deepest bruises and curling around her heart. She nodded.

The door clicked behind him. She hurried back to the boy.

On his back, muscles bared, bound, and stretched the full length of the box, he was an erotic picture. She was a criminal, and as ashamed as she was by that, the disgusting, fucked-up part of her anticipated spending the next ten weeks touching every inch of this man.

Boy.

She dragged her gaze from his body to his face, and guilt slammed into her.

He stared up at her with so much pain in his eyes. "Don't hurt my parents."

Her gut twisted. She knew that pain, lived it every day. She leaned in, lips hovering a breath away, and repeated what Mr. E had said to her. "That's up to you."

Resolve hardened his face. She knew that emotion, too. Her time in the box was permanently carved in memory, which had made Van's threats of returning her there an effective form of control in her training.

Tendrils of resentment coiled around her throat. To dwell on her or the boy's predicament would only bring irresponsible hesitation. So she did what she always did to distract her thoughts.

She reached into the cold place inside her, searching for something yearning she could sing with dispassion. The beginning verses of "What It Is" by *Kodaline* fell past her lips and shivered through the room. She sang with an icy pitch as she removed a blindfold from the trunk by the box and tied it over his wide, glaring eyes.

To deprive smell, a swimmer's nose plug went on next. He could breathe through his mouth, and the cracks in the box allowed airflow, but it wouldn't feel that way to him once she shut the lid.

The skin on his face was hot and damp, the muscles beneath jerking against her fingers. She continued to sing as she cuffed headphones over his ears, plugged them into the tablet outside of the box, and activated the timer. Twenty minutes of heart-hammering silence.

The music in her voice strangled, stopped. Twenty minutes alone with his thoughts. Then the misery would begin.

"It's just the way it is," she murmured with an ache in her throat.

His body was motionless, but she didn't miss the goosebumps creeping across his skin or the slight tremor in his jaw. The sudden desire to comfort him drew her closer, bending her at the waist, until her mouth brushed his, softly, unjustly. His lips pulled away in a quiver that she felt throughout her body.

She straightened and rubbed her breastbone, unable to soothe the ache beneath it. "I'm so sorry." A whisper, too low to pass through the earphones.

Then she closed the lid.

CHAPTER 6

Opaque fabric pressed against Josh's eyes. The clip on his nose forced his breaths through his mouth. Were there air holes? There must've been, otherwise he'd be gulping lungfuls of nothingness. His throat whistled. His mouth parched. Maybe he *was* suffocating.

Were his captors standing right outside the box? He couldn't hear a damned thing beyond the covers on his ears and the thump of his heart.

The unforgiving wood dug into his shoulders and hips. The thousand-pound chains pinned his hands and feet. The too-close walls caved in around him, firing the nerve endings along his skin in concentrated chaos. It was the kind of tactile assault he imagined could only be experienced within the deafening suffocation of a coffin.

Fear boiled in his stomach and hit his throat with searing acid. Great, he still had the sense of taste, which meant he could savor his puke as he choked on it. He squirmed, tilting his head to the side in case his stomach emptied.

This had to be a depraved prank. They wouldn't leave him chained like this for long. The girl in the next room didn't have visible wounds on her fragile frame. There weren't any instruments of cruelty hanging on the walls. Hell, the gun wasn't even loaded.

He should've grabbed the blonde and threatened to break her neck. Why hadn't he kicked the gun from Van's hand as soon as the man walked in? His chest tightened. He should've left Liv on the road to tow her own effing car.

His pulse elevated, and his body burned and itched. Mom and Dad would be looking for him. How many calls had he missed? His heavy breaths congealed the air around him. She'd done something to his phone.

He bucked against the box, yanking and twisting at the restraints. His stupid freaking impulse to help a stranger had put his parents in danger. He'd left them unprotected and abandoned them with a farm they couldn't manage alone.

He was idiot. His cheeks burned, and his body fevered with sweat and chills. He tried to punch his legs. The shackles held. So frigging stupid. He kicked again, and pain jolted through his ankles.

Could they hear him struggling? He bit down on his lip, swallowing hard. Had his hostility sent them out to hurt his parents?

A roar clawed from his throat, thundering in his head. How could he have let this happen? Why hadn't he sent his own text to Mom? Why hadn't he noticed these people watching him? He should've investigated the problem with her car himself. He could've prevented this.

His muscles clenched against another bout of trembling. Dad would retrace the route from the stadium to home. He'd find nothing. Likely not even her stalled sedan. She was too well-prepared, luring him with a story, sabotaging his phone while he sat beside her, and coercing him with Mom's routine and her stolen .22. How long had they been watching?

Why him? Oh God, what had he done to earn their attention?

Helplessness ricocheted over his limbs, thrashing against the chains. Mom was probably pacing in the kitchen, wearing down the linoleum, overworking her already fragile heart.

A sob erupted in his chest, taking him by surprise as it escaped with his gasps. *Please, dear God.* He closed his eyes, trapping wells of moisture. *Please take care of Mom and Dad.*

Prayer saturated his thoughts. He stammered through his favorite hymns, filling his heart with the inspirational, joyful words. He desperately needed the power of God to overcome this and to ensure he rose whole and confident and alive.

The walls of the box crept impossibly closer. He thrashed. Useless. He widened his eyes beneath the mask, trying frantically to see, and met a shroud of black. So cramped. Dark. His lungs panted. He needed to focus, to keep his head.

He tried to recall the meditation techniques he'd learned at his retreat. Sucking air through a dry throat, he pictured light filtering through the box's wood planks, spreading a glow over him, chasing away the shadows. The walls around him expanded outward. The coffin doubled in size. Oxygen flowed in. His pulse slowed. He swiped his tongue over cracked lips. Bless the depth of his imagination.

Time stretched. Was it minutes? Or was it hours? They should've released him by now. What were they doing out there? Sharpening knives? Laughing about what a sucker he was? Or were they planning to move the box out back and bury it with him inside?

No, not death. She'd said he would be sold in ten weeks. He would have to be alive for that to happen. He latched onto the hope of survival, even as the implication of his body being auctioned for money brought its own horrors.

A violent shudder ripped through him. Purchased by what kind of person? For what purpose?

He knew. He knew the answers and shoved them away, stretching his jaw to accommodate a panicked rush of breath. *Heavenly Father, please help me.*

Despair gave way to anger and frustration. His prayers weakened in conviction, losing their appeal. He had put himself in this situation. God had nothing to do with it. Doubt trickled in. Doubt in His divine rescue. Doubt in himself.

Too many terrible things could happen to him and his parents. The air thinned, and his lungs struggled against images of Mom and Dad's bodies gutted in their bed and painted in blood.

He curled his hands into fists, picturing Liv slicing off his fingernails with a razor blade. Nausea coiled in his stomach. The glaring possibility was rape. Was he strong enough to prevent Van from taking him from behind?

His heart pounded. His virginity was his to give, dammit, not to be stolen and dehumanized. The thought girded him, even as he knew his restraints enabled them to do whatever they wanted.

He rolled his head back and forth over the wood. What had he learned during his spiral of mistakes? Beyond his stupidity in blind trust? He was in the *Two Trails Crossing* neighborhood in Temple. His captors went by Van and Liv. Calm, physically fit, and armed, they posed a difficult barrier to break through.

Besides the mention of a Mr. E, she seemed to be the one in control. Who was she? Clearly not the girl who cried a sob story on the street. Hindsight punched him hard in the gut.

But she couldn't be a sociopath. Hadn't he glimpsed the real girl in his truck in her moving song? No one could fake the gravity he'd heard in her voice. What was driving her? Money was the obvious reason, but her aim seemed...more profound. Was she motivated by something deeper? Something attached to her?

A deep-rooted sadness had flooded her eyes and creased her mouth when he asked her not to hurt his parents. Then it was complicated by that second kiss, the one she took while he was pinned in the coffin.

Maybe he was only seeing what he wanted to see? Scrambling for the only thread of optimism in his reach? Perhaps the kiss was a design to mess with his head. Except it had conveyed a hesitancy the first kiss did not.

There was nothing hesitant about Van. His composure was fortified by piercing gray eyes, so sharp they didn't blink. Which made the calculation in his chumminess obvious—and confusing. Even as Josh had recognized it for what it was, he couldn't deny he felt a little less tense when Van traded his steely gaze for a full-faced grin.

And the girl, who must've been some kind of slave, had somehow earned a respite from restraints and supervision. A reward for good behavior?

Sweet Jesus, one week in this nightmare and he might be drooling applesauce. He writhed in the chains, his hips banging against the sides. How much longer before they let him out of the freaking box?

He tried again to calm himself, catching his breath, rolling his neck and shoulders through the burgeoning pangs of muscle cramps.

There was a way out of this. Somehow. He just needed to man up and figure it out. Field experience in instructional ministry had taught him how to associate with people, how to listen to them, and guide them through tough situations. He would concentrate his attention on observing what she was hiding and hearing what wasn't being said. He would study her face and learn her expressions. Once he discovered the heart of her, he would offer advice, befriend her, discover her strengths and weaknesses, and predict her next moves.

What if she injured him? Raped him? What were his limits? How much could he endure before he despised her so much he lost himself in hate?

Adrenaline burned through his veins. If he could survive the next few hours or days, he could survive ten weeks. Maintaining composure was paramount.

A sudden ringing sound pierced the silence. It was a consistent lonely tone, like the lingering bong of a brass bell. Was it some kind of tinnitus?

He rolled his head side-to-side, and the frequency seemed to ripple around his ears. It was definitely streaming through the headphones. The volume wasn't elevated enough to hurt. Just one loud, relentless blare.

Minutes passed, and the sound continued. His fingers tingled, as did the skin around his lips. Panic and irritation robbed his ability to catch his breath. He yawned over and over, popping his ears.

No change in frequency. No relief. He buckled down, fought the tremors in his body and the furor of emotions pushing against the backs of his eyes.

"Make it stop!" The scream shredded his vocal chords. "Please, stop."

He counted to one thousand. He couldn't calm his heart.

When would it end? He counted to five thousand.

All that existed was the certainty in one demanding tonality. He couldn't focus.

Stop, stop, stop.

"Please...Please turn if off...Stop!"

His throat scraped, his shrieks unraveling his hold on his mind.

Liv found Van downstairs in the sitting room, reclined in the armchair, a lit cigarette drooping from his lips. She stiffened as he patted his knee in invitation, his eyes twin sparks of silver in the glow of his phone, the room's only light.

The way he looked at her chilled her skin, even as his smoke-curled smile made her heart ache for things he could never give.

Spine steeled against the brutal beauty of his face, she put one sneaker before the other, plucked the cig from his mouth, and perched on his knee. "Ready?"

Moving his arms around her waist, he rested his chin on her shoulder and reached for the device. "Been ready since the day I met you."

Her skin itched where his breath touched her cheek, where his leg pressed against her ass, where his arms brushed her hips. He was both an infectious rash and a soothing touch.

She finished the final drag on the cigarette and squashed it in the ashtray, eyes on the blank screen.

He launched their e-mail account, the inbox empty. Empty for nine weeks. She stared at it, willing it to beep, her exhale trapped in her chest.

A tap on the screen made the phone call. Another tap, and he switched it to speaker mode, his free arm draped over her thigh. The call connected on the first ring.

"Any problems?" Crisp and deep, the voice dragged a shudder from her lungs.

"No, sir," she and Van said in chorus.

The inbox dinged, announcing a new message with an attached file.

"The recording is five minutes old," Mr. E said, "and two minutes long. I'll wait."

Van clicked on the video file and leaned back. She bent toward it, where it perched in his outstretched hand.

On the screen, a woman in her late-forties sat at a table in a kitchen that had become familiar from this camera angle. Wisps of gray curled through her short brown hair, her hands folded around the mug she stared into. If she glanced up, her eyes would be a deep warm brown, set in the determined expression of a woman who had birthed a child on the heels of an abusive relationship. A woman whose passion for skydiving came second to her love for her only child. The woman who said that anyone could fall; the skill was in landing.

When she'd learned her missing daughter's remains had been found in an abandoned house, she'd cried for weeks as Liv watched through video footage from her attic prison. But Mom knew how to land. A few weeks before Liv's one-year incarceration as a slave ended, Mom moved on to a new job and a new home.

The ache to find that kitchen in the video festered inside her. While Liv had the freedom to run errands, scout for new victims, and—not often enough—skydive, her movements were monitored. With anxious discretion, she slipped in and out of public libraries, hunting the web for Jill Reed the skydiving instructor, the pilot, the grieving mother. There were too many skydiving schools, too many Jill Reeds.

She scrutinized Mom's sleeveless shirt. Tepid climate in October? Could've been anywhere along the Gulf. Were the creases in her hair from long hours beneath a skydiving helmet? Or a ponytail holder, pulled back for any job? The print on the newspaper at her elbow was too small to read, and the blinds were closed on the window. No new clues, every recorded clip too meticulously selected before delivery.

The sudden impulse to demand her mother's location from Mr. E cramped her gut and heated her face. Last time she did that, he slapped her with his two-week version of house arrest. So she crushed her reckless notion behind pinned lips and traced a fingernail over the beloved image on the screen.

She earned three video sessions per slave. One on the evening of the capture. One after a successful first meeting between buyer and slave. And one when she made the final delivery and the funds were transferred to Mr. E's account.

Only once had she received a video outside of this schedule. It had arrived after she'd forgotten to take her phone on a grocery errand. Her failure to respond immediately to one of Mr. E's texts while she was out had earned her a video of Mom's demolished car, lying on its side in a ravine. Mom survived with three broken ribs and a shattered femur.

Her chest tightened at the memory and squeezed harder as she watched Mom stand from the table and move out of view of the camera. The video ended, frozen on the empty room.

Each time she watched the videos, she was reminded that she'd sold her soul and the lives of her captives to a man she couldn't trust. Didn't stop her pulse from strumming excitedly as her attention flew to the phone's notification bar. One more email would come, the video meant for her and Van.

"I expect," Mr. E said, "you'll meet your next deadline. Or your future viewings will only include one of the two videos."

A knot lodged in her throat. It was a threat he could only use once. If he killed the only two people she loved, she would no longer have the incentive to work for him…or to go on.

"A camera was installed in the bedroom," Mr. E said. "The recording is three hours old."

The line disconnected.

The lump in her throat loosened. "Did you hear that? Her bedroom, Van." For six years, she'd imagined what it might look like.

"I heard." There was a smile in his voice.

A new message alert popped up. She reached for the screen, colliding with his hand. Chuckling, he offered her the device. Then he wrapped his arms around her waist and leaned them forward on the edge of the seat, hunching over the small screen. She tapped the file, and the video player opened.

Red and brown whimsical birds winged a painted pattern over the bedroom wall. White lacy curtains draped the window, the shroud of night swallowing any clues that could point to location or climate. A red-checkered quilt blanketed the twin bed and the six-year-old girl within.

Liv's breath stuttered, and she felt Van smile against her neck.

The girl grinned, front tooth missing, eyes heavy-lidded with trust and love. Her smile was for the blond woman who sat beside her.

Liv wanted to rejoice at seeing her happy and safe, but bitter jealousy was a noose, strangling her air and failing her heart.

He gripped the back of her free hand, lifting it with his and cupping their twined fingers around the screen. Their fingers an inch from the girl's pixelated face was the closest they'd ever been to touching her. In her mind, she'd named her Mattie.

Warm breath flitted over the curve of her neck, his other arm a brace around her waist. At that moment, his affection was a quietude in shared happiness, their connection suspended in a twinkling of peace.

"She's beautiful," he murmured against her skin.

Dark brown hair curled from Mattie's sweet face and fanned over the pillow. She laughed at something her adoptive mother said and rolled to her side, shut her eyes.

Liv imagined herself a mother, saying silly things to incite that beautiful, toothy smile. She wanted to call her name just to look into her eyes. She wanted to know her *real* name and hug her when she cried. What would it feel like to pick her up when she fell, to help her with homework, to watch her blow out birthday candles? It would have been a complete life.

A burn erupted behind her eyes, her fingers dragging Van's up and down the edge of the screen. She breathed deeply, tried to swallow the choking hopelessness.

The blond woman reached for the bedside lamp.

"No." A whimper escaped Liv's lips. "Not yet."

Van moved their twined hands, hugging her arm to her waist. Her other hand held the device in a death grip.

On screen, Mattie's shoulders rose and fell with restful breaths, her little hand fisted in the blanket.

Then the lamp clicked off, drenching the screen in black. The video stopped.

Liv's heart plummeted. She wanted to restart it, tried to untangle her arm from his, but he held it pinned against her body. She balanced the phone on her leg to punch the play button, and he snatched it away.

"No replays, Liv." He forged his voice in an iron tone. "You know the rules."

Watch it once and delete it. Their phones were monitored and swapped out each time Mr. E visited. No cameras and recordings allowed on the property. No evidence. No replays. No saved or copied files. No distractions from the job.

The job, the job, the job. Focus on the job. Be the job. *Or else.* It was all she was, a mechanical, hollow nothing that did anything needed to prevent the *else.*

A violent shudder snapped through her bones. As long as she lived, Mom and Mattie would be in danger.

Liv's death could set them free. So many times, she came close but couldn't do it. She was a weak, selfish cunt.

She pushed against his chest. "Let me go."

His arm tightened against her waist. "The child will be fine."

The child.

"She's *your* child." Spit flew from her lips, her

voice rising. "*Our* child."

He dropped the device and spun her off his lap. Her back hit the couch, the weight of him holding her down. Her pathetic struggle ended with her arms above her head, shackled by one of his hands, his other pointing at the phone on the floor.

"She's *not* our child!" His volume hiked, matching hers. "She belongs to that woman."

"A woman who probably works for Mr. E!"

In six years and twenty-one videos, the blonde's face had never been revealed. Mattie's life depended on Liv. A failure during the job or a fracture in the rules promised another accident. Mom had been meant to die in that car. Mattie wouldn't be so lucky. Only Liv could protect her, and the safest way would be to hide her from Mr. E. She could be anywhere in the world. Liv desperately needed her name.

"Wipe that look off your face." He pressed his hips against hers, the steel of his irises resistant and unfeeling. "Even if you could find her, you can't take her from the only mother she's ever known."

"The way you snatched me from my mother?"

His lips thinned into hard lines with clenched teeth in the middle. "Back to this again?"

"You started this when you accepted his proposal. You *chose* to ruin people's lives."

He released her arms, standing tall and imposing, and glared down at her. "Mr. E started it when he freed me from that goddamned slum."

He stabbed a finger at the front door as if indicating the direction of his crackhaggot mother. She slung drugs in El Paso, assuming she still lived. Liv knew he didn't care either way.

Mr. E had freed him from his victimized life, trained him to be a deliverer, and paid him to kidnap a girl of his choice. Lucky for Van, his choice ignorantly roller-bladed up to his car.

Her chest ached, and her body felt cold. "You broke his rules."

Van took her virginity not long after capture. Eight weeks later, he delivered her to the client, claiming she met the requirements of obedience and chastity. The former was accurate. Van had well and truly whipped the insolence out of her and replaced it with the trap of fear. The chastity, however, was disproved when the buyer brought in a doctor while Van waited for the exam results and the money transfer. The positive pregnancy test was a shock to everyone. Except Van.

She sat up, unable to glance away from the scar that perforated his prominent cheekbone, his face otherwise model-perfect from his clear, round eyes and full lips to the high, smooth bridge of his strong nose. His complexion glowed so vibrantly with health, one could almost overlook the four-inch red cut. The laceration Mr. E had given him when the buyer returned her without payment. The mate to the one she'd received minutes after his.

He watched her with a toothpick in his mouth and the harsh lines of intention etched around his eyes. "I saved you."

Did he save her by impregnating her before she was sold? Or when he pleaded for her life as Mr. E held the gun to her head upon her return? What did a human trafficker want with a pregnant slave? In the end, Mr. E gave Van what he'd wanted: Her.

"Yeah, you saved me." She clenched and

unclenched her hands. "Instead of a life as a sex slave or a bullet in the brain, I got a disfigured face, my tubes tied, an illegal job, and a promise that I will never hug the only two people who matter to me."

His darkening expression blasted her anger to her stomach. That look had trained her to avert her eyes and drop to her knees. But sometimes, in the dark, the intensity of his stare and the openness of his lust almost felt like love.

A muscle jumped in his cheek. "Someday, I hope to matter to you, because you are the only one who matters to me. You will always be mine, Liv."

The promise propelled her to the night he'd preyed on her fear of him, comforting her while piercing past her virginal barrier. In that moment of frailty, wrapped in his strong arms, that scared, lonely girl had wanted nothing more than his devotion. She should've fought, should've retained some inkling of dignity.

That girl had realized, too late, something wasn't quite right with his adoring smile. After that night, the matching scars, and the loss of Mattie, that girl fell so far the hand of God couldn't pull her back. If manufacturing sex slaves in the house of evil was the only way to protect Mom and Mattie, to hell with God and everyone else.

Van rolled the toothpick between his lips and knelt in the *V* of her legs. "Shall we head to bed?"

The desire in his eyes knocked her backward.

She pulled her knees up and pivoted, scrambling off the couch. "I have a job to do."

He caught her before she reached the stairs, slamming her back against the wall, his lips a toothpick away from hers. His hand moved over her waist, fingers slipping beneath her waistband.

The way his breath hitched and the heat melting his steely eyes swept an uninvited warmth through her womb. When he spit the pick on the floor and slanted his mouth toward hers, she jerked her face away. *Damn, his fucking lips.* His kisses were potent, and she was too emotionally exhausted to pretend they weren't.

A strong finger on her chin turned her face back to his.

"Don't you dare look away from me." He captured her bottom lip between his, nuzzling, and pulled back.

Her heart raced and her weak fucking knees wobbled.

His gaze roamed over her eyes, hair, and mouth, gorging on every detail. "Christ, Liv, you're so fucking beautiful."

She shivered at the compliment. Or was it the nausea tumbling her stomach? Why wasn't she fighting him? Spitting and punching and running away? Was it his strength holding her against the door? The conditioning instilled in her as a slave? The connection they shared through Mattie? Or was it as shallow as lust in the proximity of those stark gray eyes and talented lips?

He shoved a hand through her hair and licked the corner of her mouth. "I won't touch your defenses. Just give me everything else."

Yet he'd already taken everything, and her walls against him were splintering. Even if she could bring herself to kill him, she was restrained by the contract on Mom and Mattie's lives. A contract that would mobilize a hit man if he or Mr. E died suspiciously.

Her chest hurt, and her heartbeat thrashed in her ears. Sure, she could run. She could disappear somewhere they couldn't find her. But Mr. E had promised that if she vanished, he'd make Mom and Mattie's death so vile, it would reach national attention. Just to ensure it reached *her* attention.

Trapped in paranoia, she was terrified to make a mistake, her every action watched, judged, and used to threaten her family. Her nerves were so raw, she trusted nothing, connected to no one, and her loneliness was exasperated by her complicated fucking relationship with the man peppering kisses over her lips. She wanted to love him even as her fingers twitched to run a blade across his throat.

She spoke against his persistent mouth. "If the boy is suffocating on his own vomit, I won't be around long enough to give you anything."

His face tightened. "Very well. Go check on him."

He stepped back to give her just enough room to slip around him. As she did, a recognizable pang assaulted her scalp. She didn't have to look back to know he held a ripped-out chunk of her hair in his fist.

His creepy hair-thing fueled her race up the stairs, to the safety of her bedroom and to the boy she would destroy to keep her family alive.

Liv rested her head against the box, absorbed by the rueful tune braiding through her mind, her ass numb from sitting on the subfloor. She should check on the boy, but the sight of his suffering would shred her already crumbling composure. The raw groans echoing from within the box were doing that enough on their own.

The other captives had fought her with vicious desperation. This boy's determination was quieter, more calculating. She heard it in his steady, low-pitched voice, saw it in his alert gaze and tightening fists, and felt it in her increased body temperature and rapid heartbeat.

Dammit, she'd trained herself not to get attached to these boys. She uncrossed her knees and straightened her legs along the floor. She would need extreme mental focus to smother her attraction to this boy and maintain her icy indifference.

The lid was closed, but she could imagine the terror creasing his beautiful face. It set off her own memories, shooting pain into body parts that had been shackled, whipped, and violated by Van's hand.

She pushed that aside. Self-pity would only earn her a stumbling misstep and a black-eye from Van's fist. Her own punishments certainly wouldn't make this experience easier on the boy. He needed a confident hand to guide him through the next few weeks. She climbed to her feet, her muscles tight with reluctance.

She opened the lid, knowing he wouldn't hear the squeaking hinges nor would he sense her leaning over him. The Solfeggio frequency piping through the headphones overpowered his perceptions, his ability to reason, his entire universe. So much so, he probably wouldn't even sense the change of air.

His lips stretched back in misery as he panted through his teeth. Perspiration wet his skin, streaking drips down his ribs with the heave of his chest. A lonely, weak moan reached from his throat and penetrated her chest.

As his body writhed against the walls in the narrow space and a pang of guilt cramped her gut, she forced herself to evaluate his distress. His rush of breath was panicked but not unrestricted. The chains confined his flailing but didn't cut off blood flow. As for his mind, she just needed it intact enough to be trained, to pass the introductory meeting with the buyer, the final delivery, and receipt of the client's payment.

After she delivered him, he would be dead to her. The same way she thought of the others.

Her eyes caught on his sculpted pecs, traveled along the dips and juts of his abs, and lingered on the impressive length of his cock where it lay against his thigh. Her fingers burned to touch him.

She gripped her stomach, disgusted with herself. He was even more attractive than the others, but he wasn't like them. His matured masculinity was prominent in the thickness of his build and the determined set of his jaw. Most importantly, he had a family and community that would miss him. What a godawful choice she'd been forced to make.

The turmoil inside her hardened into resolve. Ten weeks, a disciplined slave, and Mom and Mattie would be safe for another few months. It was how she measured her life, wasn't it? In ten week increments, in the trade of slaves, one body at a time.

She checked the music player. The one-hour recording rolled through its second of twenty-four repeats. He'd only been in the box for an hour, but it would've felt like days to him.

Ironically, the drone of the 528 hertz was used in meditation as harmonic healing. When Van had shoved her in the box and slapped the earphones on her head, he'd said, "That's a load of new age bullshit. After twenty-four hours of the same goddamned electrical wave passing through your skull, you won't be healed. You'll be fucking manic."

He'd been right. She'd emerged wild-eyed, delusional, and willing to do anything he demanded to avoid another minute in that box.

Fuck Van and his thrills. When she'd fled from him downstairs twenty minutes earlier, the desire in his eyes had been vulgar in its blatancy. Why had he let her escape so easily? He didn't give a shit if the boy vomited in the box, and he was too damned calculating to accept that excuse.

Always, he fucked her when he wanted her. Never did she participate with a willing heart. Yet their scrimmages didn't involve physical force. He'd wear her down with a skilled tongue or prey on her guilt through the mistreatment of a slave. Sometimes, he'd simply threaten to alert Mr. E of her disobedience. It wasn't until she'd met him that she'd understood the meaning of coerced consent.

She stared at the door, terrified to open it, terrified not to.

Surely he went to bed in his room downstairs instead of following her to the attic. If he'd followed her, he'd be out there with that poor girl, who had been asleep when Liv had dashed by in the race to her room.

Fucking hell. Checking on the girl was the right thing to do, no matter how badly she didn't want to open the door. Mr. E didn't give a shit how Van treated the captives as long as they met the requirements at the end of ten weeks.

Her stomach turned as she agonized leaving the boy alone. Goddammit, she was weakening already, and it was only his first night. Her chin trembled. He had to remain in the box. She couldn't bend the rules and expect to mold him into an acceptable slave. But the girl was already trained and didn't deserve Van's needless tormenting.

She closed the lid and jogged to the keypad. If he was waiting on the other side, she could shut it quickly. If he was messing with the girl, she'd have to distract him. Deep breath. She entered the code and cracked the door.

Across the room, the incarnation of her fears sat on the cot, back slouched against the wall. The girl's head dipped up and down between his spread legs, her face and his dick shrouded by her hair.

Vicious memories ripped in Liv's mind, sharp and desolate. She saw her own brown hair instead of the girl's blond. She felt his cock punching the back of her throat and his fingers digging into her scalp. An echoed sensation of their baby moved inside her, stretching her belly, making her bent position agonizing to endure.

Her blood pooled away from her core, leaving the frigid numbness of her year as a slave—nine of those months pregnant.

She swallowed the apparition of her past before it consumed her. The girl sucking him still retained her virginity, yet she was adept with her lips, mouth, and tongue. As one of the buyer's requirements, Liv had spent the prior eight weeks teaching her the skill on Van. And in two weeks, Liv would deliver her to a man whose hand was as heavy as his wallet.

Van looked up and caught her eyes, flames of greed blazing in his. "Come out here and show her how it's done, Liv."

God, she hated him when he was like this. When he watched her with such hunger as he pumped his dick in whatever hole he could command. This wasn't a training session for the girl. It was about Liv and him, and he was using the girl to tunnel Liv's guilt.

She could tuck her chin, shut the door, and fall asleep in the musty familiarity of her mattress inside the safety of her room.

And let the girl stroke and suck him until he was done with her. She'd blown him a dozen times before during practice. Did one more time really matter?

Van pushed down on the back of her head, and her hands convulsed on the mattress.

Compassion was lethal to Liv's well-being, but she couldn't stop it as it shuddered over her skin and swallowed up her heart. She opened the door, passed the cot, another keypad, another code, and down the stairs, her insides bucking and tumbling. At the end of the hall, she stopped at the only closed door and dropped her forehead against it.

What was more horrifying? The footsteps pounding down the stairs after her or all the creepy shit waiting on the other side of his bedroom door?

His body slammed against her back, his exhales hot on her neck, his erection stabbing her tail bone. He hadn't bothered to put his pants back on.

She mustered a stoic tone. "Let's get this over with."

"Oh, the sweet seduction of your words." He slapped her ass, lighting fire through her jeans, and swung open the door.

CHAPTER 9

Liv stumbled into Van's bedroom, unable to look away from the antique gun cabinet on the back wall, with walnut crests carved around the double glass doors. One might've expected a dozen prized shotguns displayed on the racks within. This was Texas, after all.

Instead, the cabinet was crammed with a menagerie of dolls and mannequins piled atop one another. Arms and legs askew, some still attached to molded bodies. Most were not. All of them bald and nude.

She rubbed the chill prickling her arms. "Little girls everywhere want to know, *Where do all the broken dollies go?"*

"Shut up, Liv." He sidled around her, and his foot sent a tiny headless torso careening under the bed, its jointed legs tumbling after.

Why wasn't that one with all the hollow-eyed faces pressed against the glass of the cabinet? Some of the heads were upside down. Others leered to the side or stared out into the room from beneath hinged eyelids. Dust-laced cobwebs drooped between the dirt-smudged body parts. If she shook the case, how many eyes would wiggle and blink back? She shivered.

"You need to"—she cleared her throat, tried to put *oomf* in her voice—"do some housecleaning."

"Nah." He threw himself on the bed, naked from the waist down.

His erection hadn't lost interest. It stood tall and unabashed between the flex of his thighs as he reclined on one elbow and watched her with his unnatural patience.

His interest in his collection, however, didn't appear to be sexual. None of his plastic friends were anatomically correct nor did they look well-loved. Much the opposite, in fact. A hairless mannequin slumped in the corner of the room, grime coating its nippleless coned breasts from years of inattention. One arm lay beside it, unattached. Its face was punched away, exposing the dark cavern of its head.

Above him, another mannequin hung from something like a meat hook jutting out of the wall. Bent at the waist, its arms and head lolled forward as if reaching for the bed, the far-away gaze on its face frighteningly reminiscent of young Pat Benatar.

"Van..." She jerked her chin at the aberration above him.

He'd never answered her years of questions about his fetishes, but he'd agreed to tuck away the ones that chilled her the most. He knew Plasti-Pat Benatar topped the list.

He rose, unhooked it from the wall, and tossed it under the bed to join who knew how many others. Then he turned to her, gripping the base of his cock, and pulled, one long lazy stroke. "Your turn, Liv. Show the pink."

A shudder bunched her shoulders to her ears. God,

she couldn't do this. Her panties were bone-dry, and her throat felt like a fucking Texas drought. "I can't do this."

His expression hardened, his thoughts likely sifting through his arsenal of manipulations. Of course, he could punch her or choke her, but he never had to. She wagered he'd either return to the girl or call Mr. E.

She moved to the narrow bed and perched on the edge. "Not like this."

The muscles in his jaw relaxed, and he sat beside her, dragging a blanket over his lap. He didn't touch her. They both knew he would fuck her before she left that room, and his ability to endure her dawdling was something she always used to her advantage. Which was stupid. It never helped her in the end.

He leaned forward, elbows on knees, and stared at the dirt-matted carpet. A wrinkle creased his brow, his tone hesitant. "You want foreplay? Seduction?"

She wanted real. She wanted to feel an essential, basic emotion that wasn't bound to the wounds he'd inflicted on her, the ones that wouldn't heal. "What I want, you can't give."

He swung his head toward her, eyes alight with pain. "I dried your face when you cried. I held you when you screamed. I haven't left your side once in all these years. You have *me*. All of me!"

She masked her flinch with the stillness she'd perfected. The absence of motion made her feel less visible under his constant attention. She didn't want him ogling at her. She didn't want *him*. How could she? His kisses haunted her, the grip of his voice too painfully familiar in the dark. He was the cause of those tears, those screams, her fears.

The cup of his palm on her cheek drew her eyes to

his, and the tenderness in his tone snagged her breath. "Sing to me."

His other hand caught her chin, preventing her from looking away. She shook her head in the cage of his fingers.

"If you need your distraction, your defense tonight, then by all means, sing." His timbre dipped, a sultry intrusion in her ears. "Your voice makes me so fucking hard." He shifted his hands to curl around her neck, thumbs caressing her cheeks, her scar. "Sing to me while I'm fucking you."

She hated that he'd figured out her *defense.* There were two mournful truths about their intimacy. One, he understood why she didn't want to fuck him. Two, he was able to convince her to do it anyway. He knew her feelings for him were as complicated as her situation. He also knew that if he led her to that dead place inside herself, she would hide there without struggling while he fucked her. It was a tactic she resented and appreciated.

"Which song?" she asked, defeated.

A happy hum vibrated in his chest, his scar a macabre extension of his smile. "Bring Me To Life."

His requests never strayed from *Evanescence,* the essence of grace in despair.

She let the trembling dread roll off her spine, drew in a long breath, and warbled through the first verse. Slipping into steady, lilting tones, her reluctance to fuck floated away with the notes. She held his eyes and sang the words he wanted to hear as he removed her sneakers, shirt, and jeans. When he traced her c-section scar, she kept her mind on the song, on its expression of the life she couldn't have and the broken shell she'd become.

He touched her hip bones with reverence, kissed

the lace that covered her most private parts, and stripped the material with a ragged groan.

"I can't wake up..." she sang, the lyrics infused with a longing he couldn't sate.

In the next heartbeat, she lay bare beneath him, her disloyal body lubricating his entry, programmed to respond. He fisted the sheets, panting and rocking his hips to the rhythm of her faltering vocals. Against her will, his thrusts woke her hunger, massaging sparks of pleasure along her inner walls. She lost her voice and burrowed into the remote pocket of her mind.

He raised up, shed his shirt, and lowered the sweat-damp heat of his chest to hers. Circling his pelvis, he dipped his dick in and out and dragged his teeth over her throat. "Your pussy's so hot, clenching around me." He nuzzled her neck, his arms stretched above them, fingers linked with hers, his biceps contracting beside her head.

"Your voice makes me want to shoot my fucking load. I'm going to come so hard inside you." He sank and withdrew, his girth a piston of stretching, hammering power. His exertion intensified, pounding her raw. "Keep singing."

Beneath a different man, in another life, she might've sang with a passion to match the intimate connection. With Van, she was a cold voice in a warm embrace, her pussy an entity of its own. The needy slit existed objectively, disciplined to accept and serve. She sang from that carnal place of flesh and superficial appetite. The place where emotions didn't dwell.

His grunts deepened, the roll of his body sliding and slapping against hers. "Come now. Come all over my dick."

The command tore the orgasm from her well-conditioned body. She focused inward, singing in her head, safe behind the shield of her mind as the sweep of unwanted sensations overtook the rest of her. She knew it could be truly pleasurable, and it had been many times with him. But she was too jumpy that night. She didn't trust her feelings because every damned nerve in her body irrationally pulsed for the boy in the box one floor above.

Van arched his neck and shouted his release to the ceiling, his pelvis slamming once, twice, and done. Then his mouth covered hers, moved over her jaw, and latched onto the curve of her neck.

"I love you." His whisper laved her shoulder, hot and wet.

It was the part she dreaded most about these unions. Those gentle words bore the strength to shatter her from the inside out. He believed what he said, but she only had to think of him with the girl who, less than an hour earlier, was sucking him toward the same neck-arching finale.

So she responded the way she always did, with thick bitter silence.

He flicked off the bedside lamp, gathered her in his arms, and trapped her hips with a leg. She lay on her back, her face angled away from his, and her cheek pressed against the edge of the mattress.

Her gaze locked on an arm poking from beneath the bed frame.

The night could've gone worse. That could've been a real arm, decaying into the carpet and stinking up the scenery in Van's garden of crazy. Despite all his cruelty and creepiness, he'd never killed anyone. She couldn't say the same for herself.

But obsessing about her felonies was dangerous in this business. Human sex traffickers were systematic and violent. Didn't matter that Mr. E's three-person operation wasn't linked to the realm of nationwide organizations. The punishment was the same. Mr. E could easily be some douche of a car salesman in nowhere Texas, but he was a douche with Mom and Mattie's addresses. The minute she lost her focus, one fucking slip, and they were dead.

Van's breathing steadied into the rhythm of sleep, and the weight of his arm and leg relaxed into pliancy. She eased from beneath him and caught herself before sitting up. Following the curve of the arm beside her pillow, she found his hand entangled in her hair, each finger meticulously coiled through its own strand.

For the love of all that's psychotic. She stifled a sigh.

After a long-suffering endeavor to extricate her hair without waking him, she collected her clothes and crept into the hall.

As she walked to her room, her thoughts churned around the newest threat to her arrangement. Over six years, she and Van had captured five boys and two girls. All of them from ghettos along the Mexican border.

Her first slave—a young Hispanic girl—worked side jobs for a cartel, but the girl's business connections hadn't seemed to care when she went missing. None of their captures had been attached to families who would miss them.

None until Joshua Carter.

Not only would his parents devote their lives to finding him, his community would sponsor a massive rally to search for their football star. But the buyer's demand for chastity had given her little choice. Boys without parents lost their innocence at young ages. There were no twenty-one-year-old virgin males among the sediment of broken families.

The virgin boy in the box would be missed.

She reached the top of the stairs, her fingers finding the keypad with ease in the dark as Van's words whispered through her head.

The job's the same. The slave we deliver will be exactly *as he ordered.*

The goddamned job. She coded herself into the attic, tiptoed to the closet beside the sleeping girl, and selected tomorrow's costume. Time to put on the mask. One that would hide her face and the fears it might show.

Chapter 10

Boy. Eyes down, boy. Strip. The haunting voice in Josh's head penetrated the never-ending tonality blaring in his ears. The flat line of sound wouldn't shut up. Not for hours. Not a single breach in range or volume. Hours and hours and hours.

Your name is whatever I want it to be. Boy. Boiyyyyee. He knew he was imagining the voice, angelic in melody, cutting in its intent.

No matter what they planned to do, no way would he become a sex slave. He would not break.

His thoughts stumbled into stunned silence, battling through the horrifically endless tone. How far would he bend if pushed? Especially without the strength that came with food and sleep. He'd dozed a bit off and on, but his body was flagging. His mind pounded to exhaustion.

He yearned to hear her sing, to invade his isolation and twine her soulful harmony around him. He needed to speak to *that* girl. Surely whatever lay beneath her chilling exterior wouldn't hurt his parents.

That's up to you.

Anger lashed through him, curling his fingers around the chain. An achy, unrelenting pain hammered his hips, back, and legs where they pressed against the wood. He wanted to choke her with the unforgiving chain and watch her stillness ripple with useless spasms.

He sucked in a breath, swallowing that hideous thought into the recesses of his gut where it could soften and disintegrate. Why? Because it was God's place to judge her? Or because he'd been raised to look for the best in people? Or was it his need to believe there was a virtuous quality inside of her that he could free and possibly use to escape?

The voice faded. His ears told him the single note stopped, too, but its echo left a lingering shard in his mind. Would the tone begin again at any moment? Had they returned to pull him out of the box? Had they ever left? His ears were playing tricks on him. Or had his sanity finally fled?

Seemed like days had come and gone since the pangs of a full bladder began their unrelenting jabs. He wouldn't be able to hold it much longer, but focusing on not pissing himself had diverted his mind from the weight of the chains, the eternal time in the box, and Mom and Dad's safety.

His throat and tongue withered with each intake of waterless air. Maybe they already buried him in the box out back. Maybe his next exhale would be his last.

No, he would've felt them move the box. And his life was valuable. They couldn't sell him if he was dead.

Something tickled his face. Another delusion. They'd left him alone for so long, his muscles were stiff from inertia, his fingers and toes numb from loss of circulation. Had they forgotten him? But the noise that had embedded itself in his brain was…silent. Nothing. Gone. In its place was the galloping thump of his hopeful heart.

The press on his ears vanished, replaced by the tingle of cool air. Then the blindfold lifted away. Blinding light stabbed his crusty eyes. He blinked, blinked, blinked, gasping, the chains clattering with his spasmodic attempts to free his arms.

Fingers touched his nose, removed the clip. His nostrils responded with greedy pulls of air, widening, clearing the snot, and filling with the scent of sweat and fear.

As his vision adjusted, the figure towering over him took shape. A gas mask encased its head. Three plastic circles darkened where the eyes and nose should be.

Was the air poisoned? Were they gassing him, drugging him? His heart hammered against his ribs, his lungs struggling to keep up.

"What are you—?" He coughed, harsh and painful. "Am I—?"

"Drink."

The voice was a muffled tinkling of ice. He thanked God it was her under the mask but didn't understand why that knowledge had coaxed his joints to relax. *She* had put him in that box.

She palmed his nape, raising his head. Cool water sluiced over his parched lips, his tongue, trickling down his throat, both abrading and refreshing.

The pressure in his bladder twisted tighter. "Bathroom."

"You shouldn't have held it." The mask's filter concealed her mouth.

He couldn't read her and wondered if that was the intent.

"Your bladder is breeding bacteria as we speak." She worked the chains quickly, tugging at his hands and feet.

She'd chained him in a box and was worried about a UTI? The restraints slackened, but his wrists remained locked together. He pulled up his legs, bending at the knees and trembling through the effort. He didn't have the strength to drag his hands to his chest.

Releasing latches at both ends of the box, she let one side fall open and lay flat on the floor. He rolled out in a haphazard tumble, arms bound together, legs free but weak as hell.

A random pattern of eyehooks protruded from the subfloor around him. There were hooks everywhere, the ceiling, the walls. They dangled padlocks, chains, and cuffs of leather and steel.

She left him lying there, heeled boots encasing her calves and clicking on the wood. His view from the floor arrested on the black PVC-like corset dress molding the curves of her waist and hips and stopping just below the creases of her muscular backside.

Wrapped in pleather, she was a promise of suffering and ecstasy.

The sudden stirring in his groin shot a burning stab to his bladder and spurred him to his knees. He slid one foot forward, his muscles screaming, and rose, swaying on his feet.

"How long was I in there?" He swung his cuffed-together hundred-pound arms toward the box.

Her silence magnified his heartbeat thrashing in his ears.

With unmoving eeriness, her blacked-out lenses watched him stagger toward her, his toes catching on the hooks. He could physically feel his body tensing with hatred for this woman, who regarded him without a twitch to assist his clumsy advance.

When his shins hit the porcelain rim, he dropped his shackled fists on the wall behind the tank, and lost the fight with his bladder. He'd meant to sit. Too late for that. Needing his hands on the wall to hold himself up, he melted into the relief pouring from him, the stream of urine spraying unguided. Thanks to his shaking legs, his aim was marginal at best.

Her mask tilted downward. At the mess he was making? At his nudity?

Let her stare. He'd showered and peed in the presence of others every day in the locker room. This was different on so many levels, but he didn't have the strength of mind to care.

He'd never been drunk, but it probably felt like this. His brain struggled to engage, his perceptions clouded by fatigue, his legs and arms wrestling to respond. He was nude and helpless before a woman who meant to sell him as a sex slave, and he grappled to keep his eyes open.

Bladder empty, he dropped the weight of his head on a braced arm and angled his face to glower at her. "My parents?"

Her vinyl-wrapped head cocked. "Last check, Mr. Carter was celebrating his empty nest at the kitchen table, wrinkling the lacy tablecloth and toppling over that godawful ceramic rooster centerpiece as he pounded his cock into Mrs. Carter's ass."

Anger spiked, and he swung his bound arms—*to shut her up? Make her hurt? Knock off the mask?*—and missed. His sideways motion sent him careening into the spot she vacated, tottering past her and into the open shower stall.

The boot slamming into the back of his knee brought him stumbling to the ground in a discombobulation of limbs and defeat. Flopping to his back, he could only glare up at her. Even his frustration required more effort than he could manage.

She squatted over him, a boot on either side of his hips, the gap of her thighs wide enough to expose a swath of black lace. He jerked his eyes away, disgusted with her and himself.

"You can look," she said.

"No, thanks." He tried to buck her off his hips and failed.

"Soon, you won't be able to stop yourself." She grabbed his jaw and shoved her mask in his face. "Requirement number five. Slave will not touch Master or Master's property in a sexual way without permission."

Master's property? She didn't mean—

"For the next ten weeks, I am your Master, and this is my property." She released his chin and gripped his penis, sliding downward, stretching brazen fingers to cup his testicles.

Blood rushed to his groin. No one had ever touched him there and definitely not like that. He hated the visible response of his body but couldn't stop it. Nor could he stop his fury.

"You're a rapist." He scuffed his heels on the tile, breaking her grip. His back hit the wall.

Holding her crouched position, she dropped a forearm over one knee. "The first requirement set by the buyer was your virginity. You will never put your cock in me or any woman."

Her definition of virginity was too specific, or perhaps not specific enough. That did *not* sit well. He clenched his butt cheeks, a sheen of sweat icing his spine.

She stood and reached for the yard of chain hanging from a hook beside the shower head. "Raise your arms."

He tucked them to his chest and stared at the drain, fighting his eyes to stay open. Twenty-four hours in the ear-numbing, sleep-deprived box. Leading up to that had been an exhaustive day of hauling cotton bales, classwork, and the big game. He didn't have enough steam left to stop her from hanging him in the shower, but he refused to make it easy.

"If you concentrate every breath on anticipating my orders, your time with me will be much less painful." Her voice reverberated against the tiles, hollow and robotic. "If you swing at me again, I'll suffocate you with much, *much* more discomfort than you experienced in that box." She bent over him, boots shoulder-width apart, hands on her hips. "If that doesn't penetrate your thick skull, I'll collect another keepsake from your mother. Perhaps something attached to her little gray-haired head."

His heart sped up, heated with anger, knotted with dread. When he recovered his strength, he would escape, and he might knock her across the room on the way out.

Straightening to her full height, she slid the chain through her hands. "Swallow your fantasies of escape and rescue. The house is soundproof. There are keypads on every exterior door. I've ordered Van to stay in the garage all day to dismantle your truck. When the parts are dispersed to various dumps and junk yards, they'll be untraceable." She held out her hand, waiting for his. "No one is coming for you, boy."

A guttural, sick hatred for her spread its poison inside him, twisting and taking over. What was next for him after she strung him up in the shower?

"My virginity… You said…" Dear God, he didn't want to say it out loud, but he had to know. "What about sodomy?"

Her hands dropped to her sides, the chain slapping against the tile wall. She strode to the door and raised her finger to the keypad.

Was she bringing in Van? To beat Josh? To bend him over in the shower and pump away in his backside?

"Wait." His attempt to stand on jelly legs collapsed into a bone-crunching sprawl on knees and elbows. "Please. I'll follow orders."

She tapped in the code.

CHAPTER 11

"Please, wait." The effort to stand had depleted Josh.

His head swam, and his body screamed for food and sleep. He stood no chance. This had been the aim of the box, he realized. A total mental and physical shutdown. He raised his bound arms and his eyes, reaching toward her goggled mask.

She entered the final digit on the keypad, and the door clicked open. She stared into the outer room, statuesque in her posture. "Requirement number six. Slave will use the title *Master*."

His extended arms shook, the lump in his throat sprouting jagged edges. "Please…" It was just a word. *Too tired to fight. Just a word.* "Master."

She made him wait another agonizing moment before closing the door and returning to his side. In a practiced movement, she locked the end of the waiting chain to one of his wrist shackles with a combination lock and removed the existing chain that squeezed his hands together. One arm dropped to the floor; the other tied to the shower wall.

He probably looked like hell, but he was a strong guy. Even in his weakened state, he could overpower her. Wasn't she afraid he might trap her and squeeze his free arm around her neck? The confident, relaxed pose of her body told him she expected it.

"*Master* is how you'll refer to the man you are training to serve," she said. "With me, you'll use *Mistress*. Say it now."

The bite in those last three words snapped his teeth together. His breath hissed past his lips. "Mistress."

Was she smiling behind the mask? Did she get off on binding and selling men?

Didn't matter. He would *never* serve a man. *Never*. "How many times have you done this?"

She moved to the perpendicular wall of the corner shower. A chain dangled from another hook. "Other arm, boy."

How many had she forced through the horror of this exact moment? Where were they now? Did she even see them as human? What about the kiss he shared with her in the truck? Her actions seemed so genuine at the time.

"How many people have you ripped from their lives, their dreams, their families?" He squinted into the lenses of her mask, his muddy reflection glaring back. "Mistress," he spat.

Her fist slammed into his mouth, spiking fire through his jaw and knocking him off balance. His back smacked the cold tile floor. His arm, chained to the wall, twisted. Pain tore through his shoulder, ripping a shout from his throat.

"Other. Arm."

Well, that was stupid. *And incredibly satisfying*. He'd found a nerve to pick at.

Crawling to his knees, he spat blood on the floor at her feet and offered his arm with a belligerent smile.

She made quick work of tightening the chains to the walls, the pull of the restraints stretching his arms out to the sides like Jesus on the cross. Naked, on his knees, his chin hanging on his chest, he didn't feel the forgiving virtue of Christ filling his heart. It pumped, instead, with the spirit of revenge and loathing.

The cold spray of water pounded ice pellets on his back, and her hands rubbed soap into his skin and hair. He acknowledged that the movement in his muscles wasn't the flex of courage but the trembling of fury. He'd never felt more subjugated in his life.

Worse was the swelling arousal between his legs. She only needed to touch his backside, his hip, or his inner thigh, and his penis stood at half-salute. He stared at the jerking thing, grimacing. At least she pretended not to notice it, though her eyes could've been directed anywhere from within that terrible mask.

The tap shut off, and he wished he'd stolen a few gulps of water. She untied him and led him by the chains to the mattress that sat on the floor. No frame or box springs in this hell hole. He dripped water onto the room's only rug, shivering like a wet poodle, and waited to see what she'd come up with next.

Maybe she'd command him to perform a tumbling act, sing karaoke, or wear a toga and feed her grapes. Hopefully, something low impact. Dehydration, chills, and exhaustion were riddling him with all sorts of irritable problems, from blurry vision to unmanageable mood shifts. He was so recklessly angry and tired his brain was spinning out of control.

"Requirement number seven. Slave will kneel when Master is present."

Hallelujah. His legs were wobbling anyway. He

lowered, and his knees gave out before he made it to the rug.

She connected the chains to a padlock and eyehook on the floor in the center of the room, spun the combination to secure it, and dragged a cardboard box to his side. "Eat."

With enough slack in the chains, he raised the lid, and the sights and smells of cheese, sausage, yogurt and hard-boiled eggs sliced through his haze. He went for the bottled water first, the metal links connected to his wrists snagging on the cardboard. He suspected the menu was intentional. High protein, high fat, likely meant to give him energy for activities he didn't want to think about.

When he finished the water and reached for a second bottle, she grabbed the cuff on his wrist. "Slow down or it's all going to come back up."

He yanked his arm away and dug into the food, using the spoon provided. His body responded instantly to the yogurt, as if it contained magical little sugar motes that seeped into his system, clearing the fog from his head and soothing the quakes in his bones.

She watched from her perch on the mattress, legs crossed at the knees, breasts threatening to tumble from her corset with each inhale. She looked absolutely uncomfortable. He decided to make it worse.

"Are you supposed to be seducing me with that outfit, Mistress? Because I got to say"—he pointed at his soft penis, cold and shriveled as it was—"epic fail."

A total lie. If he hadn't reached his mental and physical limitations, he would've been battling arousal and his outrage over it.

A sound huffed behind the mask. Could've been a gasp. Impossible to guess since he'd heard very few reactions pass her lips.

He swallowed down three hard-boiled eggs, chewing on his original game plan. Making friends with her, unholy creature that she was, gave him the best chance to glimpse beneath the mask and, with time, influence her. To do that, he needed to shed some of the superiority his buddies teased him about and consort on her level.

He bit into a slice of cheddar. "Does th— I mean, *Mistress*, does this job ever fuck with your head?"

"Wow. That's a pretty vulgar word for you, Jesus boy. First time trying it out?"

The cheese stuck in his throat. The muffling of her voice through the mask only made her words more aggravating. She might have known some things about him, but she didn't know enough to judge him. And calling him a Jesus boy wasn't an effective way to get under his skin.

"I couldn't habituate myself to using bad language," he said. "Imagine if it slipped out in the company of a parishioner."

"The horror." Her tone was deadpanned, bored.

His shoulders stiffened. His social circles were comprised of people like his folks, who so willingly devoted their lives to holiness they took their rules to another level. Study the bible daily, never miss worship, and live in perpetual fear of everything: other religions, gays, cursing, bikinis, pop music, alcohol, smoking, premarital sex, and hell. It was as if they believed humans were demons in the flesh.

The laid-back Christians on the opposite end of the spectrum were content to simply have a relationship with God. Without the obsessive focus on rules, they seemed to better appreciate all the good in the world. It would crush his parents if they knew this was the sort of Christian he wanted to be.

He also wanted a career in football, but his decisions had never been up to him. Especially not now. Given Liv's job, he knew discussing his future in ministry would not help her relate to him. "You didn't answer the question, Mistress."

A motionless tension fell over her. She shot to her feet and kicked the box of food across the room. "I do not answer questions."

Her boot swung again, aimed at his head. He caught it, tucked it to his chest, twisting her leg and rolling her. Using her loss of balance and the taut rope of chain to trip her other foot, he dumped her face-down on the floor and threw his weight over her. Strangely, she lay like the dead, arms trapped beneath her body.

Without thought, his hands went to the mask, released the buckles on the back, and chucked it to the side. He'd already seen her face, so the disguise must've been meant to conceal her expressions. *Screw that.* He wanted to force her responses to the surface and bare every twitch and twist of her gorgeous features.

She didn't try to free her arms or raise her face from the rug. Her breath whispered evenly through the mane of brown silk tousled around her head.

He lifted his chest, pinning her legs with his, and flipped her over. "Do you and Van anally rape your prisoners?"

Arms limp at her sides, her expression was a blank canvas. But her detachment seemed to make her eyes look even more dangerous as they drew into slits and locked on his.

The length of chain gave him enough range of motion to strangle her with his hands, but then what? He didn't have the code to the door, and she didn't seem concerned about her safety, which meant she was prepared. Did she have a weapon hidden in her bodice?

"You're a pimp and a rapist," he said. "How many slaves, Liv?"

"It's *Mistress.*" She slammed her brow into the bridge of his nose.

A blaze of fire burned through his nostrils. He wrinkled his nose, fighting the hurt from her hard head, worrying about the costs his parents would pay for his temerity. He needed to make certain the risks he took didn't touch them.

She slid a palm up the back of his thigh and parted his cheeks. No amount of clenching dissuaded her from touching that forbidden place between. If he swatted at her, he wouldn't be able to hold down her shoulders. He could roll off her and lose the upper hand or he could endure her probing finger.

He did his best to control his breathing, and failed.

"What would you call this?" he panted. "Seduction or rape?"

Holding his gaze, she tried to pull her knees to the outside of his legs, but his weight held them in place. So she used the only freedom she had and pressed a stiff finger against his rectum, her eyes hard and fixed on his.

"Try again." She prodded deeper, a dry invasion that crushed his molars together. "With. The. Title."

His blood boiled, and his mouth dried. "Are you going to rape me, *Mistress*?"

"*You* are restraining *me*."

Her finger, toying shallowly where no finger

should go, garbled his brain. He wouldn't give up his position, and as much as the violation made him squirm, it wasn't dampening the heat stirring in his naked groin where it rubbed against the apex of her open thighs.

"You like this." Her lips curled up, perversely smug. "They all do. By the end of the first day, all of my boys beg me to fuck them." Finger in his backside, she ground herself against his traitorous hard-on. "You'll beg, too."

He wanted to roar *Never*, but the way his fatigued body responded to her touch, he knew it would be a lie.

Her finger vanished, and his muscles relaxed but not for long. She slid her hand between their hips, and he jerked his groin out of her way. But she wasn't reaching for him. She cupped herself beneath the lace, massaging and throwing her head back with a moan.

Heat swarmed his face. He'd kissed girls. He'd groped a breast once above the shirt, but he'd never seen a girl naked before him, and this…this open display of masturbation he'd never dared to imagine. Yet he couldn't stop his gaze from clinging the dips and arches of her body and the hand circling between her legs. Was this why the others begged her for sex?

"You rape them." He thickened his voice with accusation, wanted her to hear his objection.

Her hand froze, and her glare slammed into his. The darkest reaches of her eyes seemed to rotate while her pupils remained steadily locked on his.

"You're my first virgin cock, boy, which means you will endure your training without any hope for a charity fuck." A cruel expression bent her face, catching light along her scar. "And you'll address me correctly, you stubborn prick."

She yanked her hand from between them and slapped her fingers over his mouth, trailing a smear of tart moisture on his lips and tongue.

The shock of it arched his back, his restrained hands tightening the chains and halting his backward flinch. She used the distraction to slip from under him and shove a finger into her cleavage. As he scrambled forward to recover his position above her, she whipped out a metal wire, snapped it taut between her hands, and caught him in the throat.

In the next breath, he was on his back, his neck ensnared by the garrote she'd unleashed from her corset. His arms were yanked to the side by the chains clapping against the floor. Just an impulse away from hindering his airflow, he held himself as still as possible.

Her knee dug against his chest. "Requirement number two. Slave will service Master sexually with exceptional skill, and his body will be prepared to make it easy for Master." She tilted her head, a tangle of curls snaking around her chest. "Your cock doesn't belong to me, but if you beg nicely, I'll take your virgin ass before Van gets a hold of it."

It wasn't her words that chilled him so much as the conviction that punctuated them.

She released him, and his hands went to his throat, rubbing the unbroken skin.

On her way to the door, she glanced over her shoulder. "You'll find your restraints don't quite reach the mattress. Sleep on the rug. And if you bend just right…" She pointed at the toilet. "You can balance your tight little asshole on the rim."

The rim that was splattered in his urine. His fingers gouged into his palms.

"If you don't shit before I return, I'll use a rectal bulb syringe to clean you out." With a flick of her finger over the keypad, she left.

Hatred, his new friend, swept through his veins, promising delicious acts of retaliation against every foul fiber in that woman's body. He shook with a violent contraction of muscles, his blood raging. He wanted to shove her against the wall and pummel her.

Sweet Jesus, what was wrong with him? Violence didn't justify violence. He needed to talk with her, dig through the vicious mess of her mind, and show her there was a healthier way to overcome whatever was dragging her into damnation.

He rose on shaky legs and tested the chain's four-foot length. Didn't reach the bed or the door, but if he backed up and doubled-over like she'd said, he could use the toilet. As he stared into the bowl, he knew why she'd want his bowels clean. He also knew he'd follow her orders if it meant forestalling an enema.

As for the heat she'd stirred in him when he'd held her down, that couldn't have been real. She'd concocted those feelings with the curves of her body, the shadowy depth of her gaze, and the musical way she spoke. God help him, her voice was so captivating it could reach over a hundred tortured screams and call a man to kneel beneath her garrote, mesmerized and brainwashed... *Yeah, brainwashed.* His attraction to her was certainly not genuine.

Who was he kidding? Her taste lingered on his lips. His backside still tingled from her invasion, and his erection throbbed merely by conjuring thoughts about her. At what point did he go from exhaustion to full-on erection? Was it a testament to the power she held over him? Maybe it was the yogurt giving him the fuel he needed, because no way in hell was he that easily controlled by her.

Blowing out a breath, he tried to calm himself. She'd awoken things inside him, things he'd kept repressed for the sake of his parents and career.

Assuming it was nighttime, the morning would bring a whole lot more ugly. He could be a pussy about it, or he could shut his eyes and wake energized and ready to break through her vile mask. Without using his fist.

The door snicked behind Liv, and her lungs released in a noisy whoosh, her heart thundering unguarded. She clawed at the hooks on her corset, the heaving expansion of her ribs hindering the effort. "Girl!"

The girl leapt from the cot and crawled over the floor on hands and knees, her lean naked body swaying sensually through the movement, just as she'd been trained.

"Get me out of this thing." Liv's chest heaved.

Shifting behind her, the girl's fingers worked deftly, loosening the ties that cinched the back of the corset. A moment later, the bodice gaped enough to free the hooks. Liv tossed it to the floor and turned.

Blond hair curtained the kneeling girl's face and shoulders. This captive was so docile and innocent, Liv found her hand moving to stroke the bowed head. She caught herself before she made contact.

Eyes down, the girl rubbed her palms over her bare thighs. Nine weeks earlier, Van lured the eighteen-year-old beauty from a seedy neighborhood in southern Texas, where she had lived with three older brothers. Perhaps they could've been commended for warding off horny boyfriends and protecting her chastity. The sad irony was, her innocence and virginity had set her in Van's sights.

A shiver assaulted Liv down to her bones. Whether it was from dwelling on the girl's future, Liv's damp skin from the boy's shower, or the exchange of words she'd had with him, she needed the warmth of a gentle voice. "You have permission to speak."

The girl lifted intelligent blue eyes. "Are you okay, Mistress?"

The question, although touching, couldn't keep Liv's mind off the boy's allegation.

You rape them.

Two girls. He was her sixth boy. She'd shared sexual intimacy with all of them, including the girl blinking up at her. But she'd never allowed sexual intercourse. She'd never considered the other *stuff* rape.

"I'm fine." She smiled, and it felt strained, achy.

What if she was wrong? She'd permitted the boys release countless times, removed from the purpose of *training,* without Van's knowledge. There were no cameras in the house to monitor her actions. They'd pleaded for sex. She'd responded with hand jobs. During those moments, she only meant to offer them comfort. Perhaps that was how Van viewed his unions with her.

Uncertainty twisted her up, and within the turbulence arose an even more unsettling thought. None of her intimate encounters compared to the moment she'd just vacated. Lying beneath that boy, pinned by the burnish of his defiant green eyes and the unwitting seduction of his physique, she'd felt a new kind of stirring. It was accidental in its creation, but the inconvenient truth was she wanted him. Not only that, she wanted him to want her.

Startled by her vulnerable thoughts, she angled her head away so the girl couldn't see the emotions creasing her face.

"You're cold and wet, Mistress. Would you like me to prepare the shower to warm you?"

The bathroom in this chamber was enclosed and, more importantly, out of reach of the boy's studious gaze. Swallowing the bitterness of the job, she made herself answer in the severe tone the girl was conditioned to hearing. "Yes. Don't make me wait."

Twenty minutes later, showered and dressed in an oversize t-shirt, Liv returned to her room.

He lay on his back on the rug, arms above his head to accommodate the chains. His soft snoring thrummed through the room, thanks to the sleeping pills she'd diluted in his water. But even in the grip of sleep, he wore a brooding look that pulled at his eyebrows and sharpened the bones in his chiseled face. A fringe of lashes shadowed his cheeks, and the lines on his forehead drew deep grooves.

Humans adapted quickly, and when they understood the boundaries, they worked within them. His aggressive attempts to overthrow her had been expected. All captives emerged from the box demanding answers and tossing clumsy punches. But there was something subtly different about his temperament. He wasn't desperate enough.

He wasn't scared enough.

She flipped off the light, submersing the room in darkness, and stretched alongside his body on the floor. The whisper of his breath and the clean scent of his skin navigated her toward his face. Lost so deeply in sleep, he didn't stir as she speared her fingers through the thick muss of his textured hair.

The first meeting with the buyer was in two weeks. Two weeks to mold this boy-man into some semblance of a boy-slave, one who would be deemed satisfactory by a misogynist whack-job. Could she beat the contempt and righteousness out of him in that short amount of time?

It was a psychological battle she intended to win, because the boy wouldn't suffer for his disobedience the way Mom and Mattie would.

Resolve guided her hands, lifting the edge of the rug and unfurling a thin latex sheet from beneath it. Half of the sheath was held down by his body. It was also glued to the subfloor. She folded the loose half over him, crawling quietly to his other side.

He coughed as she hefted the closest shoulder and rolled him on his side, the bones in his arm indiscernible through the hard layers of compact muscle. A few careful tugs on the carpet, his breathing stuttering and steadying, and the rug pulled free from his weight. She set it behind her and returned him to his back.

At his feet, she pulled a zipper around the edges of the latex, sliding it toward his head and removing the chains from his wrist cuffs as she went. Through the night, it would be a plastic sleeping bag. With the sides zipped together, she cinched the latex around his shoulders.

That done, she curled up on the mattress, lit a cigarette, and walked through her preparations for the next day. The nature of mornings in captivity was either they woke up remembering where they were and what was expected or they were punished and dropped in hell. The captive's first day was always hell.

CHAPTER 13

The gravity of confinement bore down on Josh's sleep-dazed utopia. It was a relentless press, dragging against his skin and nudging him to wake.

Lying on his back, he reached up to rub the fog from his eyes and couldn't move his hands. He tried to lift his legs. Couldn't move those either. His heart rate exploded, ripping the haze of sleep from his brain.

The oblivion behind his eyelids was replaced with the blank stare of a masked face. It floated above him, a ghastly-white monition against ruffled waves of chestnut hair.

Arms pinned at his sides, he blinked to clear his vision as her brown eyes watched him through the eyeholes of the opaque disguise. A nondescript nose, pointy chin, and cheekbones molded the white, oval-shaped, plastic face. It would've been androgynous, except for the puckered, red-painted mouth, the upper lip arching in two dramatically-peaked points.

He lifted his head, dragged his focus from the mask to where she straddled his ribs and arms, and wasn't sure which had his heart pumping faster. The blood-red bra and panties that bared her body or the latex body bag that sheathed his.

"What is this?" His voice shrilled, and an impending sense of doom sparked the compulsion to fight.

His muscles tightened, heating his skin and constricting against the stretchy rubber. He could give into his rising panic and shout, writhe, and wear himself out. Or he could conquer his impulses, behave with reason, and deny her the satisfaction of his fear. At least his backside was safe at the moment.

He peered into the eyes behind the mask and searched for a human being. The pupils, lifeless and frozen, might as well have been painted glass.

His jaw tightened. "Damn. I'm still in this nightmare?"

There, a flicker of raw umber in the glass. His heart danced in his chest. Then the flicker disappeared with a sweep of latex as she stretched the covering from his neck to the crown of his head.

He gulped against sudden claustrophobia, catching pockets of air in the see-through plastic wrap. Bucking and kicking and straining his neck, there was no room to maneuver. The transparent rubber clung to every inch of him, his skin sweating and slipping along it uselessly.

His inhales thinned, every other breath sealing the bag against his mouth and nose. He squirmed toward the top opening, but it cinched around the top of his skull. He could lift his head to scan down the expanse of his body through the bag, but he couldn't roll, couldn't sit up. It was as if he was cemented to the floor.

The whine of a motor screeched through the room and vibrated the wood against his back. Oxygen vanished. The latex shrunk, compressing his arms to his sides and sinking his body to the floor. His nerves rampaged with realization. She was sucking the air from the bag with a vacuum, trapping him, suffocating him.

He grunted, tried to scream at her to stop. Breathless. Constricted. Fire lit his lungs, and his heart exploded with terror.

The motor shut off, and the bag loosened. She peeled back the flap, cool air stroking his face and filling his lungs.

She smoothed his hair from his forehead. "If there's a definition for waking up on the wrong side of the bed, this is it."

Was that a joke? Was the vile witch mocking him while she tortured him?

He mustered his most sarcastic tone and smiled. "I'll pray for your soul, Liv."

Her fist slammed into his cheekbone.

Ow, dammit. A jolt of pain seared through his skull and burned his eyes.

The bag covered over his face again. The motor roared. He fought for air, his chest burning. The suffocation seemed to double this time. *Trapped. Can't breathe. Too long.* Black spots speckled his vision.

When she turned it off and pulled back the plastic, he couldn't catch his voice. He didn't want to.

One of her cold, heartless fingers traced his jaw. "You failed two of the simplest requirements."

He panted, his lungs on fire. The requirements…the requirements… Strip. Kneel. No sex with her. No touching her. No masturbating. *Eyes down.*

His gaze dropped, taking his heart with it. Chest heaving, instinct screaming to insult her with every curse word he knew, he tried to shed the fear from his face.

"That's one." She placed a hand on his groin, the

heat of her palm seeping through the thin barrier.

A moan caught in his throat. He didn't want to feel her hand there, and he definitely didn't want to like it. Dammit, which requirement was he missing? Sifting through the list, he grit his teeth. "Mistress."

"Good." She stroked his penis through the latex with a skill that infused his body with lust and fury.

Keeping his eyes averted from hers, he flexed his muscles, drew calming breaths, and blanked his mind. Years of practice in controlling his desires should've overpowered the sensations she was weaving through him, but with each twist of her wrist and drag of her fingernail, the traitorous erection swelled.

Her touch disappeared. His pulse tapered then hammered anew as she shifted down his body. Her mask hovered over his crotch, her hands braced on either side of his hips. The long silk of her hair curled around slim, bare shoulders. If his hands were free, he could snap her in half.

She slid the mask to her forehead, her face angled out of view, and the heat of her breath penetrated the thin material, sweeping over his groin. He arched, straining against the compression of the bag. His legs trembled as quivering energy tingled over his thighs and tightened his balls.

This couldn't be happening. He couldn't stop his release from building. He must've looked ravenous, the transparent latex adhering to his genitals, revealing every detail under her close inspection.

It was wrong. She was violating him, molesting him…

Her tongue dragged over his length from root to tip, wrenching a moan from deep within his chest.

Despite the layer of latex between them, all he could feel was the concentrated heat, the soft stroke, the atrocious pleasure of it.

With an invasive grip, she adjusted his erection to lie flat between his pubic mound and the latex. "You have permission to speak. Tell me what you want me to do with this monstrous cock."

"Mistress, release me."

She raised up, shifting the mask to cover her face, and straddled his hips. "I'm so wet. If you weren't wearing a full-body condom, you'd slide right in."

She ground against him, and he thought, for a terrifying second, he might come just from the contact.

"My pussy would stretch to accommodate your girth. It would grip you like a vise and cream all over your cock as you rub in and out, sinking deeply, withdrawing reluctantly." She leaned toward his face, her breath whispering behind the mask. "You would finish with hard, hurried fucks, punching every inch of my cunt."

Vulgarity could be a form of torture, along with character assassination. He knew she was taunting him, trying to coax him into abandoning his beliefs and begging her like those before him. Even knowing this, he couldn't stifle the overwhelming desire gripping his body. He'd never wanted to come so badly, but he would *not* beg.

She slid the red satin crotch of her panties to the side and rolled her hips up. The sight of her plump, pink creases of skin, hairless and glistening with moisture, wrestled his wildest, most insane fantasies to the forefront of his thoughts. He curled his toes and tensed against the warmth rushing to his groin. His breathing and heart rate quickened, yet he couldn't look away from her body.

No cheerleader, no pastor's wife compared to her beauty. She moved with the grace of a dancer, lithe and muscular, shifting over his privates as if she were floating. For a thick moment, he was convinced he'd found an angel. Then he remembered she was his captor, a rapist. The devil incarnate.

He squeezed his eyes shut, his fingers digging into his thighs, his penis unbearably hot and uncomfortable.

"Open your eyes, boy." Her voice was commanding, the mask adding another layer of detachment. "Watch me."

Startled by the ease at which he followed her demand, he watched her finger as it traced her slit, up and down, gathering wetness. He couldn't stop his mind from darting to the conclusion of sex, wanting the mystery of her flesh wrapped around him and not caring about his virginity or his parents' promise to God. It was enlightening and reckless.

Lowering her hips, she parted her folds with the latex-protected length of him, rocking, fingers reaching to pinch his nipples through the rubber buffer. The bulges of her chest overflowed the satin, the color of the bra accentuating the red pout painted over her hidden expression.

She was a demon in the form of the most beautiful girl on earth. If he peered into her liquid brown eyes, he might've found the cruelest corners of the world there. But when she ground against him, the lustrous sheen of her hair swishing around her, her fingers curling against his abs, she seemed more human, less wooden. She looked like she desired him the way a girl would a boy.

The thought made him needy in a way he didn't comprehend. He wanted her to slide her heat over him faster, longer, and hear her hypnotic voice cry out in bliss.

No. He blinked, tried to clear his head. He wanted her to stop.

Another bout of quakes tumbled through him, coaxing the climax that was teetering on a razor's edge. What was her true intention? Was any of this real? Could she produce moisture between her legs if she didn't want him?

If he could recognize her authenticity, he might be able to explain the meaning of her actions. "Mistress. Remove the mask."

She threw her head back, the sinews in her slender neck straining against the skin. She moaned, and the sound transformed into a harmony of *Ahh-Ahhhh-Ah*. Her voice was an offering from God and a temptation from hell, a tone so potent it could corrupt a man, or save him.

Blood surged to his penis, raising his testicles, and his inhibitions fled. His heart rate skyrocketed. His lungs labored, and his thighs and butt tightened. She continued to grind on him, hitting the right spot, the right speed. He was doomed.

"Requirement number eight." Hips flexing, she rubbed against him with the mastery to finish him. "Slave will not orgasm without permission."

A series of contractions gripped his cock. He'd reached the point where he couldn't stop, didn't care about anything but the rush of pleasure barreling down on him. It was happening, and oh sweet Jesus, his body shook with the violence of a spasmodic freefall. Sensations flooded him from the waist down, pulsing against the friction of her heat, and he forgot where he was.

Her weight vanished. Latex covered his face, and the vacuum roared to life.

CHAPTER 14

Four more near-suffocations later, Josh knew Liv wouldn't kill him with vacuum-shrunk latex. But every time she sealed it over his face and powered on the motor, he feared it would be the time she miscalculated.

He labored to catch his breath. How did she measure how long he could go without air? What if she waited a heartbeat too long? And what was the purpose of this cruelty? He was supposed to hold off his body's reactions? Wait for permission to come? If she jerked him off enough, maybe he'd run out of juice.

Fatigued lolled his muscles. Sweat drenched his skin, and the stickiness of five ejaculations dribbled into the creases of his balls, itching the crack of his backside. No way did he have the mental or physical capacity to come again.

He'd thought the same thing three orgasms ago. "Mistress, no more."

She leaned over him, her hand working his sore, yet frustratingly swelling penis. "Your cock says otherwise."

A growl erupted in his stomach. He licked parched lips, unsure if she registered his hunger. If she had any reaction at all, it was locked behind the damned mask.

Maybe some mysteries, like if her goal was to starve him or masturbate him to death, were better left in the dark.

She stroked and stroked and stroked. He was past cringing from the effect of her touch. The familiar surge of climax tightened his gut. Unable to stop it, his release surged through his body and burst beneath the latex.

The momentary bliss lessened each time with the ache of overuse, but it was still there, owning him. Though, if he was actually ejaculating semen, he couldn't sense it amidst the existing puddle.

When the haze of orgasm faded, he filled his lungs with air and braced for his claustrophobic punishment.

Her legs bent in a squat above him, the crotch of her panties damp and taunting.

"You smell like sweaty balls and spooge, virgin boy." She rose and lifted a bare foot backward to her hip, balancing without falter, stretching her muscles. Then she lowered her foot and repeated with the other leg. "I'm going to release you to use the toilet, scrub the piss from it, and take a shower."

His body melted into the floor, and his lungs collapsed in relief.

"Then you'll wash me," she said.

Maybe she wanted to shock him, but putting his hands on her might be the most pleasant thing he would experience in this room. No matter how much she disgusted him, her body aroused him. It was infuriating.

"Yes, Mistress."

She crouched beside him and rested fingertips on his hardening length, watching him through the eyeholes, allowing him to make eye contact with her.

Her inhuman stillness paired with her apparent disregard for time was hell on his blood pressure. As she squatted there, making him wait, the rest of the world went about their oblivious lives. Except his folks, but he refused to ask about them, fearing the answer.

Finally, she loosened the cinches around his neck and lowered the zipper down the side. "I'll feed you when your tasks are complete...*if* you follow the eight requirements you've been given."

No doubt she had an infinite supply of punishments planned if he lapsed on her perverted rules.

As she worked the zipper on the bag, he walked through the list. No sex with women. Service the Master sexually or some crap. Eyes down. No clothes. Did a latex toga count? No touching her or himself sexually. Use the title. Kneel. No orgasms. Never thought he'd welcomed that last one so eagerly.

When the zipper finished its rotation around the bag, she unfolded the cover and stepped back.

Careful not to meet her eyes, he lifted to shaky knees, debating the wisdom of knocking her off her feet. If he strangled her to death, he probably wouldn't live to see his next meal.

He rubbed his cracked lips. Were there cameras hidden in the ceilings? Was Van watching from another room, waiting for an excuse to kill his parents? And leading his parade of insecurities was a humiliating thought. Was the fluid crusting his pubis an indication he didn't have a chance at adhering to her damned rules?

His body was conditioned to take a beating on the field, his mind strengthened to suppress desires that didn't align with his spirituality. He could endure her punishments as long as he made progress in unraveling the evil knots that bound her soul.

He held out his cuffed wrists, hoping his

submission would garner her trust.

"I see through you, boy. Passivity doesn't take root until the first weeks or months, and stems from boredom and lack of contact with the outside world." The mask cocked. "Six orgasms in two hours does not convince me that you're bored and lonely already."

Ugh, she was frustrating. *Deep breath.* Acquiring her friendship would be a harrowing endeavor, but the first step was easy. He wouldn't lie to her. "Mistress, talk to me. I don't want to screw this up. If something happens to my folks… Just help me, and I'll help you."

The dainty bones in her collar and shoulders sharpened against her skin. He didn't dare raise his eyes above her neck.

Finally, the mask spoke. "Follow the requirements, and you'll help us both. No more talking."

Irritation skittered over his spine, but he remained on his knees with arms raised. Helping people was the one aspect of his career he'd looked forward to. Maybe God put him in this situation to test him with the ultimate challenge, to save the darkest of souls. "Mistress, I'd rather you restrain my arms than my voice."

She stepped before him and gripped the cuffs she'd never removed. He expected her to whip some hidden chain from her bra and slap it on his arms. Instead, she molded his hands around the tiny circumference of her waist and squeezed in silent command. *Don't let go?* Was this a softening in her armor? Please?

The velvet of her skin heated his palms. The wet crotch of her panties, in the direct line of his lowered eyes, filled his nose with a tantalizing aroma. Perhaps God was testing him with man's greatest temptation. His confidence in being able to pass that trial fizzled as blood rushed below his waist.

"Requirement number nine. Slave will not speak unless spoken to." Her nails scratched down his forearms. "Your hands will be free to perform your tasks."

He guessed she expected him to *try* to overpower her and was probably prepared to subdue him like last time. He wasn't going to give her the pleasure.

"I'm the only person who knows the code for this room. Stand and follow me." She pushed his hands off her hips and walked to the toilet, though the way she moved couldn't be described as walking. It was more like the uninterrupted flow of a stream, gliding forward with confident disregard.

He trailed her, dodging the floor hooks with much less grace. Though, he strode a little lighter with the knowledge that Van couldn't bust in without her permission. How odd that he didn't have access. Was it because she was in charge? Something didn't seem right about that, and the answer felt vital to understanding her. What was her relationship with that guy?

She stopped before the medicine cabinet above the vanity, swung open the mirrored door, and dropped a threadbare rag in the sink. Her weight shifted to one leg, jutting out her hip, the bottom edge of her panties creeping up the musculature of one round cheek. She was so tiny and sensually-shaped, yet he'd felt her strength in her punch and could see it contracting through the tendons in her back.

As much as he despised her cruelty, his body wanted her to exhaustion and beyond. It pulsed to tackle her, to use its extra mass to dominate her in a battle of physiology.

Heat blazed down his thighs, and he clenched his hands to stop them from massaging his persistent erection. She was raining temptation down upon him in the form of curves and satin and glowing skin. Was his state of arousal normal in this situation? Perhaps another means of intended torment?

He stood over the toilet. Prayer was supposed to strengthen the struggle against lust, so he cycled *The Lord's Prayer* in his head. Holding his partial erection over the rim, he tried to relax it long enough to urinate. *Lead us not into temptation, but deliver us from the evil one.*

Yeah, she was evil, all right. And seductive and exquisite and complex. The repeated verses did nothing to alleviate his wandering thoughts or the weight between his legs.

She turned toward him and leaned a hip against the counter. "There's no video monitoring in this house. What happens in this room stays in this room. If you kill me, you'll be faced with the decision of whether or not to eat my body to stay alive."

Good God. Seriously? Where prayer didn't defuse him, her revolting words did.

He softened in his hand and didn't waste the opportunity to aim and empty. "Mistress, are you trying to scare me or offend me? Because I'm already glutted on both."

"Shock has a way of rousing attention." She moved behind him, the satin of her bra caressing his back, her fingers creeping along his abs, circling around the root of his penis, and trailing his hips to cup his backside.

He tried not to purr with the electrifying sensations. *Lead us not into temptation…*

Smack.

A sting zipped along one butt cheek. His body shuddered. She smacked him again on the other side. He sighed, relaxing with the tingle. Damn. That was arousing and… cute. His lips twitched.

"No. Talking."

That was his punishment for talking? He freed the grin squirming to escape and flushed the toilet. A slaphappy fog of delusion must have settled in his brain. He didn't *know* her, yet he was dangerously close to letting her see his deepest urges. Surprisingly, he wanted her to dig around inside of him, but the notion raced his pulse. What would she do if she knew he savored physical pain?

If only she'd remove that mask so he could search for a hint at what she was thinking and feeling.

Crouching behind him, she rubbed the heat in his gluts. "You have two sexy handprints on your ass cheeks, boy." She rose, clutching his biceps, and whispered over his shoulder, "Wonder what your God thinks about you grinning while I spanked you."

His smile fell. No way she saw his reaction. He glanced over his shoulder and followed her gaze to the mirrored door she'd left angled open. The reflection of her mask stared back.

He blew out a breath. He was a rookie in this demented game, and she controlled the line of scrimmage.

"The next time you speak without permission, we'll find out how easy your ass reddens beneath my cane."

His backside clenched, relaxed. He wasn't sure what his limits were, but that wasn't one.

She sashayed to the sink, wet a rag, and flung it

toward the floor. He intercepted it and knelt before the toilet to begin his first task.

To win this, he'd play her game until, eventually, hopefully, they played on the same side.

CHAPTER 15

Toilet cleaned and hair washed, Josh stood under the warm spray of the shower. He attempted to use the few spare minutes to meditate, but the pangs of hunger nudged him from his thoughts. Facing the wall, he soaped away crusty remnants from his ball sac.

A trickling sound cut through the whoosh of the shower head. She was peeing? He leered over his shoulder before his brain told him not to be rude.

Perched on the seat, knees and toes together, she tore off a wad of toilet paper. The mask lay on the tile beside her discarded panties. He turned slowly, not to gape while she did her business but to devour her expression.

Her lowered eyes fanned thick blades of lashes over her cheekbones, softening the elegant lines of her face. Where most complexions washed out under fluorescents, her flawless skin seemed to glow in the glare.

He held his breath, feet frozen to the floor. She appeared so very human and gut-wrenchingly beautiful sitting there doing normal things like peeing and fidgeting. *Fidgeting!*

Did she know he'd turned to watch her? Was this

another enactment to mess with his head?

Her teeth sawed along her bottom lip, and she twisted the end of her hair between a finger and thumb. No question the length and shine of her hair was exquisite, but she seemed to be eyeing it with more scrutiny than it deserved. What was she thinking about?

She dropped her hand, and her eyes slid up, finding his unerringly. Her lips bent in a conspiring smirk.

Oh no. What repulsive thing was she dreaming up? He locked his knees, waited.

Without looking away, she dabbed the tissue between her legs. Blotting? Was that how women wiped? Not that he was really watching, but his periphery caught it.

She flicked the flusher and stood. With a forearm over her chest, she reached back, unclasped her bra, and jerked it off without removing the coverage of her arm. What? No seduction or vulgar teasing? What was her game?

The red satin garment dangled from a finger at her side and dropped. On the floor. Where his eyes and knees should've been. *Craaaaap.*

He balled his fists and lowered to his knees. *Crap, crap, crap.*

*I'll feed you…*if *you follow the eight requirements you've been given.*

Pressing his lips together, he wouldn't make excuses or beg for food. Dammit.

He blinked at the bare feet beneath his bowed head. She could raise a knee and knock out a tooth. Or kick one of her deceptive little toes into his groin. He loosened his shoulders. He could take it.

Fingers touched his chin, lifting his head. "Raise your eyes."

Following the hourglass curves of her waist, the cuts of her narrow torso, his breath caught when he reached the rounded undersides of her breasts. Not too full, they seemed to defy gravity, sloping upward, reaching toward the…cutting slits of her glare.

"Next time I tell you to raise your eyes, I'll be more specific." Her fingers walked from his jaw to his temple and dragged along his scalp. "I'm surprised a big boy like you isn't more focused on the next meal."

Of course he was frigging hungry. As a linebacker, he consumed 5,000 calories a day. But apparently his sexual appetite was running things.

She patted his head. "I'll reevaluate your progress at dinnertime."

What mealtime was it now? Lunch? Dinner? She certainly hadn't fed him breakfast when he woke in the rubber bag. Straining to keep his jaw from locking in a murderous clench, he remained still and stoic.

She held out a bottle of bath wash and stepped under the spray of water. Sitting on his heels, he started with her feet. That was easy enough. Then he lathered soap up her shins. The set of his jaw loosened as he reached her thighs, his palms gliding over taut satiny skin and lean muscle, his erection an eternal aggravation.

Her legs tightened and relaxed beneath his hands, her calves outrageously defined for a girl. Maybe she ran marathons when she wasn't trafficking humans. Or maybe she kicked kittens. Into end zones painted with the blood from dead puppies.

"What are you thinking about? Look at me."

He snapped his eyes up, caught in the rich

chocolate of hers. His stomach growled.

"I asked you a question."

Permission to talk? *Thank you, oh hateful one.* "Kittens and puppies, Mistress."

Her gaze froze over. "Do not fuck with me, boy."

Not a chance, girl. Holding her eyes, he leaned up, his chest against the flat expanse of her belly, and ran soapy hands up her calves. "Mistress, I was debating whether your leg strength came from running or kicking small animals."

The fierce point of her chin softened. The icy cut of her eyes melted into liquid brown, and pink stained her cheeks. *Absolutely stunning.* But nothing on Earth compared to the mystic beauty of her lips as they curved up, stretching with abandon. Her smile was jewel-like in its discovery, sparkling and precious. And for a fleeting heartbeat, it was his to treasure.

Then it was gone, replaced with a scowl and an invisible wall. "I did not give you permission to stop washing."

Sliding his hands up her backside, firm cheeks filling his palms, the spirit of her smile fluttered inside him. He'd found her. Behind perversion and tyranny was a girl who could enjoy the humor in being teased.

Still on his knees, he lowered his eyes and met her breastbone, paralyzed by a hammering need to press his lips there. He fought the impulse and continued his ministrations up and over her slender hips.

"I run," she said into the silence.

His hands faltered on her waist. He hadn't expected a response but wasn't surprised by the answer.

The angle of the shower head immersed them both in the warm spray. The tile floor dug into his knees, but it was nothing like the aches endured on the farm or during practice. He quickly shoved those thoughts away and collected more soap from the bottle. Angling his face away from the spray, he lathered suds over her ribs. Yeah, his attention skipped the body parts that guaranteed awkwardness and discomfort. Maybe she wouldn't notice.

A sigh drifted down with the torrent of water, swirling around his ears. "I'm giving you back your voice. Use it wisely."

Why would she do that? Because he made her smile? Because she was lonely?

Please God, don't let him mess this up. "What makes you happy, Mistress?"

Her back turned to stone against his splayed hands. "Why?"

Suspicion edged her voice. Not surprising given her line of work. If she kept company with genuine friends, they were probably as cautious with their feelings as she was.

"Mistress, I love your smile. If I could free it once a day, it might make the next ten weeks bearable. Would smiling cause a conflict in your job?"

Her chest rose and fell with steady breaths. Would she punish him with silence or respond with something foul and shut him down? Or would she try out an honest answer and keep the conversation open? The way she stared over his shoulder, her brown eyes turning inward, he suspected those questions warred in her head, too.

She glanced down at him, studying his face. "Freefalling."

Freefalling? Like spiraling into hell? Or leaping from a cliff for sport?

"Enjoy the fall, or nothing at all." Her lips remained parted on the *all*, expression vacant. She must have recognized the confusion in his, because she shook her head. "Nothing seduces happiness like throwing yourself from a plane."

Fascinating. And positively unhelpful. It had been a safe answer, since he didn't have a plane to *seduce* her happiness. But he didn't think it was a lie, either. Skydiving was sporty and dangerous. It fit her.

His knees slid over the floor as he shifted around her, washing her arms, neck, and hair with an effortless reach. If he were on his feet, the top of her head would stop at his chest, a reminder that he could crush her with his size alone. Perhaps that was why she preferred him on his knees.

"What about singing, Mistress?"

She regarded him, and the molten depths of her eyes rippled, then stilled. "At first glance, you come across as a pretentious wannabe-psychoanalyst."

Uncertainty pelleted his nerves. He nudged her chin, angling her head under the water to rinse. He'd never attempted to befriend someone so misguided, and he'd definitely never washed a woman's hair. A breathtaking woman. A naked woman. With dips and mounds that molded to his hands.

Stop with the lusting, pervert.

"You're not asking the usual questions, boy. Like what's going to happen to you? How badly am I going to hurt you? Who am I selling you to?" She stared at his lips, beads of water clinging to her thick brown lashes. "I think you know those answers won't help you. When you're able to think beyond your hard dick, you're focused on your Jesus-saves-all mission. Which I admit is more appealing than fatalistic whimpering. But Jesus isn't going to save you from washing the two areas you've been avoiding."

He bit back a groan. Apparently, ignoring her privates wasn't going to make them go away.

"Eyes down. Mouth shut. Hands busy."

Her commands hovered between them, protecting her like a raised gun. This girl required a lot of patience. And prayers. A megachurch full of prayers. He soaped up his hands. Knees quivering on the tile floor, insides tightening, he looked at her chest, really let himself behold her for the first time.

Symmetrical, round, heavy on the bottoms, and tipped with pale-pink nipples, they outclassed every pair he'd seen on screen or in magazines. They weren't airbrushed or oversized or marred with tan lines. And because of his much taller height and kneeling as he was, her breasts were right at eye-level, waiting to be washed.

He started with circular patterns, both hands painting lather around and around the outsides. They were firm yet soft. Springy when he rounded the sides too fast. Heavy when he slid along the creases underneath. His heart rate kicked up, pushing his breaths faster.

He avoided the hard peaks because… Did nipples really need to be cleaned? How dirty could they get? He pressed a little harder against the supple curves, tightened the circles, brushed the taut beads. Once, twice… Ugh. Where the hell was his will power?

"Are you washing them or checking for lumps?"

Wow, was he that awful at this? It wasn't like he was trying to pleasure her. He clutched her waist and shifted her chest under the water.

"How often did you beat off?" Her voice sliced like a scalpel, dissecting.

"Once a day, Mistress." At night, alone and dreaming of girls half as pretty as she was.

"I bet you think about touching titties when you stroke yourself. When you're worked up enough, you fantasize about banging a pussy with your finger. Then you replace it with your cock. Probably missionary position. Hard, fast humping. You take her without guilt, because it's only a dream, a fleeting thought that vanishes when you come."

She only had it partially right. He didn't want to *take* a girl. He wanted to give himself to her. He wanted to watch his touch soften her eyes, hear it in her breathy exhales, and feel it shudder over her body as she arched against him. The fantasy of a sated smile on a pretty face was what sent him spinning over the edge every time.

An inferno raged in his body, and his hands clenched on her waist. It was Liv's face he'd imagined just now. It was her smile that made him tremble and harden. So very, very hard. Were his fantasies forever changed? The need to look into her eyes, to put a sated smile on her face, had his molars sawing together and his muscles straining to hold her.

He pushed his chin to his chest and focused on his breathing. *Our Father who art in heaven…*

"You used up all the hot water." Her voice was soft, distant.

Then she seemed to snap out of it and rubbed a soapy hand between her legs. That done, she pivoted to rinse and twisted the lever. The shower stopped, and she breezed past him.

The sheen of water on his skin chilled. With his

body flushed and battling arousal, he hadn't noticed the change in water temperature.

She returned to his side with a rope of chain. "Well, you're horny enough." She snapped the ends on his wrist cuffs. "On your feet. Van is waiting."

CHAPTER 16

Liv led the boy into the outer chamber and inhaled the intangible fume of rage seeping from Van's fists-on-hips stance by the door. She steered the boy around him, her defensive hackles shooting her shoulders to her ears.

Anything could've set him off. She'd sneaked from his bed the previous night. She'd made him wait too long for her to emerge from her room, and she'd come out without clothes on. Or it could've simply been one of his cruel-for-the-hell-of-it days.

She could handle Van's venom when it was directed at her, but the way he glared at the boy made her stomach knot. Granted, he was as uncertain as she was on how to convert a straight boy into a woman-hating sex slave, but she still expected him to be better than this. She needed to defuse him before they began the planned training session.

Across the room, the girl knelt on the cot naked, chin tucked to her chest and hands secured to the wall behind her. She seemed invisible to Van at the moment, and in two weeks, she would be out of his reach completely. Thinking of the man waiting to buy her wrung an entirely different wrack of tension in Liv's shoulders.

She was a fool to dwell on it. After the delivery, the girl would be dead to her. Just like the others.

Angling her back to Van, she shackled the boy's wrists to the chains hanging from the apex of the room. He must've sensed Van's volatility, because his muscles contracted against his skin, and his eyes bore a fiery path over her shoulder. Dammit, there was only one place his eyes should've been.

The simplest commands seemed to be the hardest for him to remember. Van would expect her to whip the boy for it, and of course, the sadistic buyer anticipated a battered body. But there would be enough of that after lunch.

A dull pound ignited in her skull. Her logic didn't even make sense in her own head. If she were honest, she was putting off whipping him. She dreaded it down to the marrow of her icy core. This boy was fucking with her detachment.

Using her body as a barrier between him and Van, she tapped the boy's steel jaw and whispered, "Eyes and knees down."

With slack in the chain, he descended to the floor, his exhales a hot caress on her chest. She knew he was in self-preservation mode, but the way he leaned toward her, as if trying to enfold her in the limited cage of his restraints, breathed an irrational warmth through the hole inside her.

All of the slaves had become protective of her at some point during their captivity. The captor-captive bond was just one of the many ways the mind dealt with trauma. But this boy hadn't been under duress long enough to develop that kind of psychological response.

His calm focus and rugged linebacker build was so

unlike the mold of previous slaves. He looked at her like he thought he could save her. Maybe he could.

Except he was supposed to despise her. The hammering in her head increased. What a hopeful, romantic idiot she was.

When she shifted to meet the eyes burning into her back, Van flung a sleeveless sheath dress at her face, the most demure outfit from her costume closet. She kept her casual wear in a trunk in her room, but her frayed jeans and printed t-shirts endowed her with human qualities and expressions she couldn't possess in that house.

She stepped into the black nylon sheath and rolled it over her hips and ribs, tucking her breasts in the top. It wrapped her from nipples to upper-thighs and clung to every dip and bend of her body, revealing more than it covered.

Van crossed his arms over his chest, his lips in a flat line. His unusual reticence meant he was holding in something particularly unsavory. The sharpness of his eyes matched his razored tone. "Let's get started."

The knot in her belly intensified with the pressure in her head. To soothe it, she hummed the woeful melody of "Pretender" by *Sarah Jeffe,* the lyrics reinforcing the roles they were playing. Van was supposed to be a passive bystander, but his foul mood tainted the already unbreathable air.

So she left the boy on his knees with his wrists padlocked to the chains in the ceiling and paced to the outer door. "I'm hungry."

Van's footfalls chased her down the stairs. She did her best to outrun them, which was stupid. She'd left the room to confront him, but she wasn't ready. Was she ever ready for him?

He caught her in the kitchen, an arm around her waist, a hand around her throat, and lips pressed against her ear. "Why are you running?"

The beat of her heart drummed against the collar of his hand. He wasn't choking her, but the promise was there. Thankfully, years of practice had taught her how to manage him, and keeping her cool was a vital response.

She relaxed her stance and leaned her back against the granite surface of his chest. "Why are you chasing me?"

"Because you're mine."

His hand cinched tighter with that heated oath. She coaxed her pulse to match a gentle tune in her head and waited. Finally, he released her and strode to the kitchen sink.

The turbulence rolling off him clotted the small room as he stared out the window. She rushed through sandwich preparations and blamed the lump in her throat on Van's pending tantrum, not on the fact that she'd returned the fourth plate to the cabinet because the boy wouldn't be eating with them.

Unable to meet Van's eyes, she kept her back to him under the guise of arranging potato chips on three plates. "Talk to me."

"I don't like him."

Her hand flexed, crinkling the foil bag in her grip. Apparently, his jealousy had reached a new degree of crazy. He never liked the male slaves, but this was the first time he'd vocalized it.

"I want him gone." His sharp tone punched her in the back.

Objections amassed in her throat. They wouldn't find a replacement slave in time. And they couldn't just send the boy back. He knew where they lived, had seen their faces. Van's *gone* meant one thing, an unthinkable alternative he'd never suggested before.

Somehow, she mustered an exasperated sigh and a bored tone. "Why?"

"His parents are all over the fucking news." His voice grew louder, more guttural. "Their whole goddamned town is searching for him."

This wasn't about jealousy? She shivered as he paced behind her, the air frosting with each pass, sending ice through her lungs.

"He's not like the others, Van. We knew he'd be missed."

She didn't have to turn on the news to know what love and desperation looked like. Haunting images stabbed the backs of her eyes. She squeezed them shut to trap the remembered videos of Mom grieving alone and the godawful need to reach through the screen and hug her.

His fingers bit into her bicep, spinning her so violently her hip slammed into the counter's edge.

"Why did you choose him?" He shook her shoulder, his grip punishing. "Answer me," he shouted, his fury a hot mist in her face.

She blinked rapidly, grasping at the most logical answer. "He fit what the buyer wanted." She dragged her gaze to his and flinched at the feral expression twisting his features.

"Bullshit." He captured her jaw in a steel grip, lifting her chin until she stretched on tiptoes. "A hundred other fuckers would've met the requirements. This one fit what *you* wanted."

The truth of his words paralyzed her, shriveling all

of her justifications for choosing Joshua Carter. The real reason made her throat tighten. He represented purity, beauty, family, all of the things that had been taken from her. He was a glimmer of goodness in her dark fucking world, a warm spark she could hold, if only for a fleeting span of time.

Her fingernails stabbed her palms. She was such a selfish, vile bitch.

Van shoved her away, turned her over the counter, and pressed her face against the laminate. "And the way he was looking at you really pisses me the fuck off."

When his hand tunneled between her thighs, her heart sputtered.

"No." She jerked beneath the prison of his immovable body. "No, Van. I have a job to do. I need to be in the right frame of mind."

The intrusion of his fingers speared between her labia, pinching dry flesh.

"What frame of mind is that?" His tone, as cold and penetrating as his touch, froze her to her bones.

"I am a Mistress, not your sex slave." She tried to match his iciness, but it came out desperate and high-pitched.

He yanked her from the counter and slammed his knuckles into her face. She managed to stay on her feet as jolts of pain fired through her skull. A warm trickle wet her lashes and smudged her vision. The ache in her heart was worse, but she would not give him the perception he'd hurt her beyond the cut of his fist. She kept her hands to her sides and met his biting silver gaze head-on.

Angry red splotches stained his neck and cheek, and she imagined his blood simmering beneath the skin. He clutched the counter's edge on either side of her hips, his face level with hers.

"When I dispose of your body, no one will ever find it." His voice dropped to a chilling rasp. "You know why?"

Her heart sped up, increasing the throb above her eye. She held her muscles as motionless as her glare.

"Because no one will care enough to search for it." He angled over the plates and hocked a foaming bubble of spit on one of the sandwiches. "Clean up your face." His smirk flared the bruise around her heart. "You look more like a slave than your little cunt boy." He grabbed an unsoiled sandwich, sat at the table, and dug into the roast beef.

What they were, what they'd become together, wasn't sane or healthy. It was in his blood to spew nasty things in a fit of rage, including threats on her life, and she'd conditioned herself over the years to bury it. His temper would eventually ebb, and the hurt from his words would, too. Because she didn't love him. He didn't have the power to leave a permanent scar on her heart. But that reminder didn't help the rawness of the moment as she moved to the sink and turned the tap to warm.

Ducking her head, the spray showered her face, renewing the pain around her eye. The water ran red, but no amount of cleaning would remove the evidence that she was just as much a prisoner as the ones in chains. And somehow, she would have to stand before the boy with a black eye as his Mistress.

Van finished his meal and reclined in the chair, studying her. No hint of civility, but the tension in his jaw loosened. "If you spent your allowance on makeup instead of your skydiving bullshit, you'd be able to cover that before you went upstairs."

She dried her face, blotting the hurt over her eye. Her fingers recoiled from the bubbled scar on her cheek, the cut that makeup could never cover. Not that she would waste a dime on meaningless luxuries. Their monthly funds from Mr. E paid for basic expenses, groceries, gas, and tools for training. She and Van split whatever was leftover, and she used her allotment on freefalling. Her only freedom.

As she replaced the ruined sandwich top with a new slice of bread, Van tossed a bag of frozen peas on the counter beside her. It wasn't an apology, but an offer to move on.

She held the icy bag to her eye. Too bad it couldn't numb the emotions swelling her throat.

CHAPTER 17

Josh chewed the hell out of his cheek. Fifteen minutes alone with the naked girl and she wouldn't answer any of his questions. She was probably thinking, *Fifteen minutes with the naked man, and he wouldn't shut up*. Too bad. The need to hear about her experience coiled him into a restless chatterbox. He didn't just want to make sure she was okay. He needed to hear everything she knew.

He tried to draw her in with highlights from his family farm, his coursework, and football achievements while shifting his weight from one knee to the other to transfer his discomfort on the hard floor. When she said nothing, he switched back to questioning. "Do you know what they have planned next or why Van was ticked off?"

She remained statuesque in her folded pose on the cot.

He pressed his lips together and tried to rein in his frustration. "Does anyone ever visit?"

Her hands and arms were limp, her silence ominous, indicative of psychological trauma.

He drew in a deep breath and released it slowly. "Have you ever left this room?"

She stared at her lap.

"Who is Mr. E?" His stomach growled. What he wouldn't do for Mom's biscuits and gravy right now. He winced, thinking about her safety. "Have you ever met him?"

A big empty nothing.

He sighed but refused to admit defeat. "You seem like a nice girl. Pretty, too, though I've yet to see beyond the top of your head." Okay, that last part wasn't entirely true. "I'm not looking at the rest of you, I promise."

Funny how quickly he'd become unconcerned with his own nudity. He yanked his wrists, clattering the chains, and her head didn't move from its downward position.

"We're in this together, right? I just need your help understanding what *this* is."

Was she even breathing? The threat that compelled her to ignore him could walk through the door any moment, which only fueled his impatience.

"Look at me," he shouted.

Her head snapped up. *Finally!* The deep set blue of her eyes widened, flitted to the door, and back to him.

"Hi." He kept his smile soft and unassuming. "I'm Josh."

"Your name is *boy*." A whisper. "Please, stop talking." From the thready plea, the tensing of her body, and the heave of her chest, she seemed to be crawling in her skin with fear.

Pressure swelled behind his ribs. "Hey, it's okay." He stretched his arms to reach for her. Impossible. He let them drop, his elbows bent on either side of his head. "We're just chatting. What's your name?"

"Girl."

He had to strain his hearing to make out her

heartbreaking whisper. Commands were clearly more effective than questions.

He hardened his voice. "Give me your birth name."

She glanced at the door, and the nervous twitches in her cheeks tightened his chest. At least she wasn't peeking around the room at hidden cameras. Perhaps Liv had been honest about no recording devices. Or maybe the girl was as in the dark as he was.

Her attention dropped to the floor between them. "Kate."

Kate. The excited race of his heart redoubled as he considered what to ask, or demand, next. How much time did he have? Something had been tightly stretched between their captors when they left. Perhaps they were just eating lunch. Or planning the next training session. Maybe they were having sex.

He slammed his teeth together. *Good grief.* Where the hell did that thought come from? "Tell me about the relationship between Van and Liv."

With another peek at the door, she shook her head. Did the huddle of her shoulders mean this subject terrified her?

"Does he force you or Liv to have sex with him?" he asked.

Her chin lowered, her body returning to its earlier frozen state.

Dammit, now he was glancing at the door, the hairs on his nape standing on end. What bothered him wasn't the hostility vibrating from Van so much as the song humming from Liv's throat when she ran out.

She'd sung in his truck as she'd led him into this nightmare. She'd sung when he was in the box, right before she closed the lid. Singing seemed to be a mechanism she employed when something bad was about to happen. So what was going to happen? What made her bolt from the room?

All of his questions liquefied to one conclusion. "Van's in charge, not Liv. She puts on a good show, but the fact is he's a rapist—"

"Master is not a rapist." Her eyes flashed to his, lit with fire, her words heated and rushed. "He doesn't touch me like that, because he loves Mistress, and she loves him."

What? No way in unholy hell did Liv love that man. His insides twisted and turned at the idea, and it pained him to see Kate's perception so emotionally distorted by what she'd been through. And what did she mean, he didn't touch her like that? Forcibly or not all?

"You've been here a month?" He leaned toward her. "Two months?"

She shrugged, and it was wooden and completely absent of hope. "I don't know."

Was he staring at the harbinger of his own future mental state? How would his judgment fare after ten weeks of captivity? His head ached, and his impatience with her and the chains that held him set his skin on fire.

He rolled his arms in a useless attempt to escape the shackles. "I want to help you, Kate. Please, talk—"

The door clicked open.

Rage cinched his throat and accelerated his pulse. He lowered his head with a frustrated jerk and glared at the floor.

Josh's breathing grew heavier, louder. His body temperature boiled from his blood to his skin.

Liv's bare feet skimmed over the floor and passed by his knees. Van's sneakers trailed close behind. They stopped at the cot, and the mattress creaked under Van's weight, a plate of food balancing on his lap. Josh's stomach gave a miserable groan.

"Tell me what I missed, girl." The cool clip of Liv's voice sliced the air, but there was a strained edge to it. "I want to hear every word that was uttered."

Surely her other slaves talked and even befriended each other when they were alone. Did she punish them for it?

Locking his eyes on her feet was pure torture. He wanted to read her face, observe what wasn't being vocalized. In the outer edge of his vision, Van raised a sandwich toward Kate's mouth.

"He said his parents are cotton farmers. He plays football at Baylor." Between meager bites and swallows, she repeated the conversation verbatim with much better recollection than his own. When every morsel was consumed, and all of his words betrayed, she finished with, "I told him Master wasn't a…rapist, that you love each other."

The heels of Liv's feet twitched outward so slightly the movement would've gone unnoticed if he'd been staring a couple inches higher. Her knees bent even more subtly as if she were pressing her feet to the floor to mute the reaction. A sign of objection.

He was so distracted by the dichotomy between her genuine responses and her facade that he hadn't considered the consequences of Kate's tattling until Van stood.

"Roll to your stomach, girl." He moved out of Josh's field of vision, his voice pitching through the room. "Face pressed against the mattress. Ass and pussy in the air and spread for your Mistress's punishment."

Punishment? The biting claw of dread shivered down Josh's spine. No, it hadn't been nice of Kate to tattle on him, but she didn't deserve a punishment for answering his questions.

Van returned with a thin rod that resembled the riding crop Josh had used in his horse riding lessons as a boy. His brain twisted into knots trying to piece together what was happening and what he could do to stop it.

With his eyes on the floor, his field of vision was limited to below their waists.

When Van pressed the handle into Liv's hand, she didn't close her fingers around it. The exchange was swift, but Josh was certain Van bent her pinkie at an awkward angle to persuade her to take the crop.

She traced Kate's raised backside with the leather-tipped end. "Boy, you violated requirement number nine."

Requirement nine? He didn't know them by number. Hell, he wasn't sure he could recite them all. But nine was the last requirement she'd taught him, right? The one about not talking—

Whack.

The crack of the crop left a red mark on Kate's upper thigh. Her legs trembled, and her cry muffled against the mattress.

Josh drew a lungful of air and swallowed the protests springing forward. Kate would suffer even more for his outbursts.

Van crouched beside Josh, his scar pulling at his lips, intensifying the threat of his proximity. "Hey, buddy. The Mistress is a real stickler about rules, but don't worry. The girl will accept your punishment."

A roar pummeled through Josh's throat, and he slammed his jaw shut, trapping it. This horsecrap wasn't directed by Liv, and Van knew that punishing Kate would hurt Josh the most.

Van stood, sidled up to Liv, and circled a finger on the back of her thigh, just below the hem of the minidress. "Twenty strokes. Right, Mistress?"

A battle of emotions coursed through Josh, heating his blood and rushing his breaths. He clutched the chains with white-knuckled fists and braced for the most messed up moment of his life.

And so it went. A garbled scream followed every whack, each one corkscrewing through his heart, stripping away pieces that would never be recovered. Liv kept unimaginable control of her swings, bringing down her arm in a rhythmic tempo as if moving to a cadence no one but her could hear.

He shuddered with the smack of leather on flesh, the pierce of Kate's wails in his ears and the twitch of her small body receiving his punishment under his gaze.

Guilt fisted his stomach and shoved the turmoil to his throat.

Each strike fell hard and steady, but the more Liv swung, the more noticeable the trembling became in her free hand. Her fingers pressed against her thigh and her body seemed to lose its upright, stiff posture. It was a subtle change, but something was definitely pulling at her resolve.

Finally, she lowered the crop. A pattern of red welts striped Kate's backside and thighs but did not break the skin.

Liv circled around him to stand at his back. He hadn't seen her face since she'd returned, didn't know what mask she was wearing, if one at all. What was she feeling beneath her stony exterior? What held her here, bending her to do things he knew she didn't want to do?

Maybe he was just imagining her reluctance. Lord knew he prayed for it. There were so many unyielding barriers between them. Her masks. His chains. Van.

When Van released Kate from her restraints, she lowered her eyes and her knees to the floor, crawling toward Liv, legs trembling. "Thank you for the discipline, Mistress."

Her words plunged Josh deeper into the cold clutch of his new reality. It was a terrifying feeling to be enchained by people who could break a girl so unequivocally she thanked them for it. And while Liv delivered the strikes, he was convinced she was nothing more than an instrument operated by another.

Across the room, Van leaned against the wall, arms crossed, expression slack but watchful.

No doubt there would be a profusion of defining moments in the weeks to come, but Josh suspended this one in his mind, branding it to memory, and made a vow to himself. He would adapt to this environment, but he would not become an instrument, an empty shell, or a grateful slave. His parents would surrender their lives before they'd want him to become something less than he was. His heart ached at the thought of anything happening to them, but he sat lighter in his resolve, his shoulders loosened and his jaw unlocked.

"This training session will focus on requirement two." Liv's detached voice tiptoed over his shoulder. "Given your inability to remember the requirements, repeat after me. Slave will service Master sexually with exceptional skill, and his body will be prepared to make it easy for Master."

Ugh. He never wanted to hear that rule again. He climbed to his feet. "Slave will break through Mistress's mask with exceptional skill—"

Crack.

Fire erupted on his backside, a concentrated burn in the crease of his butt and thigh. Dear God, she had an arm on her. He breathed through it and hung on the support of the chains. He glanced over his shoulder, not giving a crap about the rules. His throat dried at what he found there.

Red bled over the white of her left eye, surrounded by pink, swollen skin. His heart roared in his ears, and his fingers curled into his palms. With the ragged half-inch cut on her brow bone and the scar marring the length of her cheek, she looked like a battered mess. Worse was the pleading fragility softening the edges of her gaze. She was begging him for something. To obey her? To ignore the beating Van had obviously given her?

Van held his relaxed pose against the wall, but

there were signs of edginess. His arms were crossed too tightly, his fingers pressed against his biceps, and the skin around the indentations of his grip blanched.

With Kate in her kneeling position beside Josh and Liv at his back, a division was drawn in his mind. There was a significant intersection in the room. Josh stood with the girls and faced the true threat.

A toothpick rolled slowly between Van's lips as he studied Josh. Perhaps Van was measuring him the way he weighed Van. Josh's limited counseling experience taught him that an abuser's violence was rooted in arrogance, in a belief that no one was as good as he was. Liv was someone Van could control and possess, someone to serve him. That sense of ownership bred jealousy not love.

Van was a problem that couldn't be resolved with a few anger-management sessions, not that the man would be willing to talk through his issues. Because even if he could be rehabilitated, one harrowing fact remained. Josh was on the wrong side of the bars—or chains.

If Van moved close enough, could Josh hold himself by the chains, swing his legs up, and wrap them around the man's throat? What then? He'd seen them both remove weapons hidden in their clothes. Even if his arms were free, he would still be outmatched by muscle and whatever Van was armed with. Despite the challenge charging his nerves, there was nothing he could say or do to stop this training session.

To top it off, Liv's pleading eyes held a desperate grip around his heart. He didn't want to make this harder on her, and with that certainty, he turned toward her with his head lowered. Kneeling at her feet, the chains crisscrossing above him, he tried to repeat the requirement from memory, with a few adjustments. "Slave will service Mistress with exceptional skill, and his body will be prepared to make it easy for her."

Her toes flexed. She seemed to be digesting his wording changes. "Slaves, stand and face me."

He rose with Kate, surprised by her wide eyes when they locked on Liv's swollen face. Kate's shock flashed for only a second before she averted her gaze. Van, who appeared bored by the whole exchange, picked his teeth with the toothpick. Was his abuse a rare thing? Or did Liv usually hide the evidence behind her masks?

She pinched Kate's chin, capturing her focus. "We're going to teach the boy the proper way to kiss."

"Yes, Mistress." Kate wet her lips, pressed her bare breasts against Liv's larger ones, and tilted her head.

At a similar height, their mouths brushed with ease and familiarity. Slowly, enthrallingly, it bloomed into a jaw-stretching, tongue-touching, hands-wandering-curves pleasure to watch. The intimate slide of bodies and lips was sweet, gentle, and hell on his libido. Throughout the kiss, Kate held her mouth open and accepting, her tongue tracing her own lips as if inviting Liv to lead. The fluidity of their shared breaths drew him in, heating and hardening his groin. He gripped the chains to steady his balance.

"Very good." Liv pulled back, her smile quivering. No doubt the muscle movement aggravated her injury. "A slave's kiss anticipates her Master. It's intuitive, an articulation in submission, total perception-by-feel. Return to the cot, girl."

Beneath the delivery of her words lurked a strained emotion. It didn't sound like a scripted speech. More like a remembered feeling leaking from a deep well within her. Something akin to the inviting kiss she'd let him steer in his truck. What did that mean? How did it fit with her motivations? Those answers held the key to unlocking her.

"Boy." Liv stared up at him. "As with all your requirements, number two is commanded by your future Master, for his purpose, which means you will learn how to kiss a man the way a man desires."

Josh's pulse sputtered and his stomach bucked. He should've expected this. Van's role was suddenly and devastatingly clear.

As if he'd conjured the devil, a hot, sweaty palm gripped the curve of his shoulder and throat. Fingers added a warning pressure to his nape, punctuated by a thumb on his trachea.

Van leaned in. His mouth was too damned close, reeking of roast beef and ill-intent. The toothpick protruded from one upturned corner.

Restrained by the hand and the blasted chains, his thrashing only pressed him closer to Van's body. "No. No way in hell. I won't do this."

The swing of the crop whistled behind him, and the sharp burn of leather struck the rise of his backside. *Ow, Jesus, that hurt.* He clenched his jaw.

"Open your mouth and accept his kiss."

His muscles tightened. "No."

Another strike, harder. He sucked in a breath. "I won't kiss him." He ground his teeth and prayed for his parents' safety. "Not happening."

The lashes that followed came quicker, spreading out over his buttocks, thighs, and lower back. He held onto his resolution as his body swayed on his feet and his head swam through a haze of pain. At some point, she switched to a whip. Still, he refused the kiss.

She and Van gave him a wide berth as he fell to his knees, his torso held up by his arms in the chains, the tip of the whip cutting so sharply he felt it scorch through his blood.

The strikes turned into hours, the hours into days, and so his training lunged into full swing. As those days passed, they didn't seem like days at all. With the absence of windows and the constant pull of fatigue, it was always night. But he gaged the stretch of time by the healing of Liv's face. When he slept, it was on the rug beside her mattress. When awake, he was chained to the ceiling, the floor, the walls, or her bed.

While her tactics varied in creativity, her drive was steady, unyielding, and rife with trickery. Hours of silence would spur him to speak. Twenty lashes. A tender caress on his cheek would draw his eyes to hers. Twenty lashes. Her gripping strokes along his penis guaranteed an orgasm. And twenty lashes.

Some sessions were better than others. Sometimes the pain carried him to a strange space of unawareness where time and chains didn't exist. Where he mindlessly accepted the punishment. He anticipated that feeling of bliss. In fact, when he was in the moment, he didn't want her to stop.

On the third evening, she restrained his naked and kneeling body to the floor and opened the door. Van's swift gait sounded through the room followed by the click of her heels.

His blood pressure doubled as Van circled him. He lifted his shoulders, protecting his neck, and held his elbows close to his sides. After countless beatings, he'd learned to protect the most vulnerable parts of his body.

Luckily, he hadn't seen Van in three days. It didn't take long to find out why she'd finally invited him in.

She slammed her spiked heel into Josh's back, knocking him forward. "Accept his kiss, boy."

Violently shaking on his hands and knees, he glared at the floor and bit down his cheek. His anger boiled so hot his skin flushed with fever.

Van squatted before him, hands laced together beneath Josh's bowed head.

Screw them. He'd rather stab the bastard with a three-foot toothpick than kiss him. He would *not* become a broken grateful slave.

"No." He pinned his lips and braced for twenty new welts.

The silence in the room drew tightly around him, overtaxing his nerves as he stared at Van's unmoving hands. Finally, she spoke, using the empty voice he'd become accustomed to hearing.

"Raise your eyes and sit back on your feet." She walked around him, the pointed toes of her black heels stopping beside Van.

He lifted his upper body, his bruised muscles screaming in protest, and lugged his gaze to meet the frigid sharpness of hers.

Van rose and tucked his hands into his jeans pockets. "It's okay, Liv. He doesn't have to kiss me." His tone was casual, but his gaze was molten silver and aimed on her. "You'll give me what I need."

A flash of fear lit her eyes, and Josh's blood ran cold. The scar on her cheek seemed to draw the corner of her eyelid downward into a miserable reflection of his own thoughts. He didn't want her to give that man a damned thing.

She snapped her chin up and looked down her nose at Josh. Then her expression blanked, and she stared through him like he wasn't there. With a roll of her hips, she stepped into Van's body and cupped his groin, squeezing him through the denim. Josh slammed his teeth together.

The slide of Van's hands up the back of her thighs pushed her skirt to her waist and revealed her panty-less backside. The profile of their hips pressed together and Van's grinding and groping sent Josh's pulse careening, his heartbeat pounding, and every muscle in his body tensing. He tried to shake off the anger. It was just a game, a psychological torment meant to break him.

Van freed the button at his waistband, shoved his jeans to his bare feet, and kicked the material away. Naked from the waist down, he grabbed her hand and curled her fingers around his erection.

The chains held Josh to the floor, but it was the heaviness in his chest that pulled him down and squeezed his lungs. Would Van rape her? Was it rape if she wasn't struggling?

She captured Josh's eyes and pierced him with a look so cruel it struck harder and deeper than any implement she'd used on him.

He dropped his head, eyes burning and arms hanging numbly at his sides. What was the purpose of this?

"Watch us." The snap of her voice splintered through his spinning world.

His neck ached with tension as he raised his head.

The manifestation of her sudden smile seemed

forced, blanching along the seam despite the glaring curls at the corners. She angled her chin away, and Van caught her mouth.

He attacked her lips, licking and sucking. With a hand in her hair, the other wrapped around her fingers, stroking his fully aroused length.

Josh's throat thickened, and a guttural roar burst from his throat. "I'll do it. I'll kiss you. Just..." He trembled with the violent need to bash Van's face in. "Just get away from her."

Why did he care? She'd whipped him for days. He should hate her. Yet the pain of watching her with another man eviscerated his insides and destroyed his ability to see a future beyond that room.

Van released her lips, his arm pinning her against him, and cocked his head. "Maybe next time."

He returned to her mouth, his tongue whipping aggressively, dominating the movement of her jaw. He lifted her, hooked her legs around his waist, and backed her into the wall a couple feet away.

When Van's hand shoved between their hips, Josh barreled forward, the strain of his body caught by the web of chains.

"Mistress?" He jerked and yanked, the cuffs on his wrists scraping along his skin. "Mistress, don't let him do this."

Her glassy eyes peered at him over Van's shoulder. She lay her palms flat on his back, her shoes dangling from her toes where they hung behind Van's flexing thighs.

A vicious force of nausea spun through his gut. Why was this affecting him so furiously? There was no love between him and that woman. He sucked in a breath, his mouth thick with saliva. Wasn't this possessiveness he felt for her a method of control? Maybe he was supposed to feel sorry for her. Sympathy was more effective than hating her. The proof was in the painful collapse of his chest as Van thrust his hips, sinking inside her and grunting his pleasure.

His ears burned with the sound of his heart ripping, bleeding with loss and crushing into the shape of betrayal. Why the hell did he feel betrayed? Because she didn't fight? But the skin around her mouth blanched and strained. When he snagged her eyes, she looked away.

The hammering of Van's hips accelerated. The color drained from her face, and she pressed her grimace against Van's shoulder. Josh aged ten years as he watched beneath the weight of his chains, his perceptions grinding into a jaded palate of anguish, helplessness, and jealousy.

The fact that she wasn't struggling snarled and thrashed through his head. If he thought about it, really pushed past the shock and fury of his emotions, the truth was painfully obvious. She couldn't control him with punches and whips, but this...this would leave a permanent mark. She was doing her job by any means possible. His lungs constricted, his mind a mess of twisted conflict.

As Van pummeled into her limp body and pawed at her breasts through the bodice, a wet sheen glazed her eyes. When a lonely tear escaped, she looked at Josh, startled. She quickly brushed it away on her shoulder and averted her gaze.

His chest hitched. She didn't want this. His belief in that didn't mute the pain as Van buried himself deep inside her and released with a revolting groan. But it renewed his faith in his ability to expose her goodness and gave him the strength to keep fighting. For her.

Two days later, he lay on his stomach, stretched over her mattress, his nose burrowed in her sheets. Her familiar womanly scent warmed his inhales as the strikes of her cane pommeled his backside.

The passing of time had warped into an ugly mass of emotions, the intensity and direction of his thoughts changing as frequently as her masks. He flailed between hating her, wanting her, fighting her, and praying for her. And through it all was the incessant urge to screw her. The latter formed a knot of guilt in his stomach. After witnessing Van's treatment of her, his arousing thoughts were selfish.

The air whistled. *Crack.*

Burning pain stole through his thigh and cut his breath. He held tighter to the chains connected to the wall.

Crack.

His tender skin flinched, shuddering away from the hurt. But the warmth that remained spread tendrils of heat to his groin. When her footsteps clicked over the floor, he loosened his muscles, anticipating her next hit.

Crack.

The impact stabbed his backside, flexing and quivering his gluts. His lungs labored. He relaxed into the lingering twinge, and his arousal mounted.

Crack.

He ground his pelvis against the mattress, seeking relief. He tried to muster the shame in it and failed. He'd reached that place in his head where the pain transformed into a lofty phenomenon, his body floating through an immersion of sensations, every nerve ending devouring her attention. He rocked his hips.

Her knee pressed between his spread legs, and her hand wedged beneath his groin. She gripped his erection and stabbed her fingernails into the throbbing, sensitive skin.

"Slave will not rub Master's property against the mattress in a sexual way." Her tone was as cold as the absence of her hand as she stepped away.

Crack.

Fire seeped into his bones and smoldered in his joints. He thrust his arousal against the bed, wanting more. It was strange how badly he longed for her full focus on him, only him, whether or not that attention came with pain.

Her fingers grabbed the hair on the back of his head and yanked, exposing his neck. Her lips caressed his ear, and his penis throbbed.

"Stop. Grinding. Your dick." She released him with a shove. "Kinky fucker."

Crack.

Ahhh. He melted into the heat of her strike. He couldn't remember what the infraction was that led to the current punishment. Couldn't recall what day it was. Didn't care. It was during these highs that he trusted her implicitly. And ignorantly. The flow of his thoughts whispered in jumbled bursts of nonsense, his give-a-crap drifting beyond reach.

The mattress dipped as she knelt on the edge.

Time passed. He might've dozed. Somewhere along the edges of his drowsiness, her phone beeped. When he opened his eyes, her knees hadn't moved.

He licked dry lips. It would've been delusional to

expect leniency from her after every punishment, but sometimes, while the pain ebbed, she gave him a small window of sympathy. Sometimes, during these moments, he tested her.

"Come here," he breathed.

She sighed, and it was sexy soft. His lips floated into a smile. At least he thought they did. Her gentle response surprised him as much as it had the first time he'd given her the same order. In those rare moments when she came to him tenderly, it didn't last long before the detached Mistress appeared again. Still, he wanted her, craved her body against his, and this time she obliged.

Black pleather encased her from chin to ankle, and she wrapped all that material around the length of his side, stroking a hand over his sore muscles, soothing him as he fell out of the sky.

It was the only time she held him, and he didn't try to understand her intent. He simply savored her tender attention, turning his head to peer into her eyes.

In place of a mask was an expression he hadn't seen since Van had sex with her in front of him. Beneath the yellowing bruise around her eye was pure, unrestrained fear. It paled her complexion, hardened her jaw, and flattened her lips.

"Liv?" He raised his head, his stomach hardening. "What's wrong?"

She recoiled, clutching a cell phone to her chest. In the next breath, her face blanked, her tone equally vacant. "I'm failing. I've tried everything I can think of." She released a shuddering exhale. "You're the worst slave ever."

He wanted to laugh at that, but something was

wrong. She hadn't let up her grip on the phone.

"What's going on?" His scalp tingled. "What are you doing with the phone?"

She lowered it, staring at it like it was about to detonate. Then her eyes flashed to the door. "Mr. E is on his way upstairs."

CHAPTER 20

Josh was treated to the soft strains of Liv's a cappella as they stood side by side before the door in her room. She stared at her phone, perhaps waiting for a text. He stared at her profile, trying to capture the quiet words woven in her melody. Something about hounds and chains and teams. The tune was familiar, but he couldn't place it.

Her dark chestnut hair was smoothed into a ponytail that swung over the toned lines of her arm. Black vinyl painted her limbs and torso, giving her a sleek, wet look. The catsuit was so compressed, he could've spanned the cinch of her waist with two hands. He knew her costumes were intended to intimidate and hypnotize, but her musical voice held that power all on its own.

Her lips froze mid-verse, her attention locked on the phone's blank screen in her hand.

"Where are your eyes, boy?" The stiffness in her neck matched the aggravation in her voice.

She wasn't pleased with his wandering eyes, but his last punishment had ended with her body curled against his. It gave him enough temerity to break more rules.

"What does this visit from Mr. E mean exactly?"

He watched her beautiful, expressionless face.

She turned, facing him with her back to the door and her stony eyes packed with grim promises. He considered it an accomplishment to stand before her, as he did every day, with his wrists wrapped in chains, every inch of his flesh bared and unprotected, and his backbone proudly intact.

Her scrutiny leveled on his raised chin, and her brown eyes melted for a millisecond before hardening again.

"I saw that." He was being reckless. Despite the bumps and bruises riddling his body, the threat of her whip had lost its edge.

But she could still threaten his parents. Or have sex with Van. His jaw locked, smacking his teeth together.

"You saw nothing, boy." Her stillness suggested a disciplinary strike would follow, but her expression was hesitant, as if distracted by some inward conflict.

He stepped closer, raising his hands between them, the coil of chain around his wrists a reminder that he wasn't the enemy. "If your boss is right outside this door, why are we in here?"

Her throat twitched as if she'd stifled a swallow a second too late. "Eyes down."

Of course, she wouldn't answer him.

He'd have to make a guess and read her reaction. "He's out there with Kate. Van's probably catching him up on her training. When that's done, he'll text you to open the door, so he can inspect his new property. Do I have the gist of it?"

The flash of her eyes told him he'd guessed right. "On your knees. Now."

Arrgh. He stayed on his feet. "You always do that.

You deflect with those damned rules."

Still, she seemed off-kilter, and he might not get another opportunity to poke around for a soft spot.

"I'm just trying to understand." He searched her face.

She kept it guarded. So he rested his fists against the door above her head, no physical contact, but the bond was there.

"Step. Back." Her jaw set.

Maybe *bond* was too strong of a word, but she could've ducked out from beneath his arms. Instead, she stared up at him with an unfathomable mien on her face. Something was hidden there, an expression, a truth, etched in the delicate creases around her mouth. Her lips parted and pressed together, bending the scar that mapped the struggles in her life, the ones he suspected she fought alone.

Then it clicked. "I know that song you were singing. Isn't it about loyalty and friendship and—?"

"Team." Her eyes were wide, watchful, and maybe a little skittish.

"That's right. 'Team' by *Lorde."*

He wanted to ask what the song meant to her, but she wouldn't have answered. Didn't matter. He could guess its significance, knew it had to do with why she slept where her prisoner slept, confining herself with him for five days, only leaving to fetch food.

"Better to be enchained with someone on your side," he said, "than to be alone with a false sense of freedom."

The expression on her face transformed from that of captor to equal. Her posture loosened, her features gentled, the phone forgotten in her hand. She stared into his eyes, blinking, nodding slowly, subtly. It was a poignant moment of connection, the opening he'd been searching for.

He touched his forehead to hers, his chains rattling above her head, and waited for the punishment that never came. "We may not be trapped for the same reason, but we're looking in the same direction, reaching beyond these walls *together*. Tell me what we're up against."

A low-pitched noise groaned in her throat, and her head relaxed against his. He kept his shackled arms balanced on the door, afraid the smallest movement might spook her.

Was she considering his words or formulating a safe response? Maybe she was worried about Van hitting her again. Or raping her. His throat hurt as he replayed Van's groaning thrusts and the pain in her eyes. The two times he'd asked her to talk about it, she'd whipped him for speaking without permission.

Too soon, she straightened, breaking the point of contact. She took her time meeting his eyes, and when she did, a smile tugged at the corners of her mouth, her chin slowly moving left to right. "I give you an inch—"

"And I'd be six-foot-three." He lowered his arms, nudging her chin with his bound hands. "I love your smile."

Her lips trembled and stilled. The smile remained, but her eyes dulled. "You've got balls, distracting me despite the consequences."

He blew out a breath and retracted his arms to his waist. "So you're tallying my infractions?" He dreaded what those consequences might be and tried for a light tone. "When do I get my spanking?"

Her fingers touched his navel, sending a quiver through him. She traced the dusky trail to his groin and coiled a finger tightly through the thatch of hair.

"Spankings aren't effective." She tugged, sparking a twinge of discomfort over the sensitive skin there. "You're a pain slut."

A half-laugh, half-groan escaped with his exhale. "I am not a pain slut, whatever that is."

"Oh, please. Five welts and you fall into a hypnotic trance."

Okay, maybe he felt some out-of-body weirdness. Wasn't that normal in adrenaline-charged situations?

She glanced at her phone, and a sharp line rutted between her eyebrows. Her anxiousness was bleeding onto him.

"What is it?" he asked.

She angled the phone long enough for him to glimpse the text.

Unknown number: Open the door.

An unnerving metamorphosis washed over her, stripping the emotion from her eyes, smoothing out her breathing, and hardening her body into an armored shell.

"You want to be on the same team?" Her voice was cold and terse. "You want to save me?"

He nodded, hoping it wasn't a trick. Her sudden change in demeanor tightened the muscles in his jaw.

She dropped a hand to her side, snapped her fingers, and pointed at the floor beside her feet, an unmistakable order to kneel. "Then don't fuck this up."

Whatever was about to happen, it was evident that her bearing, as well as his, needed to broadcast that she had the upper hand. He knelt at her side, holding her gaze as he lowered. Sure, she appeared dispassionate at a glance, but the hand at her side trembled.

As she entered the code in the keypad—too quickly for him to catch the pattern—he gripped the fingers digging into her thigh. The door clicked open, and she pulled her hand away but not before giving him a tentative squeeze in return.

He kept his eyes on the floor, taking in the scuffed black boots that entered first, followed by Van's sneakers. The door shut, imprisoning the room with silence.

He'd expected trousers, paired with an expensive suit, a wardrobe that signified wealth and power. Instead, black cotton work pants gathered over the dusty boots. The mystery surrounding Mr. E compounded, surging dread through his veins.

"Raise your head, boy." Her voice was so detached, even its iciness was absent.

His breath caught as he lifted his eyes and met the drab material of a cotton jumpsuit. The kind one would zip over regular clothes to change a tire or carry out an activity that might be messy. He stopped breathing altogether when his gaze reached the man's head.

It was wrapped in a potato sack hood, cinched at the neck, with two crudely cut eyeholes and vertical stitching where the mouth should be. Rough-hewed seams rounded the skull, pulling the material taut to maintain the curvature. Then it spoke.

"Stand, slave." The mouth, stitched as it was, didn't move. The voice was soft and masculine and cruelly calm.

Van leaned against the closed door in a display of arrogant composure. Liv stared at her feet, frozen and pale, as if the masked man had chased her into some unseen recess of her mind.

Don't fuck this up.

Josh climbed to his feet and let his bound wrists loll over his groin. At his full height, he stood four or more inches taller than Mr. E.

"You'll address me as *Sir.*" Mr. E glanced at Liv and back to Josh. "Did you give her the black eye?"

His shoulders tensed. "No—"

"That was me, sir." Van's smirk oiled the tension in the air.

"Ah." A chuckle rustled through the canvas mask. Mr. E reached a gloved hand to Van's jaw and patted it. "I suppose you can't fuck up her face worse than it already is."

"Nope." Van popped the *P* with a smarmy exhale and slid a toothpick between his curved lips.

A storm of rage boiled Josh's blood, twisting and shaking his insides. She should've been defending herself. And what compelled Van to be at such ease with a man who hid behind a potato sack? The man who, Josh suspected, had given them their matching scars.

The whites of Mr. E's eyes shifted inside the depths of the eyeholes and settled on Liv. Under the decomposing scrutiny, her shoulders curled forward, her gaze fixed downward.

It was in that moment that his assumptions about her place in the hierarchy were confirmed. Just because she wasn't a slave didn't mean she wasn't viewed as property and used as such. They seemed to think of her as scarred and ruined, and she certainly wasn't sexually innocent. Her usefulness to them was limited to her proficiency in training slaves. A replaceable skill. Was Van's apparent ownership of her the only thing that held her there?

There was so much obscurity surrounding the operation, and seeing her like this shook the hell out of Josh's hope. He bit down on his cheek, checking the turbulence of his emotions, and put on his own phlegmatic expression.

"Have you fucked him yet?" The potato sack cocked toward Van, and Josh balled his fists.

The silver cut of Van's eyes sliced through Josh, but it was Liv who answered. "He's not ready."

Mr. E's stillness was deafening, cranking the room's temperature to scorching. Then those elusive eyeholes shifted to him. "Let's see how well he kisses." He curled a gloved finger. "Van."

Josh fought the heart-pounding urge to swing his bound arms into that stupid mask and stared directly into the soulless eyes. "I will not kiss that man."

Liv's finger twitched against her thigh, but she was otherwise unresponsive.

"I see." Mr. E clasped his hands behind him and spent an eternal moment moving through the room, testing the strength of a dangling chain, nudging the mattress with his boot, and building a terrible anticipation. Then he returned to Van's side. "She still sleeps in here."

A muscle jumped in Van's jaw. "Yes, sir."

"You haven't won her over yet."

"She's mine."

"I'm not arguing that."

Josh felt like he'd fallen into a state of surrealism, where crap that should never ever make sense was sickeningly transparent. They talked about her like she wasn't standing right there while ignoring the fact that Josh refused to kiss Van. It was a game, a tactic to mess with his head, and maybe hers, too.

Mr. E snapped his gloved fingers under Liv's bowed head. "Get his clothes."

Her stillness unfurled into a steady, flowing stride to the trunk by her mattress. She placed her phone on the bed and returned with the jeans, t-shirt, and boots he'd arrived in. They were just things, inconsequential possessions, yet the sight of them made his heart race.

"I'm a huge Baylor Bears fan." Mr. E scratched his chin through the mask. "The news reporters are saying you're the best linebacker in college football."

Josh's shoulders curled in. How much was the news covering his disappearance? Would they be camped out on the farm, shoving cameras in his parents' faces, and magnifying their grief?

"Get dressed." Mr. E pointed at the clothes.

The taunt of freedom thrilled in his chest as she removed the padlock on his wrists and unbuckled the cuffs. He massaged the skin that had been rubbed raw by metal for a week. Were they letting him go? "What is this?"

"Too many people are searching for you." Mr. E angled his mask toward Liv. "She picked the wrong boy and has made no progress in your training. You're a liability." He placed a hand on Josh's shoulder and squeezed. "Besides, the Bears are getting crushed. They need you."

What? No. This was crazy.

Mr. E laughed. "I was kidding about the last part. The Bears are doing just fine. Seriously though, you're a risk I can't afford." The hand on Josh's shoulder shifted to his throat, gripping his jaw to tilt back his head. "I'll drop you in the middle of nowhere. By the time you find your way to a phone, we'll be gone from this house."

Letting him go home was a risk. Even if they fled, he could identify Liv and Van. There were no suspicious bulges on the men, but Liv had proven how easily a weapon could be concealed. He imagined a gun trained on his head as they pushed him from their car. Boom! Body dumped, never to be traced backed to their operation.

His chest hitched. "You'll kill me before you'll let me go."

The grip on his throat released as Mr. E said, "Been doing this a long time, boy. Never killed no one. And this is the first time I've offered freedom."

He could taste the promise of it, felt it awakening every cell in his body. Liv pressed his clothes to his chest. He stared into her eyes, searched for the truth, and found an expression as lifeless as Mr. E's mask. Even Van was gazing at his feet.

"What about Liv and Kate?" Josh asked.

"Not your concern." Mr. E waved a dismissive hand. "Take the offer, boy."

It would be so much easier to help the girls if he were free. Even if the operation vanished, detectives could track it.

Why was he even debating this? Would he seriously choose the woman who'd been beating him over his parents' happiness?

But he couldn't protect Liv if he left. She was as much a victim as he was. His head swam. He couldn't protect her in chains, either.

He dressed, and with each piece of clothing covering his skin, he felt more hopeful, more anxious. He watched her expression as he tied his boots, wishing she'd look at him and give him some sign she understood. He wasn't abandoning her. He was going to get help. He was going to save her.

Clothed and trembling, he waited at her side while she punched in the code. Was this really happening? He was wearing his clothes. They were letting him go home. Mom and Dad's joyous faces filled his vision and spread warmth through his chest. He was going home.

The door opened. Mr. E and Van exited first. When Liv stepped through to follow, Mr. E pivoted, grabbed her throat with two hands, and shoved her back against the door jamb. Her mouth gaped, gulping without sound, hands clawing at the ones on her neck.

Josh leapt forward, pulse racing, a roar bellowing from his chest. "You're choking her." He tried to break the grip, yanking on unmovable wrists.

The barrel of a gun moved into his vision. Van jerked it at his face. "Move back. All the way into the room."

Liv stretched her jaw, her eyes squeezed shut, tears leaking down her red face.

"Let her go." Josh's heart thundered, his voice thick with spit. "You're going to kill her."

"Step. Back." Van's tone was steady, but his eyes shifted rapidly between Mr. E and Liv, as if warring with whose side he was on.

Oh God, she couldn't breathe. He was going to choke her to death. Josh shuffled back, hands in the air.

With a violent heave, Mr. E slammed her head into the jamb and tossed her limp body onto the floor at Josh's feet.

Josh dropped to his knees and put his ear over her chest, then her mouth. Unconscious, she lay listless, her breaths labored. He didn't know CPR, had no medical training. What was he supposed to do?

Van lowered the gun, his muscles flexing, his teeth bared, but he made no move to help.

"You're not going home, boy." Mr. E clutched the door handle. "You were never going home."

Deep down, Josh knew it. Didn't stop the pain from splintering his chest. He turned her head and followed the river of blood to the cut on her scalp. Head wounds bled a lot, right? Did she need stitches?

"She needs a doctor." Josh cradled her head in his hands.

"She needs to do her job. You meet your future Master in two days. If you want her to live, you'll kiss him with ardor and skill. You'll grab your ankles if he wants to test drive your ass. You'll be fucking willing and obedient."

Van stepped out of the room, and Mr. E followed. The door slammed shut, shaking loose the last forgiving piece of Josh's heart and replacing it with a sharp-edged thirst for blood. Mr. E and Van seemed to be using her in the most vicious way. Maybe she could outsmart them, but she wouldn't need to do it alone.

As he carried her to the vanity to search for a medical kit, he glared at the door. God was neither hot tempered nor did He rush to judgment. Josh could be patient, but when the time came and God delivered those bastards before him, he would defeat them.

He would utterly destroy them.

CHAPTER 21

Something warm and hard and decidedly alive lay beneath Liv's body, coaxing her awake. Her throat throbbed, and a pounding ache fired through her skull. She was face down with her cheek on a brick chest of muscle, which could only belong to the boy. She tried moving her arms, dragging them along with her thoughts from the comfort of oblivion.

Mr. E's hands on her throat.

The impending meeting with the buyer.

Her phone.

She snapped her eyes open and met the fathomless green of the boy's gaze.

His hands skimmed heat along her back beneath the blanket, his thumb tracing the length of her spine.

"Good morning." His voice was raspy, relaxed. "Or afternoon. Or whenever it is."

Her stomach told her it was afternoon. She pushed against the cotton covering his shoulders. He was dressed, and by the scratchy feel of her skin against his jeans, she wasn't wearing a damned thing.

He watched her closely, his hypnotic eyes and sensual mouth producing a tremor through her aching body. She struggled to drag her attention away from the masculine lines of his chiseled face, the thick mess of black hair, the defined cheekbones. The sudden and intense longing to be cared for by him filled her with dangerous hope. She would address that—all of that—as soon as she gathered her strength.

She pushed again to sit, but the hands on her back held her in place with gentle determination.

"Easy," he whispered against her hair. "How are you feeling?"

Her whole fucking body hammered like the aftermath of one of Van's beatings.

She reached up, flinching as her fingers met the lump beneath her hair.

"Let me go." Her command came out hoarse and thready, blazing more pain through her throat.

"Nope." Holding her with an unyielding arm, he reached to the floor and lifted a glass of water to her mouth.

He let her arch up enough to tilt her head back. The first gulp over-flexed the bruised muscles in her throat, reigniting the burn.

She continued to drink, scanning the room. "Where's my phone?"

He studied her, eyebrows shifting downward. "Why?"

Mom and Mattie. If Mr. E wanted to further punish her for the previous night, he'd give her the news in a text.

A sinking feeling pulled on her insides. "My phone. Please."

His gaze narrowed.

Yeah, her tone was desperate. She was begging. "Please?"

He set the glass on the floor, and his hand returned with the phone. He held it out of reach, watching her with those compelling pale-green eyes. "If I give this to you, will you talk with me? Let me help you?"

If he intended to take advantage of her vulnerable state and force her to talk, he would likely succeed. But there was no manipulation in the wrinkles that worried his chiseled face. His drawn eyebrows and the supportive way his arm rested against her back wasn't rooted in coercion. He seemed content with simply comforting her.

Her heart contracted, massaging an unfamiliar sensation through her chest. For the first time in seven years, someone held her in a nonsexual way. She didn't know what to do with that, so she nodded, unbalanced.

The phone dropped into her outstretched hand. He could pluck it away as soon as she unlocked it. And why wouldn't he?

He let his head rest on the pillow, studying her, and touched a tentative finger to her scarred cheek. His concerned gaze as he stroked the raised line of flesh told her escape wasn't at the forefront of his thoughts. Another thing she'd need to examine. Later.

She angled the screen away and tapped in the passcode.

Seventy-eight texts from Van. Nothing from Mr. E. She released a lungful of air.

He grabbed her wrist and jerked the screen toward his face. Her breath caught as she pressed the power button, locking the phone.

"What the fuck?" She let the phone drop from her hand, her molars grinding. "Don't I feel stupid for trusting you."

He released her hand and narrowed his eyes.

"Now you know how I felt when I learned that the stranded girl I helped was a sex trafficker."

Ouch. She deserved that. Remembering her own capture magnified her shame, stirred an old ache inside her, and shoved her self-loathing to the surface. "I already know that feeling."

Though her words were whispered, he flinched as if she'd shouted. Their eyes locked, and a long look suspended between them.

His expression hardened. "What does that mean, exactly?"

Not for the first time, she wanted to confide in him. For five days, she longed to expose her arrangement, with the hope that he'd understand her position, and trust he wouldn't use it against her. She'd never burdened a captive with the truth of her situation. At least, not while they were bound in her chains.

Her composure was wrecked, and his perceptive eyes seemed to capture every crumble and twist of her face. She needed to toughen up, put on her best mask. The scary part was she didn't want to wear one with him.

His features softened. Even when frowning, his lips formed a serene curve. "Okay, Liv. I'm going to let that sit for a minute." He blew out a breath. "First, I wasn't trying to steal your phone. You're not exactly forthcoming, and I need to know what you're not telling me. Second, why did that bastard text you seventy-eight times?"

"He's probably worried." *Or horny.*

"Really? He let the friggin' door shut while you were bleeding and unconscious on the floor." His nostrils flared at her flinch. He scrubbed a hand over his stubble. "Look, I don't know what your relationship is with him—"

"There's no relationship." She let her heavy head fall to his chest.

The protection of his body was a persuasion she couldn't resist with her mind as fuzzy and achy as it was. He felt like the safest place on Earth.

"Have you told him that?" His voice vibrated through her, powerful, dependable.

She should've been punishing his disobedient ass, whipping him into the shape of a dutiful, cock-sucking slave. Even if the thought wasn't so ludicrous, she had neither the energy nor the will to hurt him. "Let me just lie here a minute."

"Thank you, God," he murmured as his fingers combed through her hair, not coiling and yanking, just soothing the strands and stimulating the roots along her scalp. "How much pain are you in?"

"I'll manage." Every inch of her bare skin relished the support of his warm musculature. She brushed a hand down his ribs, hooked a finger around the belt loop of his jeans, and yanked it hard enough to pinch his balls with the pull of denim. "Why am I naked?"

A deep noise strangled in his throat. "Your sprayed-on leotard was constricting your breathing." He bent his knees, and she settled snuggly in the cage of his hard thighs, chest to chest. "Don't think it's passed my notice that I'm supposed to be the slave, yet you're the one lying here battered and troubled."

The beat of her blood accelerated.

"I'm just going to talk through this and hope that you'll fill in the gaps." He stroked her hair. "I've tried to figure out why I need to consent to do *things* with Van." His caressing paused and began again. "Van doesn't hit me, hasn't raped me, but he wants to. What's his deal?"

She tightened her hand on his waistband. "The buyer wants the appearance of a willing slave. One who desires a man despite his innate heterosexuality. If Van raped you, that outcome wouldn't be achieved."

He laughed, coarsely. "Thank God for that. So, that's a requirement?"

"Requirement one. Slave has never experienced sexual intimacy with a woman. Slave is heterosexual but hates women. He desires only his Master."

A soft chuckle rumbled through his chest. "I could never hate women." He wrapped his arms around her. "Nor can I hate you."

His tender embrace made her heart thump against her ribs. The backs of her eyes burned with the kind of ache she hadn't felt in a long time. Swear to God, if she cried over a hug, she'd never regain her position with him.

His lips touched the crown of her head and retreated. "If you fail to deliver a slave as prescribed…" His silence stretched for so long she raised her head and found him staring down at her. "Mr. E will kill you?"

A swallow hung in her raw throat. "Worse."

His face twisted. "What's worse than death?"

Mom always said if she could confront the wind at 10,000 feet, she could confront anything. But falling out of the sky felt a fuck of a lot safer than exposing her awful, selfish truth. "Ask yourself that question."

He stared at her with such intensity she closed her eyes against it. He was the only person who had ever tried to peek beneath her masks, and damn her, she wanted him to find what he was searching for. After a long moment, he rolled her off his chest with gentle arms and settled her on her side. Then he sprang from the bed.

She shifted to sit with her back against the wall, pulling the blanket around her chest. As he paced through the room, the contraction of his tense body captivated her.

Powerful legs stretched the denim of his low-waist jeans. His biceps flexed as he ran his fingers through cropped strands of his black hair.

"Who is he threatening? Your parents? A husband?" He stopped at the mattress, fists on his hips. With the agitation straining the tight fabric of his t-shirt, the hard line of his lips, and his eyes sharply focused, there was no way he could pass as a boy. In fact, he looked like a man prepared to take on the world. Especially when he shouted, "Who, Liv?"

Why did she feel so compelled to open up to him? She pressed her fist to her lips, stifling the song that suddenly and violently ripped through her mind. He wouldn't hurt her, wouldn't use her fears against her.

Drawing a deep breath, she swallowed her panic and whispered, "My mom."

In the next breath, he was kneeling beside her, holding her hands in his. "Your mom?"

She pressed her back to the wall, her hands sweating and shoulders stiff. "And my daughter."

She kept her eyes on his, but her voice was so small she was sure he didn't hear her nor did she want him to. She would've done the world a favor if she'd died giving birth. But her body had recovered, just like it always did. A fucking curse she couldn't bring herself to end.

His face paled, and his hands convulsed around hers. He lowered his head and tilted his ear toward her. "Say that again."

An onslaught of dizziness spread through her head. Her cheeks numbed and her throat tightened. “My daughter.”

He leaned back, searching her face as a whirlwind of emotions crashed over his.

CHAPTER 22

Liv held her breath, waiting for her revelation to sink in. She circled her thumbs over his hands. What would he do with this information? How would his reaction impact Mom and Mattie?

"Say something," she whispered.

His jaw hung. He closed it, blinked. "Who's her father? Where is he?"

When her eyes flicked to the door, he sucked in a breath, his face contorting in disbelief.

"Him?" His voice was guttural, strained. "You have a child with Van?"

A wave of nausea rolled through her, trembling her body. Disgusted with herself and his reaction to her, her eyes averted from his. She forced them back, met his steady gaze. "There's a story."

"Then you'll talk while you're eating." He cupped her chin. "But you sure as hell aren't going out there." He stabbed a finger toward the door. "Not until we have a plan."

Her back stiffened, and she jerked out of his hold. "A plan? Don't you think I've thought through every possible solution?"

He climbed off the bed and scanned the room. "Do

you have anything to eat in here?"

She pointed at the trunk. Why wasn't he badgering her with questions?

As he strode around the mattress, his eyes held hers, heavy with intent. "We'll walk through our options after you eat."

Clearly, she was no longer steering this…whatever this was. Not that she'd ever really gained control of him. The thought both petrified and thrilled her, a testament to how wildly her world was tilting on end. She knew she should order him to strip and kneel and kiss her feet. She also knew if she peeled away the layers of bullshit around her heart, she'd find a hopeful girl who wanted him stubborn and fierce and whole, exactly as he was.

He returned with an armful of energy bars, apple chips, bottled water, and surprisingly, one of her long nightshirts. "I thought this might make you more comfortable."

Her heart tripped. The shirt was a kindness she wasn't accustomed to receiving and certainly didn't deserve, considering his week-long nudity. She slipped it on, her insides quivering with the realization that he could destroy her at a fundamental level. She'd hidden her vulnerability by pretending not to care, but in the span of a week, he'd sliced a deep cut in her mask.

He unwrapped an energy bar, folded her fingers around it, and pulled her legs over his lap. Then he regarded her, one hand curled around her calf. Not eating, he seemed content with watching and waiting.

After a few deliberating moments and two energy bars, she told him about her kidnapping. Her slave training. The loss of her virginity. The day she was sold. The pregnancy and the scar.

He listened without interrupting, his hand soothing the shivers along her leg, his eyes unwavering. She maintained a steady monologue until she reached the part about Mattie's adoption and the conditions of her arrangement as a deliverer. Her voice thickened, and her heart ached with memories and longing. "The videos are the only assurance he gives me."

"Which is why you wanted your phone. No text is good news?"

She nodded, crumbling under the reminder that she still had a job to do and a slave she couldn't train. His attention honed on her change in breathing and the wobble in her chin.

He gathered her in his lap and scooted to lean against the wall. He touched her brow, her cheek, and the line of her neck, the tenderness melting her against his solid body. "You know exactly how I felt when you locked me in the box, huh?"

Guilt squeezed her gut. "Which makes what I did a hundred times worse." She stared at him, miserable and conflicted about what to do next. "I'm so sorry."

His hands gripped her waist, lifting her and adjusting her legs to straddle his hips.

"What are you—?"

His thumbs pressed against her lips, his palms cupping her jaw. Bound by the strength of his gaze, her body went completely still as his thumbs parted, sliding over her cheeks to join his fingers. There was no hint of harshness in his demeanor. His eyes shifted between hers and dropped to her mouth. His lips parted.

Oh God, was he going to kiss her? A sudden rush of hope blasted through her, and she rode that gust, the filthy perimeter of her existence sweeping away. He lowered his head, and she could only squeeze her eyes shut and anticipate the connection, his acceptance, and maybe his forgiveness.

His lips touched hers, achingly sweet, soft, cautious. A chill replaced the sensation as he leaned back. His breath released, taking hers with it. She shuddered and opened her eyes.

They stared at one another, faces just a kiss apart, and it was the most intimate moment she ever experienced. As he looked at her, the pale glow of his eyes softening, asking without words, *Is this okay?*

She nodded, her body liquefying in the cradle of his lap, molding against his tense abs and thighs.

His fingers flexed on her back, and he swept forward, taking her mouth, opening her lips with the warm flesh of his. Beneath the spice of toothpaste, she tasted his natural purity, his breath flavored with sweetness and hope.

With his hands spread over the rise of her ass, he pulled her closer, kissing her deeply, his tongue chasing and tangling with hers. She devoured the heat of his mouth, the strength of his embrace, the precision of his movements. Neither submissive nor forceful, he clutched her hips and controlled the rock of her pelvis. His strong jaw guided the speed and motion of her mouth, his lips burning a trail of sparks as his whiskers scratched a pleasurable twinge across her skin.

His chest heaved, and a moan rumbled in his throat. She savored the response, wanted to hear more, feel him closer. She wanted to crawl inside of him. She slid her hands down his chest and slipped under the hem. Gliding back up the warm taut brawn of his abs and the velvet skin wrapping his pecs, she paused over the beat of his heart against her palm.

He gripped her nape, angled her head, and intensified the kiss. She didn't know if it was her emotional exhaustion or if he was more experienced than she'd thought, but his mastery over her was assured and exquisite. Every lick and nibble tingled through her body, curling her toes against his thighs, racing her heart, and fuzzing her brain.

Too soon, they came up for air. After a few noisy breaths, she gave him a smile, which he returned with warmth and affection.

"Wow." She shook her muddled head. "You've done that a lot, haven't you?"

He captured her lips again, his mouth just as maddening and curling as before, leaving her body shivering when he finished. "Kissing is the only thing I *can* do."

Her heart pinched. Unfortunately, her bladder, too, but she refused to leave the embrace of his arms. Emotions swept through her as she snuggled against his chest, swirling her thoughts into a jumbled knot. She wasn't ready to voice her worries and ruin the moment, but he did it for her.

"Does Van know Mr. E's identity?"

Their eyes met and she nodded.

"Do you?"

She traced his strong jaw, the whiskers rasping against her finger. He held still as she followed the smooth skin stretching over his cheekbones, between his enchanting eyes and disappearing beneath the soft inky hue of his hairline. His beauty had the power to enthrall and distract.

She dropped her hand. "If I knew Mr. E's identity,

we wouldn't be sitting here." She would've tracked him down. Perhaps he had a family she could've threatened. "Van claims he's only seen beneath the mask once, when Mr. E lured him from his mother's meth house. I have my doubts." Her bladder prodded again.

Something shifted through his eyes, and his jaw twitched. "Mr. E basically pushed you into my arms last night." His embrace tightened around her, punctuating his point. "Why would he do that? And I see the way Van watches you. Why would Van let him do that?"

The answers weren't simple, most of which were based on her own theories. "I need to go to the bathroom."

He carried her to the toilet. She might've refused out of pride if she weren't so reluctant to leave his arms. He lowered her to the rim and squatted before her.

Her head spun from the sudden loss of his supportive strength, but she still mustered a glare when he propped his chin on a fist and settled in.

"You look like you're about to fall over." His tone was gentle.

Too tired to argue, she closed her eyes and released her bladder. "Van may not agree with everything Mr. E does, but he's never challenged him. He loves the cocksucker like a father." She glanced up and found him observing her steadily.

The set of his jaw matched the hardness of his eyes. "Van thinks he loves you."

That truth didn't need acknowledgment. She flushed the toilet and moved to the shower. "Mr. E's actions aren't always transparent. Last night was the first time he'd ever raised a hand against me. Other than..." She touched the scar on her cheek and turned the tap to warm.

He sat against the wall outside the open shower as she undressed and washed. Her movements were robotic, but her thoughts were an utter mess. Now that he knew her situation, what was he willing to do?

She needed to know where his head was. "Maybe Mr. E pushed us together to wrangle your sympathy for me, a ploy to persuade you to do what needs to be done, using me as leverage."

Though his eyes followed the motion of her hands, they were unfocused, turned inward.

"He's never attempted anything like this." It seemed too complicated to be worth the effort. As she washed her belly and thighs, she lay a soapy hand over the horizontal c-section scar below her bikini line. It was one scar she wished hadn't faded. "Honestly, I don't know why he's kept me alive all these years."

"Do you have sex with Van privately? Or do you just screw him in front of your slaves?" Quiet words at odds with his finger digging restlessly at a frayed hole in his jeans.

Her throat convulsed, her stomach caving with humiliation. Was he regretting the kiss they'd just shared? He wasn't glaring at her with judgment or pumping his muscles with jealousy. But he'd also been raised to approach problems with civility and grace.

She shut off the water and faced him, wet and naked, with a quiver in her voice. "It's complicated."

The hand on his leg curled into a fist, and his chest heaved. He straightened his fingers, cleared his throat, and imprisoned her eyes. "Complicated how? Is it consensual?"

Was it? She nodded. Unsure, she shook her head

then nodded again.

He stood, slowly, his expression tight, and wrapped a towel around her. "I really need you to explain that answer, Liv." He rifled through her trunk while she talked through Van's tricks, his mind games, and his threats to involve Mr. E.

"He doesn't physically force me." She felt sick, weak, frozen in the shower stall. "Having sex in front of you..." She shivered with self-hatred. "I was cornered. He'd told that morning he was going to fuck you. I convinced him jealousy was more effective."

He glared at his hands, gripping the edge of the trunk, his eyes full of pain and face red. When he returned, he handed her a t-shirt, jeans, and a pair of panties that matched the mint green of his irises.

He touched her face, his fingers lingering on her mouth. "Do you come for him?"

Shit, she didn't want to answer that, but he looked at her as if he were consumed by the need to know.

"Yes." She gripped the towel around her chest.

Tension vibrated from his body as he stormed through the room. He seemed to be trying to drive it away with his swift strides back to the trunk and whatever was distracting him there. She didn't own anything personal. Only meaningless things she'd collected while living in that room. She dressed and sat on the mattress.

While he rummaged, she told him what the news had been reporting about his disappearance, highlighting the resiliency his parents exuded during their interviews. Then she talked about her own experience with Mom's grieving and her eventually moving on. "When enough time has passed, your *fake* decomposed remains will turn up somewhere and put an end to all the searching. I don't know how Mr. E arranges such a thing, but he pulled it off when I disappeared." Her throat dried, scratching her voice. "Van says Mr. E intends to do the same with you."

During her one-sided conversation, he'd found a tennis ball in the trunk, a gift she'd *earned* as a slave. He tossed it against the far wall, caught it, tossed it again, over and over. He didn't seem to be listening.

"Am I boring you?" she asked.

He snatched the ball out of the air and jerked his head toward her, his eyes clouded under the *V* of his dark eyebrows. "Mr. E has a pretty twisted hold on me by threatening your life. How does this affect the threat against my parents?"

"That threat was my creation." She felt sick. "An empty one."

Harming his parents had never been an option. She wanted to go back to the day she took him and erase the worry she'd planted in his head. She also wanted to bury her pen knife in Mr. E's jugular and watch his stupid mask soak up the blood. Damn him for manipulating Josh into feeling sorry for her.

He watched her with eyes too perceptive for his age. "Is Van a threat to my parents?"

She pressed a cool hand against her burning cheek. "Your parents are entangled with media and detectives. He wouldn't dare go near them."

Even without the risk, she didn't believe Van would murder an innocent person.

Josh's fist flexed around the ball, his other hand scraping roughly over his face.

"What's bothering you? Besides the obvious." She gestured around the room, indicating his prison cell.

He glanced at her, the tightness of his chest visible in the muscles straining his shirt. "I work my parents' farm at dawn and dusk." He flung the ball, caught the bounce back. "At practice, I sprint, tackle, and sweat through endurance exercises for hours every day." His voice lowered. "Now I'm locked in an attic with the most gorgeous woman I've ever laid eyes on." The ball sailed through the air, returned to his hand. "Whom I just shared a very. Arousing. Kiss. With." A toss and catch punctuated each word.

A warm tendril of pleasure shivered through her. She wanted to close the distance and wrap her arms around him, but he seemed to be trying to control his arousal and pent-up energy. She had no interest in taunting him.

Lowering his head, he pressed the ball to his brow. "And there is a tyrant waiting outside that door to have sex with you. Again." He resumed pummeling the wall. Bounce. Bounce. Bounce. "I'm trying really hard to keep myself in check, Liv."

His words tied her up with heartache and compelled her to silence. She clung to the sounds of the thumps against the wall and the way he controlled his body despite his turmoil.

He caught the ball, clasping it in his hands behind his neck, and looked heavenward. "If I escape, I might be able to track Mr. E down. But he will kill you before I do. If I take you with me, he'll kill your mom and daughter."

Her breath stumbled with the acceleration of her pulse.

"If we follow all the rules, your arrangement is safe." He dropped the ball and sat beside her on the mattress. "Given my background, I think he knew you would trust me with your predicament, and he's counting on me not to put you or your family in harm's way. We're both being played, Liv."

Hearing him voice her fears churned her gut, boiling bile through her chest. "I want to kill him."

"Murder's not the answer."

Maybe he'd meant to find some preacher comfort in his response, but the sinews in his neck were taut against his skin.

She pinched the bridge of her nose. "I can't kill him anyway. He has a contract out on Mattie and Mom. It's part of our arrangement. If anything happens to him or Van, the contract will be activated."

Blood drained from his face. "A hit man?"

She lifted a shoulder, swallowed. "Something like that. He's in the business of trafficking humans. I don't doubt he has connections with an assortment of criminals. But I'm inclined to test his threat."

He leaned forward and laced his fingers through hers. His perceptive eyes projected an intrusive quality, one that could unearth her weaknesses or nurture her strengths. "You're going to teach me all the rules. Train me as your slave."

Regret pinched her chest. Mr. E succeeded where she failed. The boy would be cooperative. *What an elegant fucking play.* "I can't—"

"You will." He squeezed her hand. "And since there's no way I'll let you go out there alone—"

"*Let* me?" She pulled her hand from his. "You're pushing it, boy."

He barked an unsmiling laugh. "I've stomached the *boy* crap long enough." He stood on the mattress, feet planted on either side of her knees, and stretched out his arms. “Do I look like a boy to you?”

Dark stubble shadowed his masculine jaw. His biceps were damned near the size of her thighs. The brick wall of his torso narrowed into low-hung jeans that cupped his groin. She knew too well the shape and girth of the cock that formed that bulge, and it could only belong to a man.

“Cocky bastard.” She hid a smile.

He dropped to his knees and straddled her thighs. With a dip of his head, he stole a kiss. “You’re going to text Van and tell him to bring us food.”

“He won’t— ”

He kissed her again. “Shut up and listen. You’ll tell him I’m becoming the perfect little slave— Don’t look at me like that. I can act out the damned requirements.” Determination sharpened his eyes.

“Van will test you before the buyer’s meeting tomorrow.”

His face slacked. “Does the buyer expect to have sex with me at this meeting?”

The other boys she’d enslaved weren’t virgins, and the buyers *did* fuck them during the introductions. But this deal was different in so many ways.

“I’ll do everything in my power to prevent it.” She filled her eyes with the truth of her words. “I promise.”

“Then we’ll get through the next few days and figure out the rest.” His tone sobered. “But Liv?” He held her eyes, drew in a long breath. “Requirement number two is my limit. The only way I’d have sex with those men would be by force. Do you understand?”

She could hold her promise about the buyer’s meeting. And she could calm down Van by sending him a text. Once he knew she was okay, he’d leave her alone to do her training.

It was the rest that made her want to throw up.

She nodded, her heart lodged somewhere in her stomach.

CHAPTER 23

Josh knelt in the center of the room, naked, and fixated on the nimble movements of Liv's fingers. His insides quivered from holding still for so long.

Crouched before him in her jeans and t-shirt, she tied a long coil of rope into loose bows, sliding his arms through the loops and cinching the knots along his sternum.

Flashes of dizziness reminded him he'd only eaten a couple energy bars. He nodded toward her phone. "Send Van the text, Liv."

She'd texted him an hour earlier to check in but had yet to request food. She slid another knot in place, her eyes narrowed in concentration on the laced web that began with a noose around his neck and intertwined a dragonfly pattern down his chest.

Her tongue touched her upper lip. "We're not ready for him yet."

The urge to suckle that taunting tongue sensitized his skin where it rubbed against the nylon bindings. The knotted bows formed taut sleeves over his arms, holding his elbows in an *X* over his stomach.

"You made a straight jacket from rope." He waited for the panic to set in, but all he felt was wonderment.

"I've learned how to do a lot of awful things." Painful memories pulled at the corners of her eyes. Then they were gone, and her calmness returned, flowing through the fluidity of her fingers as they moved down his abs.

The torturous caress of her full attention both soothed him and made him antsy. Van was probably prowling on the other side of the door. Or beating on it. She'd said it was soundproofed.

"Why are you the only one with a code to this room?" he asked.

Her rich dark eyes, lashes fanning thickly through slow blinks, were as arresting as her hands on the rope near his groin. She pulled his hips closer to her. "When I was returned by the man who bought me, Mr. E put me in Van's possession." She kept her eyes on her hands, plaiting and twisting the rope. "I requested to have the only code to the door, and I think Mr. E agreed because he knew if he didn't limit Van's access to me…" Her voice wobbled, strengthened. "I wouldn't have survived all these years if I had to live every minute under Van's thumb, sleeping in his bed with nowhere to escape."

Her courage knew no bounds. Maybe it was God working through her, but she radiated an inner strength he was certain she'd never acknowledged. "You've done a hellacious job surviving. You don't have it in you to give up."

"I would have." She glanced up, eyes hard, and returned to her rope work. "But this living arrangement, this room, has kept those thoughts at bay."

For how long? Mr. E could take it away any moment.

"Van's okay with it?" He peered into her eyes.

"How long before he swings a chainsaw at that door?"

"He's accepted that this is the only way I'll be a part of his life." She yanked on a knot with more strength than was needed. "As long as I'm around, Van has an outlet for his desires. The virgin slaves remain virgin. Mr. E knows this and lets me keep the code."

His heart ached for her. She deserved a life beyond masks and locked doors and black eyes. Something about her, captor or not, brought out a fierce drive in him to take care of her, to serve her. Not that he could do anything with his hands tied, but she'd asked his permission before restraining him with rope. It was the *asking* that compelled his cooperation.

She wound the ends around his upper thighs, tightened the final knot, and sat back on her heels. Rather than studying her intricate work, she peered into his eyes, her posture motionless and her face framed by ribbons of chestnut hair.

When her silence stretched, he tilted his head. "What is it?"

A deep groove appeared between her eyes. "You're not broken or defeated." The side of her mouth tipped up into a trembling curve, making his chest swell against the restraints. "But you let me do this." A whisper.

When her gaze lowered, he bent his head to remain in her line of sight. "I have faith in you, Liv. You know how to handle Van. What's wrong?"

The furrow in her brow deepened. "This kind of bondage is about trust, not control." She traced a finger over the rope harness and adjusted a knot to line up with the others. "I would've never attempted it on one of the captives." She glanced at him through her dark lashes. "I practiced a lot on a borrowed mannequin."

Given the labyrinth of knots, it was a binding that couldn't be easily forced, a position he certainly wouldn't have volunteered before Mr. E's visit. He pressed his lips to her forehead. Maybe his trust was too soon, but somehow it had braided a bridge between them that was as complex and sturdy as the rope that bound him.

"You trust me." She wasn't asking, but disbelief creased her face.

He captured her parted lips, stroked his tongue over hers, tasting her sincerity, and straightened to behold her. "I trust your intentions."

Soft brown eyes stared back, her hand settling on his inner thigh. He felt that single point of contact through his whole body, warming and stirring. She stretched a finger and stroked down his semi-erect shaft. "You shouldn't."

His breath strangled. "Liv." He groaned, his penis jerking against her touch. "What are you doing?"

"Before I text Van, you need to memorize the requirements. A *perfect little slave* could recite them verbatim." She curled her fingers around the pulse between his legs, massaging him to hardness. "And you need to do it while I distract you."

She grabbed his nipple and twisted it to unholy hell, sparking pain through his chest. The rope between his arms and thighs halted the bow of his back.

"Arruugh!" He moaned for long seconds after she released him.

"What is requirement number one?"

He ground his teeth, reeling from the lingering bite of her fingers. "Slave can only have sex with felonious men—"

She yanked on his other nipple with a brutal pinch

and let go. The sting thrummed through his body, and his groin heated, stiffening to the point of pain.

Her hand clenched around his erection. "Slave has never experienced sexual intimacy with a woman. Slave is heterosexual but hates women. He desires only his Master." She arched a slim eyebrow.

He repeated the requirement. "How would anyone know if I've slept with a woman?"

Those gorgeous eyes roamed his face. She trailed her other hand along his hairline, around his ear, and down his neck, watching the path of her caress. "Experience. Skill. Confidence. These things surface in a man's eyes when he regards a woman." Her gaze flicked to his, the hand on his penis sliding up and down. "Don't gape at me like that."

"Seriously?" He released a ragged breath. "You're stroking me."

"When we're in the presence of others, don't look at me at all. You need to practice that now."

If he was going to be tied up and naked around Van or the buyer, he wouldn't be looking at her with anything but panic.

"Tell me requirement number two." She added a second hand between his legs, fondling his balls while she twisted her wrist along his length, her heavy-lidded gaze clinging to his.

"Slave must—" A shudder rippled over him, his biceps flexing against the rope. "Service the Master. Slave's body is prepared and—" His release coiled, tightening, threatening. "You have to stop."

She leaned in and bit his lip. Hard. Consuming. The pang snapped his control, the build up tumbling over in a powerful wave of heat and sighing relief. His head dropped back on his shoulders, his body shaking in the constriction of rope.

As the bliss of his orgasm drifted from his muscles, he realized he'd closed his eyes. When he opened them, she stood above him, her cute little nose wrinkled in annoyance. He wanted to kiss it.

His lips twitched. "Um. I guess I need to work on requirement seven."

"No. Number seven is kneeling, one of the only fucking rules you haven't broken." She rubbed her eyes and glared at him. "Number three. Eyes down. Four. No clothes."

"I've got number four covered." He tried to check his smile, but his cheeks were persistent.

"Good job." Her monotone response matched her disapproving stare.

Hard to believe he'd considered her vicious. With the set of her stubborn jaw and her lips in a plump flat line, she looked decisively non-threatening. "You're adorable."

She spun, striding to the locked cabinet where she kept her crops, whips, and paddles. "You're patronizing me, you little prick."

Oh, he'd really ticked her off. Her aggravation vibrated with the slap of her feet on the floor. He peeked at his lap, and the sight of his come tightened his chest with guilt. Dammit, he needed to try harder.

She unlocked the cabinet and returned with something he knew existed but had never seen in person. Shaped like a cone and made of black rubber or plastic, the phallic shape sent a shiver of dread down his spine.

"No." He shook his head. "No way. Go get the flogger."

"I could beat you until you're bruised and bleeding, but it's ineffective." She squatted before him, her pretty features etched in thought. "You know why?"

The ropes suddenly felt tighter, scratchier. "Because I'm a terrible slave."

"The worst." Her free hand drifted to his ball sac, reawakening his bottomless well of arousal. "How often did you get a woody after a hard hit at football practice or during an excruciating exercise?"

He shifted his weight on his knees, her question poking at experiences he never spoke about. Feelings he'd wanted to express but never had a tolerant ear to whisper them to. Until now.

"On the farm…" He coughed, unable to loosen the discomfort tightening his throat. "Some of the grueling chores worked my body pretty good." His muscles would burn with exertion, his penis would rub against his jeans. He met her eyes.

"It made you hard."

As the room filled with weighted silence, he examined the expression softening the peaks of her lips and rounding the depths of her eyes. He knew her features wouldn't harden and twist with judgment. "Yeah."

She dipped her head, her breath tickling over his cheek, lifting her hand from his balls to toy with the hair behind his ear. "You get hard every time I punish you." She kissed his jaw and nibbled on his ear lobe, whispered, "Kinky pain whore."

Her teasing tone and the playful bite of her teeth on his neck exposed the girl she kept tucked away. His already excited heart hammered against his ribs.

"The problem is…" She turned her head to glower

at him. "The whip lost its thrilling danger after the first time I used it. It takes you to an out-of-body place, and all that's left is the thrill." She held up the plug. "But this—"

"Is *not* going inside me." His pulse accelerated, and his rectum contracted.

"It is." She smiled, soft at the edges, but no less determined. "It's up to you if I'll lube it, if I'll be gentle, if I'll prepare you." She licked the tip of the plug, wetting it. "Requirement number ten."

His heart rate redoubled. Sweet mother, he didn't know that one. Sweat beaded on his nape, and his pecs twitched, ready to fight.

"Shh." She brushed a kiss on his chest between the crisscross of rope. "This is a new one. Slave will show gratitude for punishment and discipline."

His lungs sighed in relief. "Thank you, Mistress."

And just like that, their roles reverted. He understood why she rose and stripped down to her panties, why she tied a black kerchief around her nose and mouth, and why she gathered her composure into the unnatural stillness of dominance. It was her masked persona, the Deliverer who performed without mercy or emotion. To enforce the training. To deliver the punishments. To protect those she cared about.

But who protected *her*? Now he was one of the people she would come to defend. This certainty was a visceral grip of faith, and it filled him with a new sense of purpose. Her hidden expressions, costumes and nudity, and penchant for restraints were meant to disarm a slave. It was her cross to bear, and he would help her carry it.

As she repeated the rules over and over, he kept his eyes down with respect, his mouth shut in obedience, and his mind focused on memorizing her words.

Liv sent the text to Van, and thirty minutes later, she walked to the door and put her hand on the keypad. Josh was ready. As long as he didn't look at the yet-to-be-used butt plug she'd left on the mattress.

She glanced back, her shadowy gaze peering over the kerchief. "You can guess why I'm only in panties."

He raised his eyes, swallowed. The test with Van would be sexual in nature. Since she wasn't asking a question, he kept his guess to himself and drew a deep breath.

"I don't know what Van has planned, but he *will* test your limits." With her chin tilted up, she faced the keypad.

As she punched in the code, he knew she would do what was necessary for her family. He returned his attention to the floor and girded his spine.

CHAPTER 24

The aroma of greasy food followed Van into the room. Josh's mouth watered. He couldn't stop the growl escaping his stomach, but he kept his lips clamped, his eyes down, and his knees on the floor.

A takeout bag dropped within grabbing distance, not like he could steal a French fry. The rope-entwined straight jacket held his arms firmly around his torso.

Van's ratty sneakers paused in the space between Josh and Liv, and the toes turned toward hers.

Without moving his head, Josh strained his upward line of sight, marking the tension in Van's legs as they flexed against the denim.

The man's broad shoulders curled forward, his hand lifting her chin gently.

"Liv." His whisper was strained, presumably from the sight of the bruises Mr. E left on her neck.

The distraught reaction set Josh's blood afire, considering the yellow-purple marks around her eye still lingered.

"Don't." She stepped back and turned away. *Good girl.*

Van stood motionless for a moment. Then he reached for her hand. She pulled it away before he made contact.

"What can I do to fix this?" Van gestured between her and himself.

She was impossible to read with her body turned away and her voice so damned wooden. "You could've warned me what he was planning *before* you left me unconscious, bleeding, half-strangled."

Van kept his back to Josh, his fingers flexing at his side. Seconds passed, indicating some kind of deliberation. "You're right, Liv. I fucked you over, and I hated every fucking minute of it."

As much as Josh didn't want to believe him, the man's voice cracked with soft-spoken guilt.

Eyes on the floor, Josh held his spine straight as Van shifted and sat before him.

He pulled a paper-wrapped burger from the bag and addressed Josh. "Sorry about the gun thing last night. That was a dick move on my part. We cool?"

Was this guy for real? If he glanced up, he'd probably get nicked by the sharp silver gaze of crafted bullshit.

"She's starving you, isn't she?" Van held the burger beneath his nose, taunting him with the heady fragrance of grilled meat and ketchup. "Go ahead. It's yours."

Not gonna lie. It was going to chafe like hell to eat from that hand, but he needed energy more than his pride. He opened his mouth.

"That pleasure belongs to his Mistress." Liv's bare feet moved into his periphery.

God love her. He would thank her later. With his mouth. On her satiny skin. Something to anticipate. His penis jerked.

Van lingered, the burger hovering before Josh. The hesitation produced a burgeoning hum that dragged beneath the skin. Unable to see their expressions, Josh was excluded from whatever unspoken communication passed above his head. Not peeking was torture.

At last, Van relinquished the food and traded places with her.

The soft curves of her bare breasts filled Josh's view. The impulse to reach out and run a fingertip over one of those pink nipples was consuming. Good thing his arms were restrained.

She took two bites for every one she gave him. From the unhurried offerings she placed on his tongue to the possessive hand curled on the juncture between his shoulder and neck, she radiated an aura that compelled lowered eyes, humbled gratitude, and an unquestioning desire to please her. No wonder the girl, Kate, had fallen so spectacularly into her subservient role.

But he was not a terrified slave, crawling in compliance to escape the bite of her whip. Initially, he was supposed to be emasculated, hopeless, empty. Mr. E changed the game when he threatened Liv. Now he was supposed to be the slave so consumed with fear that he would risk his life to make sure nothing happened to his Mistress. Instead, his heart drummed with faith in the power of God, in her courage, and in his ability to save her.

As she fed him, Van perched behind her on the mattress, hands clasped between his bent knees. "How did you get him to hold still for rope bondage?"

She brushed a thumb over the corner of Josh's mouth. "You may speak. Tell him how I did it."

They had discussed how the questioning might go.

Since their plan didn't extend beyond surviving the buyer's meeting, they'd agreed honesty was the best approach.

He swallowed the fry she'd placed in his mouth, savoring the fried, salty taste. "I trust her." Oh, how he wanted to meet Van's eyes when he said that.

"Really?" Van's voice punched in disbelief.

"And I don't want to see her harmed again." His words, though rehearsed, came from an empowered place inside him. She'd already been hurt so much, but she was not beyond saving.

"You and me both, buddy."

His veins heated with rage. Did the hypocrisy burn Van's mouth as it huffed out?

The conversation fell quiet as she kept the food coming, brushing his lips under the guise of catching crumbs. With the hard floor grinding into his knees, he wanted to remove the distance between them, wanted to strip the kerchief that covered her nose and mouth, and plunge into her eyes. He wanted to be alone with her. Hell, he yearned to speed forward into the future. A future free of shackles. A future with her in it. He dared God to challenge his desires.

Two burgers, a cola, and a bag of fries later, his stomach settled.

Van lifted a foot and nudged her back. "Let's see what he's learned, Liv."

She stuffed the trash into the bag and set it aside. "Say the requirements in order with an eagerness and accuracy that will please your Mistress."

While Van made a decidedly sucky *buddy* in this ridiculous game, he seemed to have his temper under wraps. In fact, he was shockingly passive. Why?

Josh's shoulders stiffened with realization. If he messed up the buyer's meeting, if Liv was killed, Van would suffer the loss. The volatile bastard had just as much at stake.

He exhaled, "Yes, Mistress," and recited rules one through ten slowly and carefully, imagining himself performing each one for her, trusting her not to use his obedience against him.

Her finger caressed a warm path over his knee, her body blocking her affection from Van's predatory eyes. She removed her hand.

"Impressive." Van rose. "Show me how he will service his Master."

A flinch jerked Josh's insides, but he remained outwardly still on his knees. He knew this moment would come and told himself if she could endure Van's touch, he could, too. He waited for her command.

She reached back toward the mattress, but he couldn't see what she grabbed. She touched his jaw. "Look at me."

With pleasure. Connecting with her, by any means possible, would make this more bearable. As he raised his head, he leaned forward, subtly, into her personal space, inhaling the peppermint and lavender scent of her shampoo. Peering over the black kerchief, her magnetic eyes pulled him in further. Her pupils widened with an indiscernible emotion.

She held up the butt plug. "Requirement number eleven. Slave will wear and accept toys Master chooses to adorn him with." She paused, seemed to wrestle with her words. "You can open your mouth to Van's kiss or spread your ass for the plug. Both prepare you for your Master tomorrow, but which would please your Mistress now?"

The movement of her mouth paused beneath the cloth as if she were considering the answer, but he suspected her diabolical mind had already choreographed the proceedings from beginning to end.

Van crouched behind her, his eyes alight with interest, his toothpick seemingly forgotten as it lolled in the crook of his lips.

Josh's breaths quickened, his eyes searching hers. One flawless eye, one bruised, the surrounding skin furrowing as her eyebrows drew together. In the complexity of her gaze, he saw concern, a sense of responsibility, and maybe even possessiveness. If he read her correctly, she didn't want Van near him. Or maybe he was just projecting his own desire.

The kiss would be the least intrusive, and if it were with any other man, it might've been his preference. She'd warned him the plug would be used *eventually*, and he'd resolved to accept it *eventually*.

"The plug for now." Her tone was bored, bordering cruel, but the gentle look she shared with him helped smooth the tumble in his gut. Meanwhile, his nerves were shrieking in horror.

With a strong voice and an open expression, he embodied his consent. "Yes, Mistress."

She and Van rose, and she angled her mouth toward Van's ear. Whatever she whispered sent him bolting to her cabinet of tools.

Minutes later, Josh lay face down on the mattress, knees on the subfloor, arms roped around his torso, backside in the air. Shifting into his line of sight, she squirted gel from a tube over her fingers, making sure he saw her apply it to the plug.

He wished he had the tennis ball to slam against the wall and distract his impulse to scream and fight. Instead, he focused on something more soothing. Like the tender touch of her hand as it eased between his crack. The measured caress around the entrance she'd only ventured in the one time. And the fact that it was *her* pressing against the barrier and not the man climbing onto the mattress and reclining beside him.

Face-to-face, Van stroked the back of Josh's head. "Relax your rectum and push against the plug. I know it's scary, but you're in good hands."

He flinched inwardly, burning to crack the guy's skull. The cold hard tip of rubber pressed against the ring of muscle. He tensed instantly then forced his butt and legs to loosen. It must've been the work of God that kept his heart from tearing out of his chest.

The plug inched in, stretching, burning, building a terrifying pressure. He slammed his teeth together, his breath hissing, loud and fast.

Van released a long exhale. His eyes glazed over, and the torment etching his face was startling. "I bled a lot my first time. I was young. He was…huge." His hand cupped Josh's nape, twitched, his gaze refocusing on Josh. "My mom didn't keep good company. She was too blitzed to notice her companions' interest in me." His voice was soft, horrifyingly serious.

A sudden burn sparked in Josh's anus, followed by a dull fullness. She rubbed his gluts as his body adjusted to the intrusion. Breath by breath, his muscles relaxed.

Her footsteps retreated, and the bathroom faucet sputtered on. His legs trembled. With relief that it wasn't as bad as he'd expected. With Van's revelation.

Josh met his eyes and willed himself to listen if the

man wanted to talk about it.

"You probably want to counsel me, yeah?" Van leaned up on his elbows and watched Liv's approach. "She's dragged all the messy details from me over the years. No counseling needed."

That was debatable. She'd said there was no relationship, but they shared a history, an intimate one. Hell, they had a child together. The thought turned his stomach. He resented their bond, whether or not it was fused in tragedy. Remembering them having sex made him sick with jealousy.

The direction of his thoughts was ludicrous in his trussed up position, face in the mattress, his rear plugged and clenching. Didn't he have enough to worry about?

Van moved to sit on the edge of the mattress. "I think my girl's going to put on a show for us."

My girl. Jealousy burned anew, hot and painful. But she didn't want Van. She hid in her room to escape him. The reminder cooled his blood but didn't extinguish the nauseating pang.

She snapped her fingers and pointed to the rug by the mattress. He'd told her he trusted her intentions. Still did. He scooted backward on his knees, the plug both discomforting and oddly stimulating.

Standing before him and removing her panties, she rested her hands on his shoulders. "Your eyes stay on my pussy."

CHAPTER 25

Josh had seen her bared sex countless times, but he'd never stared long enough to take in the details. Out of awkwardness. Out of respect. But the mastery in her command and the potency of his arousal raised his eyes from the floor.

Wrong or not, it was a picture that would be forever branded in memory. Hairless, plump, taut flesh. The slit parted just enough to give him a glimpse of the dark, alluring depth within. When he'd washed her, he'd never ventured inside the crease. Would the delicate lips grip his finger? She was so small he couldn't imagine what it would feel like to slide his penis in there. Dear God, he wouldn't last more than a few thrusts.

"He's already hard." Van's voice held way too much awe as he crouched behind one of her spread legs and curled a hand around her thigh. His other hand held a purple silicone dildo, presumably what she'd sent him to fetch from the cabinet.

Would Van use it on her while Josh watched? Would the bastard have sex with her again? His heart raced, and his blood heated. Beneath the dread of Van's participation was a selfish hope that she would masturbate right there, so close to his face.

She took the dildo from Van and held it to Josh's lips. "Wet it."

His inhibitions fled as her free hand slid between her legs, fingers separating the folds and disappearing inside. He licked the silicone with a dry mouth, tried to gather spit, and spread it over the tip. The glide of her fingers between her slit and the hitch in her breath melted his body into a thrumming pulse of need.

At the edge of Josh's periphery, Van shifted stiffly, angled toward her, his breaths quickening.

She turned, kneeling on the mattress, and thrust her beautiful heart-shaped rear so close to Josh's face, he could see the freckle in the crease between her cheek and thigh. But the freckle faded next to the sinful view of her sex splitting her from anus to clitoris.

The smooth arches of her cheeks curved into the divide and led to folds of skin so pink and velvety and enthralling. A rush of wet air whistled past his teeth. The pulse in his erection intensified, quivering sensations through his body. He jerked his arms in the restraints and tried to distract his lust with rules. *No talking. No masturbating. No coming.* He groaned.

How was this training? Perhaps over time, he'd learn to hate it or resent her for putting him through it. Was that even possible?

She lowered her forehead to the mattress and reached the dildo between her spread thighs. The tip separated her folds, the soft-looking skin clinging to the silicone as it slid in, inch by inch. Sweat slicked his palms. The rope dug into his heaving chest.

She withdrew the toy, slid it back in. Out. In. The dildo glistened with her moisture, filling the room with a sucking sound as her channel swallowed it greedily. It was torture. It was beautiful. He wanted to put his mouth on her, his cock in her. He burned to know how deep he could go, how fast he could thrust, how long he could hold on while staring into her eyes and tasting her lips.

The pull of a zipper sounded beside him. Josh kept his eyes on Liv but could make out the movements of Van pushing down his jeans and taking himself in hand.

No. No, not Van. Not with her. Rage boiled to the surface, straining his muscles, searing his skin. He ground his teeth, seething to chase Van from the room. He couldn't do this, dammit. Not again. His arms twisted in the rope. He had to get free, to protect her, to fight for her.

A grunt muffled beside him, followed by a shouted exhale. Van jerked, shoulders twitching, and groaned out a sigh.

Josh was, at once, relieved and revolted by Van's orgasm. But how quickly would he be ready to go again?

Her dark eyes flickered over her shoulder, skimming over Van's groin, and collided with Josh's gaze. There was a softening in her expression, in the skin exposed above the kerchief, as she accelerated the strokes of the dildo. The shared eye contact made him want to hold her tight and glide his length deep, their bodies so close, so intimate, he would learn everything about her. Every bump and turn inside. Every dream, every secret, hidden away in every nook and crevice of her heart. He craved that knowledge more than he'd ever craved anything in his life. He craved *her*.

His hips rocked, his erection stabbing the air, the plug sharpening the sensations. She flexed her pelvis, riding the dildo in sync with his movements. Their eyes held, her desire feeding his. Veins pulsed in his cock, his arousal coiling, straining, unable to reach the relief he so desperately needed. He couldn't come without stimulation. He couldn't come without permission.

She blinked at Van, back to him. Josh's body shuddered. His penis ablaze, it swelled further, stretching painfully.

"Hey," Van said gently, touching his leg, shooting electric sparks over his oversensitive skin. "Let me help you."

Josh glanced down at his shockingly red and swollen erection jutting from beneath the ropes, his balls so tight they'd disappeared into his body. His brain muddled, and his body overheated. Was this the plan? Work him up to the point that he'd accept Van's touch?

He raised his head, meant to search her eyes, but couldn't see past the drugging beauty of her flesh wrapped around the thrusting dildo.

God forgive him, he jerked his chin up and down, breathless, lost to lust, crazed in his urgency to climax.

"Open your mouth." Van's words breathed in his ear. "Accept my kiss."

Anything to keep that man away from her. He stretched his jaw, instantly, wantonly, his butt flexing around the plug. Lips captured his, tongues whipping and battling for control. Exhales pummeling in the hot trap of their sealed mouths. Van's breath was sour and terrifyingly sweet. They kissed like they would fight. Rough, merciless, impassioned. And seething with rage.

A large hand gripped his erection, and he surged up on his knees, slamming his cock into the clench of fingers. With Van's head angled to the side, Josh kept his eyes glued on her clasp of skin as it stretched around the toy. Was she imagining the dildo was him?

He thrust his hips, having sex with her in his mind, panting noisily, his peak coiling tighter and tighter. Almost there—

"You will not come." Her voice rasped at the edge of his awareness.

Frustration slammed into his gut. The hand on his cock was an extension of his own hand, stroking him at a hard and consistent pace. The tongue in this mouth shoved and licked.

He hung on the precipice, balancing, trembling to rush forward. Her command was unbearable. *No coming without permission. No coming without—*

Ughhh, her pink folds looked so wet, her toned thighs flexing, her fingered grip on the dildo blanching her knuckles. He wasn't going to make it. He tensed against it. Focused on the heat of Van's mouth, the coarse stubble scratching over his jaw.

"Come, boy." She panted. "Come for your Mistress."

Her command tore the orgasm from every frenzied nerve inside him, surging forth in powerful, shivering waves. He rocked into the fist around his cock, his fingers digging into the rope on his torso, pressing into the man's mouth on his, and moaned a hoarse, strained exhale.

His body tingled, trembled, sighed. He collapsed, shoulders deflating, the plug pressing against his heels, throbbing to the beat of his blood.

She set the dildo aside, squatted before him, and removed the cloth from her face. Van raised his arm, his wrist striped with come, and licked it clean in one swipe.

Josh shuddered. Seriously, that was jacked up.

Van held out his tongue, lathered in semen, and leaned toward Liv.

What the unholy hell? She wouldn't. *No way.*

Her moment of hesitation passed quickly. She caught his jaw between her hands and drew his tongue into her mouth, her eyes squeezed shut.

Every muscle in Josh's body stiffened, the urge to interfere overwhelming. He trusted her intentions. She was playing a game. He bit down on his cheek and waited.

When Van's hand shoved between her thighs, his fingers slipping inside her, Josh jerked forward.

She broke the kiss, caught Van's wrist, and pushed his hand away.

"Thanks for the burgers, Van." She rose, gathered up the trash, and entered the code at the door.

A red flush stormed over Van's expression. He stood, yanking his jeans into place, and strode toward her, his voice low. "You're sleeping with me. Get him out of the ropes. I'll wait."

CHAPTER 26

Fear, anger, and jealousy stormed through Josh, pulling at his insides and squeezing his ribs tight. He strained his eyes to keep his chin down while glaring over his shoulder.

Liv's arms lolled at her sides, her head tilted up, her face a blank canvas. "Another time, Van. I'm working." She smiled, but it was tight at the corners. "You owe me an orgasm. Don't think I won't collect."

Van raised his hand, caught a few strands of her loose hair in his fist, and yanked. His eyes flicked to Josh.

Crap. Josh dropped his gaze, praying he didn't rouse suspicion about his obedience.

"Okay, Liv." Van sighed, his voice tired. "Get through the meeting tomorrow. Then come to me."

The unmistakable smack of lips followed, colliding with wet sucking sounds. The door clicked shut.

The gravity of what Josh had just participated in settled like lead in his gut. The burger and fries gurgled to come up. He jumped to his feet. "He needs a damned padded room."

She slumped against the door, her stoic mask falling away, exposing the heartbreaking expression of a trapped woman. Her eyes fluttered shut.

He moved to her, the rope web pulling on his thighs, the plug rubbing sore tissues. He leaned into her space, frustrated he couldn't hold her, and pressed his forehead against hers. "It worked, at least."

"For now. We still have to get through tomorrow."

And the next nine weeks. He inhaled the scent of her skin at her temple and let her closeness soothe his nerves.

"Do you resent what I did tonight?" Her voice was small, unsteady.

His sins were mounting. Of course, he hadn't been given a choice, but he *orgasmed in another man's fist*. Did it really matter in the scope of their situation?

"No, Liv. You got me past some pretty big barriers. If I hadn't been so horny for you"—he dropped his head on her shoulder, laughed, groaned—"that would've gone much worse." He straightened and looked into her eyes. "What was the semen-licking thing about?"

A ragged sigh pushed past her lips. "It's his thing. He does it during training sessions. In the past, it wasn't a battle I'd chosen to fight. Changing that tonight would've stirred up questions about us."

Us. The sound of that stirred up all kinds of questions. But that was for another time.

Her hand traveled over his butt and gripped the plastic base of the plug. She leaned up and bit his lip as she pulled it out with one tug.

He blew out a breath, the muscles in his backside clenching away the tension. But his relief was accompanied by a flush that spread through his body. She'd awoken something in him, and he wanted…more. He followed her to the sink.

She washed the plug and tackled his ropes. As the

knots loosened so did his knees. He perched against the edge of the vanity and relaxed into the satiny feel of her hands trailing over his chest.

Her breasts swayed beneath the movements of her toned arms as she freed each length of rope. He wanted to lean in and lick her parted lips. He wanted to lick her everywhere, and his penis responded immediately to that thought. Her gaze lowered to his glaring arousal, and a slow smile built on her gorgeous face. She flicked her eyes to his and shook her head, grinning.

"I wasn't like this before I met you." He laughed. It was kind of true.

"Bullshit. You just wore a jockstrap to keep your endless boners tucked away."

"Actually…" He puffed his chest defensively. "I tucked it into the waistband of my briefs."

A laugh bubbled from her, and she tossed the last of the ropes on the floor. "Let's take a shower, you dirty boy."

Showering with her was a thrilling mix of gratification and torture. He knelt at her feet, caressing soap along the contours of her slender body. Every curve he stroked reminded him how desperately he wanted her. His breaths quickened, and his hands lingered on her inner thighs, his erection oh-so painfully aware of her naked proximity.

His fingers ached with the need to touch her breasts. So he did with a lather of bubbles and a devoted hand. He was in love with her body, the perfect size of her chest, the dramatic dip of her waist, the pink flesh between her legs. Simply watching her stirred a shiver of pleasure through his groin and a fluttering feeling near his heart.

There was nowhere in the world he'd rather be than on his knees, worshiping her body. It felt *right*. The thought should've made his blood run cold. Instead, it flooded his chest with a fulfilling warmth.

When they finished the shower, they turned off the lights and collapsed on the mattress.

He pulled her back to his chest and hooked an arm around her waist, her clean minty scent clearing his head. He'd become accustomed to her nudity, but with both of them bare in this position, it felt new, intense. Her belly warm beneath his hand, her feet sliding over his shins, he couldn't quiet the endless stirring he felt in her presence.

"You're hard." There was a smile in her voice.

"You're naked. And I'm going to burn in hell."

Her musical laugh lifted through the darkness. "For snuggling with the devil?"

"The devil with the voice and heart of an angel." He buried his nose in the soft damp strands of her hair. "I want you so damned much, Liv."

The curve of her body along the length of his lay motionless, unresponsive.

How many times had a captive made the same declaration to her? Damn his big mouth. "That doesn't mean I'm going to—"

"You don't want me." Her whisper cracked. "You want…someone who deserves you."

An ache tightened his chest. He heard her. Not her words but *her*. For a fraction of a moment, he heard the girl he'd been searching for. The girl who yearned to be loved. "Will you do something for me?"

She tensed against him.

He caressed his hand from her belly to her breastbone and settled it over the galloping beat of her heart. "When it's just you and me, lose all those guarded layers. Let me see you." He raised up on his elbow and strained his eyes through the dark to make out the outline of her face. "Don't hide this from me." He tapped the spot over her heart.

A noise hitched in her throat. "It's ugly in there, decayed by lies and shame, endlessly bleeding for all the lives I've ruined. You're the eighth reason I don't deserve affection."

Eight slaves worth of guilt. He wanted to ask where they were, if she could trace their buyers. But those questions would derail the conversation and dredge up the one thing they hadn't discussed. His future. "That's not who you are, Liv."

"Don't do this."

The anguish in her whisper gutted him. He pushed through it. "Don't do what?"

"Don't make me feel things for you." Her voice rattled. "It will end badly."

So much fear and hurt. He wanted to take it from her, longed to heal her. But she needed to open herself up and let him in.

"You think having feelings for someone puts them in danger?" He was in danger whether she cared for him or not.

Her breaths quickened.

"Did you have a relationship with any of the others?" he asked.

Had she fallen for a captive and sold him into slavery? No amount of praying could have prepared him for the answer.

"I've never been in love." A weighted exhale. "And I've only had sex with one person in my life."

His pulse spiked. She'd told him her original buyer hadn't touched her before he tested and rejected her, but the rest? No sex with slaves? No dating between captives? Maybe he should've been relieved, but all he could feel was outrage. The only intimacy she'd known was with a person who coerced her, raped her, and beat her. "Do *not* let him dictate your self-worth, Liv."

Her entire body went rigid. "Do *not* preach your self-righteous bullshit. This is not a therapy session."

Though her reaction made his hands curl into fists, he knew he'd plucked a nerve. It was progress. With regard to her irritation, he could fix that.

He rolled her to her back and took her mouth, tasting the mint of her toothpaste, relishing the instant stretch of her jaw. She welcomed him with a heated gasp and a teasing tongue, swirling and whipping and stealing his breaths. He ran his hands down her arms, up her ribs, lifting and kneading the fullness of her breasts.

She licked and sucked his lips, shooting tingles across his skin. Her fingertips grazed the arch of his butt and brushed a trail of warmth along his spine. Each of her caresses, every breath of her attention, flowed through him and settled between his legs, aching, hardening, needing. Too soon, she tried to lean back and break the kiss.

He surged forward, deepening the reach of his tongue, clinging to the connection, wanting more, wanting all of her. "Let me inside of you." He rocked his erection against her thigh, groaning, wanting in her so badly. "Please, Liv."

"No." Her tone was a sharp prick. The rejection cut.

He dropped his face against her neck, moaned.

There were dozens of reasons why she would refuse him. He needed to know *her* reason. "Tell me why."

She pushed on his chest until he conceded a few inches of space. "I've been where you are. I gave the wrong person my virginity and have resented him every second since." Her hand cupped his jaw and fell away.

He had a long way to go on salvaging her self-worth if she put herself in the same category as Van.

"Fine, Liv." He blew out a breath. "We'll work on righting your perceptions."

"We're not—"

He pressed two fingers over her lips. "Let me touch you. I've been here eight days and haven't seen you orgasm once." He released her mouth to trace the line of her neck.

"Just hold me?" Her request was tender in its delivery, but potent in its significance.

"Gladly." He curled around her back and tucked a knee between her legs. His hand on her breast, his heart paced in tune with hers.

Holding her, melding with her, his virginity felt so inconsequential. This connection extended far beyond a physical union. He'd give her anything. He wanted to give her everything.

"Liv?"

"Mm."

"You said there were twelve requirements. You've only given me eleven."

She laced her fingers through his and held their hands to her chest. "Requirement number twelve. Slave will not sleep in Master's bed."

His laugh coaxed hers, and they tumbled into comfortable silence.

The ceiling's A/C vent breathed a steady whoosh. He tried to sleep, but his mind wouldn't shut off as he traced through the events of the night. "You awake?"

"Yeah."

"Why did Van pull out your hair?"

A sigh. "It's his thing."

It was a common occurrence? "He has a lot of *things*."

"You have no idea." She wiggled her back closer against his chest. "Go to sleep. We've got a four-hour drive tomorrow."

The meeting with the buyer.

He would leave the attic, taunted with freedom, enchained by the threat on her life.

Crack.

Liv raised the four-foot stock whip, the rigid handle sweaty in her palm, her stomach twisting. They had to leave for the meeting in one hour.

She swung again. *Crack.*

He flattened his hands on the wall, feet spread on the subfloor, and accepted each strike with a twitch in his sculpted back. No chains, no clothes, no words. When she'd told him she had to mark him, he'd stripped wordlessly and gripped the nearest wall. The knot in her gut doubled.

Mr. E had taught Van the art of whip cracking, and they used her body as Van's cutting target. Van eventually passed the skill to her. But it didn't matter if she was on the end of the handle or the fall, she had never experienced the kind of trust evidenced in the relaxed muscles before her.

That he would find credibility in her despite the cruelty she'd inflicted upon him twisted her insides.

She snapped back the single tail, popped it forward, and let the fall lash his upper thigh. *Crack.*

His legs trembled and his back rippled, but he refused to move, bound by trust alone.

Her heart squeezed, but she kept the whip moving over her shoulder, elbow in. A hairpin wave uncurled like an extension of her arm. *Crack.*

Another welt joined the others striping his back, ass, and thighs. His head dipped between his braced arms, the hair at his nape damp with sweat.

She swung her arm back. Held it.

Every strike left a new scar inside her. No more. She dropped the whip, her blood beating cold. "I'm done."

Turning, he closed the distance, cupped her jaw, and rested a hand on her hip. "I'm kind of starting to like those feverish little love taps."

A glimpse of his erection confirmed it.

"Kind of starting?" She sighed. "You've been getting stiffies under my whip since day one."

If he weren't locked in her room, facing an unknown future, maybe she wouldn't feel so sick about her part in it. Maybe she would wrap her legs around his waist and fuck him like she'd wanted to the moment she first saw him.

But he deserved a good, clean girl. She drew in a slow breath and raised her eyes.

His smile creased his clean-shaven complexion, lighting up the pale glow of his green eyes and chasing away some of her overflowing guilt. It also wobbled her footing as his Mistress.

She glared at him, her insides melting under the warmth of his affection. "Remove your hand from my face, boy."

"What's your last name?" His hand dropped, but only as far as the bust of her corset, fingertips caressing the pillow of her breasts above the binding. He bit his lip, watching her with a lopsided grin.

Fuck her, he was so damned charming. She emptied her expression. "I'll break your fingers."

He arched a challenging eyebrow.

She arched one in return.

He ducked his head and took her mouth, lips brushing, tongue teasing, flicking, kindling a slow-burning fire. His hands traveled around her ribs and clutched her back, tugging her close. He ate at her mouth, and she met him lick for lick.

She loved his kisses, his confidence, his stubbornness. She loved every goddamned thing about him. He only had to glance in her direction, and the floor dropped away. She was freefalling, riding the wind of his breaths, hoping he'd catch her.

She rolled her hips forward, the hard heat of his desire jabbing her hip.

"Reed," she breathed. "Liv Reed."

His lips floated along her cheek, his smile tickling her jaw, one hand returning to her breast, curling fingers beneath the binding on her corset. "Are you worried, Liv Reed?"

By using her name, he was prodding her to say his. But she needed the designations to resume her role. Just needed to get through the meeting.

She stepped back, chilled by the distance she'd put between them. "My worry is none of your concern, boy. Stand straight. Shoulders back. Eyes down."

He bent his knees to meet her eyes. His grip on her hips was hard and soft all at once. "Then whose concern is it?"

Her heart fractured. *Think about Mom and Mattie.* "If the buyer is satisfied and doesn't back out after tonight,

Mr. E will send new videos." She left out the part about watching them with Van. She would deal with that detail later.

His jaw slackened, and his arms fell to his sides. "All right." He straightened, squared his shoulders, and lowered his eyes. "Will you explain why you just whipped me?"

She clicked through the room in her thigh-high boots, the stiff leather mini-skirt pinching her legs and shortening her strides. "The buyers aren't just purchasing slaves. They're paying for the training of their *property*." The cold words shivered through her.

"And the marks on my body show you've been beating me properly?" He leaned a shoulder against the wall, arms crossed, unabashedly nude.

A swallow dragged down her throat, her skin tight with a strange, intense emotion. With the others she'd delivered, she experienced remorse, regret, self-hatred. With him, she burned with a sense of possessiveness.

She grabbed his jeans from the trunk and tossed them to him. "The slave's obedience during the introduction proves the validity of the training." She moved to the cabinet. "Since the sale is not final until delivery, Mr. E claims fresh welts are a marketing tactic. *Seals the deal*." Mr. E's words. She unlocked the door and removed what she needed, avoiding his eyes. "Sadists get excited seeing a body marked up."

Her breath strangled. She couldn't tell him how cruel these buyers were at these meetings. She didn't want to give him any more reasons to run.

Clothing rustled, sounding his approach. "Look at me."

She raised her chin, fell into his eyes.

"We'll get through this."

His affirmation gave her strength. She rubbed arnica into his welts and gave him Tylenol, something she'd done for every slave after every beating. Then she held up the long rope of chain in her hand. "Ready?"

He answered her in a heady, tongue-swirling, toe-curling kiss.

Ten minutes later, he followed her into the outer chamber. The girl lay on the cot, her eyes closed. Liv suspected she feigned sleep to avoid attention. The thought didn't help the knot in her belly.

Josh walked beside her, wearing only his jeans and boots. Chains wrapped his torso from neck to waist and locked his forearms together. Metal cuffs secured his wrists to the links on his chest.

The restraints she hated most forced his hands into fists against his sternum, encasing them in a tangle of strong wire. The strands of metal twined in and around his knuckles and thumbs, preventing him from straightening his fingers. He couldn't clasp a door handle or squeeze the trigger on a gun. The gun she would carry and hoped she didn't have to use.

Van was waiting in the kitchen with lunch. She ate her burrito in silence, feeding her prisoner between bites. Van watched with panic straining the edges of his eyes. He feared these meetings as much as she.

Van wasn't allowed to join them. The first time they met a client together in her role as a deliverer ended with Van's fist in the buyer's face. He hadn't liked the way the man was gaping at her. Fortunately for Mom and Mattie, the transaction went through despite the *misunderstanding*. Since that night, she was the only face of the operation.

But without Van's overbearing protection, she was on her own. And given this buyer's expressed hatred for women, the clench in her stomach was threatening to double her over.

She forced resolution into her knees and stood. "Time to go."

With her phone, a hood, and a long scarf in hand, she snapped her fingers and walked to the garage and the waiting van.

The van's only two windows and windshield were tinted to conceal the interior but not enough to risk getting pulled over. She and Van restrained Josh on the floorboard in the cargo area. He lay on his back, eyes on his boots, retractable tie-down straps holding him in place.

She wedged a ball gag in his mouth and covered his body and face with a sheet, smothering her unproductive emotions with long, deep breaths. Then she climbed behind the wheel and rolled down the window.

Van opened the garage and approached her door. "I put the cooler in the back."

"Thank you." She meant it. She hadn't remembered to pack dinner, wasn't thinking past the meeting.

He handed her a small LC9 handgun and a disposable phone through the window. "He'll call at seven o'clock."

The clock on the dash read *3:58 PM.*

"Take 35 south until he calls. He'll tell you where to go from there."

She nodded, gut churning.

He placed a hand on her jaw and a kiss on her opposite cheek, over her scar. She held miserably still as he kissed the corner of her mouth then fully on her lips. The skin around his mouth was colder, harder than Josh's smooth complexion. The movements of his lips forced, pried, and dug in. The scent of his breath wasn't unpleasant, but it was *wrong*.

His hand fell away. "Come back in one piece."

"I always do." Key in the ignition, she started the van and backed out.

He stood in the driveway, hands in his pockets, his expression tight, worry rimming his eyes. If she never returned, that would be the last look she saw on his face. Her chest hurt, a complicated pain.

Ten minutes outside of Temple, she pulled into a vacant parking lot, tucked the gun in her thigh-high boot, and climbed into the back. A whisper in her head begged her to not to deter from the routine. Slaves always rode in the back.

Would he cause her to wreck in an attempt to escape? What if she was pulled over by a cop?

She didn't listen to logic as she yanked back the sheet and removed the gag.

"I can't…I don't want you back here…like this." She pinched the bridge of her nose.

What the hell was she doing?

She raised her eyes, clung to the calm strength in his. "Will you try to run?"

"Not going anywhere without you, Liv." The intensity in Josh's eyes slammed into her chest, knocking her shoulders loose and freeing her lungs.

She hadn't trusted another person since Mom, and experiencing that feeling again was thrilling. *And stupid.*

Releasing the straps, she waited, frozen beneath the gravity of her decision.

He rose, sidling past her, the chains straining across his back and arms, his jeans molding distractedly to his ass. He dropped into the front passenger seat.

With a glance at his wired hands, he faced the windshield and let his head fall on the head rest. "Will you buckle my seat belt?"

Her heart hit the floorboard. More restraints. More trust she didn't deserve. Maybe some day they could drive to an unknown destination without shackles and stomach-curdling anxiety. They could sing along to music on the radio and talk about the future. They could dine together in a restaurant, and maybe he would hold her hand.

Her hopes died in her chest. She'd surrendered her chance at love the day she roller-bladed to Van's car. There would be no carefree car rides or dreams about the future. There was only her videos and his chains and the man who awaited their arrival.

As she drove, he sat sideways in his seat, arms locked to his chest, watching her with a maelstrom of thoughts turning behind his eyes.

She chewed on the inside of her cheek. "What are you thinking about?"

"Why does Mr. E require ten weeks of training?"

This would be difficult to explain to a guy who didn't fit the hostage mold.

"He allows the stages of captivity to run its course. Panic and denial consume the initial seconds to hours. Hostility and escape attempts happen in the first few weeks." She swallowed. Never had she considered allowing captives to ride up front on their way to an intro meeting. Two weeks into their confinement, and their eyes burned with a desperate need to escape.

The pale green eyes studying her were patient, thoughtful, and nothing she was accustomed to dealing with.

He rolled his lips. "And after the first few weeks?"

She stretched her neck, eyes on the cars zipping along beside them. "True acceptance is gradual and doesn't fully materialize until the first couple months. Acceptance is necessary for the kind of slave Mr. E is selling. One who can follow his Master around without noticeable restraints." Complete and total submission. Broken and hopeless.

"Eight slaves in seven years, if you count me." His steady gaze warmed her face. "Nine, if you include yourself. That's little over a captive a year. What do you do the rest of the time?"

"We hunt. Our selection process is based on the

buyer's requirements, family and social situations, but most importantly, the captive's ability to conform. The latter takes months of surveillance to determine the ideal candidate."

He shook his head. "You watched me for weeks and—"

"I knew." Her stomach clenched, conflicted and lost. "I knew you weren't the right choice for this." She met his eyes and found her way. "You were the right choice for *me*. When I saw you, I couldn't walk away."

A smile tipped the side of his mouth. "There's my girl, honest and open. Was that so hard?"

Her chest lightened, her pulse pumping in an untroubled rhythm. "You're easy to talk to." *And easy to love.*

As she drove, she explained what she knew of Mr. E's network, how he never had contact with the clients, and how he'd created a referral system for new buyers. "Each buyer must pass along a reference at the intro meeting. It's Mr. E's requirement in the contract. Since I'm the only one who meets face-to-face, Mr. E preserves his and the clients' anonymity. Once the delivery is made and the transaction is sent, we never hear from them again." *There's so much more to that last part.*

His silence pulled at her skin, scratching with unasked questions. No doubt he was thinking about how impossible it would be to find her previous captives. If he asked where they were, she would lie to him the way she lied to herself. They had to be dead to her, because the truth was too risky, for him and everyone involved.

When he finally spoke, his question surprised her. "Are there female buyers?"

She imagined him growing hard beneath another

woman's whip, and a double knot of jealousy tightened her tone.

"You think a female buyer would've made this easier for you?" It was unfair to accuse, and she immediately wanted to take it back.

He sucked his teeth at her, his voice low and aggravated. "I'm struggling to understand how I'm supposed to be a straight guy who hates women."

She flicked the blinker and changed lanes. "There was one female buyer. She wanted a male slave." A corporate, power-charged bitch with a chip on her shoulder. "I don't know what prompted the unusual demand of misogyny with this one, but it's imperative you give the impression that you despise me and any other woman who might be present."

A miserable silence followed as they watched the open pastures blur by. How would someone *make* a person hate women? It was an impossible requirement, but she'd known that going in.

She grabbed a pack of cigarettes from the console, cracked the window, and lit one. "Recite the requirements. The better you know them, the easier it will be for you to embody them."

He narrowed his eyes on her cigarette. Oh, he wanted to scold her, and if they were on their way to somewhere normal, he probably would have pulled out his preachology. Instead, he smirked and dictated the rules. Listening to him practice the loathsome words, knowing he was doing it for her, made her want him with a ferocity that burned the backs of her eyes and swallowed her destination.

He repeated the twelve requirements with fewer and fewer errors, until he relayed them perfectly. His body molded to the words, his chin dropping, thighs opening, no hint of resistance in his voice. She knew he wasn't losing himself. He was acclimating. For her.

Her body heated and tightened. He was the strength and heart of the most dangerous jump. He was the soul of bravery wrapped in chains. He would never fall, no matter how much metal weighted him down. He was a man who loved selflessly and honestly, and she was taking him to a monster who would slice him open and fuck the incision.

She gripped the wheel with two fists, unable to steer off course, unable to save him from herself.

An hour into the drive, flat fields tumbled into the scattered tower blocks of Austin.

"I grew up here." Her voice sounded distant to her ears. Memories could tear her apart, but they were there, gathering in the clouds that hovered over the metropolis. "Just a few miles that way."

He turned to face her. "What was your childhood like?"

"Spent a lot of time up there." She pointed at the blue sky that spanned beyond the reinforced concrete and steel. "When I wasn't at school, I was jumping with Mom." She smiled past the burn in her throat. "I used to sing to the first-time jumpers. Mom said it calmed them, but it's so noisy on the plane—"

"Sing to me." His gentle tone competed with the hard set of his jaw.

She wanted to, desperately needing the distraction. She began with "Pretty Face" by *Sóley,* letting the misty notes rise to her lips and carry them out of her hometown.

When she hummed the song to a close, he regarded

her as a lover might, affection softening his eyes and lips, his shoulders curling forward as if reaching toward her.

"Gives me chills, Liv. Every damned time. Your beauty isn't just an experience for the eyes. It breathes through the ears and evokes a reaction so consummating it claims the soul."

Her boot slipped off the gas pedal. She regained her footing but not her voice. It was flattened somewhere beneath her galloping heart.

"I can feel you." He leaned back, inhaled deeply. "Inside me. Everywhere. You own me. You will always own me, and I will walk through hell to keep it that way."

Eyes on the road, her breath shivered from her lungs, cracking her voice. "You own me, too."

"I know." He pinned her with those mesmerizing pale eyes. "Sing another one."

She shuffled through her favorite atmospheric tunes, serenading him, drawing out every minute they were side by side, beyond the prison walls, speeding in the same direction.

An hour south of San Antonio, her phone buzzed in her lap. They both jumped and stared at one another until it buzzed again. She lifted it to her ear.

"Take 85 west toward Asherton." The buyer's voice was suave, smooth, and thick with a Latino accent. "There's an abandoned railway station." He gave the address and disconnected.

She entered it into the GPS. "One hour away." And minutes from the Mexican border.

How easy it would be to disappear. She could toss the phone Mr. E tracked her on. Maybe he wouldn't try to find her. But she couldn't escape the news coverage.

His promise to punish her with national headlines of Mattie's death made her hands shake. Her fingers turned to ice on the steering wheel.

Josh's gaze was tangible, pressing into her skin. "You okay?"

"It's just a meet and greet." She angled her head to see his sharp expression. "I won't let anything happen to you."

Muscles contracted in his arms as he tried to pull his hands from his chest. "I can't repeat those words to you, Liv. Not when I can't use my arms."

"You don't need your arms. Focus on the requirements and remember to hate me."

He reclined in the seat and stared at the roof. "Right."

An hour later, she stopped a mile outside the GPS destination on a vacant gravel road. "Bathroom break."

She released her nervous bladder into the dust-covered weeds. Then she pushed down his jeans and held his cock so he could do the same. No words were uttered when he returned to his seat in the van, when she unlaced and removed his boots, or when she stripped his jeans and left him bare.

With a tremble in her hands and an ache in her chest, she covered his trusting eyes with a black hood. "This is for both of us." An accidental glance between them could be fatal if the buyer was perceptive.

As she stepped back to close the door, she hesitated for one heart-clenching second. She didn't deserve him, but goddammit, Joshua Carter was hers.

The black shroud of night held still and patient, coaxing her to risk a stolen moment. She climbed onto his naked thighs and lifted the hood just enough to expose his lips.

The first kiss was for him. A brushing of lips, a promise of protection. The second kiss was for her. A deep-reaching dance of her selfish tongue, a curl of love with a man who deserved so much more.

She lowered the hood, slid off his lap, and left him panting.

"Liv?"

"The requirements begin now. Who am I? Say it."

"Mistress."

She shut the door on the hiss of his breath through his teeth, wrapped her hair, nose, and mouth in a long scarf, and drove to the red dot on the GPS.

A single story building squatted, tired and alone, beside overgrown railroad tracks. Surrounded by shadowed fields and woods, no one would stumble by this end-of-the-road depot. A black sedan parked in the empty lot. No license plates. It looked outrageously sleek and out of place beneath the sagging gloom of the unkempt property.

She checked the handgun's concealment in her boot, tucked her phone in the other boot, and guided Josh to the door.

Her strides glided over the crumbling sidewalk with precision, shoulders cut back, lungs regulated, her thoughts beating to the seditious hymns of "Ghostflowers" by *OTEP.*

She was a deliverer, a killer, a soulless captor.

She shoved through the door.

CHAPTER 29

Over the years, the intro meetings had instilled certain expectations in Liv's mind. The buyers were paranoid, often armed and protected by bodyguards, and always masked. As Liv led Josh inside behind her, gripping the chain at his waist, her sphere of preconceptions evaporated, along with the air from her lungs.

The door creaked closed, and she tried and failed to shield his too-large frame with her smaller one. He bumped into her back, his head hooded and his body tight with tension.

A man reclined in a dusty chair at the center of the room, seemingly unconcerned with the grime rubbing onto his expensive suit. He wore no mask, and there were no obvious bulges marking concealed weapons. Even more unnerving, there were no bodyguards. He was either stupid, confident, or planning to kill her. Maybe all three.

Fifty extra pounds lolled over his belt and tested the button threads on his shirt. Late-forties, round nose, bald head, his oily gaze greased through the air, slicked past her, and clung to Josh's nude body.

But what made the hairs on her neck bristle was the naked woman restrained to the ceiling. She stood off to the side, in the shadowed edge of the room, staring out of twitchy, unfocused eyes. Her arms stretched over her head, tethered to the rafters, her feet weighted to the floor with chunks of broken sidewalk.

Thank fuck for the hood over Josh's head. He was temporarily oblivious to the depravity she'd led him into.

A ring gag held the woman's jaw open, secured in place with straps around her tangled black hair. Her tongue rolled in her mouth, pushing saliva through the ring and down her chin. A reflective orange collar cinched her throat. Belts fitted around her waist and upper thighs, connecting a wide strap that covered her vaginal and anal entry points. To fuck her, he would have to remove the three padlocks dangling between her legs.

If he hated women, why did he have a female slave? Most likely, misogyny was the reason he kept the woman confined in a chastity belt. So why did he want Josh?

Her stomach tightened painfully, but she forced her most dominant voice through the scarf on her mouth. "This is an introduction only. You will view what I've brought. If you approve, your down payment is required in the form of a phone number. As you know, we operate on referrals only. Call me Deliverer. What do I call you?"

"Traquero." His accent slithered with his gaze, his neck arching so he could steal a better look at Josh.

A yellow bulb drenched the wood floors and plaster walls in a dirty glow. At the perimeter of the light, the bound woman began to writhe. A moment later, she shrieked, muscles convulsing, drool stringing from her gaping mouth.

Behind Liv, Josh's breath hitched. She tightened her grip on his chain, a silent command to remember his role.

The woman's chin fell upon on her chest, and she drooped in her restraints. Traquero held up a remote, pushed a button, and the woman screamed again.

As Liv made the connection to the shock collar, images assaulted her—Josh collared under the hands of this man, his beautiful face shattering in agony, his faith in humanity shredding with each press of the button. *No fucking way.* Not while she still sucked air.

She jutted out her hip, creased her eyes with a calloused smile, and laughed. "Who the fuck is she?"

"My wife." Traquero flared his nostrils. "She used to be my life. Until I found out she was just a fucking whore." He stood, yanking the tie loose at his neck, his accent clotting with long *i*'s. "Fucking all my colleagues. Making me a goddamned laughingstock, the filthy fucking bitch."

He strode toward his wife, rolling up his sleeves, and backhanded her face.

A normal person would've regretted asking the question. Hell, a kind person would've ran for help. But Liv was neither. She needed Traquero's commitment to the deal to ensure her family's safety, and she *couldn't* leave without it.

Marketing 101. Know the customer's needs and use the information to influence him.

She met his eyes. "You want a lover who won't"—*can't*—"undermine the dominion you've worked so hard to establish?" *Fucking lowlife.*

"Yes." He folded his hands behind his back and swaggered toward her. "Move. Let me see him."

She didn't want that motherfucker anywhere near Josh. The thought alone spindled around her lungs, tightening its oxygen-depriving tendrils. But she couldn't shove her gun down his throat and pull the trigger. She could not. She could not. She breathed through it, focusing on the reason she'd stripped Josh of his clothes. He was there to be viewed. Seal the deal.

She stepped aside and exposed Josh to the man's sickening gaze.

"At last, I see you, *mi belleza*," he said, referring to Josh's cock. Traquero's attention was fixated and slack-jawed. "Out of the way, whore." He shooed her with a hand, his voice thick with spit.

"It's Deliverer, you sexist cunt." Her lashing tone was a pitiful attempt at maintaining her position.

Didn't matter who she was. She had a vagina. He considered her no more important than the woman he strung up and electrocuted, and he glared at Liv now like he might hit her.

She backed up, hands at her sides, fingers resting on the edges of her thigh-high boots.

He circled Josh, his gaze scouring the flexing muscle encased in chains, and paused with a hand over the raised welts.

"Magnífico." He reached up and yanked off the hood. "Face me."

Never had she expected to become so overwhelmingly possessive of a man, and it terrified her. The fear of losing him was as painful as her loss of Mom and Mattie.

Josh kept his eyes down, but she knew he could see the woman hanging in his line of sight. Other than the twitch in his shoulders, he kept his reaction to the horror behind an empty expression. When he turned and Traquero cupped his lowered jaw, her heart pounded wildly to smack the touch away. She locked her knees, forced herself to wait it out.

"Has your dick been corrupted by pussy?" Traquero breathed. "Speak. Give me your eyes."

Josh was several inches taller and regarded the sweaty, suit-clad man with a calm expression, his tone admirably smooth. "I'm a virgin, Master."

"Good. Good. *Muy bueno.*" He caressed Josh's bicep and followed the chains over his chest. An unmistakable erection bulged below the girth of his gut. "The slut I married will watch me fuck you. She will see honor and respect as you accept my dick, my rules, my power. *Then* she will know what her cunt has lost."

So fucked up. His requiting desires should've made his twelve requirements more plausible. Instead, the perversity of his oath and the lust smoldering in his eyes magnified his madness.

When he palmed Josh's cock, she grappled for an excuse to stop him. She hadn't told Josh that fondling was acceptable at these meetings. Stopping it would raise suspicion.

Josh held still with a heavy-lidded expression and intense patience, but that didn't mean he wasn't cracking beneath his stoic exterior. Her helplessness was an agonizing knot in her throat.

"Your limp pecker pleases me." He cupped Josh's balls, weighing them in his hand. "Not interested in men, no? Since I only employ men, you won't fuck my colleagues? My servants? Answer."

She shook her head, inwardly. Traquero liked the idea that Josh wouldn't be tempted to fuck his colleagues, but what the megalomaniac wasn't considering was that also meant Josh wouldn't willingly fuck him, either.

"No, Master." Josh's voice was soft, but a vein pulsed in his forehead.

"No, you won't." Sick satisfaction congealed in the crook of Traquero's grin, his eyes locked on his groping hand. "I want him."

The three words she needed to hear and had dreaded with every fiber of her existence. Time to get the fuck out. "Delivery will be in eight weeks. Do you have the down payment?"

His referral would be her next client. One with a new list of requirements for a new captive. An endless cycle she couldn't break.

"I said, I want him." Traquero hardened his jaw.

The force of his declaration punched through her, stealing the strength from her legs. Did he mean—?

"Right now." He continued to molest Josh's cock, his audacity slicing through her rising fear.

She brightened her eyes with the vicious smile he couldn't see beneath the scarf. "He hasn't been prepared for you, and he'll fight like hell." She hoped she hadn't misunderstood his desire for a willing victim. With her hands on her hips, she rolled her head on her shoulders and stretched her mouth in a yawn. "He needs more conditioning." She yawned again. "Hence, the eight weeks." *Now get your fucking hands off him.*

"He's not leaving until he gives me something. No deal without this." He squeezed Josh's cock, stretched it from his body. "I want you to come for your Master."

Her heart skipped a beat. How would she stop this? Mr. E didn't care what happened during these meetings as long as she secured the deal and the contact info for the next client.

He grabbed the chair, scratching the legs across the

floor, and slammed it down in front of his wife. He pointed at the seat and frowned at Josh. "Sit."

Josh's muscles strained against the chains as he paced to the chair, head down. His wire-wrapped knuckles were bloodless, his jaw a hard line of anger. She stayed on his heels, the weight of her promise to protect him a splintering pang in her chest.

When he sat, she stood in front him. His heavy exhales rushed against her back. He was pissed, probably scared, but he hadn't done anything to foul up the meeting.

She needed to wrap this up by any means possible. Strike that. By any means but one. "You will not fuck him tonight." *Or ever.*

Traquero removed his suit jacket. "Then I'll fuck you."

The room was fetid, reeking of desperation, the air thickening every second she hesitated. Vibrating through the stench was the silent wall of rage behind her. Josh's knees tapped against the backs of hers, bouncing violently, begging her attention. It was a terrible reminder of the horror she'd subjected him to. At the same time, she found comfort in his jostling presence. He didn't want this for her, and his concern was a fiery spark in her chest, a pulsing light that energized her with so much warmth.

She glared into the eyes of a monster who didn't respond kindly to disappointment and dragged her response, bucking and sour, from the pit in her gut. "You want to fuck my filthy cunt? I'm just a whore."

Traquero stepped into her, toe to toe, his exhale scorching her face. "That's why I'm fucking your ass. I'll come in your bowels while my property comes in your face. Turn around."

The floor tipped. Her ankle gave out, and she righted herself. She was teetering in unchartered territory. Josh was her first virgin boy. The other boys had not only been promiscuous but also experienced in anal sex. And by the time they'd attended their intro meeting, they'd been conditioned enough to accept the kind of demand Traquero was making.

If she denied Traquero, would he pull out a hidden weapon? Would he back out of the deal? Even if he let them leave unmolested, her rejection would wound his sense of superiority. An unhappy client meant a death warrant for the two people she'd sacrificed everything to protect.

A shiver chilled her blood. *Shit. Fucking shit.* She swallowed, held her spine straight. Van had taken her anally countless times. She was already ruined and would do anything to spare Josh that fate.

As she turned, a moan bellowed from the woman hanging beside them. Her mewls transformed into an ear-piercing shriek. Good God, he was shocking her again. Her body thrashed and fell quiet. Liv choked back the bile burning her throat.

"Bend over." Traquero's hands gripped the hem of her skirt, shoved it to her waist, and fisted her panties, ripping them off. "Eyes on me, slave."

Fuck, fuck, fuck. No way could Josh look at him without a face full of emotion. If he lost his shit, they might not leave there alive. If he showed any concern for her, the raping twat-hater would see through their facade. She hoped to hell Josh was working this out in his head.

As she bent over his lap, their gazes collided. The

connection lasted a fraction of a second, but it was all she needed. He wanted to fight for her. It was there in the pink rims of his eyes, in the blotch of red staining his cheeks. His lowered chin was fiercely set, his mouth a pale line of anguish.

He raised his head, blinked up at Traquero, the emotion gone. He'd swallowed his struggle deep inside where it would fester and eat him alive. He did that for her. For Mom and Mattie. Her eyes filled with tears. Not for the pain she was about to endure, but for the man who would suffer it with her.

When a zipper sounded, reality slammed into her in violent waves of tremors. Her teeth chattered behind the scarf, and her stomach heaved bile through her chest. *Think of Josh. Protect Mom and Mattie.*

She bolstered her voice with steel. "Condom."

Traquero's pants rustled, and a foil wrapper fluttered to the floor. Sweat trickled beneath her corset. She grabbed hold of the seat back and planted her elbows on Josh's thighs. His body was a stone pillar to which she clung, every hard inch of him bracing her.

Fingers singed her hips. The cold, hard tip of Traquero's dick pressed against her rectum. Her muscles tensed on the verge of springing. He shoved.

The burn ripped through her and cut her breath. Pinpricks seared the backs of her eyes. He didn't give her time to adjust, pounding her in a relentless beating. Oh God, this wasn't how Van fucked her. Not even close.

Dots blurred her vision. Her fingers cramped around the chair back.

"Slow down, goddammit." Her command was thick with saliva and cracked with tears.

The vicious gouging in her ass sped up. *Cruel,*

motherfucking prick. She shook with so much hate, her thoughts swarmed toward rash decisions, all of them involving Traquero's insides splattered over the room. As his dick punched a fist of fire inside her over and over, she tucked all those images into the harsh, broken chambers of her soul and soothed herself with a promise. The son of a bitch would die. Her throat burned, her eyes smearing. Maybe not tonight but very fucking soon.

His punishing stabs punctured and branded. Fire and ice. Stretch and rip. Fuck, it hurt so much. She was sure her skin was tearing. She wanted to die.

Eventually, her mind recoiled, pulling her into that lonely corner inside herself where it was just her and her songs and numb paralysis.

She searched for the right tune, a calming verse, fumbling, arms outstretched. But instead of her voice, she found Josh's waist, hugged it, pressed her forehead against the chains on his abs, the velvet skin on his back warming her fingertips.

The hurt in her rectum was a dull burn, rising through her. She cleaved to Josh with her hands and her heart. He was all around her, his breaths singing for her, his shackled arms floating above her, his tensile muscles absorbing her pain.

Traquero's grunts punctuated each forceful jab. "Come with me, slave."

Josh's cock remained unresponsive beneath her chin. He wouldn't be able to come, not like this.

A hand fisted the scarf on her head, tangled with her hair. Traquero used it to angle her to the side, exposing Josh's flaccid state. "Damn you." He panted, slowing his thrusts. "Make him come. Use your mouth, whore." He released her head with a shove.

A shiver swept through her. He was either mindless in his methods or he was testing her. Did this violate the first requirement prohibiting sexual intimacy with women? No, she'd jerked him off countless times in training. Blow jobs were allowed, and Mr. E expected her to do *anything* to seal the deal.

"Do it," he bellowed and slammed into her so hard the chair screeched backward.

She balled her hand until the trembling subsided then tugged the scarf from her nose to her neck.

Josh would hate her for doing this. In this place. While her ass was getting fucked. Guilt gnarled in her chest as she gripped the base of his soft cock. The merest lift of his hips nudged her hand.

She glanced up at his face, hoping to find acceptance there. But his eyes were on Traquero, his features heartbreakingly blank. He flexed again, the clench of his ass and thigh muscles urging her.

It wasn't consent, but it was enough to lower her head. She kissed the tip of his cock, closed her eyes, and drew him into her mouth.

CHAPTER 30

Oh, sweet God in heaven. Josh's boiling anger shuddered off his body the moment Liv's lips wrapped around him. Every molecule of thought descended into the wet clasp of her mouth. He swelled against her tongue in a violent surge of blood, his balls alive with electric shocks.

Nothing compared to the unfathomable suction of her lips, and he would've been lost in the pleasure if Traquero weren't brutalizing her backside. It required a double-backboned power of will to stare into Traquero's eyes of soulless black and regather his brain cells.

Maybe if he hadn't lived such a sheltered life, he could've predicted this, would've been able to stop it. Now all he could do was trust that she'd made the best decision for her loved ones without destroying herself in the process. No matter what happened, he intended to be there to help her heal.

He squeezed his fists so tight the wires broke skin, grounding him in a way his prayers hadn't. Why didn't she just let Traquero force *him* instead? Didn't she know watching her suffer was a torture worse than experiencing it firsthand? Perhaps the same rang true for her. She'd promised to protect him, and he hadn't realized what it would cost her.

What could he do? He didn't have his arms, but if he stood, kicked high and hard in that vile face, he might... Might what? Buy them time to run? That wouldn't save her family.

Her trembling fingers clutched at his waist, and he was thankful for the cage of chains and the command that held his eyes hostage. One downward look at the savage motion of hips, or worse, if he found a haunted expression on her face while she sucked him, his obedient slave routine would shatter.

"Come now." Traquero's voice was an abrasive rasp, bred by a hundred stolen thrusts.

She responded by accelerating the speed and intensity of her sucking, pumping her fist in sync with her mouth, urging him to comply. And he would. He would end this for her.

He kept his eyes on Traquero but didn't see him, his mind chasing every beautiful and painful thing he loved about this girl. Her guarded brown eyes, her rare smile, the purity of her voice, the cut of her whip, her lips sliding over his length. The grip she held on his heart and her control over his body made him ache, sped his pulse, tightened his groin, gathering, reaching.

Traquero grunted. "Come."

Only for her. He held it, let it coil, until she pinched his backside in a silent command. His climax barreled through him, strangled his breath. He gave it to her, all of him, raw and willing, his release in her mouth so intimate the room melted away. He was on her tongue, dripping down her throat, fusing with her body. Just the two of them. He was hers.

The horrors around him snapped back with Traquero's gasp. "Unnngh."

The bastard's body doubled over her arched spine, trapping her chest against Josh's thigh. The wife wailed a pitiful moan, and he laughed. Then he stood, stuffed the used condom in his pocket, and tucked himself into his slacks.

"Get up." He jerked his bald head at Liv.

She replaced the scarf over her nose and mouth. Josh ached for her, and that ache erupted into a burning rage. He wanted her to remind Traquero she wasn't a slave, even as he knew she wouldn't be able to reason with a man whose evil bled from his skin to his bones.

She adjusted her skirt and rose with shoulders stiff, hands fisted, and eyes smoldering like embers of a dying fire. "Boy, go stand by the door."

Dammit, Liv. He knew she was sending him out of harm's way, but what about her safety? If he disobeyed, the deal would fall through and her family would suffer.

He fixed his gaze on the floor and crossed the room, sweat dripping down his back in his effort to obey. Every step away from her killed him.

"Give me the referral, and we have a deal." She wielded her voice like a blade slashing the air, but there was a slight hitch in the inhale that followed. Pain from the brutality she'd endured? Fear of what might happen next?

Traquero paced a circuit around the room, gathering his suit jacket and straightening his tie. "I don't like what I see."

Her laugh was a cold shiver. "What, his cock's too big for you? His face is too pretty? What the fuck do you not like?"

"He comes for you, not me."

The man just did unspeakable things to her and

had the balls to sound petulant. Josh was a hairsbreadth from body slamming him. He locked his legs. To stand there and do absolutely nothing flung his nervous system into a havoc of messed-up signals. His muscles pumped to use physical force while his brain bellowed the consequences.

Despite what just happened, she'd dealt with predators like Traquero before. She was their best shot at getting out of this. So he kept his eyes down, his periphery rising no further than their waists.

"You wanted a straight boy. Of course, he's going to come for me." She leaned a shoulder against the wife's suspended body as if she were a lamp post. Her fingers rested on her thigh, just inside the top of her boot.

Traquero's pacing stopped behind a narrow counter. "Get away from her."

Liv straightened but didn't step away. "After ten weeks of training, he will crawl to you on his belly, lick the cheese from your nut sac, and plead for your cock in his ass, all while quivering with anticipation to come on your command."

The godawful image boiled bile into Josh's throat. He stood by the door, his distance from her a heavy frustration, his chains equally so. At least, the width of the room separated her from Traquero.

"There's something else going on." Traquero buttoned his jacket. "You're protecting him."

"I protect my assets, you delusional fuck. Until you pay, he's mine to keep undamaged and unused. If you're not man enough to want him, another Master will be. Do we have a deal or not?"

Her voice was ice, but beneath her taunting, Josh could hear a crack. If Traquero were listening past her words, he would've heard it, too.

"No," Traquero said. "No deal."

Silence, so stagnant it clotted Josh's inhales and clung to his skin. His muscles contracted, preparing. What was she thinking? What would she do? Her temerity scared the ever-loving crap out of him.

"Go to the car, boy," she growled.

She was out of her mind. He rooted his feet to the floor.

"You go." Traquero shifted against the counter. "He stays."

Josh snapped his head up as Traquero pulled a snubnosed revolver from beneath the counter and trained it on Liv. Blood thundered in his ears. He jerked forward and crashed to a halt when he saw the gun in her hand.

She shoved the barrel through the ring that held the wife's mouth open. "Are you a good shot, Traquero? Maybe you'll hit me at that distance. Maybe you won't." Her dark eyes blazed with ruthlessness, but flickering in the depths was a hint of desperation. "We both know *I* won't miss."

Josh's heart died in his throat. Liv was gambling on Traquero's caliber of bullet, his accuracy from thirty feet, and his level of duress. If he didn't hit her with the first shot, chances were he'd kill her with the second.

The room stood still, waiting for Traquero's response.

CHAPTER 31

Josh's breathing shallowed. His heart knocked against his ribs. Every frenzied thought concentrated on the aim of Traquero's gun.

The glow from the filmy bulb gilded Traquero's distorted face in a putrid yellow. "Don't shoot her." He tipped the revolver's nose down, just an inch. "Please."

There was nothing shocking about a man begging for his wife's life. Unless that man was Traquero. But Liv didn't seem shocked. Somehow, she'd figured him out.

"Empty the gun. Toss it."

She spoke as a Deliverer, a Mistress, a cold criminal. But that wasn't who she was. No matter the mask, Josh had never wanted anything more than the courageous, reckless woman trapped beneath it.

Falling bullets plinked on the floor. Traquero chucked the revolver, and it clambered somewhere beyond the reach of light.

Holding her gun in the woman's mouth, she removed her phone from her boot. Probably the same place she'd concealed her gun. "The referral."

As he rattled off a phone number, she typed with her thumb and, given her subtle exhale, sent off the text.

"Don't fucking move." She stared at the screen, her

gun hand unwavering. A moment later, she said, "Confirmed."

Thus, securing the lives of her family. Her drive to protect was fierce. Josh wanted that same kind of protection for her. He wanted to be that for her.

She returned her phone to her boot and kept the gun aimed on the woman as she backed toward the door, her feet gliding smoothly and confidently. "I need a phone number for the delivery."

Traquero stared at his wife like he wanted to run to her. "Maybe I want a different boy. One who doesn't look at you like that."

She stumbled and resumed her backward walk. "They all look at me like that. You'll change your mind when the training is done."

"We'll see," he said, absently.

There was no indecision in her need to get out of there. She held the door for Josh and quickly followed him out and to the car.

For five minutes, she drove, silent, eyes darting to the side mirror. Josh wanted her to fall apart the moment she hit the gas. He needed to see *her*, not the damned Deliverer. The stink of fear and sweat oscillated through the dark interior, but somehow she held it together.

His nerves stretched, and his pulse refused to slow down. He tried not think about the battered wife, the botched deal, or Traquero raping her from behind, but his thoughts surpassed turbulent. His hands ached in the wires. He wanted out of his chains. He needed to hold her. He felt so damned useless. "Liv? Talk to me."

She turned off the road and followed a long dirt path through a thick cluster of trees. Deep within the grove, she stopped and turned off the engine, her eyes hidden by the moonless night.

Wrestling with the scarf, she untangled it from her hair and tossed it to the side. The screen on the phone in her hand awoke, casting a soft light over the dash as she knelt in the space between their seats.

A flash of pain sparked in her eyes. "I have to call Van."

He clamped his teeth together. He knew she'd need to check in. The nightmare was never-ending.

She connected the call, her gaze watery and heartbreaking. She squinted at the screen, at Josh, then switched it to speaker and set it on the dash.

"Already talked with the referral." Van's voice prickled across his skin. "He wants a girl. The usual requirements."

Kate was still at the house, waiting for her delivery day. So another girl would be ripped from her life. Dread clamped Josh's stomach.

"I'll leave in the morning," Van said, blandly.

Leaving? A rush of possibilities jump-started Josh's brain.

She touched his fists with trembling fingers and untwisted the wires. "I didn't secure the deal."

"What do you mean?" The question dripped from the phone, a slow ominous reverberation.

Her face paled in the screen's dim light, her expression tight. "He wants a heterosexual boy to come for him on demand. It didn't happen the way he wanted."

"What the fuck *did* happen, Liv?"

She sucked in a sharp inhale. The wires loosened between their hands. Circulation rushed to Josh's fingers in biting stings, but the sensation dulled with the rush of her next words.

"He fucked my ass, Van. Then he fucked me again by rejecting the deal." She pulled the wire free and flung it at the back of the van, her teeth grinding so violently Josh could hear the enamel scraping.

The line went quiet for a heartbeat, two… The sound of shattered glass crashed through the speaker. "Goddammit, Liv. God fucking dammit." Heavy exhales. "Get home. Now."

She winced then recovered with squared shoulders. She unscrewed the quick links connecting Josh's chains and paused on the last one. "The videos."

"There won't be any fucking videos." The line went dead.

She ducked her chin, hiding her face. A surge of anger rocked Josh backward. He knew Van didn't have any control over the videos or what would happen to their daughter, but the man sure as hell wasn't putting his ass on the line to fight for her. Josh suspected he was more afraid of losing Liv and this fragile arrangement than anything else.

The chains fell off his chest and arms and pooled around his waist. His freedom swept through him in ragged breaths.

She gazed at him with stiff lines of determination on her face, an expression he'd seen a hundred times, the unwavering glare that tortured him, aroused him, conjured his nightmares, and filled his dreams.

He memorized each twitch of her lashes, the delicate point of her raised chin, every faltered breath. He was consumed with having her and terrified to lose her.

"Tell me what you're thinking." He reached up to brush his fingers through her thick dark hair.

She recoiled before his hand made contact. A blank mask fell over her face, a wall of ice slamming between them. She moved to the driver seat and faced forward.

His momentary calm burst into a roaring fire. Hands fisting, heart pounding, he didn't know what do with the fury burning through his veins. He tagged his jeans and boots from the floorboard and jumped out.

He dressed as he walked, jerking on his boots, kicking branches out of his path. His muscles heated, and sweat slicked his bare chest, chilling in the night air. He wasn't angry at her. He was angry *for* her. The abuse done to her body. The helplessness of her situation. His inability to free her.

He slammed a fist into the nearest tree trunk. Again. Again. Pain ricocheted through his hand, down his arm, and fed his breaking heart.

Out of the corner of his eye, he caught her silhouette standing a few yards away. A slender shadow, shrouded by darkness. And in her raised arms, she held a gun, trained on him.

He threw another fist. Absorbed the burn. Expelled the rancor. He knew she was holding a gun on him to prevent him from running and putting her family at further risk. Regardless, she wouldn't shoot him. Not because she needed a slave, but because she loved what was hers with a self-destructing passion.

He faced her and held out his arms. "I'm yours."

The girl and the gun didn't move.

"Lose the damned mask and stop hiding from me." He raked his throbbing hands through his hair. "Scream, cry, hit something. Hit *me*. But for God's sake, let it out."

The shadowy lines of her body wavered. The gun lowered, returned to her boot.

He stretched out his arms, savoring the cool breeze brushing over his unrestrained skin. "I stand here without rope or chains, Liv, tethered to you by my own will." His blood beat with the ferocity of his words. "I won't be free until you are."

Her head jerked back, her body rigid. Then she walked straight to him and unleashed her fists on his chest. She clobbered him over and over, her gasps accelerating with each fall of her hand.

The lashing didn't hurt. Not like the whimpers rising from her chest. She was hurting, lashing out for the wrongs that had been done to her. A sharp pain swelled in his throat. The only thing he could do was take it in, try to bear some of it for her.

He held his arms out and his body open. When her hits ebbed into weak slaps, she stumbled back, hugging herself and clutching her elbows.

His heartbeat slogged through the ache in his chest. He kept his arms outstretched and whispered, "I'm here."

Disbelief widened the whites of her eyes, and her breath caught. He waited.

In two running steps, she launched at him, climbed up his chest, and curled her hands in his hair. He lifted her, pinning the curves of her thighs around his hips, and took her mouth. His knuckles burned with fever, but the heat from her lips was overriding. She whispered kisses over his jaw, around his mouth, caressing, assuring.

He angled his head, deepening the reach of his tongue and drinking her in lick by lick. Her hands in his hair, the sweetness of her breath filling his mouth, there will never be another kiss like hers. She knew how to suck his lips and trap his tongue in a way that stroked every nerve ending in his body. More than that, she knew how to reach inside him. She found him, her ferocity defying the odds and pivoting them into place, perfectly interlocked.

Her thighs squeezed around his waist, her breasts soft against his chest. He palmed her backside with a cautious gentleness, and chased her tongue, spiraling, stretching deeper, falling heart-first into an existence where only she mattered.

When their mouths separated, gasping for air, she cupped his cheeks and pressed their foreheads together. "I'm so sorry."

He knew she was referring to the atrocities of the meeting, and she had nothing to be sorry about. "You should be sorry. Getting a blow job from you was a real hardship."

She rested her lips on the corner of his mouth and sighed. "We need to go."

"I'm driving." He shifted her, hooking an arm beneath her knees, and carried her to the driver's side door.

The way she curled against his chest and hugged his neck produced an obscene amount of pleasure for his emasculated ego. She was finally turning to him for comfort. Though, the fact that she didn't protest him driving was a testament to her physical and mental state. She trusted him not to cause a wreck or drive to a police station. He kissed her head, let his lips linger there, branding her peppermint scent in memory.

He scooted behind the wheel, sliding back the seat to accommodate his longer legs, and found the keys in the ignition. She snuggled into his chest, settling in, exactly where he wanted her. Her knees folded under his arm and allowed him plenty of room to see and steer. Holding her like this, her soft body half the size of his, she didn't seem so tough and intimidating. In fact, the quiet tremor shaking her breaths made his muscles heat with the need to avenge her.

He veered onto the main road, the tires kicking gravel into vacant fields. No cars. No buildings. Only a black dome of sky and a thousand questions beating against his skull. He stretched his hands on the steering wheel, igniting a burn through the gashes. "What happens now?"

Her lips moved against his neck. "The intro meetings are always strained with tension, but I've never walked away from one without securing the delivery." Her voice wavered. She cleared her throat. "Mr. E will try to sell you to another. Though, the next buyer wants a girl."

"And Van captures the girls?"

She nodded, fingers curling against his chest. "He'll be gone a few days. Maybe a week. Scouting only. Watching. We hunt as far from home as possible. You were an exception."

She'd already explained her reason for choosing him, one he'd accepted with ease. Better him than someone else. He hated to ask, but they needed to talk about the ramifications of the meeting. "Does Traquero's referral safeguard your family?"

"I don't know." Her voice was desolate, tearing the lining around his heart.

"We *need* to know." He tried to choose his next words carefully, but there was no way to soften what she needed to hear. "If they're dead, you will be, too." Mr. E would no longer have a means to control her. "We can't go back there."

She stiffened. "I have to go back for Kate."

Kate. She'd never used her name, and doing so now was monumental. And terrifying. Was she giving up? Or giving in? "Then we'll go back, wait for Van to leave, and make our escape."

"Her delivery to the buyer is in two days. If Mom and Mattie are still alive, I *have* to deliver her."

He slammed a hand on the steering wheel, and she didn't even flinch. For the love of God, this was so jacked up. "How is delivering her better than not returning for her?"

The passing fields illuminated with the flickering lights of the emerging town. She slid out of his lap, dragged the cooler to the front, and perched in the passenger seat.

"When I deliver her, I'll kill the buyer." She held a forkful of salad to his mouth and looked at him as if she were talking about football stats.

He accepted a few bites and tried to consider her suggestion with an open mind, but he couldn't be moved from the conviction ingrained in him. Murder must always be a last resort. "You're not killing anyone. Murder is a *big* sin, Liv."

She stuffed another bite in his mouth with more force than necessary. "So if it had come down to leaving you with Traquero or pulling the trigger, you would've preferred the former."

"Yes." He would've found another way out, God willing.

"You're an idiot." Her tone was scolding, at odds with the weariness sagging her eyes.

"Repay no one evil for evil. We *will* overcome evil

with good."

"Ugh. Shut up." She threw the salad container into the cooler. "I *am* evil. Destined for hell. What the fuck am I saying? I'm already there."

"I'm not even going to respond to that." He glared at the road.

Her self-perception punched him in the chest, but he wasn't helping her, either. She needed a solution, not a bible study session.

"Contact Traquero and request another meeting," he said.

"We only get one-time-use numbers. A number for initial contact. And a number to make the delivery. Outside of that, the buyers call Van. Mr. E's rules. He prides himself on buyer confidentiality." She leaned back in the seat and stared out the windshield. "Traquero will have a change of heart and call Van again."

She seemed confident, and he wasn't sure how to feel about that. His self-preservation objected to the notion of Traquero making that phone call, but his trust in her was unremitting. If it had come down to leaving him with Traquero, she would've pulled the trigger, damning herself to hell.

They passed through San Antonio and Austin, and the conversation circled around ideas that wouldn't form into a plan. She put holes in every suggestion until there was only one option left. One he couldn't accept. Premeditated murder was not a solution. Nor would it save her family and return him to his.

As he drove, he evaluated his feelings about resuming his old life. Returning home meant exchanging twelve requirements for a hundred more. Did he really want to go back to their rules? Mom and Dad's restrictions were morally acceptable but no less confining.

When he exited the interstate at Temple, edginess stretched between them. Her mask fell in place, and her posture gathered into that unnerving stillness.

He pulled off into the same vacant lot she'd used ten hours earlier and climbed into the back. They were no closer to a solution, but they were together, bound by a connection that was deeper and stronger than keypads and shackles.

He lowered to the floorboard, and the chains went back on.

CHAPTER 32

The next twenty-four hours tested Josh's faith in God's presence in Temple. As Liv sank slowly and deeply inside herself, he questioned if maybe this was hell. Perhaps she was right. God had abandoned him on a threadbare mattress, locked in an attic, with his heart hemorrhaging in his hands.

He fed her the meals she retrieved from downstairs, showered with her, and tended his swollen knuckles and the small rip on her rectum. But his single-minded outpouring of questions, affection, and worry were failed attempts in breaking through her steel-plated chest, which grew colder and more rigid with each passing minute.

She curled in a ball on the mattress and clutched her phone. Waiting for the videos that never came. Watching the blank screen as if, at any moment, it would stare back with lifeless eyes.

If Mr. E intended to kill her Mom and daughter, he would do it *after* she delivered Kate. Van had left Temple before they'd returned early that morning. Mr. E needed her and wouldn't risk her dissent. Josh knew she knew that.

He dropped the tennis ball he'd been throwing for

the past hour and stood over her, hands on the waistband of his jeans. "What time is it?"

Her thumb tapped on the phone's screen. "11:48 PM."

Only fifteen minutes had passed since the last time he'd asked. He was out of excuses to coax her out of the attic. Kate was free to roam the outer room, and Liv had brought up enough food to hold the three of them over until the delivery tomorrow.

He knew Liv intended to kill Kate's buyer. Every time he counseled her against this decision, he was met with a litany of colorful words. Liv seemed completely unconcerned about her own safety.

Numerous times, he'd considered calling his parents to let them know he was okay. He would've had to trick her into unlocking her phone, but that wasn't what quashed the idea. He didn't know the outcome of their situation until she delivered Kate. Giving his parents false hope would be cruel.

"No more waiting." He perched on the edge of the mattress. "We need to leave. Escape with Kate."

"No." Her answer was cold, final. She turned away and stared at her phone.

It hadn't passed his notice that she was the only one going downstairs for food. With Van gone, there was no need for pretense. Beneath that icy mask, she still believed he would leave her.

He drew in a breath and matched her chilly tone. "If you haven't heard from Mr. E before the delivery, then what?"

She'd said Van would send her the address for the delivery when he received it.

"Are you still going to deliver Kate?" he asked.

Her body turned to stone, her voice grinding. "I'm going to do what I have to do."

He rubbed his temples. He couldn't ask her to choose whose lives to protect. It was an impossible decision. One that would make the strongest person lose her bearing.

Laying on her side with her back to him, she folded in on herself, arms and bedding wrapped around her belly. She needed someone to hold her on the shore of decision, to cradle her fears, to contemplate what was best for *her*.

He leaned in and touched her bare shoulder with his fingertips, with his lips. "If you need a place to go, Liv, I'm right here."

A shiver twitched down her arm. Her hair swept over the pillow in ripples of mahogany. The naked curve of her spine disappeared beneath the sheet that bunched at her waist. He was conscious of her lack of clothing under there, and while her nudity was no longer a mystery, it was no less alluring. Even in her misery, he wanted her, in every way possible.

He trailed a knuckle along the dip of her waist, over the rise of her hip, taking the bedding with it. He expected her to jerk away as she'd done all day, so he decided to surprise her. He yanked the sheets to the floor, exposing her slim lines and milky skin, stripping her bare.

She rolled to her back, her lips parting in disbelief, her phone seemingly forgotten at the edge of the mattress. What a gorgeous opportunity. He pinned her chest with his and captured her mouth before she could close it, swiping his tongue, finding hers on the second pass, warm, wet, and so damned promising.

She arched into him, the heated satin of her flesh molding to his hands as he caressed her backside. He was instantly hard, his balls tightening with an achy need. He palmed her breasts, his thumbs rolling over her nipples, his tongue licking and stroking the sensual reaches of her mouth.

The most private part of her body ground against his, her calves hooked around the back of his thighs, her fingers clutching his biceps. As their mouths moved together in synchronized surrender, he wished he'd had the foresight to remove his jeans. He wanted to feel her against his skin. He wanted *in* her.

Her hands twisted through his hair and tugged, breaking the kiss. Her lashes lifted, carrying her gaze from his mouth to his eyes, and held him, heart and breath, in eternal suspension.

She licked her bottom lip, and he felt it pulse through his erection. She blinked and something shifted over her expression. Angling her chin to the side, the hands in his hair pulled his face to her chest, and her thighs tightened around his waist. "Please don't give yourself to me."

He broke the crush of her embrace and gripped her face with two hands, forcing her to look at him. "I already have. This"—he rocked his groin against hers—"is part of the deal."

Her eyelids shuttered closed, and a breath spasmed through her chest, her lips in a flat line of rejection.

His hands fisted in the pillow. He couldn't, wouldn't, force her, beg her, or otherwise guilt her into it. He lowered his forehead to her shoulder, inhaling the clean scent of her skin, savoring the intimacy of her body against his.

A haunting melody strummed from her lips. He recognized it immediately. "Possession" by *Sarah McLachlan* was a sad but fitting choice, its tune reflecting the tragedies in Liv's life. He shivered against the sweet breeze of her vocals, holding her tight as she expressed herself the one way she knew how.

She sang about trapped memories and solitude, but when the lyrics shifted to aching bodies, her huge brown eyes moistened, welling in the corners, staring up at him, piercing. Her conscience emerged through the words, her voice cracking, yearning. He realized she wasn't rejecting him. She was beseeching him. Asking him to love her.

He sat back on his heels, curled her legs around him, and beheld the beauty of his world. Uncertainty misted her eyes. He drank in her fading hymns, her feminine allure. The parted seam of her mouth, gentle swells of breasts, flat expanse of belly, vulnerable spread of thighs. Her fearless heart.

His chest swelled, overcome and pounding frantically, as her love gathered before his eyes, twining her fingers around his, rolling tears down her cheeks, whispering a word he'd ached to hear in her angelic voice. "Josh."

Not *boy*. She called him *Josh.*

"Liv… I want this. I want *you*." He bent forward and collected a tear on his fingertip.

His pulse beat in his throat as he lowered his finger and traced the slit between her legs with the teardrop, sliding deeper and deeper with each pass. His lungs panted. His finger breached her opening, and warm, slick flesh sucked him in.

Just thinking about putting his penis there sent a shock wave to his groin. He sank to the knuckle, her channel flexing and gripping. A moan tumbled out with his exhale, and he fell forward, catching his weight with his free arm beside her, laughing at himself, overwhelmed with desire.

He pressed in and out, and added a second finger. Her eyelids dipped to half-mast. Her lips freed a smile, her body glowing with life. He cherished every breathy gasp, marveled at how wet and hot she was, and couldn't let go. He wanted in, and given how violently his muscles shook, it would happen quickly and with a great amount of energy.

The naked light bared her arousal in all its curves and glistening flesh. His hand braced his larger frame over hers, his other exploring her sex with fumbling urgency. "Wish I had ten hands. I want to touch you everywhere while I'm doing this."

"Just keep doing exactly what you're doing." She reached down, found the button on his jeans, released it, and lowered the zipper. "You'll have me coming in no time."

Oh, those words stroked him, made him harder. He concentrated on the depth of his touch, the velvet heat of her folds drenching his palm, and the sound of her exhales. When she pulled him from his pants and glided a fist up and down his length, he quickened the thrust of his fingers, wheezed on his laboring breaths, and felt his release barreling down.

He bucked out of her grip, pulling his fingers from her, squeezing the base of his erection and halting the orgasm.

"I…uh…" A ragged laugh shook from him. "Wow. I'd like to get at least one thrust in before I embarrass myself."

Stretching her arms above her head, legs spread in offering, she grinned. "I'll keep my hands here." She sucked on her bottom lip, her gaze sobering. "I'm all yours, Josh."

Ahhh, his name on her lips. The arousal straining her face and the sultry caress of her voice accelerated the gallop of his heart and the throb between his legs. He lowered his face to her mound, slid his hands under her butt, and kissed a path down the line of her sex.

The sweet scent of her moisture infused his inhales. His mouth watered as he spread his lips over her, licking, sucking, imbibing the salty, sugary essence of her. He kissed her like he would her mouth. Deep, hungry pulls with his lips, burying his face, his tongue circling and lapping. The more he explored, the hotter her flesh grew, her entrance swelling, widening, wanting. He was doing that, tweaking her body, giving her pleasure.

Her legs flexed around his shoulders, her inner muscles pulsing against his tongue. Fingernails scraped the wall above her head. "Ohhh, fuck, fuck. Don't stop."

No way. He ground his hips against the mattress, working his jeans off with one hand and kicking them away. His heart raced toward implosion, his hard-on so hot and painful, he was consumed with the primal need to fill her, to make her his. He curled his fingers around her thighs, spreading her further, deepening his kiss.

Her curvaceous backside went tight in his hands and loosened with her full body sigh. "Ah, ahhh, I'm coming. Oh fuck, Josh, I'm coming."

He devoured her through the twitches and pulses, the muscles inside of her beating against his tongue. Soon, she melted into the mattress, her breaths falling like lingering tears. She gazed down the length of her torso, eyes heavy-lidded and clinging to his.

One more tongue-delving kiss, and he crawled up her body, taking his time, dragging his mouth over her quivering belly, capturing every bead of sweat, following the dips of her ribs. He got sidetracked when he reached her nipples, flicking and biting until she pulled his hair and covered his mouth with swollen lips.

She drew in his tongue, humming, hands sweeping down his back. Her fingers burrowed into his butt crack and pressed against his rectum. Fire sparked in her eyes. "Take me."

He shivered, his voice strangled. "Yes, ma'am." He rolled his hips forward, cock in hand, and lined it up to her opening. They'd tied her tubes, but… "Condom?"

A smile shook the corner of her mouth. "Van doesn't sleep around and has blood tests to prove it. I trust him on that." Her eyes asked, *Do you trust me?*

He nodded, his heart hammered. This was it. He found her eyes, smoothed the hair from her face. She touched his lips then his chest, over his heart.

He thrust, a hard breathless slide, and they bled into one. Hot and wet. Soft and tight. Freedom. It was everything he'd wanted and nothing he expected. Her body stretched around him, gripping him, spinning stars through his brain. Buried to the root, he inhaled her breaths, sweating profusely, afraid to move.

She stared up at him with a yearning look, her dark eyes framed by wet lashes, the corner of her mouth trembling.

Connected inside her in a way he could've never imagined, he tasted her lips, a caress of soft, swollen bliss. "You okay?"

Her fingers speared his hair from his temples to his

nape.

"I never thought…" She drew in a deep breath, tightening her hold on the back of his head. "This tenderness...you and me..." She blinked rapidly, her inhale hitching. "This is an intimacy I never thought I'd experience."

A deep level of satisfaction washed over him. He was able to give her something she'd never received from another man. Hope fluttered in his stomach. Maybe his love for her was big enough to heal her emotionally.

Her warm sex clenched, spurring him into motion. He withdrew, dragging his length along her walls, igniting a million sensations, and slammed back in. His hands scrambled for purchase on the mattress. Oh, God. His vision blacked, and his release tore from deep inside him, pummeling through his cock, shredding his throat.

"Ah, ahhh, ughhh." He shouted incoherent sounds over and over, his muscles jerking in spasmodic bliss, his heart tripping in his chest.

His head hit the pillow, the remnants of his climax thrumming through him, tingling his skin. When he regained his voice, he shifted his weight to his arms, bracketed her face, and searched her eyes.

"I intended to last longer than two thrusts." A smile pulled at his lips, and he let it loose with a laughing sigh. He circled his hips, still seated deep inside her, with no plans to pull out. Ever.

She shook her head, biting down on her own smile. "Just like a teenage boy." She kissed him, gliding her tongue and heating his mouth. Then she pushed her hands through his hair and leaned back. "But you fuck with your heart."

"Then my heart is aching to move." He rocked his

hips, relishing the connection. Grinding harder, he circled his pelvis, feeling her everywhere, and worked into a furious tempo.

She cupped his jaw and arched a brow. "Again?"

"As long as you'll have me."

Her legs and arms hooked around him, and she rolled them. With his back against the mattress, she straddled him, folding her arms behind her head. "My turn."

What a glorious vision. With her body bared before him and a gleam in her eyes, she rotated her hips, breasts swaying, waves of dark brown hair cascading around her. "You gave me a gift, Joshua Carter. I'm keeping it. Always."

He gripped the curves of her butt, holding her to him, lifting his hips, and sliding deeper. "Good. Because I'm yours. Always."

When she came, she took him with her, milking him, crying his name. He would never forget that moment. The merging of their passion, peaking together. Two parts of a whole, lost together.

They curled up in silence, her back to his chest. She laced their fingers and brought them to her mouth, kissing the cuts on his knuckles.

A few moments later, her musical laugh tiptoed through the room. "You're hard?"

He bit her shoulder, stroked his erection along the crease of her butt. "I'll never get enough of you, Liv."

She angled her hips, reached between her legs, and guided him inside. He was home.

Hours passed. Outside, the sun would've been climbing the sky, but he didn't care. He had so much light in his arms, it was easy to pretend nothing else mattered. Just for a little longer. They made love incessantly and intensely, slow and fast, hard and soft. He was lost in her body. Lost in *her.*

Eventually, exhaustion pulled him under with her curves against his, limbs entwined.

When he woke, it was with a head full of sexy dreams and blood swelling him to a full hard-on. Never enough. He grinned and reached a hand over the mattress, searching for her. Not finding her.

He lurched to his knees. The mattress was bare. The room empty of life. His heart went wild, his thoughts crazed. Maybe she was checking on Kate. Or making breakfast. He climbed to his feet, and something crinkled beneath his toes. A white piece of paper with scrawled handwriting. Beside it, a car key.

He dropped to his knees and a picked up the letter with shaking fingers.

Joshua,

Van called with the buyer's pickup location. Meet me at the Sleepy Inn on 35. If I don't make it there by tomorrow morning, go home. Go home to your family.

The code is 0054. The key belongs to the black Honda parked out front.

Liv

The letter wadded in his clenching fists, a fog of red clouding his vision. All business. Nothing from the woman he'd spent the day in bed with. She might as well have signed it *Deliverer.*

He spun to the trunk and found his clothes inside. Hers were gone. She wasn't coming back. He shoved his hands through his hair.

The code is 0054. Number fifty-four. She was freeing him. What would happen to her Mom and daughter?

His heart collapsed, spilling panic through his blood. What the hell was she planning?

CHAPTER 33

Liv drove the van out of Temple, with Kate strapped to the floor in the back as she headed west on 190 to make her seventh and final delivery. Darkness descended over the horizon. Street lights flickered on. Her pulse beat a frenzied vibration in her ears.

Josh would be driving to the motel by now. A motel that would never be one of her destinations. *If* he obeyed her instructions, and hopefully, without revealing his identity to the motel clerk. God, she needed him to just wait somewhere safe and hidden until morning. By then, everything would be done. Surely, he wouldn't go to the authorities before going to the motel?

Fuck, it was a risk, made more excruciating after spending the previous seventeen hours in his arms. She'd tried to keep him at a cold distance when they'd first returned from the meeting. She'd been fighting through her uncertainty about Mom and Mattie's future and trying to come to terms with what she had to do. She needed to protect him from her, refused to endanger him with the details. But most of all, her plan would've devastated him.

When they became entangled, they brought with them all their convictions, pursuits, and pains. Whether it was scriptures from religious study, record-breaking interceptions, or delivery deadlines with sex traffickers, he'd taught her that one's purpose in life had no sway on who the heart latched onto. And while she'd managed to keep her plan hidden, he exposed the rest of her with a fierce loyalty behind his gorgeous green eyes and a blaze of determination burning in his touch.

She yanked the seat belt pinching her chest, strangled and trapped by the tragedy of her miserable fucking life. She loved him, goddammit, but she had to let him go. Covering her mouth, she smothered a sob between trembling fingers. Fuck, it hurt so damned much.

Focus. Breathe. Don't fuck this up. Gripping the wheel with two hands, she glanced at the passenger seat. A mask, change of clothes, the LC9 pistol Van left for her, the pen knife he didn't know about, the phone Mr. E would be tracking her with, and her letter to Van. What was she missing?

Josh. His absence was a bleeding fucking hole inside her, the stitches around her heart unraveling and ripping. She inhaled deeply. Gasped noisily. *Fuck. Keep it together.*

A glance over her shoulder revealed Kate's heaving chest beneath the restraints on the floorboard. Liv's throat burned, stinging pinpricks of pain through her head. She wiped at her nose and eyes, hands shaking.

A few miles later, a gas station emerged, the lot half-full with customers. The first stop.

She pulled off and parked at a pump beside a minivan. Bright lights fringed the canopy over the pump islands, flickering with winged insects and bleaching the starless sky. A woman leaned inside the minivan's sliding door and hollered at the wailing kids within.

Liv approached her with her thumbs hooked in the front pockets of her jeans. "Excuse me, miss?"

The woman turned her head and blew a wayward hair away from her face.

Liv shaped her mouth into a friendly smile. "Sorry to bother you. Is there any way I can borrow your phone for a minute? Mine's out of juice, and I really need to check on my dad."

The woman shifted to face her, and her eyes widened, fixed on Liv's scar. She looked away quickly. "Uh, yeah. Let me grab it."

Funny, Liv never really thought about her fucked-up face until she ventured into public. Her internal damage had always been much more distracting to her.

"Here you go." The woman offered the phone, the pity in her eyes negating her smile.

"Thanks. I'll just be a minute." She stepped away from both vehicles until she was out of hearing distance and dialed the number she knew from memory. It was the sixth time she'd called it, and it'd been eight months since the last call.

"Who is this?" Camila's sultry voice, though always straight to the point, had a way of warming Liv every damned time.

"It's me."

"Where?"

The reason for her calls was always the same. "Brady Reservoir." She gave Camila the GPS coordinates Van had sent. "10:00 PM."

"Shit. We're three hours away." A muffled noise scratched down the line. Then Camila's voice came back. "We'll make it. How many?"

"At least one extra man. Maybe two."

"Stall them. We'll be there." The line disconnected.

Stall them? Buyers and their bodyguards did not stall, and it was eight fucking o'clock. Camila would have to make up a full hour. Liv sighed, rubbed her eyes. It wouldn't be the first time Camila overextended.

Fear crept in, like it did before every delivery. Deep breath. This was the last one. She pinched the bridge of her nose, drew in another calming breath, and returned the phone to the woman.

For the next two hours, she smoked one cigarette after another. The stimulant intensified her edginess, so she sang while she smoked. When the tears sneaked in, she changed up the song. The towns grew smaller with each passing mile, stretching farther apart, separated by rocky scrub land. Fifteen minutes outside of Brady Reservoir, she stopped on the side of the road and changed into her costume.

The Deliverer wore a silver under-bust corset over a bra and boy shorts, both made of black latex. The gun went into her thigh-high boot. The knife's scalpel blade folded in, and the pen-like design fit down the center of the bodice, snug in the corset casing that had originally held a steel bone.

With a few minutes to spare, she knelt beside Kate and brushed the girl's hair from her sweaty forehead. "I delivered another girl once. Six years ago." Her chest tightened, testing the seams of the bodice. "She was very brave." She leaned down, pressed a kiss on trembling lips. "You remind me of her."

Thanks to the pitch-black interior, she couldn't see the fear in Kate's eyes. She didn't need to. It breathed through the van in a ghastly shudder, desolate and needful.

She returned to the driver's seat, a sheen of dread dampening her skin and chilling her spine, and faced the next phase of the plan. As she maneuvered the winding roads, dipping and curving around hillocks and banks, she couldn't escape the grip of doubt.

The emotionally detached letter she'd left Josh weighed on her the most, but she couldn't leave him with the damaged whispers of her heart. He might've clung to her words, searched for her, tried to save her. There were too many people involved in her deliveries, too many identities to safeguard. The less he knew in his freedom the better for everyone.

Stunted bushes crowded the landscape, forming smudges against the inky backdrop of barrenness. The last building was ten miles back. The occasional headlight bobbed in her side mirror and vanished behind the bends in the road. The desolation preyed on her nerves.

The navigation system directed her onto a narrow path that faded into a gnarled expanse of wilderness. As the clutch of trees closed in, she put on her mask, tying the strings to hold the round white face in place.

Up ahead, an arced glow rose through the dark, striping through the skeletal branches. Her boot shook against the gas pedal, and her palms slicked the wheel.

"Glory and Gore" by *Lorde* invigorated her lungs and heart as she scanned the trees, searching for a sign of her secret saviors.

Ricky, Tomas, Luke, Martin, Tate, and her very first captive, Camila.

She knew them by the names she'd once refused to use, by the bruises on their skin, and by the strength of their forgiveness. Her six deliveries in seven years were dead to her. Until she called. Her freedom fighters always came when she called. And they came for blood.

A car blocked the road, its headlights aimed at her and cut by the silhouettes of two men. She shielded her eyes with a forearm, turned off the engine, and grabbed the phone. In the back, she unstrapped Kate, straightened the girl's knee-length cotton dress, and led her out.

"Stay beside me," Liv whispered. "Shoulders back. Eyes down."

"Yes, Mistress." No chains or cuffs. The girl was broken in her despair.

With the confidence of the Deliverer, she swayed her hips and flexed her bare thighs with each stride toward the waiting predators.

Liv closed the final few feet with her chin held high and her strides wide and easy. Her insides, however, shook with a violence that strangled her breaths.

The shorter of the two men wore a Guy Fawkes mask, painted with a mustache, goatee, and a cynical smirk. The bodyguard didn't share his employer's creativity, his face distorted in a transparent sleeve of nylon.

"Good evening." Guy Fawkes cocked his head.

"We'll see." Her cool voice tangled in the autumn air.

The bodyguard approached her, and she remembered the drill from the intro meeting. She stretched out her arms, her phone in one hand. Beside her, Kate stared at the ground.

He prodded around Liv's mask and hair and patted down her bra, corset, and skin-tight shorts. When he reached her boots, he lifted the gun as she'd expected. Pocketing it, he moved to Kate and repeated the search. That done, he stepped back.

The Guy Fawkes mask turned toward Kate. "Come to your Master."

Liv clasped her wrist and walked a step ahead of

her, holding her to the side. Was Camila there yet? Could Liv cut the fucker before his bodyguard shot her? Stall, stall, stall.

She released Kate's arm. "Kneel."

As the girl descended to the ground, Liv arched into Guy Fawkes' suit-clad body, inhaling the stench of musk and greed. She cupped his groin.

He swelled in her grip and held a palm out, halting his guard's advance. "How much for both of you?"

Same question he'd asked last time. If he saw her scarred face, he'd probably choke on his persistence to buy her.

"Pay me for one slave." She tightened her fist around him. "Then we'll discuss the prospect for two."

He pulled out his phone, his fingers tapping on the screen over her shoulder. She stroked his erection, bile burning through her chest and challenging her steady breaths.

"Sent." He pocketed the device and slammed a hand down on her ass. A heavy fucking hand.

The sting rippled down her leg and burned through her muscles. He reared back and hit her backside again. Her fingers fell away from his dick to clutch his hip. She was sure he broke blood vessels, the sadistic prick.

Her phone vibrated in her hand. She held it between their chests, unlocked it, and glanced at the text.

Van: Funds received

Her heart soared. It took a great amount of discipline to hold in the relief blubbering to escape. She breathed to the beat of "Glory and Gore" and lowered the phone to her bodice. As she worked it beneath the binding, she slipped the pen knife free, her body pressed to his in a wretched embrace.

The bodyguard stood a few paces away, his nylon-smashed expression skimming the surrounding woodland.

She flicked the blade open, her hand hidden beneath the rise of her chest, her pulse thrumming wildly. Trusting that the Guy Fawkes mask limited his field of vision, she swung the scalpel upward, and sliced his carotid artery. He shuffled back, cupping the spray of blood beneath his mask.

The bodyguard straightened, drew a pistol from his hip. She stopped breathing.

One shot fired from the trees. Two. Three.

He jerked back, stumbled. *Oh, thank God.*

The beam of headlights illuminated a crimson stain at the center of his white shirt. He snapped his gun up, aimed at her, and fired.

The bullet whistled past her. She leapt on him. Took him to the ground. Landed on his chest, the knife slick in her grip, her heart beating at a dangerous velocity.

The buyer hit the ground beside them, one hand squeezing the flow of red at his throat, the other clawing through the dirt to grab her leg. His fingers caught her calf in a blood-slicked grip.

She jerked her leg free and stabbed downward, hitting the bodyguard's chest. The blade sank an inch and stopped. The sternum? A rib? Shit, shit, she couldn't push it in. He shoved her away, raised his gun.

A gunshot cracked from the brush.

The beige of his nylon hood turned red, seeping blood. His gun dropped, and his body slumped.

A ragged breath tore from her throat. She unlocked

her limbs, shaking violently, and checked the pulse in his throat. Nothing. She scrambled toward the buyer.

He lay on his back, arms lolled to the side. She tore off his mask and stared into the lifeless eyes of a weathered face.

She sat back on her heels, removed her own mask, and choked on the copper-tainted fumes of death and defeat. Nausea gripped her insides. The torture of her first seven captives had fattened Mr. E's off-shore account, but they were free and their buyers dead. And her eighth captive…

A sharp pain ripped in her chest. She inhaled deeply. Josh was safe.

Kate knelt a few feet away, curled over her thighs, shoulders trembling. Liv needed to go to her, but her legs wouldn't move, the gravity of what came next weighing her down.

One more kill. In Van's bed. Where he would find her dead and rotting and clutching her letter.

The stampede of foot falls crashed through the trees. A moment later, arms wrapped around her, Camila's familiar spicy scent a temporary comfort.

"I'm sorry, Liv. We tried to get here in time."

Shoes scuffed the rocky terrain around her, sounding the movements of young men gathering the dead and cleaning up the evidence. Young men she'd abducted, humiliated, whipped, and jacked off.

Killing herself would free them for good. It would also free Mom and Mattie. Mr. E would have no reason to harm them if she weren't around to experience the horror of it.

She should've ended her life years ago, but Josh had been the push she needed. Releasing him back to his parents was the right thing to do. Perhaps it was his integrity that had given her the strength to be honorable.

She hugged Camila's slim shoulders and dropped her face in the black silk of hair. "Don't be sorry. You still managed to fire a kill shot. Thank you."

Camila pulled back, shaking her beautiful round face, her eyebrows drawn in confusion. "We didn't shoot anyone. We just got here."

Her blood ran cold. "What do you mean?"

"Liv?" The deep accented voice behind her belonged to her second captive.

She pulled to her feet and came face to face with Ricky, who aimed a gun at a pair of pale green eyes. Eyes she never thought she'd see again.

Josh.

In his hand, dangled a Taurus PT-22 with a pink wood-grain grip.

CHAPTER 35

Six guns aimed at Josh's head. Five men, one woman, all of them young, irrationally attractive, and glaring at him with fight in their eyes. He should've been scared shitless, but the cold blood settling around his heart suspended him in a state of shock.

He'd just killed a man. Even as he feared God and shunned evil, he knew without a doubt he'd do it again. For her.

Liv watched him, her eyebrows in a stark *V*, her complexion pale and splattered with blood. "Lower your guns."

The weapons lowered, disappearing in waistbands and pockets. Her friends, whoever they were, shifted closer, forming a bulwark at her back.

The Latina woman opened her mouth, and Liv held up a finger, silencing her and glaring at him. "How did you find me?"

"You might call it a lucky break. I call it divine intervention." He flicked the safety on the gun and held it up. "Why'd you leave this in the Honda?"

"So you could return it to your mom." Her eyes flashed. "I did *not* expect you to use it in a reckless gunslinging rescue." She spoke low, repeating her question. "How did you find me?"

He tucked the gun into his waistband at the base of his spine. "I left as soon as I woke. Got to the front of the neighborhood, and there you were, in the van, only a few blocks ahead of me." God hadn't abandoned him after all. "I followed you."

Her lips pinched in a line. "I freed you."

The woman at her side covered her mouth, eyes wide. "Oh my God. He's that missing football player from Baylor." Her head snapped to Liv. "He's one of us?"

They were three hours from Baylor in the middle of nowhere. It was surreal that news of his disappearance had traveled that far. And what did she mean, *one of us*? His vision prodded through the nighttime shadows, searching the faces of her gun-toting, backup team. "Who are you?"

Liv pulled out her phone and squinted at the screen. "I have about twenty minutes before Mr. E wonders why my phone isn't moving." She blinked up. "Josh, this is Camila."

Camila gave him a chin lift. "I was her first delivery."

The hand of darkness seemed to lift from the trees, the stars singing together and the world crashing into place in a duh-faced moment. He took in their handsome features, their muscular builds, and their youth. Some were of Spanish descent, and they all fit the same desirable mold, including Kate. All seven of her captives. Here. *Free.*

All the signs had been there. She had never shown remorse over the fate of her captives, refused to talk about rescuing them, never veered from her plan to deliver Kate. And Van's inability to attend the transactions made it all possible.

Camila gave Liv's hand a squeeze. "Liv gutted my buyer the minute he sent the transaction. I screamed like a maniac, covered head to toe in his blood." She half-laughed, half-groaned. "When she calmed me down, she told me her story. Her history with Van. Her Mom. Her daughter." A sad smile touched her lips. "I refused to abandon her, so she let me dispose of the body and gave me an anonymous e-mail address. I sent a phone number there, one that couldn't be traced to me. A year later, she called. That's when I met Ricky."

The man closest to him held out a hand. "Ricky. Slave number two."

Josh accepted the handshake, awe-struck, his tongue not functioning.

Another guy flicked up three fingers. "Tomas. Number three. Her favorite."

Someone coughed, "Bullshit." Then each of the remaining men stepped forward, their names threading around him, pulling him into their huddle. Luke, the only redhead, number four. Martin, who had to drag his eyes from Liv, number five. Tate, huge smile, number six.

A familiar blond head emerged through the wall of men, her hands twisting in the front of her dress. She peered up at the strangers with a shell-shocked expression. "I'm…my name is Kate." She stared at Liv, her lips parted and eyes wide. "Does this make me number seven?"

"Yeah." Liv moved to her and cupped her face, bending to meet her eyes. "You okay?"

With a jerky swallow, Kate raised her chin and nodded. "I'm still trying to catch up. I…I had no idea. I thought I was going with that man." Another swallow. "I didn't expect you to kill him. Have you ever lost a slave?"

A deep inhale billowed Liv's breasts above the cups of her bra, and a quiver skipped over her arm. "No, Kate. We're all here."

We. They were all free, yet Liv was still a prisoner.

Liv smoothed Kate's hair from her face and spoke to her in a low, rushed tone about her mom and daughter, the significance of the other slaves being there to help her, and why she does what she does. The whispered conversation went back and forth for a moment longer, and Liv turned Kate toward Camila. "I trust them with my life, Kate. They'll protect you with theirs."

Camila embraced Kate in a hug. "Finally, a girl. And blond?" She glanced at Liv. "Still hunting in the border towns?"

"Until Josh." Liv moved to the hood of the sedan and picked through the cash, weapons, and phones that had been gathered from the dead men's pockets. "Kate's buyer wanted blond and innocent. Took Van a year to find her in the southern slums." She turned toward Kate. "Your brothers were protective of you, but they're drug dealers, and they're involved with some really bad people."

Kate's face pinched. "I know."

"It'll be fine." Camila grinned and waved a hand at the men. "You can help me air out the testosterone in our house."

Josh startled. "You live together?" Were they still considered missing?

Ricky strode around the buyer's sedan and shoved the lolling arm of a body into the trunk. "We come from broken families and ghettos who wrote us off as runaways." He slammed the lid shut. "If we return to our hellholes, it might initiate investigations that led to Liv." He walked back toward the group, eyes on Kate. "You can't go home."

She stepped away from Camila's embrace and rubbed her head. "I…I know."

Martin pointed a finger at Tate. "You know, that guy threw a fit when we told him he was stuck with us. Look at him now. He's been trying to fuck me since he moved in."

Hands laced behind his head, Tate glared at him. "I come into your room at night, because the entire house can hear you shouting Liv's name while you're jerking off. You need to get over her, man."

Martin flipped him off. "Fuck you." His eyes lit with laughter then shifted back to Liv with unmistakable longing.

Liv's shoulders squared under Martin's gaze as she blinked up at Tate. "You look well." She smiled. "Happier."

"I *am* happy, Mis—" He coughed in his fist. "Liv."

Tate was number six, so he would've been her last delivery, which she'd said was eight months earlier. Thick black hair and one of those boxy jaws women love, he smiled like he was posing for a camera, but it was warm and sincere when he regarded Liv. Josh believed she'd never had sex with him, but she knew him intimately. She knew all of their bodies intimately. With her hands. And her mouth.

Jealousy surged through his lungs and tightened his muscles. It was ill-timed and immature, but it couldn't be helped. His fists clenched, itching to drag her away and pretend that none of this existed.

Ricky nodded at him. "Liv, your boy's about to pop a vein in his forehead."

She closed the distance, her shadowy gaze caressing his face, her nearness replenishing the oxygen in the air. She clasped his fists and uncurled his fingers, her hands sticky with blood.

"Why'd you free him without a transaction?" Martin crossed his arms over his chest.

Her eyes didn't waver from Josh. "He's stubborn, disobedient, and untrainable."

He saw so much behind those words. Her spine straightened defensively, her lips flattened with fear, and her eyes hooded with affection.

"He failed the buyer introduction." She raised their laced hands to her chest. "You would've failed the next one, too. It was only a matter of time before Mr. E and Van saw this..." Her lashes lowered, her gaze on their hands, and fluttered back up. "They would've killed you."

A mass of regret clotted his throat. He didn't mourn loving her, never that. But he wished he was smarter. There had to be a safe way to end this with her family protected, but he couldn't see it.

The guys continued their road cleanup, but their attentions lingered on Liv. Without hesitation, his possessive heart led his lips straight to hers. With a hand on her neck, his other clasping hers against her chest, he kissed her deeply, nipping, licking, stealing her breaths, swallowing the hum in her throat. She was his, and he owned her mouth with a kiss that would leave no misunderstanding.

When he released her lips, her eyes clung to him,

dark and hungry. Exactly how he wanted her. *After* all his questions were answered. "You freed me. Freed Kate. How does this save your mom and daughter?"

Camila paused in her effort to kick gravel over a patch of blood-stained dirt. "That's what I've been trying to figure out."

The crimson gore slicking Liv's cleavage gleamed in the headlights as her chest heaved. She unwound their hands and walked toward the van. "We need to wrap this up."

He shoved his fingers through his hair, watching the uncharacteristic wobble in her retreating strides. "Camila, why didn't she tell me about you? About this?" He gestured at Ricky and Luke, who were pouring jugs of acrid-smelling vinegar over the crime scene.

"She freed you," she said, softly. "When you return, you'll be swept into the investigation of your disappearance. Lots of interrogations." She jerked her chin at the group. "How are you going to keep this a secret? We're killing people, Josh. And Liv is crazy protective of our identities. In fact, she's terrified her expressions or reactions around Mr. E and Van will give us away. So she lies to herself when she's in that house. She thinks of us as dead." She turned toward Kate, whose eyes were glazed and distant, and stroked her hair. "Until she needs us."

Across the road, Liv leaned against the passenger door of the van, stripping her boots and wiping the blood from her chest with a t-shirt, her expression downcast and inwardly focused. He never once suspected this endgame, and he liked to think he knew her better than anyone else did.

He watched her with a renewed appreciation for

her mystery. She was a complicated puzzle, one he planned to enjoy for the rest of his life.

A new life. What did that look like? He wouldn't return to his old life without her. Yet, she'd sent him on his way as if she expected him to do just that.

His spine tingled. "She wouldn't have freed me unless she had a solution to save her family."

Kate's shoulders bunched as she watched Liv wrestle with the front clasps of the bodice. "She's going to kill herself."

His nostrils flared, his pulse spiking in objection. "Did she tell you that?"

Her head shook as she hugged herself. "I was just thinking about her behavior since we left the house. She cried a lot on the way here. Then her voice grew cold and weird. She started singing "Last Resort", you know, that suicide song by *Papa Roach*. Definitely not her usual genre of music."

Muscle-clenching fear shot through his legs. He sprinted toward Liv, watching her movements, his entire body aware of her fingers on her corset and her feet pacing in a tight circle. Did she have a weapon on her? Would she attempt it right there? In front of him?

He skidded before her and slapped her hands from her belly. "Do you have a blade under your clothes?" He wiggled the remaining hooks free, dropped the corset, and tackled her bra, searching the seams. "Answer me."

"Fuck you." She gripped his arms, tried to stop his hands from unclasping the back hooks.

The bra dropped, her breasts bare and streaked with red. No weapon. He dropped to her latex shorts, shoved them past her hips.

"What the hell are you doing?" She glowered

down at him, kicking off her shorts like she was going to kick *him*.

Well, screw her. He was a breath away from tying her up. He opened the passenger door and shifted her until the door gawk-blocked her nudity from the nosy onlookers.

With her arm twisting in his grasp, he pulled her chest against him and pinned her back against the inside of the door, his voice low and vibrating. "Did you consider me in your suicide plans?"

A gasp shuddered through her. *Good.* Let her feel some of his wretched horror.

Her shoulders rose, and her eyes sparked. "Yes, I thought of you. So much so I made a covenant with my heart to stop cutting you with its jagged, damaged pieces." She spat the words, her voice growing louder, her eyes watering. "Don't you see how wrong I am? I'm a kidnapper. A murderer. A fucking monster."

"I see all of you." He wrapped his arms around her and pressed his lips to her temple. "I claim every jagged piece of you."

She shoved at his chest, tears escaping, screaming, "I freed you. For you."

His feet dug in, his arms caging her against the door. He put his face in hers and stared directly into her eyes. "And I will free you. From you."

Her eyes fluttered closed for a moment. She seemed to be struggling to hold her composure in place. Then a heartbreaking sound keened in her throat. She grabbed him, clinging, her arms twining around his neck, her thighs climbing his body.

He hoisted her backside and wrapped her legs around his waist. His heart fractured and bled out, but as he held tightly to her trembling body, his fortitude strengthened and beat anew.

With her face against his neck, her rushed breaths stroked his skin. “Staying alive is the most selfish thing I’ve done. Every day I live risks them.” She gestured behind her. “And you. Mom. Mattie.”

“Yet you rise out of the storm, faultless and upright.” He gripped her chin, angled it until he won her eyes. “With every delivery, you release another captive. Then you return to your cell to begin the cycle again. The buyers exist with or without you. You lure them out and stop them from preying elsewhere.”

She peered up at him, lips parted, her body going soft in his arms.

He kissed her lips, treasured the salty tears there, and rested his forehead against hers. “Let the one who has never sinned throw the first stone. You were the first slave. The one who has never been freed.” He cupped her beautiful, tear-stained face, and traced the scar with his thumb. “Don’t give up. On me. On us.”

The hammer of her heart against his chest slowed with her breaths. She hugged him tighter, nodded. “Thank you for coming. For shooting that man.” She trailed a finger over his lips, watching the movement. “You saved me.” She glanced up. “You can mark that off your to-do list.”

She still needed saving, as did her family.

Camila strode toward them and held out Liv’s handgun. He snatched it before Liv could and set it inside the glove box, along with Mom’s PT-22.

Camila’s face creased with concern. “You won’t come home with us, will you?”

The others talked amongst themselves in the

background.

"She sure as hell ain't going to kill herself."

"Fuck no. But she can't go back to that house."

"He's right. We need her. Our lives, this whole operation, is fucking pointless if she's dead."

Liv untangled her body from his, wiped her cheeks, and shook her head. "I have to go back."

Using the wet rag Camila held out for him, he wiped Liv's face, neck, and arms, removing the remnants of blood. The others hovered around the sedan, grumbling, dismantling the cell phones, and pocketing the cash and other valuables that had belonged to the dead men.

Questions piled up in his aching head about the dangers of this operation. "What do you do with bodies and evidence?" He tossed the rag back to Camila.

"I'll explain on the way back." Liv grabbed a t-shirt from the passenger seat and pulled it on. "We need to go."

"What do we do with the Honda?" He handed her a pair of jeans.

"Where is it?"

"About a quarter-mile back." He pointed down the road. "Keys are in the ignition."

"It's yours," Liv said to Camila as she dressed. "I was supposed to get rid of it anyway."

With the bodies stuffed in the sedan and the road cleared of blood, they said their good-byes. The guys hugged Liv a bit longer than he thought was needed, but there was no talk of future contact. Everyone knew the stakes, and no one had a solution.

Kate lifted a hand to him and gave a small smile. Her demeanor seemed to already be transforming, her chin lifting higher, her shoulders relaxing. She would be fine. Probably better than fine with that fierce pack of protectors.

"I'm driving." Liv climbed in the van, her gaze lingering on her friends.

Some of them slid into the buyer's sedan. The others faded into the woods. Her expression was wistful as she watched them leave, her fingers curling around the wheel.

"You'll see them again." He would make sure of it. "Under better circumstances." He hoped.

As he moved her extra clothes from the passenger seat to the floor, his hand brushed a folded piece of paper. He held onto it.

The van crunched along the gravel road, the same path he'd taken by foot in his race to catch up with her. At the time, he'd had Mom's pistol out and ready with no intention of using it. But when he saw that gun aim at Liv, it was a terrible ache, a flashing of his own life, a loss of breath. There was no falter in pulling his trigger. No guilt. She was alive.

He put on his seat belt and unfolded the paper in his hand.

"Don't read that." She stared straight ahead, navigating the winding road, her expression lost in the darkness.

When he flicked on the ceiling lamp, she tried to grab the paper from his hand. He caught her wrist, pinned it to her thigh, and held up a letter that was addressed to Van.

Van,

The reasons that chained me here were my reasons to go.
I've never asked you for anything. I'm asking now.
Keep them safe.
Liv

Every mournful word stabbed Josh in the gut. As he read to himself, Liv stared straight ahead, her jaw locked in unapologetic stubbornness. He folded up the note, turned off the light, and spoke as calmly as he could. "You were going to do this at the house?"

"Where he'd find me." Liv's whisper was cautious.

He let that sink in. Would he have done the same to save his parents, damning himself to hell?

Maybe. He didn't know, couldn't wrap his mind around it.

His throat burned as he freed the heartache piling up there.

"I would've missed your smile, how it lifts your eyes and rounds your cheeks. And your voice. God, Liv, your voice is so mystical and arousing. I've never experienced anything like it." He pinched the note between his fingers, loathing its purpose, feeling its strength. "I would've missed your kiss, that incomparable connection when your lips brush mine. But most of all, I would've missed our future together, the one you would've taken from us." He turned in the seat to face her. "You said you freed me, but freedom isn't defined by chains or walls. You, alive, with me. That's my freedom."

Her profile nodded in jerky movements, and her hand reached out for his.

He caught it and entwined their fingers. "I need a promise, Liv. A promise to survive."

She glanced at him, swiped at her cheek, and steered onto the main road. "Wish I could say that if I went back to the day I first saw you, that I would've looked the other way." Her hand tightened in his. "I can't. I found my redeemer, and I know where you'll still be in the end. I won't give up. I promise."

Damn, those words felt good. He traced her knuckles with his thumb and settled into a comfortable silence until a hundred and ten questions penetrated his solace. "How did it start with Camila?"

"She has associations with a cartel. Not family relations. It's some kind of business connection. I don't know the details. She was doing side jobs for them before Van took her. When I killed her buyer, she drove away with his body, saying she knew people." She let go of his hand and raked her hair from her face. "I was so damned scared, unsure if I could trust her. She went back to work for her connections, and now they help her dispose of the bodies, cars, weapons. I don't know. I only talk to her on delivery days, and our interactions are as brief as you saw tonight."

His heart raced, his mind spinning. "Has she

looked for your mom and daughter?"

With her connections, Camila should've been able to trace Liv's mom at the very least.

"She's tried. I don't know my daughter's real name and there are no Jill Reeds that match Mom's description."

He drummed his fingers on his knee, gathering his thoughts. "Did you plan to kill Camila's buyer?"

She nodded. "Camila didn't know. I think she thought I was going to kill her, too."

No doubt. Liv was the fiercest woman he'd ever met. "How does Mr. E not know about this? With every buyer disappearing after his purchase, someone would notice."

She stretched her legs and reclined behind the wheel, eyes flicking to the side mirror. "The buyers are supposed to disappear. They crawl out of whatever hole they come from, make the transaction, and return to their holes. Which happen to be in shady places south of the border. They're all from Mexico."

That part made sense. Traquero had the accent.

Josh shuddered, knowing the fat freak was walking the streets then going home to torture his wife. "What about the referral system? They're all connected."

"Wrong. Camila is the connection. When she drove away with the body of her buyer, she also had his phone. And the contact number for his referral. She used it to create a network, initially on her own and now with the help of the guys. They sell referrals to potential buyers." She took a breath, bit her lip, and glanced at him.

Yeah, he was listening, shocked speechless, his head pounding.

"They lure would-be slave owners," she said,

"often acting as previous buyers, collect the contact number, and sell it to the next client in line. The buyers aren't connected to each other. They're connected to Camila." She barked out a laugh, rubbed her eyes, and sighed. "Camila actually charges each fucker for the referral number of the next fucker. Then he sits back and waits for Van's call. A year later, she's emptying his pockets and disposing his body."

Jesus. He scrubbed a hand over his mouth. Fields of black whipped by the window, passing him by, leaving him reeling in another dimension. "What is Mr. E's role in this?"

Her gaze ping-ponged between the side mirror and the road. "He started this horrific operation. I think he owned slaves before he brought in Van and me. I mean, he taught Van how to train slaves. Why would he know that?" She tugged at her ear, her expression pensive in the passing headlights. "Now he just sits on his greedy ass and collects money while Van and I scramble beneath his blackmailing thumb."

Nausea rolled through his gut. What would've happened if he'd been the obedient slave she'd intended him to be? His own delivery would've played out. Traquero would've been gutted. Then what?

"I'm not like the others." His chest tightened. "My parents are searching for me. I would've wanted to go back."

She flinched. "I know. I chose you anyway, without a clue on how to deal with the aftermath."

The whole operation was risky. So damned risky. One misstep, one slipped word from the buyer to Mr. E, and the whole thing would fall apart with Liv at the center. Yet they'd pulled it off six times.

"Where does Mr. E think these referrals come from?" he asked.

"Why would he care as long as he has his next paycheck lined up? Van makes the initial call, gathers the buyer's requirements, and establishes Mr. E's rules on anonymity. Mr. E never deals with any of them."

"It takes months to hunt and capture a new slave? Ten weeks to train him? And you're doing this, knowing the slave will never see the inside of a buyer's prison?"

"Hoping." Her voice wavered. "Never knowing. Van was banned to tag along after Camila's intro meeting. That ban could've been lifted. Or I could've been overpowered during a delivery. Or my freedom fighters could've been delayed…like tonight." She peeked at him from the corner of her eye.

"Freedom fighters." His lips twitched. "I like that."

"I've been thinking." She glanced at him and back to the road. "Van knows who Mr. E is. What if he also knows where my family is? Maybe we could tie him up and torture him until he tells us everything he knows? We'd keep him alive so the contract isn't triggered."

Wow, that was the thinnest idea he'd ever heard. "You're serious?"

She shrugged. "I've got muscle now." She gave his arm a pointed once-over. "What would Jesus do if he was built like you?"

"Cast the first stone?" Honestly, he didn't know. "What if Van doesn't know anything?"

"Then we're fucked either way."

For the next two hours, she answered his questions about Camila's operation, and he still wasn't sure he understood all the intricacies of the process. When she turned into the *Two Trails Crossing* subdivision, she stopped the van a block from the house. "Meet me on the front porch. He's not due back for a few days, but we're running out of luck. If he's there, I'll find a way to sneak you in." She left him on the curb with a heart-pounding kiss and trust in her eyes.

The walk was quick, but the wait on the porch dragged ten minutes too long. Drapes blacked out the windows. There was no light peeking through the creases. No sounds coming from within. What if Van was in there? Hurting her? His nerves stretched by the second until he finally snapped.

Down the driveway, past the garage, he stopped at the back door, found the keypad, and punched in 0054. She'd said all the doors but hers opened with multiple codes. Van and Mr. E had their own.

The door opened into the kitchen, lit by the lamp over the sink. Soft sobs crept from behind the bar and tore through his chest.

He sprinted around the counter and found her curled up on the floor, clutching a photo and a newspaper clipping. "Liv? Liv, what happened?" His pulse roared in his ears. "Are we alone?"

She nodded, expression pallid, voice empty. "Mr. E was here." When he jerked back, she grabbed his t-shirt, her face twisted in horror. "Oh God, Josh. It's…it's…" Her gaze was lost to the papers shaking violently in her hand.

Stomach plummeting, he pulled her into his lap and wrenched the pages free. The photo showed a small smiling girl, her dark brown hair the color and length of Liv's. Same milky complexion. Same delicate chin. The date and time printed on the bottom indicated it was six hours old. On the back, neat cursive scrawled, *Do not fail again.*

Liv coiled her arms around his ribs, her body trembling. "Mom got married." Her voice was hoarse, desolate. "That's why I couldn't find her."

He kissed her head, his lips numb with dread, and dragged his eyes to the news article printed by the *Key West Examiner,* dated today.

Local woman killed in plane crash

The pilot killed in a plane crash near Key West is being described as a skydiving adventurer and a generous volunteer in the community.

"It's devastating," said Wyatt Keleen, husband and co-owner of her skydiving school. "Jill was a warm-hearted woman and well-known in the Keys for her charitable efforts with families of homicide victims and missing persons."

Keleen said Jill's only child was kidnapped and murdered seven years earlier.

Jill's body was discovered off the coast of Lois Key in a swampy area. The wide cavity surrounding the wreckage indicates her life came to an end after a high-speed impact.

The Transportation Safety Board is investigating the crash. Officials have yet to confirm the cause. Memorial services were held today at 2:00 PM at Summerland Key Cove Airport.

Liv lay on her side on the mattress, showered, fed, and *depleted*. Josh had kept her talking through the night, prompting her to share memories of Mom and preventing her from crawling inside herself. Eyes itchy and sore, she'd cried more than she had in seven years. If she didn't stop, she would find herself ass-up in the prison of her own self-pity.

Mom had survived Liv's death. She could survive Mom's. And she would. With Josh's hand in hers.

He'd run their dirty soup bowls downstairs two minutes earlier. Her fingers were clenched so tightly in the sheets, one would've thought he'd been gone for hours. Her lungs didn't seem to suck enough air, her focus blurring on the door, awaiting his return. When had she become so fucking needy?

The angel in the photo she'd tacked to the wall smiled down at her with eyes and hair as dark as hers. So much better than a video. She had a snapshot of her daughter's face, forever looking back at her. Perhaps Mr. E gave it to her to cushion the murder of Mom. Or to lessen his own regret. But she knew that was bullshit.

She'd failed to nail the deal with Traquero, which earned her Mom's death. But he'd still given the referral, which earned her Mattie's photo. His motivation for not sending a video had to do with the fact he didn't trust her with access to e-mail without Van present.

That thought awoke an unwelcome feeling about Van's departure. It wasn't odd for him to hunt immediately upon receipt of a buyer's specifications. But given his enraged reaction to the meeting with Traquero, why hadn't he waited for her return and the opportunity to punish her?

What if Van had left to kill Mom himself? Was he cruel enough to not only let it happen but *make* it happen? Despite his violent nature, she struggled to believe he was the hand that brought down Mom's plane, but how well did she really know him?

She and Josh had discussed going to the FBI to request an investigation into the plane crash. Hell, they wanted to divulge everything. How closely was Mr. E monitoring them? How easy was his access to Mattie? Could the authorities hunt down a masked man before that man hurt her daughter? It was too much risk.

The door clicked open, and Josh's broad frame brimmed her horizon. Relief whooshed from her lungs. He tilted his head to the side, and his alert eyes narrowed on her fists. She uncurled her fingers.

A muscle jumped in his bare chest. "You still think I'm going to leave you?"

She shook her head swiftly. No, the stubborn bastard wasn't going anywhere.

"I think I'm just feeling a little raw." And exposed. Definitely not a feeling she was used to.

The sharp lines in his face softened. He closed the door and strode toward her, the towel around his waist hung low beneath crowded bricks of abdominal muscles.

He bent over her and planted his fists beside her hip, the mattress depressing beneath the weight of his vascular arms and upper body. Jesus, his proximity was distracting to a fault. It wasn't just the cuts of his body, crystalline green eyes, and strong lips that demanded attention. His pursuit to please her was a perceptible aura that charged the space around him.

Looking up into the face of a man who would damn himself to protect her, she knew she'd found her sanctuary, her deliverance, her future.

He swooped in to kiss her, and she got a lungful of his nourishing scent. Clean, pure Josh. She kissed him back, licking his mouth, tasting the familiar intimacy, and clinging to his love.

His tongue trailed fire around hers, leaving no part of her mouth untouched. It was impossible to be afraid when he was so close, so intense, that the barriers between them burned away. He moaned against her lips and kissed her with a pressing necessity, stoking a flame in her belly and coaxing a curl of something she hadn't felt in years. *Joy.*

Guilt breathed through her, a foul-smelling intruder, whispering her failings. Seven years of slavery, chained by a threat, and she still lost Mom.

Her lips stretched back. Their teeth tapped. She turned her chin away, but he caught it. Then he caught her eyes.

Fingers pinching her jaw, his expression swam in contemplation. He stared at her, panting from the kiss. "What would your mom say to you right now?"

A quiver interrupted the rigid set of her chin, her lungs pumping to hold in a thousand clogged tears. She closed her eyes and saw Mom laughing, jumping into the wind, her hair whipping around her smiling face. "She'd say, use a condom."

He huffed. "I think your mom was much more profound than that. Try again."

She opened her eyes, diving straight into his. "She used to say, what defines us is not how we fall but how we land."

He leaned in and stroked his nose along her scar. "You've survived the hardest landings. You'll survive this one."

Was that what she'd been doing all these years? Landing? "Feels more like plummeting out of control."

Every harrowing moment was chained to the next one. What if the cycle was finally broken? If she could find Mattie, then what? She'd never considered a future outside of the attic walls.

Until Josh.

He stood and adjusted the towel at his hip, watching her. "You're hurting, Liv. I want you to give it to me. All of your hurt."

Her eyebrows snapped together, her chest pinching. "What?"

He studied her, rubbing his jaw, gears spinning behind his eyes. Then he turned and paced to the cabinet. The round brawn of his ass flexed beneath the towel. The muscles in his back compressed and expanded as he worked the combo lock. Clearly, he'd figured out all her lock codes were the same. He opened the door. What the hell was he doing?

With a length of chain and a flogger in hand, he returned to the mattress. "You feel like you're plummeting? Like you don't have any control? Then control me." He grabbed her wrist and put the implements in her hand. "Do this on our terms. Not Traquero's or Mr. E's or anyone else's."

She glanced at the flogger and chain then searched his hopeful eyes for a long moment. He wasn't just new to sexual submission. He was new to sex. He might not have consciously known what he was asking, but it was a request voiced from a sequestered part of his identity, one she'd seen rise to the surface with the first cut of her cane. Of course, he wanted her to fuck him. But he also wanted her to hurt him. His hard powerful body seemed to crave the rough handling, being pushed to its limits.

Letting the chain spill into her lap, she slapped the leather tips of the flogger against her palm.

He didn't flinch, his eyes hooded and penetrating as he crouched before her. The towel separated at his thigh, the downward angle of his legs hiding what was between.

"You want to explore your naughty side, Josh?"

His chin tilting slightly, his cheeks sucking in with a steady inhale, he traced a knuckle over her nipple where it tightened against her t-shirt. His eyes didn't waver from hers, a luminescent glow beneath the determined mantle of his dark eyebrows. "I want to explore everything with you."

The idea sent a tremor through her, fanning a needy blaze between her legs.

It was around three in the morning, but they were both too restless to sleep. They had nothing but time on their hands until Van returned. She could either spend the days wallowing in misery or…

She let her gaze take a leisurely stroll over the messy spikes of black hair raking away from his forehead, the stubble roughing his jaw, the vein pulsing in his thick neck, and the taut skin stretching over bulges of shoulders and biceps. His cock jerked beneath the towel as he watched her devour every gorgeous detail.

Fuck, he was a lot of man. Chiseled, powerful, perceptive, and his attention remained resolutely fixed on her. She gathered the chain and rose to stand beside him. He'd said she needed control, but he'd initiated this, and he held the power to end it. The moment he said *no* she would stop.

There were a few things she could regulate, however, and she would use her mastery of dominance to help him find his boundaries. Her ratty, thigh-length t-shirt didn't exactly exude an authoritative air, but she didn't need a costume or mask. Not with him.

"You want me to have control? I'm taking it. Now." A stillness swept over her, measuring her breaths, loosening her shoulders. "I decide the how, the intensity, the purpose, all for my pleasure."

The depressions outlining his shoulder blades twitched. His hands flattened on the mattress. "Yes, Mistress."

The appellation was shockingly arousing, fluttering through her belly with nipping tingles. The title had never stirred a response in her. But now, it was given willingly, on his terms. For her and no one else.

At the center of the room, she connected the chain to the latch in the ceiling. "Stand here with your back to me."

She didn't wait for him to obey. She returned the flogger to the cabinet and gathered a pair of cuffs and three things he would've never chosen.

He stood where she'd directed, arms crossed above his head. The vertical indentation down the length of his back led erotically to the rise of his firm ass peeking above the towel. His torso, wide on top, narrowed to a slim waist, its appeal punctuated with two dimples where his back met his hips. The sight alone rolled the heat between her legs into a pulsating clench.

She wanted to just stand there, relish the burgeoning rise of desire, and stare at him. So she did, taking in the carved angles of his body. The backs of his ears twitched, probably from a flexing jaw. Oh, she knew he was squirming with impatience, but he remained where she'd told him with his back to her. Still and silent, awaiting her next order.

After another long, taunting moment, she crossed the distance and stood behind him. Not touching but close enough to let him feel the heat of her body. "Are you hard?"

"Yes, Mistress." A rasp.

Her heart thumped. It didn't matter how rare his innocence was, how fast he ran a football, or how respectable he behaved among his parishioners. It was the sexy, honest pain slut under it all that enthralled her now.

She placed the toys on the floor and strapped the cuffs on his wrists. Once his arms were restrained to the dangling chains, she grabbed the blindfold from the pile. "I'm going to open your eyes."

She tied it around his head and smiled, certain his imagination was running rampant. What kind of dirty thoughts were spinning through his mind?

A tremble skated down his back. She chased it with a fingertip, sliding through beads of sweat, memorizing each dip and peak of muscle. "You won't come without permission."

He tensed, relaxed. "Yes, Mistress."

Feeling his skin creep beneath her touch and controlling him with just her voice and the pad of her finger was intoxicating. She ran her hands down his sides, caught the towel, and dropped it to the floor. Circling him, she trailed her fingers over his warm flesh, touching him everywhere. Everywhere except the very swollen erection jutting from between his legs. She caressed his thighs, the indentions in his hips and abs, savoring his shallow gasps.

She returned to the items on the floor and raised the rattan cane, the most advanced tool in her cabinet. It took her years to learn how to use it without splitting the skin and leaving a scar.

It whistled through the air as she swung it back.

Thwack.

The single strike of the cane's rigid width formed two side-by-side welts on his ass with a narrow depression of skin in between. The nerve endings in that depression would be stinging like a son-of-a-bitch.

He drew gulps of air, his fingers curling around the chain above him. He was likely feeling a fire of pain spreading outward from the impact site, blazing through his legs and back.

She whacked him again, an inch above the first marks. He breathed, clutched the chain tighter. Three more thwacks. Ten red lines striped his ass. His head dropped forward, his body shivering.

Shit, did he not know he could end this at anytime? What was the protocol for consensual beatings?

"Tell me *no,* and we're done." She rubbed her eyes, nauseous with guilt. She should've talked this out with him before they started.

He stood taller, raised his chin. "Don't stop." His voice was thick with arousal.

She walked around him to see his face. The blindfold hid his eyes, but his lips were parted, his jaw slack. Between his legs was the hardest, longest cock she'd ever seen. She squeezed her thighs together and returned to his backside.

Pacing back and forth, she varied the cane strokes between hard and soft so that he wouldn't know what to expect. "What does a future with you look like, Joshua Carter?"

Thwack.

"A lot of prayers." His ass flexed.

Thwack.

"Bible study three times a day."

Thwack.

He lifted up on his toes, his voice hoarse. "No smoking and cussing."

Very funny. *Thwack.*

"Missionary position only."

A laugh burst from her throat, and she stumbled, her swing missing him completely.

"No sex until we're married," he said.

Oh my God. Did he really just mimic her practiced deadpanned tone?

She moved to stand in front of him, so she could watch his mouth. "You're going to hell."

His lips twitched then erupted into a full-faced smile. "Oh, good. I was worried you'd be there without me."

Her heart swelled, tightening her chest. Fuck her, but she loved this man.

Dropping to her knees, she set the cane on the floor

and lowered her lips to the tip of his erection. A gentle kiss pulled a moan from his lungs and a bead of pre-cum from his cock.

She grinned. "No coming without permission."

His head fell back on his shoulders, his thighs quivering. "You're going to kill me."

"Over and over again."

Gripping the root of his cock, she drew him into her mouth, the velvety skin burning against her tongue. She sucked him greedily, drinking in the flavor of salt and man. She ran a hand over his contracting muscles, squeezing the back of his thigh, careful to avoid the welts. The throb in her pussy intensified, releasing moisture along her inner thighs.

When his hips started rocking, she didn't scold him. His movements were confident, needy, stubborn in his desire to please her. Exactly how she wanted him. She ran her teeth along his cock and twisted her fist in time with the long consistent pulls of her mouth.

His breathing strangled, and his thrusts ceased. He was holding back his release. She was mesmerized. And trembling with desire.

She tormented him with a few more dragging suckles along his length and breathed around him, "Come."

Taking him over with a one word command was the ultimate high, exceeded only by his willingness to give her this. He groaned as he came, filling her throat, the steel of his cock jerking against her tongue, his body shaking violently. She licked him clean, humming, smiling, so damned pleased.

She rose and stepped behind him as he slumped in his restraints, catching his breath. She didn't give him time to catch it for long. Shedding the t-shirt, she grabbed the last item on the floor, stepped into it, and cinched the straps around her waist and thighs. Next came the lube, on her fingers and the attached dildo.

She'd never enjoyed the strap-on with the boys she'd trained, which was why she'd chosen to do it now. This was Josh, and it was on their terms.

Her body thrummed as she pressed against his back and prodded his crack with the dildo.

"What are you doing?" There was no hint of alarm in his voice, only curiosity. Evidently, the butt plug had chased away his fears.

"I'm going to fuck your ass." She kissed his shoulder, her pussy slick and pulsing. "Tell me *no*."

He pushed against the strap-on. "I'm yours, Liv. Inside and out."

She didn't have to see his eyes to know what was behind them. He was once a captive in her attic. Now she was the one held captive, enraptured by his unwavering trust.

She took great care stretching his tight ring with her lubricated fingers, stroking and circling the opening. She nipped at his back, and finger by finger, he loosened around her intrusion. His feet stepped farther apart, his body settling into complete submission.

Pressing the tip of the dildo against his rectum, she reached around his hips and gripped the stone-hard girth of his cock. She smiled against his back. "You're an incredible man."

"I'm a lucky man." He panted and rocked against her, helping her work in the first inch. His voice choked. "When you're done having your way with me, I get to return the pleasure." He bucked backward. "Now quit talking and work those hips."

She half-gasped, half-laughed, and smacked his thigh. With a few strokes up and down his erection, she teased him into a trembling frenzy. Then she thrust and held still, her pelvis flat against his ass, allowing him to adjust to the pressure.

His sigh filled the room. That was her cue. She did work her hips, driving into him, her fist jerking his cock, her other hand roaming his chest, his abs, his balls. The leather strap behind the dildo ground against her clit, building her into a panting mess.

Maybe she hadn't reached his limit, but after a few minutes, she'd reached hers. She pulled out, untied his blindfold, and released the chain on his wrist cuffs. As she washed her hands in the sink and stepped out of the strap-on belt, she felt his eyes searing every inch of her skin. But he remained where she'd left him, waiting, watching.

"Where did this obedience come from?" She dried her hands and turned to face him.

He tapped his fingers on his chest, directly over his heart, a fire flickering in his eyes.

She nodded, her throat swelling. "I relinquish control." Not that she'd ever fully had it.

In four swift strides, he was on her, lifting her, and slamming her back against the nearest wall. His hand pushed between their hips, gripping his cock, and aligning their bodies.

He drove hard and true in one long stroke. They groaned in unison. She hooked her legs around his waist, her arms around his neck, and let him pound her against the wall. He moved in urgent thrusts, his lips finding hers. She felt the joining in every part of her body.

The wet slapping sounds of their lovemaking echoed around them, their bodies moving together as one. Guttural breaths. Heated moans. His muscles bunched around her, supporting her, his hips hammering to the tune of her heart.

The hands on her ass clenched, fingertips digging in. Their tongues swiped and slashed and curled together. Her release was climbing hard and fast. Her toes flexed. Her arms around his shoulders wobbled. Her desire knotted, double knotted, and tightened.

"Josh," she gasped into his mouth.

He released her lips, worked his hips, and cupped her jaw, staring into her eyes with an intensity that pushed her over.

The sensations lifted her up, up, up, and burst outward. The ecstasy of stimulation softened her bones, melted her body, and robbed her breathes. He continued to thrust, her pussy convulsing around him, her skin tingling.

Grinding his pelvis against her, his hands squeezed her ass and his smoldering gaze collided with hers. "That was so damned beautiful."

Then he took her mouth again, gently, letting her feel his words. She kissed him with the same tender tempo, rotating her hips against him, ratcheting his already labored exhales.

A moment later, he dropped his head on the wall beside hers and thrust once, twice. A long groan vibrated his body. His arms coiled around her waist, tightening. His muscles quivered, and his cock jerked deep inside her.

The hum of contentment whispered through them. At last, she was exhausted enough to sleep, and it would be a restful sleep with him wrapped around her in a blanket of protection and love.

They showered, she treated his welts, and they lay between the sheets, chest to chest, sharing breaths. Their legs entwined, and his toes caressed her ankle. She felt him with her entire body, every nerve ending reaching for him.

Through the absence of light, she found his eyes. "You freed me."

His fingers stroked down her back and rested in the crack of her butt. "Then we'll tackle the next few days knowing we're already free."

The strong beat of his heart against her breast filled her with hope, something she'd never depended on until that moment. "We need to find Mattie."

"We will."

She drifted to sleep with a heart full of trust in those two words.

CHAPTER 38

Liv woke however many hours later, sweating, panting, her mind fluttering with erotic images of Josh. Face down on the mattress, her breaths steamed against the pillow. Her pussy was a furnace of wet heat, throbbing with its own demanding heartbeat. And sliding along its slit was a strong and skillful tongue.

The bathroom light cast a subdued luster through the room. She glanced over her shoulder and met Josh's sparkling eyes peering above her ass cheeks.

With his hands under her hips and his body stretched out between her legs, his gaze burned into hers. He lifted her pelvis, rocking her against his mouth and kissing her pussy with a single-minded ferociousness. He glided his lips through her folds, sucking, curling his tongue, his hips grinding on the mattress.

His groan hummed through her core as he pushed her thighs farther apart and deepened the kiss. His intensity was contagious, shuddering over her spine and coiling her body inside and out.

Her climax exploded, wrenching a moan from her lungs and rolling her eyes into the back of her head. He licked her through the sweep of sensations, thrusting a finger inside her, his breathy noises magnifying the ecstasy.

Then he bit her ass. She shrieked, and he laughed, dragging his lips over her back, nipping and pecking as he crawled toward her head. She buried her face in the pillow. Apparently, his libido was making up for lost time.

She sighed, smiling, her voice muffled in cotton. "You're such a horny slut."

Chuckling, his mouth reached her nape, sucking the skin below her ear. He covered her body with his hot leaden weight, his thighs bracketing hers. His palms slid beneath her chest, massaging and cupping her breasts. Oh God, the sensation of his touch combined with his body pressing down on her was indescribable.

His cock prodded, wedging into the tight space between her thighs. He reached between them, guiding the connection, and thrust. She clutched at the pillow, arching her back and pushing against him to deepen the drugging stimulation.

The position and angle of her legs pressed together limited his thrusts to short, shallow fucks. She couldn't get close enough and bowed her body into his. She wanted him to fuck harder, though he was hammering his hips, his cock filling her with each forceful drive.

He was inside her, his body enveloping her and shaking violently with need, yet she wanted more. Couldn't get enough of him. Her heart pounded against the mattress, and her ribs felt bruised inside. Needy and crazed, she twisted her neck, seeking his mouth. He met her tongue and responded with the same urgency, feeding her his desire, swallowing her exhales.

His toes curled against hers, his powerful body rubbing along the length of her smaller one. One hand shifted beneath her hip, his trembling fingers fumbling around her clit. He found it, circled through her wetness, and flicked it with precision. *Right there. Oh fuck, right there.*

"Come," she breathed against his lips. "Come with me."

He rotated his hips, rubbed her clit, and ate at her mouth until they stiffened, gasped, and fell together.

When they caught their breaths, he leaned in and nibbled on her earlobe. "Morning."

"Morning."

An hour later, they realized it was, in fact, afternoon. They stood at the keypad, showered, dressed, and stared at the digital *3:18 PM* on her phone. Despite their shared smiles, unease buzzed between them. Their bodies needed to be fed, so they were forced to leave the room.

She stuffed her phone in the back pocket of her jeans and clutched the door handle. "Let me go down first. I'll make sure he's not back and return to get you."

He reached around her and punched in the code. "We went through this last night. You're not going down there, or anywhere, without me."

The door clicked open. She flashed him her most threatening glare. "Then stay behind me and out of sight."

Through the vacant outer chamber, another keypad, and down the dark stairway they went. Silence greeted her at the bottom. Daylight leaked in through the kitchen window, spreading a sparse glow into the hallway.

She reached back, placed a hand on his chest, and gave him a silent command with her eyes. *Stay.*

In the kitchen, dirty soup bowls filled the sink. The refrigerator hummed. Outside the window, the trees rustled beneath the afternoon sun. With a stuttering heart beat, she opened the door to the garage. The van sat alone. She held her breath as she checked the driveway and the front curb through the windows. Van's sedan wasn't there, and he had no reason to hide his car from her. Her edginess loosened, but remnants of uncertainty remained.

Returning to the stairway, she found Josh gripping the door frame, his impatient eyes blazing from within the shadows.

She touched his abs and met a wall of rock-hard tension. "He's not here. Follow me."

Leading him down the hallway, a familiar dread gripped her gut. She needed to check Van's room of horrors, if only to ease some of her lingering anxiety about Van being there. But she didn't want to go in that room alone.

Hand on the knob, she inhaled deeply. "This is his room. As you know, he is…" How did one sum up morally, mentally, aesthetically, and theoretically damaged? "Fucked up."

Impatience vibrated from Josh. "Open the door, Liv."

She did. And gasped. Stumbling through the room, she spun in a circle, hand over her mouth. An empty mattress. An empty gun cabinet. The drawers hung from the dresser. Empty. The closet door stood open. Empty. No mannequins. No clothes. There was nothing but worn carpet and the musty reek of vacancy.

"He's gone." Huge fucking alarm bells blared in her head. Her heart raced and senses heightened.

Why would he leave? Was it fear? Was all hell about to break loose?

Josh clasped her fingers, his forehead furrowed in thought. "Tell me what you're thinking."

She rubbed her head. "Van's a sadistic dick, but he wouldn't have left me if my life was in danger. Something prompted him to leave in a hurry, though."

Shards of glass littered the carpet in front of the gun cabinet. The door was a toothy frame hanging on its hinge.

Her stomach turned. "That's what he hit when I told him about Traquero." Had he been angry *for* her? Or *at* her? It shouldn't have mattered, but when it came to Van, her feelings gnarled and bled in complication. She thought back to the last conversation she had with him. "He said he was leaving in the morning to begin his scouting."

"Only, he left before we got back." Josh strode out of the room and into the spare bedroom.

A square of ratty green carpet buckled between the walls. The metal blinds on the single window hung lopsided and yellowed by age.

"This one has always been empty," she said. A room reserved for her, one she'd refused to move into.

He turned and walked down the hall, his gait quickening as he approached the kitchen. "He was pissed about what happened with Traquero. He must've packed immediately and blew out of town."

She ran to keep up with his longer strides. "Why? To kill my mom?" She flinched and clenched her fists against the stabbing reminder. "Or to protect himself from Mr. E?" *But why would he need to do that?* "Van's a lot of things, but he's not a coward."

Josh veered into the kitchen and opened the fridge door, scanning its contents. Of course, the linebacker was focused on his stomach. Her thoughts were on a crash site, somewhere off the coast of the Keys, and the man who might've caused it.

Josh tossed deli meat and cheese on the counter. Then they sat through a nerve-stretching meal. She picked at her sandwich, her stomach souring with each bite. He barked at her to eat when she sat still too long, his anxiety feeding on hers. They finished in silence, staring at the door to the garage as if it would open any moment and let in all the answers.

Thirty minutes later, they tackled the filing cabinet in the hall closet, the only place in the house that could've held a clue to Mr. E's identity. She'd dug through it countless times, but maybe she'd missed something amongst the bills, receipts for generic items purchased for the house, tax filings, and news articles.

"Who is Liv Smith?" Josh held up two hands full of paperwork.

"The fake identity Mr. E gave me."

"Everything is in that name. The rental agreement for the house. Liv Smith." He thumbed to the next one. "The titles to the vehicles. Liv Smith." His face twisted beneath clenched eyebrows, his voice rising. "The friggin' repair bill for the A/C unit. Liv Smith."

She looked up from her drawer. "I see that."

"You see that?" His cheeks burned red, and his eyes widened in a state of disbelief. He wiped his forehead with the back of his paper-filled hand. "Not a single document shows Van Quiso paying taxes, consuming groceries, or living here at all. Ever."

Her hackles rose in defense. "He told me to sign

stuff. It was legitimate stuff related to the house. I signed it with a fake name." But she didn't realize the name was on *everything*.

"What about the neighbors? Do they know him?"

"No. He comes and goes from the garage. Tinted windows. Just like Mr. E." She picked the edge of the paper in her hand and said, dejectedly, "I cut the grass."

He blew out a long exhale. "It's like he doesn't even exist." He returned the papers to their hanging folders, none too gently. "What does it mean, Liv?"

It meant Van was smarter than her. "He can disappear." And she couldn't. Not if she wanted to keep Mattie safe.

"Why would he do that?" He slammed the drawer.

She lifted her chin and collided with the sharp green of his eyes. "Mr. E could be planning to shut this down and kill us. Or Van could've decided on a career change after my fuck up and bolted." Without saying goodbye. Her heart squeezed. *Stupid asshole heart.*

Josh crouched beside her, shifted her hand from the thick file hanging in the drawer, and pulled it out. Her swallow clogged in her throat, along with her breath. How would he react to the news clippings about his disappearance?

Kneeling, he leafed through each one, his face paling, his brow furrowing. She'd skimmed through all of them. Seemed Van had added more in his paranoia about Josh's notoriety. The file was filled with reports about the dead-end investigation, Baylor University's on-going support, search parties, and walk-a-thon's to raise money and awareness. Her heart twisted as she imagined all the pain and resentment barreling through Josh.

Scooting closer, she straddled one of his knees and

wrapped her arms around his neck. He welcomed her with an embrace around her waist, holding her tight as he read.

When he finished the pile, he returned it to the drawer. "Where's yours?" His voice was quiet and strained.

She reached in the back of the drawer and handed him the thin dossier. "My disappearance didn't get the publicity yours did." She offered a smile, but it quivered at the corners.

With a kiss on the crook of her mouth, he opened the file. They read the first article in silence.

Body of missing Texas girl found in Del Valle

Officials in Texas say that remains found in an abandoned house this weekend are those of a 17-year-old girl who has been missing fourteen months.

Austin police confirmed Monday that the remains were burned beyond recognition. Police said that autopsy results indicated they belonged to Liv Reed. A 9mm shell casing and two unfired .38 caliber bullets were discovered at the crime scene.

Reed's mother, Jill, told KRPC-TV that roller blades were found in the house. Liv was wearing them when she disappeared from Fentress Airpark. Her class ring from Eastside Memorial High School was also recovered.

Austin Police Chief, Eli Eary, said it's believed that Reed was shot and killed in the abandoned Del Valle house, and her body was burned to destroy any evidence.

Her eyes blurred, unable to read further. An old ache clawed through her throat. Regret for Mom having suffered through her death and the terrible frustration for not being able to prove she still lived. And searing the edges of that ache was a harrowing sadness for the nameless victim who died in her place.

Josh stuffed the documents in the drawer, closed it, and shifted her legs to wrap around his waist. His lips stroked across her brow, his hands rubbing over her back. He held her as if he'd never let go. She held him the same way, arms tightening, fingers curling into flesh and muscle.

"There are no articles on the other captives." His tone was distant, somber.

A ragged inhale hitched through her. "There was no fanfare with their disappearances. Those who did miss them wouldn't have involved the police. Kate's brothers are criminals. Camila was a gopher for the cartel. The others came from crack houses or no homes at all." She kissed his neck, inhaling his scent to chase away the toxicity of the conversation, and leaned back. "What now?"

He rose, lifting her with him and standing her on her feet. His jaw was hard, his eyes equally so. "Now, we wait for Mr. E to come looking for Van. Or for us. And when he does, we'll be ready."

Her pulse kicked up in approval. She wanted him to color his words and fill her mind with images. *His* images. "Ready to do what?"

"To trap him and beat the ever-loving crap out of him until he exposes Mattie's location. Then we'll slice his throat from ear to ear."

Hope spun around her, curling her lips. It continued to lift her through the night as he led her upstairs, fucked her, cuddled her, fed her, and fucked her again.

They remained in the safety of the attic for two days, waiting for Mr. E's text, closing the door only when they were sleeping, planning and exploring each other. The latter was a new experience with whips and ropes and creative sexual positions. She only egressed for food, and her sentinel was always an arm-length behind her. They never emerged unarmed. He carried his mom's .22 in his hand. She carried the LC9 in the waistband of her jeans.

On the third afternoon, she crept down the stairs and stopped. Her toes touched the bottom step, illuminated by a glow of light. Josh bumped into her back.

Her scalp tingled. The hairs on her arms stood on end. The kitchen light didn't reach the staircase.

Fuck, fuck, fuck. She stretched her neck to peer into the sitting room. The lamp drenched the dated decor in a sickening yellow wash. She never turned that damned lamp on.

Her heart thundered in her ears. Mr. E hadn't sent her a text. He always sent a text.

She spun and pressed a finger against his lips, shaking her head. His eyes narrowed, his body vibrated, and his stomach hardened to stone against her hand. She drew the 9mm from her waistband, flicked off the safety, and turned back. Choking on the thickening dread in her throat, she stepped into the hallway.

With a final glare at the silhouette of aggression vibrating in the staircase, she pointed a finger at him and strode toward the kitchen with the gun at her side.

She tripped in the doorway, her heart stumbling with her breath. A mannequin sat at the table, a naked woman with a head of hair, holding a doll. All the blood in her face dumped to her stomach.

She scanned the corners of the room for Van, unsure what to do with the gun. Raise it? Conceal it? Should she go for business as usual? She held it at her side. Where the fuck was he?

Her eardrums throbbed, straining for the sound of footsteps. She positioned herself so that she could see behind the bar, the entrance to the sitting room, and the mannequin at the table.

"Van?" She shouted loud enough to dissuade Josh from charging after her.

But what if it wasn't Van? What if this was one of Mr. E's games?

A few feet away, the brown marbled eyes of the plastic woman stared back at her. A painted red line connected one glass eye to the pink hand-drawn mouth. Propped on the mannequin's lap, the doll was the size of a small child, clothed in a red checkered dress.

Liv's scar tingled in her cheek, her muscles stiffening to the point of pain. Staring at the morbid reproductions of her and Mattie, she tried to keep the contents of her stomach from painting the floor.

Gut-twisting curiosity shuffled her feet forward. With the gun rattling in her hand, she slid her other hand through the sparse hair on the heads. Each strand was different from the other but also…the same. They varied in hues of brown, intricately combed together and sewn into some kind of mesh cap glued to the scalps. The fibers between her fingers weren't glossy like synthetic hair. They felt thinner, some damaged, realistic. *Familiar.*

She jerked her hand back, her stomach bubbling toward her throat. *Oh God.* Her hair. Why? Jesus, fuck, what did it mean? She pressed a fist against her belly, backed up, and slammed into a hard body.

A hint of cologne touched her nose. The width of torso was too big. She turned, but Van's arm around her chest caught her, pinning her back to his chest. His hand squeezed her breast, and she sucked in a breath. If she shot him, the contract on Mattie's life would be activated.

She pressed the side of the gun against her thigh to thwart the shaking in her hand.

His lips touched her shoulder, her neck, the scar, creeping goosebumps over her skin. "I know you don't approve of them, Liv. But I needed something to remember you by."

Chapter 39

"What are you doing with the gun, Liv?"

Van's voice was a low, strumming pulse in her ears. But there was an unraveling edge to it that scared the shit out of her. She drew in a breath and hoped to hell Josh stayed out of sight.

She trailed her fingertips over the back of his hand where he cupped her breast, to soothe him, to reestablish their fucked-up connection. "I thought you'd taken a permanent vacation."

He sank his teeth into the side of her throat, not enough to break skin, but the sharp pinch stole her breath and raised her on tip-toes. One shift of his hand and he could break her neck.

She leaned into the bite. "Did you come back to kill me?"

His arm and teeth released her with a jerk. She fell forward, righted herself, and spun with the gun raised in both hands.

Three days of stubble darkened his jaw. His steely eyes were void of their usual glint, sagging beneath his hood. His smirk seemed forced as he slid a toothpick in his mouth. "You're the one pointing a gun."

She aimed at his chest. His jacket concealed the

strength of his body, but she knew every muscle, every twitch, every scar. He'd taken her virginity, trained her as a sex slave, whipped her, fucked her, and loved her. She wasn't any different from him. With one exception. She responded to the word *no*.

The light in the doorway behind him rippled. She didn't shift her eyes, fearing it would give away Josh's presence.

To distract Van, she backed to the wall, until the length of the room separated them, and jerked her chin at the dolls. "Do they mean you won't be pulling my hair anymore?"

"I won't have a choice." He searched her face longingly, desperately, as if collecting every detail into a special pocket of memory made just for her.

I needed something to remember you by.

She shivered and steadied the gun. "Why did you come back?"

The heat in his eyes said, *To fuck you*. His suspicious non-answers said, *To kill you*.

"Just say it, Van."

If she shot him, Mattie was dead. If he killed her, Josh would kill him. Mattie was dead either way.

"I'm sorry about your mom." Sincerity wrinkled the skin around his eyes, but his voice was a monotone hum.

His lips clenched on the toothpick, flattening into a line. His gaze hardened.

He was planning something cruel.

Her molars sawed together, her nerves stretching. She bit down so hard on her cheek the taste of copper filled her mouth. "You murdered Mom."

His face clouded, his timbre scratchy. "I'm sorry.

I…" His expression blanked. He reached behind his back.

Jesus, he was going to kill her. Her heart stopped, and her finger slid over the trigger.

Time throttled into a series of choices, measured by the slam of her heart and the cascading motions that followed. Van tugged at something in the back of his jeans.

She squeezed the trigger, and Josh yelled, "No!"

The recoil reverberated down her arms, and Van stumbled sideways.

He slumped against the bar. A dark circle of blood spread on the shoulder of his black t-shirt. He frowned at the crumpled paper in his hand, and the toothpick fell from his slack mouth.

"Oh, God." Her voice was an echo in her fuzzy head.

She lowered the gun, blinked. He hadn't been reaching for a weapon.

He laughed, coughed. "I deserved that." His legs slid out from beneath him, and he toppled to the floor.

Josh skidded through the room, tucking his gun in his jeans, his panic jolting her to move. Numb with shock, she handed the gun to him and knelt beside Van.

A river of blood soaked his shirt, coursed down his arm, and pooled beneath him. He lay on his back and peered up at her with the most heart-breaking expression on his contorted, beautiful face. No hint of anger or blame. It was as if he knew he was dying, and he was okay with it.

She pushed his hood off his forehead and cupped his damp cheeks. "You killed my mom. I thought you were going to kill me."

He shook his head in the frame of her hands.

"Tried to save her." His chest heaved. "Drove...wasn't fast enough." He gripped her wrist and held her eyes, his nostrils flaring. "I was too late." His eyebrows clenched together, and his breaths rushed out as he squeezed his shoulders against the floor. "I'm sorry."

A low, agonizing hum vibrated her chest. He wouldn't lie about that, and the realization tore through her in a barrage of buckshot.

"Oh no, Van." Her chest convulsed, and a sob climbed her throat. She stroked his cheek, staring at the blood soaking his shirt. "Oh, God. What have I done?"

His eyes fluttered closed for a moment and snapped open, glassy with pain. "It's okay. There's no—" His spine arched, and he moaned. "No contract."

She gulped at the thinning air and pressed her hands to the bullet hole. "No contract? No hit man to collect on your death? Or Mr. E's?"

She glanced at Josh, his eyes wide and locked on Van.

"A bluff." The corner of Van's mouth wavered as if attempting a smile. Sweat trickled down his temples. His gaze landed on Josh, and his lips bowed downward.

A bluff. She knew Van's coercions intimately, and this wasn't one of them. He would never fuck around with Mattie's life. Tears rose up and burned trails down her cheeks. "If he doesn't hire hit men then who killed Mom?"

"He arranged it." His voice quaked. "His job—" His chest caved in, and his teeth snapped together in agony.

Warm streams of red pumped over her fingers. The steel in his eyes dulled, his complexion a pallor of white. He was losing too much blood. Josh disappeared behind the bar, banging things around in the cabinet.

The paper crinkled in Van's fist. "You love him?" His chest stilled as if he weren't breathing at all.

She didn't glance away as she nodded, slowly, confidently. If anyone understood the connection between captor and captive, he did.

He closed his eyes and released a slow, easy breath.

Josh returned with an armful of dish towels, pressed them against the wound, and lifted Van's shoulder to see beneath his body. Van hissed, his lips pulling away from clamped teeth, his eyes rounding in shocked pain.

"There's no exit wound." Josh lowered him to the floor and held the towels in place.

She caught Josh's eyes, and they shared a harrowing look. The bullet was still in there. She reached in her back pocket and handed him the phone. "The code to unlock it is 0054. Call 911."

"No cops," Van murmured. He raised the wadded paper in his hand. "He'll know."

She flattened the edges of the news clipping, watching at Van's shallowing breaths, and read the first sentence of the article.

Austin Police Chief, Eli Eary, stood at the podium during a recent celebration to honor his career…

"Mr. E." Van's voice jolted through her.

Her veins seized with shock, her body shivering. "Eli Eary? The police chief who handled my disappearance? *He's* Mr. E?"

Van nodded, his hand gripping her knee. "My

dad."

She choked, her throat thick with tears, panic sprinting through her blood. She gave the paper to Josh and wrapped her hand around Van's cold, sweaty one. Her thoughts wheeled violently around the axis that was her arrangement. "That's why he gave me to you, why he's so lenient with you."

It also explained why Mr. E hadn't punished him for his stunt at the intro meeting with Camila. He'd simply banned him from future meetings and deliveries.

Van's eyes flashed, his voice straining. "He turned me into…this." His lips curled into a weak snarl. "He killed your mother. I never—" He coughed and slapped a hand over Josh's, adding pressure to the towels. "My mom was one of his."

"One of his…" She searched his red-rimmed gaze and found a haunting, deeply rooted pain. "She was a slave?" She looked at Josh, seeking his reaction and perhaps his comfort.

Josh pressed one hand on the towels, the other settling on her back. His gaze formed a grim mirror of her own, creasing at the corners.

Was that why his mother fell into a life of drugs? Because she'd been a slave? Resentment engulfed Liv, shaking her limbs. Mr. E had ruined so many lives.

"I came back to kill him." Van panted. "Needed your help."

Across the room, the dolls waited at the table, his morbid things to remember her by.

Her lungs shuddered. "Then you were going to disappear. You were going to let me go." Guilt ravaged her insides, twisting and fraying.

"Have to kill him." His eyes glassed over, his gasps

weakening. "He'll avenge me." He choked. "He'll kill Livana."

"Livana?" The unfamiliar name hit her where she breathed. A name formed from… *Liv. Van.* "Mattie's real name is Livana?"

He closed his eyes, his nod so devastatingly subtle beneath his short, bucking exhales. She was losing him.

"Van? Where's Livana?"

"She's…" His eyes flickered open, unfocused, and confused. He reached for her face.

She leaned in to meet his hand, eyes blurry, heart collapsing. "Van." Her voice rasped, clogged. "What's Livana's last name?"

His clammy fingers fumbled over her scar, across her lips, and lingered on her chin. He opened his mouth and strangled on an incoherent noise that died in the air. His eyes drifted closed, and his hand dropped.

He's gone.

"Nooo." She scrambled atop him, fingers trembling over his bloodless face. "No, Van. No, don't go," she screamed.

Anguish took hold in a series of wails, raging in her throat, shaking her limbs. He'd tried to save Mom. He was a fucking victim of his own father's greed. Why had she thought he'd kill her? He never would've done that. He loved her.

Oh Jesus. Fuck. Fuck. Look what she did to him. "Oh, Van. I'm so sorry."

She couldn't take it back. The bullet. The blood. She clung to his limp body, weeping, nose running, her heart shredding.

Arms came around her chest and pulled her to her feet. She elbowed Josh, dropped to her knees, and hugged Van's waist.

Josh gave her a few more minutes to release a torrent of sobs. Then his arms were back, wrapping around her and dragging her up.

He half-walked, half-lifted her to the sink, dragging her blood-soaked hands with his under the water. "I know you're not thinking clearly, Liv, but we need to make a decision and act quickly."

She wept in breathless starts and stops, staring at the pink-tinted water spiraling down the drain.

With his body wrapped around her back, his hands slipped over hers, rubbing her arms and rinsing away the evidence. "We have two choices. One, we go to the cops. Mr. E is brought in for questioning. His corruption may be embedded amongst his peers or he may be working on his own."

"And Mat— Livana? If he were incarcerated, he could still kill her." Goddammit, she hurt. Her head. Her heart. This shit with Van shouldn't hurt this badly.

Josh tore off some paper towels and dried their hands and arms. "Two, we look up his address and stop him ourselves. By whatever means possible. Right now. Before he tries to call Van. It's the safest option for Livana."

Turning to face him, she gathered strength from his eyes and curled her hands around his neck. "Then it's the only option."

"Agreed." The resolution in his taut expression matched his voice. "Mr. E tracks both of your phones?" He pulled her phone from his pocket.

"Yeah. Leave it on the counter." She scrutinized their clothes for blood. Both in dark t-shirts, the smudges were inconspicuous. With a final glance at the blood-soaked body on the floor, she pressed a fist to her chest and blinked away the watery ache in her eyes.

"There's a handwritten Austin address on the back of the news article." He held it up. "Mr. E?"

She closed her eyes. "God love you, Van." And goddamn him. He wasn't making it easy to walk away on sturdy legs. She grabbed his car keys from the counter and headed toward the garage. "Van's phone stays here. Mr. E is in contact with him hourly."

Josh remained a breath behind her. "If his phone is here, Mr. E will know he's here. You're hoping he doesn't call?"

She punched the code in the keypad and grabbed two long scarves from the hook beside the door. "Yeah. It'll buy us some time to make the drive to Austin. Or if he does try to reach us, maybe he'll think we're asleep."

Van was asleep. *Forever.* Fuck, she should've been relieved, but the ache behind her breastbone burrowed in with brass knuckles.

Fifteen minutes later, she parked Van's sedan in the *Daddy's Grill* parking lot outside of town. The sun clung to the horizon as the gray cast of night crept in.

She left the engine running. "I'll be a minute. Try not to let anyone see your face."

He glanced through the tinted windows at the three cars in the lot and said, sarcastically, "I'll do my best."

Inside, the waft of cigarettes and bar-b-que thickened her inhales. She stood before the only pay phone in the area, pumped it with coins, and lifted the receiver.

"Who is this?" The smooth, feline voice answered on the first ring.

"It's me."

Silence.

"This isn't—" Liv cleared the rasp sticking in her throat. "This isn't my usual call."

"No, I don't expect it is." Camila's tone was casual, but worry lurked beneath the surface.

"I need the house cleaned." The tears broke through. She wiped them away. "There's a mess on the kitchen floor."

A gasp pushed through the line. "Your boy?"

"No. This one was never mine."

"Oh." A pause. "I feel like I should be happy." Camila sniffed. "I feel…"

"Same here. I'm on my way to finish this. You have about an hour before the house gets crowded. Two hours tops. Code is 0054."

In a perfect scenario, Liv would kill Mr. E and sneak off with Josh into the night. If she were busted during an assassination of the police chief, she would use the slave house as evidence in her defense. But she didn't want to explain two bodies. If she failed in her attempt, she didn't want Van discovered by Mr. E.

"Is the time-frame doable?" she asked Camila.

"It will be."

Liv thought the line disconnected, but Camila's voice came back. "Be careful."

"Thank you." *For everything.*

The phone went dead.

Liv drove in silence for ten minutes before Josh breached the conversation she'd been expecting. "I'm trying to understand what you're feeling right now and what you felt for him exactly."

"I'm not sure *I* will ever understand it."

Van protected her from Mr. E in the best times, and her body bore his bruises on the worst days. Above all, he gave her a daughter.

"I loved him and hated him with damaged devotion," she said. "He was embedded in my life for seven years. You don't rip that away and feel nothing."

He nodded, unbuckled his seatbelt, and gave her exactly what she needed. Twisting in the seat to face her, he slid a hand over her belly and clenched her hip. His other hand combed her hair from her nape, gripping the strands at the back of her head. With his body curled around her side, he dropped his head on her shoulder, the warm tendrils of his breath twining around her neck. He didn't move for the length of the drive, and it was in that loving clench that she found the strength to forgive herself for killing Van.

Forty-five minutes later, they sat in the car, glaring across the street at a two-story home. Middle-income neighborhood, manicured lawn, well-lit walkway, and hanging flower baskets, it resembled every other house for ten blocks.

Dusk had settled. Cars lined the curb on both sides of the sparsely lit street. Van's sedan blended in, but if Mr. E glanced at the car from his front window, he would spot them. The sedan was a generic car, but he knew what Van drove. He could make the connection if he were suspicious enough.

Josh caressed a warm palm over her thigh. "Mr. E hasn't spent a dime of his illegal money, huh?"

She wrinkled her nose at the simple lines of his lackluster home. "He's a police chief. How would he explain million-dollar luxuries?"

Josh's strong profile watched the street. "He

could've cut ties, retired to the French Rivera, and lived off of his fortune. Why is he doing this?"

She blew her cheeks out. "Maybe he likes trafficking humans. The power. The corruption. Maybe he's just greedy and wants more money before he retires." She grabbed the two black scarves from the backseat and coiled one loosely around Josh's neck. "Better than chains, right?"

He leaned in and stole a kiss. "I love your chains, Liv."

A flutter lifted in her chest. She looped the second scarf behind her neck. They would sneak in with their faces concealed, shoot the greedy motherfucker, and leave before anyone noticed. Easy as gutting all the other millionaire slave-owners.

Across the street, the front door opened. Josh gripped her hand as an older man strode along the walkway, shoulders squared, eyes on his phone. The outdoor lighting accentuated the streaks of silver in his black hair. She recognized the police chief in the news articles.

The road was free of traffic noise. If she rolled down the window, they'd be able to hear his footfalls. Could she shoot him at this distance? A shiver licked down her spine.

"What if he's texting Van? Or me?" Her blood pressure skyrocketed. "What if he's on his way to the house? Fuck, what do we do?"

"Deep breaths, Liv." Josh squeezed her hand tighter. "We'll follow him."

When Mr. E reached the SUV parked in the driveway, the front door opened again.

A little girl ran out in blue-jeans and light-up

sneakers with long brown hair winding around her shoulders. Her tiny chin pointed up, her eyes alight with laughter.

Fear and joy collided in a rush of nausea. "Josh. Her smile…Oh God, her smile." Liv slapped at the button that rolled down the window just in time to hear, "Daddy! Daddy, wait up!"

A disgustingly familiar chuckle bounced down the driveway. "Come on, Livana. We're in a hurry."

"No, no, no, no."

Liv's whisper seeped into Josh's pores and chilled his bloodstream. Hooking his arms around her chest, he pulled her away from the window.

"Are you sure that's her?" He hoped to God she was wrong.

"Yes." Her voice was a tearful hiss, whipping through the dark interior of the car.

He pressed his lips to her cheek in an attempt to soothe her, holding tight to her heaving body. "If he's going to Temple, I don't think he'll bring your daughter with him."

Liv's daughter. The daughter Mr. E raised. His son's daughter. His granddaughter. It made the decision to kill him a cluster of confusion.

Josh dragged his nose through her hair, his head swimming. Fifteen days ago, he'd sat in his Christian Ethics class, rooted in the belief that murder was a grave moral evil. A capital crime punished with eternal damnation. That was before he'd met Mr. E and the buyers' network of soulless greed. Before his convictions had been tested.

He stroked his thumbs along her rigid arms. He

certainly hadn't felt unclean after shooting the bodyguard. Killing that man had been a last resort, one that saved her life. As for Mr. E...the bastard strangled Liv. Bashed her head against the wall. Scarred her face. Stole her child. Enslaved Van's mother. Trained his son to kidnap and torture people. He was beyond saving.

Hell, there were countless examples in the bible that justified homicide to protect one's self and the lives of others. A heady sense of responsibility heated Josh's blood and tightened his muscles. Liv was his to protect.

Across the street, Livana interlaced her tiny fingers with those of a man who trafficked sex slaves. A man who followed through on his threats, evidenced by Liv's dead mother. A reminder that, once again, there were no nonviolent options left. As long as Mr. E lived, that little girl's life was in danger.

As Mr. E looked down at the child, it was difficult to interpret his expression in the dim light. If there was love there, tenderness even. What would killing the only father she'd ever known do to her?

A soft mewling noise rattled in Liv's throat, her round panicked eyes locked on Livana's affection toward Mr. E.

"Oh God, Josh, why did he raise her as his daughter?" She pressed a hand to her abdomen, rubbing, her body shaking.

His arms locked around her waist, hugging her close. He wanted to believe Mr. E raised Livana because she was his granddaughter, but he suspected the reason was more perverse. What better way to keep his arrangement with Liv tightly fastened than to keep her daughter as close as possible?

"What if he figures out Van is gone? He has my

daughter, and I killed his son."

"He'll investigate why neither of you are answering your phones before he eliminates the only hold he has on you."

Maybe Mr. E considered Livana his daughter, but it wasn't a mercy Josh would count on. The man had abandoned his own son to a woman who was too stoned to prevent her child from being raped. What kind of life was Mr. E giving Livana?

He buried his rising panic and kissed Liv's head. Leaning her backward against his chest, he lowered their bodies below the windows.

The front door opened a third time. A blond woman stepped out, slender frame, hair in a pony tail. She was maybe a decade younger than Mr. E given her swift strides, the muscle tone in her arms, and her trendy jeans and blouse.

With her purse in hand, she strode toward Mr. E. "I'm starving."

Mr. E stared at his phone. "Change of plans. I need to be somewhere." His gaze shifted to Livana who yanked on his hand in a futile attempt to move him forward. He untangled their hands and patted her head. "I'm going to drop you and Livana off at the station. We'll pick up dinner on the way, and you can eat there."

For a heart-stopping moment, Mr. E glanced at the street, his eyes probing the lines of parked cars. Then he climbed in the driver's seat.

Josh's muscles ached with tension. "Why would he take them to the station?"

"He's paranoid." She stroked his fingers absently. "For the first time in seven years, we're not answering our phones. My mom's murder gives me a damned good reason to revolt, and he knows the first thing I'd do is search for Livana."

The woman clasped Livana's arm, holding her in place. "We'll just stay here."

"Get in the car," Mr. E barked from within the SUV.

The woman jumped and hustled Livana into the backseat. As she slid into the front seat, the engine started, and the brake lights illuminated the driveway.

"Shit. He's backing up." Liv slumped lower on his lap, dragging him down by his shirt. "Josh, he's going to Temple. We need to be there."

His pulse raced. "Shh. It's okay." He hugged her against him. "As soon as they leave, we'll head back. We'll beat him there."

She pressed her face against his chest, nodding, her body trembling. "She'll be safe at the police station. We'll kill him at the house and…Jesus, what if he doesn't come? It's a huge risk."

He stroked her hair as the rumble of the SUV grew closer. "This is a blessing, Liv. We're captives. We'll end this where he imprisoned us. It'll be self-defense. We won't have to run or try to cover it up."

Josh would see his parents again. Liv could live a normal life. His muscles clenched, his heart thundering. He wanted that for her so badly.

The rumble came to a stop beside them. Was the darkness and the tinted windows enough to conceal them? He popped open the glove box where the guns were stored and held his breath, his pulse drumming in his ears. Her fingers dug into his ribs, her body heaving against his.

The engine growled and the soft whir of tires on

asphalt sounded the SUV's retreat down the street. He blew out a shuddering exhale.

She melted against him, rubbed a hand up his chest, and curled her fingers around his neck. Raising her head, she blinked at him with watery eyes.

"I"—she kissed the spot over his heart, leaned up, and kissed his lips, softly, breathlessly—"you."

His heartbeat catapulted, strumming every cell in his body. "You, too, girl." His mouth moved against hers, and during that brief, stolen connection, he felt her lips curve up.

For the next hour, they detailed their plan as they drove. The setup. The strike. The aftermath. When they pulled into the driveway in Temple, they had the story they would give to police ironed out and rehearsed.

She used the remote to open the garage door, and the emptiness within tingled down his spine. "Where's the van?"

Her forehead furrowed as she parked the car and climbed out. "Camila probably took the van to transport..." She rolled her lips, chin quivering, and rubbed her nose. "To transport the body."

The tingle on his spine receded, replaced with a fortitude to do anything needed to ensure they survived the night. He handed her the LC9 from the glove box, grabbed the PT-22, and followed her to the kitchen door. His muscles burned through his strides, amped up and ready.

Her pass code released the door, and he slipped in before her, gun raised in two hands. He had three bullets left. He'd only need one, unless someone was waiting for their return. Did Mr. E have a larger network? Would he have called someone to meet him here?

The silence in the kitchen stood as still as the dark. She moved behind him, her footfalls trailing to the sink where she flicked the switch. Light flooded the room.

The yellow linoleum floor showed no evidence of blood. The matching yellow sink was also scrubbed. The chairs were pushed in at the table. No body, no bloody rags, and no dolls.

"I'm glad they took the mannequins," she whispered.

No joke. In the end, Van had surprised the hell out of him. Perhaps Liv's influence in Van's life had altered his journey to one of redemption. Nevertheless, the memory of that man would be an eternal prickle creeping over the back of Josh's skull.

She lingered above the spot where Van had bled out, eyes on the floor, her arms wrapped around her torso. Her pallid expression produced a sympathetic ache in his chest.

Trusting that her friends had been thorough, he gave her the two phones from the counter and pulled her by a hand up the stairs, his gun out as he scanned the sitting room and hallway. The absolute stillness of the house was both reassuring and nerve-wracking.

She checked her phone as they climbed the stairs. "Mr. E sent one text, a little over an hour ago. All it says is, *Where is Van?*"

"He would've sent that around the time he came out of his house." At the top of the stairs, he entered the code with his gun hand. "You're not texting back, right?"

"Of course not."

Good. No communication would force him to show up. "What about Van's phone?"

"I've tried every code I can think of to unlock it."

She walked through the outer chamber and snagged a black costume from the cabinet. "It's a no-go."

Fifteen minutes later, he knelt in the middle of her room, facing the closed door, his naked body prickling with goosebumps. With his wrists crossed behind his back, he was her slave.

She stood by the keypad, phone in one hand, the LC9 concealed in her thigh-high boot, the sheath of her minidress clinging to her curves. Holding her body motionless, she was his Deliverer.

Chains spread out around him and locked to the hooks in the floor. They led to the cuffs on his arms, but it was all a ruse. They didn't attach to the cuff rings. Instead, they wedged beneath the leather straps. One jerk of his arms, and they would fall away. With his hands hidden behind his back, he held the PT-22.

The minutes stretched, his heart beating to the unfamiliar melody floating from her lips. Her lyrics were indiscernible, but the beauty of her haunting voice massaged its way into his muscles and invigorated his blood.

Their foremost priority was to lure Mr. E far enough into the room to close the door. Once locked inside, he wouldn't be able to escape if something went wrong. And while she'd been adamant about being the shooter, he'd denied her pleas to relinquish his mom's gun. No way would he allow her to defend them on her own.

Finally, her phone buzzed. She glanced at it and tossed it on the bed. "It says, *Open the door.*"

Sweat formed on Josh's skin. His heartbeat thundered against his ribs. He dropped his chin to his chest and rested his finger beside the trigger guard, the gun held tight against his back.

Liv opened the door and stepped back.

Black boots stopped in the threshold. The door opened all the way, and a bath towel landed on the floor. Mr. E kicked the terrycloth until it was wedged beneath the crack, propping the door open. "Van's phone is somewhere in this house. Where is he?"

Josh's blood pressure spiked. There went their plan to lock him in.

Her heeled boots shifted a step backward, her silence constricting his chest. If Van had planned to kill his father, he certainly wouldn't have told the bastard where he was going or what he was doing. Why wasn't she answering him with some kind of lie?

Josh raised his chin as subtly as possible, and his breath caught in his throat.

Mr. E wore his cotton jumpsuit and that godawful canvas mask. His body angled toward Liv. She stood a few feet away, staring down the barrel of his semi-auto pistol.

Josh locked his jaw in a painful clench, his entire world a trigger-squeeze away from death. His fight response pummeled at him to attack, hardening his muscles and heating his veins. Timing would be everything.

A tic bounced in her cheek as her fingers stretched along her thigh, dipping into her boot and grasping her gun. "I'm not Van's babysitter."

The pistol swung, colliding with the side of her head. She fell to one knee, and her gun clattered on the floor.

Josh jerked so hard one of the chains fell loose from his wrist cuff. It clanked behind him, drawing the mask's eyeholes in his direction.

She lurched for her gun and collided with Mr. E's boot as he kicked it toward the shower stall.

"You gonna shoot me, you fucking whore?" He shoved the barrel beneath her chin, forcing her to lift on her knees. "Where the *fuck* is Van? You've got one second to answer. One—"

"Dead." Her eyes burned, wide and fierce.

The compulsion to protect her wracked Josh with indecision. His pulse raced. No way could he level his gun before Mr. E fired.

Mr. E crouched and shoved his canvas mask into her face. "I don't believe you. Last chance." His gloved finger began a slow squeeze of the trigger.

A tremor gripped Josh's spine as her throat bobbed against the press of the barrel.

Her fingers curled against her thighs. "Your son cleared out his room before I killed him. Go see for yourself."

Oh, God, Liv. Josh tightened his grip on the gun.

"You're dead," whispered from within the hood.

In that everlasting second, as Mr. E's finger pulled the trigger and the hammer released, Josh plummeted, gutted. Lifting his arms, he met his breaking point with a single-minded focus to join her in death and take the son of a bitch with him.

His heart roared with fear for her as he snapped his arms forward, clattering the chains and aiming the gun.

Mr. E's semi-auto clicked, a jarringly quiet sound.

Josh stopped breathing. It clicked? The pistol jammed? *It misfired! OhGodOhGod, thank you, God.*

Liv swung her arm, knocking the barrel from her neck, and Josh trained the .22's sights on the mask. He squeezed the trigger as Mr. E jerked his hand to readjust his aim. Both guns fired.

The double *boom* pierced Josh's ears. He choked on his terror as Liv's eyes widened, her hand cupped around her neck. *No, no, no.* She couldn't be hit. He bit his tongue, tasted blood, and forced his attention on the threat.

Mr. E's pistol dropped. Red spouted from a hole in his canvas-wrapped neck, and he collapsed beside her. Josh had aimed true.

He scrambled toward them, his pulse thrumming in his throat.

"Liv? Are you hurt?" He kicked Mr. E's pistol, skidding it across the room, and pulled her hand from her neck.

Milky, unblemished skin stretched against the delicate lines of her throat. She glanced at the ceiling, and he followed her gaze. The bullet hole marring the sheetrock sank a surge of relief deep into his lungs. His eyes ached with the aftermath of jumbling emotion, and he wanted nothing more than to hold her.

The masked head twitched on the floor. Josh clenched his fist, vibrating with the need to take away the last of the man's power. He found the ties on the back of the canvas hood and yanked it off.

Silver striped through thinning black hair. Bags of wrinkles hung from pain-filled eyes. The older version of the man in the news articles worked his jaw, unable to drag in a breath.

She leaned over the police chief, her nostrils flaring. "Van flew to the Keys and tried to save my mom."

His eyes flashed, and his head rocked side-to-side.

"That's right, cocksucker. And he came back to kill you." Her voice strained with tears.

Kneeling beside her, Josh uncurled her fingers from Mr. E's jumpsuit.

The man's jaw opened and closed soundlessly, red trickling from the corner of his mouth. From the neck down, his body lay limp. Maybe the bullet damaged his spinal cord. He was definitely choking on his own blood.

"I went to your house and found Livana." She grabbed his bobbing chin. "When your pretty blond wife returns from the station, I'm going to show her all the things you taught me to do. Then I'm going to kill her."

Josh probably should've been bothered by her taunting a dying man, but his righteousness was buried beneath the huge freaking desire to crush the bastard's skull with his fist.

A gurgle of blood bubbled from Mr. E's mouth, followed by a strangled sigh. His face slackened, and his head fell to the side.

She checked the pulse in his neck. Josh pulled back

the edge of a black glove and felt for a pulse on the wrist.

With her face only a few inches from his, he could feel her tension releasing with the slowing of her movements. He waited for her to glance up. When their eyes collided, a surreal moment hovered between them, fueled by their unified breaths. It was over. He leaned in, touched his lips to her trembling ones.

Her face crumpled. "I wanted him to die in a horrible way. This..." Her voice scratched. "This was too merciful."

His heart fractured for all the torment Mr. E caused her. He spoke against her quivering chin. "He'll be judged and spend eternity suffering for his sins."

She shifted, staring at the body, her eyes welling, blinking. A quiver rippled across her lips. She turned toward him and coiled her arms around his neck, her lungs hauling tearful gulps of air.

"It's done, Josh." She cried, quietly, her cheek against his. "I'm so sorry you had to be the one to kill—"

"Don't, Liv." He cupped her face. "I'm not sorry, and you won't be either."

"Okay," she whispered, nodded. "Livana…" She pressed her face in his neck, her fingers clenched in his hair. "She's free."

And so was Liv. Free of fear. Free to live. Free with him.

As he held her, wiping away the streaks of tears on her face, he let fifteen days of tension twist free of his body, muscle by muscle, exhale after exhale. He waited for the guilt, for the darkness, for some indication to show him the wrongfulness of his path, but all he felt was liberation breathing through this passionate woman and the salvation that kept her heart beating.

God's will led him to that house, but it was love that bound him within its walls. He was born with choices and would die with his decisions. Looking down into her huge brown eyes, her emotions so raw and beautifully exposed, he knew she was the most important decision he'd ever made.

He scooted to the mattress with her curled in his lap, snagged her phone, and dialed. Pressing a kiss to her salty lips, he lifted the phone to his ear.

"Bell County 911. What is your emergency?"

"This is Joshua Carter. I just killed the man who abducted me."

CHAPTER 42

Ten hours later, Liv shuffled out of the interrogation room in the Temple police station, her boots scuffing along the stained carpet squares, the arches of her feet igniting pain with each step. *Damned heels.*

The highlights of the detectives' examination swished through her weary brain. *We believe Eli Eary acted alone in his crimes. Killing him in self-defense is permitted by the law. Your actions are not legally punishable. No* actus reus. *You and Mr. Carter are free to go.*

The investigation was far from over, but for now, they were free. She and Josh had been separated the moment the driveway flooded in blue and red flashing lights. They were transported to the station in handcuffs, separately. They were questioned for hours, separately.

She stepped into the corridor, searching the unfamiliar faces for pale green eyes and came up empty.

No one followed her as she walked, but detectives and uniformed men stopped mid-conversation to watch her pass. *Fuck them.* She tugged down the short hem of her dress, feeling awkward and really fucking exposed.

She hugged her mid-section, dropped her arms, crossed her arms again. This feeling…this insecurity was so foreign. The last time she lived in a free world, she was just a kid. But in her twenty-four years, she'd never been unsupervised, never went anywhere without checking in with someone...Mom, Mr. E, Van.

As she passed offices and holding rooms, looking for Josh, she felt lost. She needed his hand on her hip, his fingers laced through hers, his eyes studying her with his bold affection. She missed him with every dry, achy breath.

Turning the corner, she entered a long hallway, anxious to see how he was doing after all the questioning. Their carefully crafted story to the police painted Eli Eary as a sadistic slave owner, not a slave trafficker. They claimed he acted alone when he abducted and imprisoned them. The detectives were overwhelmed with the discovery of the allegedly-murdered Austin girl from seven years ago and the nationally-mourned linebacker from Baylor.

She and Josh had agreed to omit the existence of other slaves, the dead buyers, and Van. Too much murder, way too many complications. In their story, Eli Eary used her and Josh—his only two slaves—for his sexual, sadistic pleasures. No one knew she abducted Josh. And no one mentioned Mr. E having a son.

Her longer captivity was more complicated. To expose her connection to Livana, she accused an unknown man of raping and impregnating her a few weeks after her abduction. She'd told them Eli Eary threatened the child's life as a way to control her. She was allowed limited errands outside of the house but lived in constant fear for her child. When she'd revealed that truth to the room of detectives, her painful tears fomented the story. The seven-year-old scar on her face might've garnered some sympathetic votes as well.

When they told her she was free to go, she asked for a visitation with Livana. They promised to do what they could with a cautious message. "Mrs. Eary is struggling with her husband's death and his crimes. Give her time."

They'd said the wife and daughter were safe in Austin. Mrs. Eary had been oblivious to her husband's corruption, which meant she'd raised Livana as a legitimate mother. It was good news, right? Livana was loved and taken care of. Yet a deep ache flared in Liv's chest. Her limbs felt heavier, her body colder.

It wasn't as if she had aspirations to take over the role of Livana's mother. God, she'd been so focused on just keeping her baby alive. But if she were to examine her dreams of the future, they did include her daughter. Losing Livana had left a hole inside her, and perhaps that hole would always be there, but she needed to see her child. Needed to understand Livana's relationship with her adoptive mother.

At the end of the hall, she paused at the doorway of the waiting room, halted by the hiccuping sobs tumbling from within. Across the room, Josh sat on a couch between his parents with their backs to the door. Their heads bowed together, their private huddle enveloped by a chorus of whispered prayers.

It was four in the morning. Her stomach hurt at the thought of them waiting for her. They should've gone home. Of course, Josh would never leave without her. But would they be together the next day? Or next month? Would he go back to school, live with his parents, work the farm, and become a minister?

What was her place in his life? She was a master at rope bondage. She could crack a whip without splitting skin. She knew how to suck a cock. As for the Bible, well, that was just an anthology of well-written fairytales. She wasn't a minister's wife.

He clasped his mother's frail shoulder, his broad back twice the size of hers. At least, they let him put clothes on before hauling him to the station. They hadn't given her the option.

Emily Carter's graying brown hair had unraveled from her bun. Her flowery collared smock dress fell loosely around her skeletal frame. The woman Liv used to watch through binoculars had lost a lot of weight.

Guilt landed like a bullet in Liv's stomach. She'd caused his poor mother so much grief.

Daniel Carter grasped his son's neck. The humped curve of his spine and the weathered skin on his nape reminded that most of his sixty-six years had been spent beneath the unforgiving Texan sun. Silver peppered his full head of black hair, and she knew if he turned around she'd see Josh's pale green eyes in the older man's face.

The sight of the three of them together, praying, and crying happy tears produced a sharp pain in the back of her throat. For a flickering moment, she entertained an unrealistic desire to receive some of the love they shared between them, but she didn't deserve it. Taking him from his parents was the most selfish thing she'd ever done, but she would *never* regret choosing him.

She lingered in the doorway, unsure where to go or what to do. Should she interrupt their private reunion? Her fingers shook as she adjusted the clingy top over her nipples. The bottom hem reached just below her ass. One of the detectives had offered her his suit jacket. Now she regretted declining it. She resembled a homeless skank.

The truth in that thought clawed through her chest

and burned her eyes. She *was* homeless. Also penniless, jobless, and without a family. Hell, she didn't even have a change of clothes. Aching for Mom, miserable on her lonely side of the room, she backed out of the doorway.

What the fuck was wrong with her? She was free. Livana was safe. Josh's parents had their son back.

Pull your balls out of your cunt.

Van's words steeled her strides down the hallway. She'd wait on the bench at the end of the hall until Josh was ready. Her toes pinched in her boots, and her stupid eyes burned with stupid tears. She slapped at her cheeks and pretended she couldn't hear the desolate echo of her heart in her ears.

Halfway to her destination, an arm hooked around her waist. She gasped and inhaled Josh's clean familiar scent. Tension shuddered from her body. She let her head fall back on his shoulder and compulsively reached for his hand at her hip. Christ, she hadn't realized how badly she needed him to hold her.

"What are you doing?" His breath caressed her ear, and his other arm crossed her chest.

She turned in his embrace, wrapped an arm around his muscled back, and pressed her palm to his whiskered jaw, savoring his heat seeping into her skin.

"I don't know where I'm going." Her nose thickened with tears. Fucking hell, she was sniveling.

"Hey, it's okay." He was heartbreakingly beautiful, even more so when he regarded her as if he were searching, not her eyes but what lay behind them. "I'm not going anywhere without you." He touched a knuckle under her chin and raised it. "The worst is behind us. It's just you and me. Everything else is trivial. Got it?"

Her insecurities dimmed in the intensity of his

gaze. She traced the curve of his bottom lip. "How do you do that?"

With his arm braced around her, he dipped two fingers inside the front of her dress and pinched her nipple. Leaning in, he kissed the corner of her parted lips. "I'm a horny slut, remember?" He adjusted her top, twined their fingers, and led her back to the waiting room. "Time to meet my parents." He peeked back at her, grinning.

She shook her head and followed that gorgeous, confident smile. She'd follow him anywhere, even if it was to meet his parents with her tits creeping out of the minidress.

"Mom, Dad, this is Liv."

The air shifted with the horrified widening of their eyes. Judgmental energy prickled over her cleavage and down her legs. They didn't openly gawk at her body. It was a flash, a gasp, a quick glance away.

Holding their chins stiffly upward, their eyes locked on Josh as if another accidental glimpse in her direction would damn them to hell. What had he told them about her? Not the truth, certainly. But had he told them he loved her? His fingers were laced with hers, but that could imply friendship. She rubbed her sweaty palm over her belly, stared at the exit longingly, and met their narrowed eyes.

Emily clutched a wad of tissues to her chest, her face etched in wrinkles. Her gray gaze flicked to Liv's scar and returned to Josh.

"Oh dear." Her voice was cold, forced. "You poor thing."

Liv cringed. "Nice to meet you, Mr. and Mrs. Carter." She held out her hand.

Daniel clasped it, his fingers gnarled from manual labor, and let go. The hue of his eyes were indeed the same as Josh's but duller and surrounded by dark circles. Worse, those eyes studied her as if they were putting her in a box labeled, *Things To Keep Away From Josh.* "You're welcome to stay with us until you get on your feet. We don't have a lot of room, but we'll make it work."

"She's staying with us." Josh gripped her hip, pulled her chest against his hard body, and rested his lips on her forehead.

She hooked her thumbs in his belt loops and kissed the hollow of his throat.

Daniel's harsh squint was slightly more subtle than the ugly twist of Emily's mouth. They knew their son had been imprisoned and used as a sex slave. She doubted Josh had gone into details with them, but imaginations were limitless, even for church-goers. They would've been told that she was a victim like their son, but she was still part of the evil that defiled their virginal boy.

"Excuse me, Mr. Carter?" A uniformed officer poked his head in the doorway. "If you're ready to leave, we can escort your family to your car. There's a lot of activity out front."

Minutes later, she stepped into the cool evening air with Josh's arm hugging her shoulders. A small assembly of news reporters lined the walkway to the parking lot, flashing bulbs and shouting questions. But their voices were smothered by the cheers of college kids, waving *Welcome Home* posters and Baylor Bears memorabilia.

"Somebody's pop-u-lar." Liv squeezed his waist, and his chuckle vibrated through her.

They walked behind his parents and two officers, weaving through the crowd that spilled into the parking lot. The college kids stared openly with wide eyes, likely imagining all the horrors of their star linebacker's captivity. Some shouted friendly greetings. Others held candlelit prayer circles.

Suddenly, Josh's muscles stiffened around her. He stopped their forward movement and turned them toward a huddle of pretty twenty-something girls.

Seriously? "Josh, what are you—?"

A flash of long black hair caught her attention.

Camila shimmied between two girls and held out a plastic grocery bag filled with clothes. Her huge dark eyes were cautious, flicking over the crowd.

Josh grabbed the bag, and Camila vanished behind the crowding bodies.

"Keep moving." He held her tight to his side, his height allowing him to see above the bystanders. His eyes were focused straight ahead. He must've spotted the car.

A knot formed in her stomach. Camila wouldn't have risked exposing her connection with them just to bring a change of clothes. The thought niggled as she followed Josh into an old station wagon and shut the door. His parents climbed in the front, and she sat directly behind Mrs. Carter. Josh reclined in the middle, his big body crowding the bench seat.

He set the bag of clothes on the floorboard and whispered in her ear, "We'll talk when we get home."

She nodded, agreeing that a conversation about Camila in front of his parents would raise questions.

Headlights from passing cars flashed across his face as Mr. Carter pulled out of the lot. Something was working behind Josh's eyes, and it had her sitting on the edge of the seat. He buckled their seat belts and tucked her close to his side.

The drive to Waco was filled with his parents' gossip about church, accolades for the community's support after his disappearance, and updates on the farm's crop losses. Josh assured them everything would resume to normal soon, and Liv's doubts about where she fit in sat heavy in her chest.

As Mr. Carter brought Josh up to speed on the business side of the farm, Josh caressed the skin above her thigh-high boots. Sliding toward the hem of her skirt, his fingers slipped between her legs and traced the edge of her panties. She held her breath and stared at his profile. Why was he doing this?

His attention seemed fully absorbed in the conversation with his dad as he eased beneath the crotch of her panties, found her wet, and pressed his index finger in to the knuckle.

She released a soundless breath and gripped his wrist, her body flooding with warmth. Still, he didn't look at her.

"You fired the contractor, right?" he asked his dad, curling his finger inside her.

Her head dropped against the seat back, her thighs parting. Nerve endings tingled along her inner thighs. She realized he was telling her without words that nothing would change between them. The church talk, his parents, his previous life wouldn't sever their connection.

She relaxed around his grinding hand, her lap shrouded in darkness. Her breaths quickened. Her mouth moistened.

He stroked her until she couldn't contain her panting. His hand pulled away, and he drew his finger into his mouth, watching her with a smile playing at the corners. "Liv will be sleeping in my room."

"That's fine, honey," Emily said. "I'll make up the couch for you."

He leaned back and closed his eyes, his arm resting over her lap. "No, Mom. She'll be sleeping in my room *with me*."

That was not how she'd envisioned him exposing their relationship. She slipped down in the seat, wishing she could disappear.

Tense silence pulsed through the car. He squeezed her thigh, and his eyes remained closed.

"Son." His dad shifted, his gaze on the rear view mirror. "I don't know what you've been through, and we'll work through that. But the rules haven't changed. You ain't gonna be hitched and not churched. Not under my roof."

Josh sat forward, slowly, his eyes narrowed on the mirror. "Your rules haven't changed, but mine—"

"I'll sleep on the couch." Fuck, she didn't want to cause this family anymore pain. She turned toward him and cupped his face, shifting his attention to her. "Please, Josh? I want to sleep on the couch."

He'd hear the lie, but she trusted he'd understand her intention.

He reclined against her, shoulder to shoulder, and traced the skin between her fingers. For a stubborn pain in the ass, he let the subject drop too easily. Which meant he was probably going to do whatever the hell he wanted.

Emily shifted the conversation back to church stuff, promising that the ministers held all the answers to helping him heal. Forty minutes later, they shuffled into the Carter's small, single-story home. The front half was split between a sparsely decorated sitting room and a galley kitchen. A short hall led to two bedrooms and a bathroom in the back.

Josh stopped Liv at the bathroom door. "Take a shower if you want. My room's right there."

He pointed at the door across the hall. Following her in, he set the bag of clothes on the counter and dug through the jeans, cotton dresses, and t-shirts.

A comfortable warmth tingled through her chest. She owed Camila for so damned much.

"Can you sleep in this?" He pulled out a camisole and sleep shorts.

She nodded. "What happened back there with Camila?"

"She said something to me. The crowd was loud. I don't know. I read her lips." He scraped a hand through his hair. "I swear she said, *Watch your back*."

What? Her spine tingled. "Why would she say that?" *Their enemies are dead.*

He unfolded the camisole, and a piece of paper drifted to the floor. Handwritten scribble bled through the thin folded stationary. Her shoulders tightened as they stared at it.

He picked it up, his eyebrows pulling together, and handed it to her.

Her heart raced as she unfolded the note. "Camila has no way to contact me."

Why would she need to? Liv gripped his arm and held up the note so they could read it together.

We're so happy for you! When you're ready, our home is your home.

A couple lingering concerns...

The kitchen was clean when we arrived. The job was gone. No cars in the garage. Were you able to take care of this on your own?

Traquero and his wife are dead. Found two days ago. We're not sure who did it, but the how was passionate. Definitely personal.

CHAPTER 43

Van's death replayed through Liv's head in slow motion. The gunfire. The river of blood on the floor. His final words. *He killed your mother…Needed your help…He'll avenge me.* Leading her surge of emotions was the overwhelming relief that Traquero's depravity had met a bloody end.

Josh closed the bathroom door, his complexion a sheet of white. "You shot him in the shoulder." He rubbed the back of his neck, studying her. "Is it possible he survived that?"

She opened the toilet lid, flushed the note, and tried to keep her argumentative voice to a whisper. "He bled out."

"Or passed out." He shoved his hands through his hair and dropped his head back, staring at the ceiling. "So stupid." He shut his eyes. "We didn't check his pulse."

Her mouth went dry. She closed the toilet lid and collapsed on top of it. Her chest felt hard and cold inside. "We left him there to die."

"Except he didn't die." Stunned realization cracked his voice as he crouched before her and tucked her hair behind her ear. "When he returned to the house last night, he already killed Traquero."

She blinked, the movement irritating her gritty, tired eyes. "He must've *flown* to the Keys to help Mom." She nodded to herself, swallowing past a tight throat. "He could've killed Traquero on his way back. But how did he know how to find him?" A horrible thought clenched her stomach. "What if he knows about Camila and the others?"

His hand wrapped around her neck, his thumb stroking the skin below her ear. "Think about *why* he killed Traquero."

The only things predictable about Van were his jealousy and his hypocrisy. "Traquero hurt me."

Van had no qualms raising a hand to her, but Traquero had overstepped, recklessly. Van probably killed the wife in front of him just to make him suffer.

Her breath stuttered. "I think he packed up and left with the intention of protecting Mom and disappearing. When he failed, maybe he came back to avenge Mom's death."

Would he do that? For her? The ache in her chest said, *Yes*.

"I despise Van." He tilted his head. "But his behavior in the kitchen when you shot him…" A line formed between his dark eyebrows. "I got the sense that he was done. With Mr. E. With the whole operation."

She sifted through her memories of the prior night when Van was bleeding all over the floor. She couldn't pick out a single word, expression, or action that suggested ill-intent.

"If he knew about Camila and the others, he'd have no reason to harm them." Her shoulders loosened. "He's not a threat."

Josh pulled her to the edge of the toilet seat, wrapped his arms around her waist, and rested his forehead on her belly. "You're not leaving my sight."

Her hands went to his hair, raking through the messy black strands. "I can work with that." She lowered her lips to his head and filled her nose with his warm, comforting scent.

A fist knocked on the door.

"Joshua?" Emily called. "Are you in there?"

His moan rumbled through her. He raised his head and kissed her lips. "I'll be right outside that door."

CHAPTER 44

Twenty minutes later, Liv was showered, dressed in the pajama set Camila gave her, and wrapped in blankets on the couch. The kitchen light trickled into the sitting room, accompanied by low murmurs. Josh and his parents were still awake, gathered at the kitchen table around the corner.

She declined the biscuits Emily made, too exhausted to eat. Stretching out on the sofa, she closed her eyes. It must've been around seven in the morning before sleep finally took her.

Not long after, she woke, cradled in his arms, her body pressed against his chest as he carried her through the brightening house. Stubborn man was breaking his parents' rules.

"Aren't your parents due to get up?" she whispered.

"We've already done all the morning chores. They just passed out."

She hooked her arms around his neck and found his mouth.

His tongue met hers eagerly, his lips wet and inviting. In his unlit bedroom, he closed the door with a quiet click and dropped her on a mattress. The shades blacked out the daylight, drenching the room in darkness. She hadn't been in there yet, and when she scooted back to make space for him, she quickly learned how damned small his bed was.

Her head thumped against the wall, and she cringed, hoping she hadn't awakened his parents. "How the hell do you fit in this?"

Clothes rustled, his breaths deepening, growing closer. "You're about to see how both of us fit."

The mattress dipped and hands grabbed her top, stripping it over her head. Her sleep shorts went next. Then he was on her, spreading her thighs, his naked body sliding over hers, his cock prodding between her legs, coaxing a delicious spark of fire.

His teeth caught her nipple, tugging and stretching. Her hands fisted in the sheets. His fingers swept along her sides, his weight wonderfully heavy, his hips grinding against hers.

Her back arched, and she bit her lips to trap a moan.

"Josh," she whispered.

The box springs creaked as he lifted his body and flipped her to her belly. Kneeling between her legs, his fingers skimmed up her inner thighs, dipped through her wetness, and entered her.

Pleasure shivered through her. He thrust his hand, his fingers dragging along her inner walls, his panting so incredibly erotic. Her hands ached to touch him. Her body burned to be stroked harder. When his fingers slid out, she held her breath, expecting his cock. Instead, a soaked fingertip pressed against the pucker of her ass. She looked over her shoulder but couldn't see him through the dark.

"Van has taken you here?" His whisper was hoarse.

"Yeah." She closed her eyes, knowing his jealousy would be rising to the surface and stirring his instinct to claim her.

"Are you healed?"

"Yes."

It had been a week since Traquero had hurt her. A couple times, during moments like this one, she'd watched Josh spread her cheeks and stare at her anus while fucking her. She knew what he wanted. She'd never willingly given her ass to anyone, but he wasn't just anyone.

"It's yours," she whispered.

His breath stammered, and his finger pushed past the ring of muscle, intensifying the throb in her pussy.

"Holy hell, Liv. You're so tight. And hot." He moved his finger in and out, and his thigh trembled against hers. "I want this. Badly."

"Take it, Josh. Do you have lube?"

"No." He groaned, circling his finger. His other hand held her waist in a death grip.

The sensations from his invasion vibrated across her skin, electrifying every cell in her body.

"Use spit," she panted.

The hand on her waist vanished. She heard him spit and pictured him stroking himself, lubricating his cock as he fingered her ass. Fuck, she was going to come quick. She dropped her head to the pillow.

His finger slipped away, and something much larger nudged her opening. Lifting on hands and knees, she pushed back against him. He swept a warm palm up and down her spine. His fingers lingered on her tail bone, pressing down, and he worked his cock in slowly, cautiously, despite his quickening exhales.

They gasped in unison as his hips bumped her ass, his length buried fully inside her. He bent over her back and cupped her breasts. "Not gonna last long."

"Me neither." She rotated her hips. "Now move."

He moved. Oh God, did he move. She gripped the edge of the mattress and smothered her yelps in the pillow. He pistoned his hips, filling her over and over with an overwhelming tempo of speed and power. The bed squeaked. She didn't care. Her body was on fire, her desire for him tunneling through her and awakening all her pleasure points.

His tongue dragged up her spine, and his fingers slipped into her pussy. She exploded in a spasm of quivering limbs and stammering breaths, her inner walls convulsing around his fingers. His strokes slowed, his mouth open and panting against her shoulder. He came with his face buried in her neck and his arms locked around her, clutching her back to his chest.

She sighed, smiling, as he rolled them to their sides. "You just fucked my ass with your parents on the other side of the wall."

"At least, they didn't come in." He pulled out, rubbed something soft and cottony between her legs and cleaned himself. "There's no lock on the door."

Her gaze flew to the vicinity of the door. Was he *trying* to get busted?

"Did you just clean your dick with your t-shirt?" she asked.

"Yep." He tossed it through the dark room, and it landed with a thud in the corner. "I'll make sure it gets in the hamper."

"Let me guess. Your mom does your laundry?"

He curled against her back, enfolding her in his arms. "She's been washing my cum filled t-shirts for years. Go to sleep."

She lay awake with her cheeks stretched in a silly grin and a flutter in her chest. Sleepless minutes passed, and her thoughts drifted to Van. He'd been a bastard to her for seven years. If he hadn't abducted her, Mom might've still been alive. But there would've been no Livana. She would've never met Josh.

For the first time since Van entered her life, she thought of him with a tiredness that was fulfilling rather than draining.

When Josh's breaths evened out, she carefully untangled his arms and kissed his temple, inhaling the scent of his skin. Then she crept back to the couch.

The next three days rolled into a repetitive cycle. She used the Carter's phone every morning to inquire about a visitation with Livana. She helped Josh haul bales and clean farm equipment. In the evenings, they ran together, just the two of them, the dirt road beneath their sneakers, and acres of freedom.

After his parents retired each night, he carried her to his bedroom and showed her how much he loved her. When he fell asleep, she crept back to the couch. But his irritation with the sleeping arrangements was mounting, if his narrow-eyed glower at his parents every morning was anything to go by.

When she approached him about his attitude toward his parents, he said, "They're more concerned about what happened to the farm while I was gone than what happened to *me* during that time. You'd think they'd be more invested in what I need and less concerned about church gossip and farm chores."

While his parents pretended his time in captivity never happened, the news stations begged for details. They called from all over the country, buzzing the phone so often the Carters turned off the ringer. A number of times, Josh had to run off reporters who were rude enough to show up at the house. He wanted to avoid the press for as long as possible, which meant he was also avoiding school, football, and church. All his attention was on the farm and catching up on the tasks his parents had fallen behind on.

On the third morning, her call to the Austin police department was answered with a message from Carolyn Eary. Mr. E's wife finally agreed to meet with her.

The next day, Josh drove her to Austin in the family's station wagon.

She sat beside him in a spartan holding room at the police station. Her palms sweat, and her mouth dried as Carolyn stared at her with pink-rimmed eyes.

Liv swallowed, tongue-tangled, and searched for the appropriate thing to say to the woman raising her child. "Thank you for seeing me."

Carolyn raised a trembling hand to her face, brushing away an invisible hair. "I'm trying to come to terms with this." The woman gestured at Liv and Josh. "But my primary concern is for my daughter. She's lost her father and—" She choked on a sob. "She's all I have."

A maternity test would prove Liv's parentage. A court order might give her custody. But what was best for Livana?

Liv leaned forward, the long table separating them. "I'm not here to uproot Livana's life. I just want to meet her and, with time, get to know her." She closed her eyes, opened them. "I have so many questions."

"You can ask me anything." Carolyn smiled, though it faded quickly.

"How and when did she come to you?"

Carolyn rubbed her forearms, her blond eyebrows gathering over her blue eyes. "We adopted her. She was only a few days old."

Had Van kept her during those first few days? Or had she gone to the hospital for care? She pressed a hand to her abdomen. She couldn't ask those questions and reveal Van's part in this.

Carolyn's lips pinched in a line. "My husband claimed he had an estranged son who contacted him and asked him to raise his child. Said the mother didn't want her." She averted her eyes and took her time dragging them back to Liv. "My husband and I couldn't have children, so of course I was ecstatic. He dealt with the paperwork." Her cheeks flushed. "It all seems so very obvious now. I should've questioned more. He never mentioned having a son before Livana came to us, and now I know it's because he never really had one."

Josh grabbed Liv's hand under the table, and she laced their fingers, squeezing. Did that mean Van had never met Livana or Carolyn? Was that Mr. E's doing? Isolating his son from the only family he had? Remorse sat heavy in her stomach.

Carolyn leaned back in the chair, her eyes cold, flat. "It was all one big lie."

Not exactly. Liv believed Van and his confession to being Mr. E's son, but she wasn't going to correct Carolyn.

"My husband never paid attention to Livana." Carolyn's firm eye contact held Liv immobile. "Please believe me when I say I have loved her enough for the both of us. And she has *never* been mistreated."

Warmth circulated through Liv's body. Fuck, she'd needed to hear that. "Who named her?"

Carolyn tucked her hands behind her elbows. "He told me his son chose the name." She shrugged stiffly. "I guess my husband named her after you." She blinked away.

Van named her. Liv was sure of it. A bloom of warmth curled through her chest, and her lungs filled with a deep, content breath. "Can I see her? Is she here?" Hope bottled up inside of her, quickening her pulse.

"Yes, of course." Carolyn rose and left the room.

Liv clutched her chest. "Oh my God, Josh. OhmyGodOhmyGod. Pinch me."

She swallowed rapidly, light-headed and giddy, gulping deep breaths. Her hands shook over the front of her cotton dress, straightening it. She combed fingers through her hair. Should she brush the strands over her scar?

He hooked an arm around her, touched his lips to her cheek, and chuckled softly. "Stop fidgeting. You're breathtaking. Livana will adore you."

She leaned her forehead against his. "Thank you. I'm so glad you're here."

The door opened, and she stopped breathing.

CHAPTER 45

Liv's heartbeat boomed through her body. She leaned forward in the chair, her *Hello* strangled.

Huge brown eyes scanned the room and collided with hers. Livana blinked, tilted her head. A dimple appeared in her pink cheek and a beautiful, shy smile stretched across her face.

Liv had waited six years for that moment, imagined it every day, and never expected one smile to connect her to life so completely. It was a floating sensation, as if all her past and future failures were lifted. Her soul had everything it needed right there in that room. She tightened her fingers around Josh's hand.

Livana entered before Carolyn, her dark hair swishing around her shoulders in long waves. Ladybugs embroidered her t-shirt, and her tiny hand clutched a tablet, which connected to the ear buds poking from her ears.

"Livana?" Carolyn closed the door and regarded Liv. "I'm sorry. She has this thing with music. Always singing."

Josh's thumb brushed over Liv's fingers, and a sense of unity drifted through her, balancing her pulse into a slow, happy beat.

Livana approached, her mouth moving silently, her knees bouncing to some unknown melody. She paused a hug away, and her delicate chin raised. Her lips parted as she stared into Liv's eyes.

Carolyn tugged an ear bud from Livana's ear and sat two chairs away. "Livana, this is Liv and Josh."

A tentative hand reached toward Liv's face with starts and stops until tiny fingers brushed her scar. Too soon, the gentle touch fell away.

She couldn't breathe, her throat too thick. She gathered her voice. "Have you seen a mark like this before?"

She tapped her scar. Carolyn wouldn't know why she was asking.

Livana shook her head. "Nah uh."

It was a sad confirmation. Livana had never met her father.

Liv hunched down to peer at her daughter's dainty features. "What are you listening to?"

Those brown eyes widened, fringed with Van's thick lashes. "Katy Perry. She's really pretty. Like you."

Oh God, that sweet voice. A tingle burned her nose. "May I?" She gestured at the dangling ear bud.

Livana nodded enthusiastically and shifted to sit in her lap. Carolyn watched with tense shoulders, but a small smile touched her lips.

Liv's pulse thrummed in her throat as she released Josh's hand. She lifted the beautiful girl, hugging her close and adjusting the ear buds. One in her ear, the other in Livana's. A tiny finger swiped through Katy Perry songs on the tablet and selected "Unconditionally."

The tune clapped through the ear buds. When Livana's vocals launched, strong and perfectly pitched, a shiver crept over Liv's skin, raising the hairs on her nape. She sought Josh's eyes and found him studying them, his arm propped on the table, a knuckle resting against his lips. Behind his hand, the corners of his mouth curved, his gaze warm with affection.

The chorus kicked in, and she joined Livana's voice in a higher octave, their tones harmonizing as if they'd sung together for years. They watched each other, smiling, laughing when Liv stumbled over the words.

When the song finished, Livana flashed a toothy grin. "You sing good. Let's do another one." She swiped the screen on her tablet.

Carolyn pressed her fingers to her lips, her eyes watery. "Well." She smoothed her skirt and gave a shaky smile. "That explains Livana's beautiful voice."

Liv felt taller, stronger. She'd passed on something of herself, something that was considered beautiful. And she'd done it without meeting or touching her daughter. Her heart froze then pounded with overwhelming wonderment.

A dozen Katy Perry songs later, Livana said goodbye with her arms wrapped around Liv's neck.

"Would you like to see Liv and Josh again?" Carolyn asked.

Liv's heartbeat thrummed heavily, sluggishly. Ripping Livana from the only mother she'd ever known would be so damned selfish. As badly as Liv wanted to demand custody, no one would benefit but herself.

A tingling sensation fluttered in her belly. She wasn't a self-serving monster. Not anymore.

Livana grinned, looking up at Carolyn with love and trust. "I'll bring the music."

Carolyn clasped her hand. "I bet they'll come see

you whenever you want."

"Thank you," Liv mouthed to Carolyn.

Two hours later—and after a stop behind a deserted building where she thanked Josh passionately for coming with her—they walked into his parents' house. Actually, she danced. She wiggled her hips, bumping into his as he walked. Her heartbeat drummed in her chest. A light-hearted feeling dispersed through her body, loosening her muscles. She was high on laughter, and his beautiful smile and playful shoves spurred her elation as she spun around him, rejuvenated by the best day of her life.

As they flitted around one another through the sitting room, his hands tackled her ribs, wrenching a laughing scream from her lungs. She pivoted away from him and collided with the hard, narrowed stare of Mr. Carter.

He stood in the kitchen doorway, his distaste evident in the pressed line of his lips. "This was in the mailbox."

With a stiff arm, he handed her a confidential envelope, addressed to Liv Reed in typed font. No postage stamp. No return address. Her stomach tumbled.

Josh led her to his room and closed the door. His hard jawline sawed side-to-side. "I don't think I can handle any more surprises."

He paced the small room, pivoting between the spartan furnishings. A twin bed with a handmade quilt. A dresser with a bottle of aftershave. Shelves lined the walls displaying years of football trophies. He stopped in front of her, crossed his arms, and waited.

Adrenaline flared through her veins, firing her brain to act. She sat on the bed, tore the seal, and slid out a single letter.

The name, address, and phone number of an international bank in the Cayman Islands printed across the top. The body of the letter included three lines.

Liv Reed
Account number 00145481720
Balance $6,000,000

CHAPTER 46

A flush of dizziness swam through Liv's head.

The mattress shifted. Josh sat beside her, his hand curling around her wrist, angling the paper. "Am I reading this right?"

"Hand me the phone." Her voice trembled.

She called the toll-free number, confirmed the account and the balance, and disconnected.

He rose from the bed and resumed pacing. "Why would Mr. E put his money in your name? Your *real* name."

She stared at the letter, the words blurry. He'd put the house and everything else in her fake name. He and Van had been ghosts in the slave business. She was the face and the name connected to the entire operation.

"So I could take the fall?" Her chest pinched. "But someone personally delivered this to your parents' mailbox."

His mouth slackened, voicing her assumption. "Van."

Van. He'd spent seven years trying to break her, and it had only taken him a few minutes of near-death honesty to make amends. She'd already forgiven him. She didn't need the money to mend things between them.

"There were seven transactions, at least a million each. He probably kept a portion." She sucked in a breath. "Regardless, I can't accept it."

Josh stared down at her, his fists on his hips. "Why the hell not?"

"Eight lives, including yours"—she ground her teeth, her voice rising—"were torn apart for this money."

He crouched between her legs, tugged the letter from her fist, and set it on the bed. "Nine people, Liv. You're one of us. And you *know* our lives are better for it." He placed his palm beneath her ear, his thumb caressing her cheek. "*My* life is so much more damned meaningful. Because of you."

Her head ached and her chest squeezed. She rubbed the middle of her forehead. What were her options? She couldn't send the money back. She could donate it to charity. Or… "I can divide it among the eight of you."

He searched her eyes, his hand lowering to tap his fingers on her thigh. "You'll divide it between the nine of us, and I'll give my portion to my parents."

She smoothed a wayward lock of hair from his forehead, mesmerized by the iridescent glow of his eyes. He wouldn't need his own money if she kept a portion of the account. Neither of them knew what the future held for them, but one thing was certain. They would be together.

She wrinkled her nose to thwart the sudden burn of emotion. She had a future to look forward to. With him.

"Joshua?" Emily's voice muffled through the walls. The door opened, and her gray eyes darted between them. "Son, I'm not comfortable with the door shut when there's a girl in your room."

Liv bit her lip. Good God, they treated him like a child.

He flattened his hands on her thighs and drew a deep breath. "Sorry to hear that, Mom. And the *girl* has a name."

Emily raised her chin. "Yes, of course. I didn't mean to be rude."

"Anything else?" He squinted at her over his shoulder.

Her chest hitched. "Can I see you in the kitchen?"

"No. If you have something to say—"

The door hit the wall behind it with the force of her shove. She turned on her heels, her strides fading down the hall.

He bowed his head in her lap. "God grant me the serenity to accept the things I cannot change."

Liv combed her fingers through his hair, massaging his scalp. "There's going to be churchventions all over McLennan County praying for your soul tonight, Joshua Carter." She touched his rock-hard jaw and raised his head. "Go talk to her." She gave him her coldest Mistress glare.

A laugh barked from the back of his throat. He held up his hands.

"All right." He rose, smiling. "What's a churchvention?"

She shrugged and batted her eyes. "Interventions for churchy people?"

Shaking his head, he scratched his jaw and lingered in the doorway. "You're splitting that money between the nine of us."

She picked up the letter, hugged it to her chest, and

fell back on the mattress, biting back her smile. "Fine."

Early the next morning, he caught her waist with a determined arm as she tried to sneak from his bed. "Not this time."

Twilight bled a faint glow beneath the window shade. She swatted at the hand creeping between her legs. "Your parents will be up soon."

He rolled to his back, shifting her over him, chest-to-chest, and gripped the sides of her head.

"Then muffle your moans." He pulled her mouth to his and used his tongue to awaken her from the inside out.

Ten minutes later, she faced his feet, straddling his thighs and riding his cock. His body trembled beneath her. Each rock of her hips made his toes curl. She wanted to bite them.

His hands skimmed her back, spreading tingles of sensations over her skin. His pelvis lifted to meet the grinding slide of her ass, the motion bouncing her breasts and tightening her nipples. The fullness of his girth dragged along her inner muscles, her body flooding with warmth.

She stroked his balls between their spread legs, and the sight of him gliding in and out coiled her release to a teetering edge.

"Josh, I'm close," she whispered.

His fingers dug into her hips as he slowed his thrusts. In the next heartbeat, they came together, their sighs floating through the room.

A fist knocked on the door.

"Joshua," Emily hollered. "That girl didn't sleep on the couch last night. I think she's gone missing."

Liv's hands flew between their legs where they

were joined as he shouted, "Be out in a—"

The door opened, and a laundry basket tumbled to the floor.

Emily covered her horrified gasp with a trembling hand and slammed the door, her screams penetrating through the wall. "Daniel! Oh dear Lord, Daniel!"

Liv slumped over his legs, her heart hammering in her throat. "I miss my keypad."

His body jerked beneath her, vibrating through his hitched breaths. Oh God, was he crying? She rose off his cock and twisted around.

His forearms crossed over his face, his chest heaving. She crawled toward him, yanked his arms down, and found his mouth curved and his eyebrows crawling up his forehead. He was laughing?

She smacked his chest. He laughed harder. She smacked him again. "Shame on you. Your poor mother is probably out there rallying an exorcism."

He regarded her with a dimple in his cheek and light in his eyes. Why was he so nonchalant? Then it dawned on her. "You wanted her to walk in on that?"

A sigh rippled from his gorgeous lips. "I want them to see *me*, not who they want me to be." He tucked her hair behind her ear. "A really pretty girl told me once that shock has a way of rousing attention."

She caressed his jaw, her fingers lingering on his mouth. "She's a stupid girl."

His eyes hardened. "Bull." He scooted to the edge of the bed and perused her body over his shoulder. "As much as I love you without clothes on, you should probably get dressed for the family meeting."

In the kitchen, Emily sat stiffly at the table, holding a tissue to her nose. "You just haven't been right since the kidnapping. You need to talk to a minister." She nodded. "You need the influence of *good* people."

Liv hovered in the corner. Fuck, she didn't want to be there, but when she had emerged from the bathroom in her jeans and t-shirt, he dragged her along behind him, saying, "This needs to be done."

He leaned against the fridge, arms crossed over his bare chest, his legs clad in low-hung jeans. Despite his casual pose, there was a fire burning in his eyes. "Liv is good people."

She and Josh had discussed their options the night before. With their financial issues resolved, they could go anywhere, and they would. He wanted to ease his parents into his impending departure.

Her insides quivered with anxiety. This was ripping off the band-aid before they'd healed from his last departure.

Daniel sat beside his wife, his green eyes narrowed on Liv. "We have rules in this house, and we expect you to follow them."

Josh's nostrils flared. "Don't you dare blame her."

"She's as loose as ashes in the wind," Emily whispered, as if only Josh could hear her.

Liv caught her sigh before it billowed out and dropped her head on the wall behind her. His parents were hurting. They'd lost their son, and he'd returned with his own view on life, one that had veered from their belief system.

"Be careful, Mom." He straightened and stormed toward the table, the muscles in his back flexing and hardening. He raised an arm and, for a fearful moment, Liv thought he might sweep all the dishes to the floor. He snagged the gaudy ceramic rooster centerpiece.

"Apologize to her or the rooster's gonna get it."

Liv bit back her smile and tried to imagine how her mom would've reacted to catching her in bed with him. She honestly didn't know and that realization tugged at her chest. She was a seventeen-year-old virgin when Van took her. Her relationship with Mom had never reached this kind of trial, and it never would.

Emily fanned her fingers over her breastbone and flicked her eyes to Liv. "I'm sorry. It's just...my boy's going to be a minister. He has schooling and farm work. He doesn't have time for—"

"That was an embarrassing apology, Mom." He set the rooster on the table and strode toward Liv with wide steps, his eyes roaming her face. Placing his hands on the wall on either side of her head, he leaned down and kissed her forehead. "I love you."

Her heart wobbled. "Love you, too."

"Let me remind you that you're *not* married." Daniel rested his forearms on the table. "Tell me this was the only time you...shared a bed."

Liv sagged against the wall. Their son was kidnapped and trained as a sex slave. Jesus, they were in serious fucking denial about his captivity.

Josh turned and hooked a thumb in his belt loop. "I love her, Dad." He pointed at her. "And I'm *sharing a bed* with her every which way to Sunday. Because I. Love. Her."

Daniel paled, and Emily gasped, her face crumpling. "You need to go to church. And you need to finish your religious studies."

He let out a booming laugh. "No amount of church is going to keep me from sleeping with her."

Liv pressed a fist to her lips, her chest swelling. She

wanted to kiss him for standing up to his parents, but her stomach sank as she considered what it might do to his relationship with them.

"You've changed." Emily straightened her spine and pursed her lips. "That man who took you put something bad in you. You need help, Joshua."

He raked a hand through his hair and groaned. "I need *her*." He sat in the chair beside Emily, turning it to face her. "I'll finish school. *When I'm ready*. I'll worship God. *On my own terms*. As for the farm, I'll help you financially." He twisted and met Liv's eyes over his shoulder. One dark eyebrow lifted.

Oh God, he wanted her to step in here? They already hated her. She rubbed her forearm, wrinkling her forehead. He wanted her support, and she had a sure way to give it to him.

Two confident strides put her behind his chair. She rested her hands on his shoulders. "I inherited some money when my mom died." She rubbed her thumbs over the skin on his back. "We'll leave you with more than enough to retire."

Daniel stiffened, his eyes on Josh. "What is she saying? You're not leaving."

"I am." His shoulders rolled back.

"You will not disobey me." Daniel jumped up, his face red. "You're not leaving. That's final."

Josh stood with his hands in his pockets, chin lowered, and his body angled toward his parents, but his eyes cut to the side and met hers. A small smile played around his lips. "No more requirements."

She swallowed around a lump of guilt and moved to stand beside him.

He reached for her hand and looked at his dad.

"I'm not leaving *you*. I'm leaving your rules."

He was telling his dad, man-to-man, how he was going to live his life. She was certain he'd never done that before. She wished his parents could see what she saw. Joshua Carter would never be enchained by someone else's rules. He was a man of strong convictions. His *own* convictions.

Emily sagged against the chair back. "You don't even have a car."

"I'm taking the bike."

CHAPTER 47

Josh moved through his bedroom with a high-energy buzz and an overwhelming lightness in his chest. Before Liv, his path was narrow and predetermined. Now it was a wide open field that reached the horizon and beyond. He wanted to fling his arms up, break out into a run, and whoop like an idiot.

Liv lingered by the door with a gleam in her eyes and a smile struggling to punch through her stern expression.

"What bike?" She closed the door and crossed her arms. "I stalked you for weeks. I would remember a bike."

He transferred her clothes from the grocery bag to his backpack. "I've got an engine strapped to two wheels."

"That sounds safe."

Said the girl who threw herself out of airplanes.

"I started putting it together out in the shed when I was fourteen." He grinned. "Old school pipes. Uber fat tires. It has enough torque to make my parents stutter through their prayers."

"They wouldn't let you ride it?" She joined him at the bed and helped him fit her clothes in the bag.

"Nope." Not even slow in the driveway. "But it still runs. I fired it up yesterday when you were in the shower."

She stuffed the last shirt in and put her hands on her hips, staring at the sum of every possession she owned. "Where are we going?"

He opened a drawer and tossed a few shirts, briefs, and jeans on the bed. "We need to go to a bank, open an account, and transfer your funds. We need phones so my parents can call us. Oh, and helmets for the bike." He sidled in front of her, prompting her to look up and meet his eyes. "We can go to Austin and live near Livana. Or we could call Camila. You think they have room for two more in their house?"

"Nine adults in one house?" She threw her head back and laughed, her gorgeous brown eyes alight with amusement.

Probably not the best idea, especially given the way the guys longingly tracked her every move.

"Tonight…" He wrapped his arms around her lower back and squeezed her addictive backside. "We're staying in a hotel with no keypads and no parents and…" He scanned his room, his attention snagging on the hook behind his door. That would work. He released her, grabbed a leather belt from the hook, and held it out to her. "And this."

She could strap him to the bed or shackle his wrists or whip his backside. A pulse of warmth curled through his groin. He needed to buy more belts.

She took the one from his hand, folded it, and whacked her palm. Her upturned face glowed, her soft cheekbones curving with her smile. "You want me to beat your ass, you dirty slut?"

Her cool voice sent a shiver down his spine and stiffened his penis to a throbbing hard-on. "Yes, Mistress."

She twisted her fingers through the hair at his nape, her long lashes blinking slowly. Then she pulled him down for a kiss that tunneled his vision and rocked his hips.

"Finish packing." She released him and stepped back.

He adjusted himself and returned to his dresser for one more thing. Digging beneath the clothes he would leave behind, he pulled out his favorite childhood toy. He clutched her wrist and set it on her palm. "I want you to have this."

Her slim eyebrows pulled together, her face arranged in an adorable expression. "A Rubik's Cube?"

The square stickers peeled at the edges, each of the six sides grouped by color.

"I solved it when I was eight." He laughed, shaking his head at the memory. "Took me a year. I refused to undo it after I figured it out."

"Wow." She stared at it, confusion lingering on her face.

"It wasn't the satisfaction of solving it that was meaningful. It was the experience in pursuing an endeavor of my choosing. I never found another puzzle I connected to the way I did with this one." He touched her chin, held her eyes. "Until you."

She clutched the cube to her chest and pulled his forehead to hers. "Thank you."

He kissed her nose. "My jersey number was based on that cube. There's fifty-four squares."

A huge smile spread beneath her glistening eyes.

"My name."

Roman numeral LIV. His favorite number, his fate, his freedom.

An hour later, he hugged his dad in the driveway. The bike rumbled a few feet away. Liv stood beside him with everything they owned on her back.

"Love you, Dad."

Dad squeezed him until his ribs complained.

Mom's embrace was gentle but no less caring. "You call us as soon as you have a phone."

"Yep." He climbed on the bike under the remorseful gazes of his parents.

Their lips pressed tight, their expressions stony, but they were there to see him off. They loved him, and time and patience would sand away their disappointment.

Liv straddled behind him and curled her arms around his waist, her thighs clenching his hips. He licked his lips and pointed his feet forward. A breeze ruffled his hair. The sun warmed his skin. His heart beat a steady, peaceful tempo.

He twisted his neck and collided with her eyes over his shoulder. "Where to?"

She didn't look at the road. Didn't gaze at the sweeping hillside. She raised her eyes to the sky and smiled.

CHAPTER 48

Three months later, Liv gulped the cool air rushing through the open door and gripped the bench seat beneath her. The aluminum walls of the narrow cabin vibrated with the roar of the wind. Her palms collected sweat in the thick gloves. Her goggles steamed with humidity. And her smile was so big her cheeks hurt.

Josh sat on the bench across from her, his complexion a kaleidescope of grays and greens. He looked like he was going to throw up all over his red jumpsuit.

Mom had always said to reach for the sky, so Liv decided to do just that and followed Mom's jump boots. Liv's instructor position at the skydiving school outside of Austin enabled her to take Josh on his first jump without the nervous chatter of other newbie skydivers. It was just her and him and the sun-bleached sky.

She leaned forward and shouted over the shrill of the engine. "Changed your mind yet?"

He snapped his arms out and bellowed some kind of indiscernible battle cry. Then he flashed her a panty-soaking smile.

The man had balls, and fuck her but she loved those balls. She'd had them bound in a ball stretcher the previous night while she paddled his ass to a gorgeous shade of red. The memory kindled a damp heat between her legs. She wiggled, grinding her pussy against the seat.

His boot nudged hers. "You thinking about me?" he yelled.

She caught her lip between her teeth and shook her head, the whir of the turbo-props piercing her ears.

He'd transferred his classes to Austin University to pursue a teaching degree. He wanted to coach high school football. With only two semesters of schooling left, playing college ball wasn't feasible. He shrugged it off, saying that wasn't part of his *Freedom Plan*.

Mr. and Mrs. Carter called daily. They were warming to her but had yet to visit their rental house of bed-sharing sin. The freedom fighters, on the other hand, popped in frequently. Overwhelmed with their sudden wealth, they spoke of the future with glimmering, wide eyes. A future that included her and Josh.

She visited Livana several times a week. It was surreal, sitting in Mr. E's house, in the rooms she'd memorized from the angle of his camera. Her time with Livana filled that empty hole inside her. Some of that happiness included thoughts of Van. Despite the painful memories, she focused on his goodness with a tingling warmth in her face. Sometimes, while running errands or working in the yard at the rental, she'd feel a prickle on her spine and would catch herself squinting over her shoulder, scanning the street for a charcoal hoodie. He was out there somewhere, and she deeply hoped he found something worth living for.

Her gloved hand reached for Josh, and he caught it, squeezing her fingers, his smile cartwheeling through the wind.

The pilot shouted over his shoulder, "We're one minute to drop zone."

"Ready?" she mouthed.

"Yep." He shook his head, still holding onto that sexy grin.

They shuffled toward the open door, weighted down by gear. She checked his emergency parachute one more time, spending unneeded seconds adjusting, tightening, and readjusting the harness between his legs. He laughed and ground his cock against her hand, the horny slut.

Satisfied with the buckles and position of the vest, she shifted his back to the open door with his heels touching the threshold. She grabbed his face, pressed her cheek against his, and shouted into the wind, "Trust me?"

He answered her with his tongue in her mouth, slashing and whipping, his lips strong and determined. His hands clutched the door frame with nothing but empty space behind him.

She pulled back with a kiss on his bottom lip, cocked her head, and shoved his chest.

With an *Oomph*, he was gone.

The wind slapped at her body, thrashing her hair around her face. She sucked in a breath and leapt into the sea of blue, surrendering to the turbulence as it shot her through the air. She watched the plane fly away, her pulse thundering and her lips pulling away from her teeth. The shock to the heart was such a fucking thrill.

She flipped to face downward and spotted her entire world coasting above the curvature of the Earth. He arched his pelvis, limbs out and steady, adapting to his environment so easily, just like he always did. Christ, she loved him, and she would never let him get away.

She arrowed her body, her arms balancing her legs. Using velocity and angling to manipulate the aerodynamics around her, she gained on him.

With the wind deep in her ears and flapping her clothes, she reached out her arms and caught him. The gusts smothered his laugh, but his smile tangled around her, his eyes flickering through the goggles.

He entwined their legs, locked his hands around her back, and covered her mouth with his. Spinning them to descend heads down and feet up, she matched the elated movements of his tongue, answering his affection with the slide of her smiling lips.

Nothing compared to the freedom of floating in his arms.

He would say the hand of God was holding them up, delivering them.

She called it love. Her heart didn't fall. It flew.

The **DELIVER** series continues with:

VANQUISH (#2)
Van's story

DISCLAIM (#3)
Camila's story

DEVASTATE (#4)
Tate's story

TAKE (#5)
Kate's story

LOVE TRIANGLE ROMANCE

TANGLED LIES TRILOGY

One is a Promise

Two is a Lie

Three is a War

DARK PARANORMAL ROMANCE

TRILOGY OF EVE

Dead of Eve #1

Heart of Eve #1.5

Blood of Eve #2

Dawn of Eve #3

STUDENT-TEACHER ROMANCE

Dark Notes

ROCK-STAR DARK ROMANCE

Beneath the Burn

ROMANTIC SUSPENSE

Dirty Ties

EROTIC ROMANCE

Incentive

PLAYLIST

"Gods and Monsters" by *Lana Del Rey*
"Lullaby" by *Sia*
"What It Is" by *Kodaline*
"Bring Me To Life" by *Evanescence*
"Pretender" by *Sarah Jaffe*
"Team" by *Lorde*
"Pretty Face" by *Sóley*
"Ghostflowers" by *OTEP*
"Possession" by *Sarah McLachlan*
"Glory and Gore" by *Lorde*
"Last Resort" by *Papa Roach*
"Unconditionally" by *Katy Perry*

ACKNOWLEDGMENTS

To my critique partners and beta readers—Author Dana Griffin, Author C.K. Raggio, Author Lindsey R. Loucks, Lindy Winter, Jill Bitner, Cristen Abrams, Aries75, and Angie Halteman—for your scolding, your cheers, and your high standards for quality. You pushed me when I slouched and called bullshit when I rushed. I couldn't have asked for a better critique group to kick my ass through every chapter of this book.

To Author Leila DeSint, for beta reading with a very wise and naughty red pen. Your advice is honest and crisp and exactly what I need to hear. I cherish your intuition and your friendship.

To Author Barbara Elsborg, for beta reading amidst your countless projects. Your mastery of the craft shines in your stories, and I'm so honored to be on the receiving end of such insightful advice. I'm forever your fangirl.

To my editor, Jacy Mackin, for appreciating the tone of the story, annihilating my serial commas, and identifying the scenes that needed more roar. Your counsel never disappoints.

To my proofreader, Lesa Godwin, I's cant' publish in error free book witout you're sharp eyes. I love you so damned much!

To my best friend, Amber's Reading Room, for being a pillow to snot on, the PA who works for free, and the bestest companion for an old curmudgeonly writer. I wouldn't have survived this writing cycle without your support. You're stuck with me, oyster.

ABOUT THE AUTHOR

New York Times and USA Today Bestselling author, Pam Godwin, lives in the Midwest with her husband, their two children, and a foulmouthed parrot. When she ran away, she traveled fourteen countries across five continents, attended three universities, and married the vocalist of her favorite rock band.

Java, tobacco, and dark romance novels are her favorite indulgences, and might be considered more unhealthy than her aversion to sleeping, eating meat, and dolls with blinking eyes.

EMAIL: pamgodwinauthor@gmail.com

Made in the USA
Middletown, DE
17 February 2019